THE EARTHQUAKES

THE EARTH QUAKES

Late Anti-Stories

Subimal Misra

Translated
from the Bengali by
V. Ramaswamy

HARPERPERENNIAL
An Imprint of HarperCollins *Publishers*

First published in English in India by Harper Perennial 2024
An imprint of HarperCollins *Publishers*
4th Floor, Tower A, Building No. 10, Phase II, DLF Cyber City,
Gurugram – 122002
www.harpercollins.co.in

2 4 6 8 10 9 7 5 3 1

P-ISBN: 978-93-5699-176-7
E-ISBN: 978-93-5699-216-0

Typeset in 10.5/13.7 Sabon LT Std at
Manipal Technologies Limited, Manipal

Printed and bound at
Nutech Print Services - India

For Michael Hofmann

'I know the man that must hear me,
to him my tale I reach.'

Contents

The Great Renunciant

> 'On the way to the marketplace, surrounded by a bunch of inquisitive boys, a *yampatak* (Yama-scroll seller) displayed his scroll. The scroll hung from a long stick which he held in his hand, and with an arrow-like staff in his right hand, he pointed to the pictures. On his left hand – the terrible Lord of Death astride a buffalo was the principal image.'
>
> – Gurusaday Dutt (*Patua Sangeet*)

One

Jharuprasad Naskar was probably born in the month of March in the year 1918 of the Christian era, in the village Jamiya, located midway between the Kalindi and Mahananda rivers, at the farther end of the old quarter of the town of Malda. (By another account, he was born in the ninth ward of English Bazar.) His grandfather, Prahlad Chandra Naskar, and father, Ganesh Chandra, belonged to the Mahaldar or Malo community of fisherfolk. Some people say Jharuprasad belonged to the Tiar caste of fisherfolk (see 'Jharu Babu and His Songs' by Haradhan Chattopadhyay, in the magazine *Sahitya-Sanskriti*, March 1975). But in an interview, Jharuprasad identified himself as 'kshatriya'. From the time of Ganesh Chandra, the family's livelihood kept changing, and he eventually left for the village of Borboriya, under the Kandi subdivision. Once there, he took up the work of puppet making. Eventually that became his sole occupation.

Jharuprasad attended the Borboriya Primary School in the Malo hamlet and later studied briefly in Akrumoni Coronation School. But whenever he got the chance, he used to go off to sing with *bishari* or *alkap* folk performance groups. He was also initiated into *jhumur* songs at this time.

Jharuprasad returned to the village of Jamiya (his birthplace) in August 1934 and became a member of Paresh Dutta's *gambhira* group. Recognizing an equally capable singer in him, Paresh inducted Jharu into the group. It was from Paresh Dutta that Jharuprasad received his primary education in singing and composing songs. And it was Paresh whom he acknowledged as his guru all his life. Besides singing *gambhira*, the various occupations Jharuprasad took up in his variegated life included singing *bishari* and *jhumur* songs, performing *khemta* dance, puppet making, pith craft, working as a lawyer's clerk, cinema ticket checker, etc. Towards the end of his life, he came in contact with a Baul, Motichand, and became a disciple of Shonkhomoni. But he was not a full-fledged Baul, he had only come in contact with Bauls at a specific stage in his life. His life manifested a wonderful assemblage of all this. Scholar Haradhan Chattaopadhyay's view merits close attention: 'All his life, Jharuprasad searched in his own way for the real meaning of life – who knows whether or not he found any meaning anywhere.'

Two

Jharuprasad's artistic life can be divided into five broad phases:

1. Paramananda Mistri's group: He was with this group from 1937 to 1938. The leader of the group composed the songs, sometimes Jharu too composed the songs. Among his associates in this phase were Dharani Malo, Mahadev Malo, Baira Sardar and Uncle Haru (Fatik Babu).

2. Potu Daam's group: Jharuprasad was in this group from February 1938 to March 1940. It was while he was in this group that his fame spread in the nearby villages. That was when he began to compose patriotic songs, influenced by the poet Mukunda Das, and sang these in various performances. On a special request, he joined a *gambhira* group for a few months. His companion then was a sixteen-year-old boy called Nidu. It was from this time that he earned the displeasure of the British authorities for his song lyrics and performances. He was arrested in 1939 while singing the anti-British song 'Thrash and drive out the English from this land' in Bandhgoda village. With him were Nidu, Mohammad Giyas and Kudno Majhi. They were, of course, released afterwards.

3. Rakhari Daam's group: After the death of Potu Daam, his younger brother, Rakhari Daam, started a new group together with some of the disciples. Jharuprasad was with them from the moment of conception. Nidu, his only disciple, accompanied him here too. But Jharuprasad did not see eye to eye with Rakhari regarding the management of the group. Rakhari was in favour of composing songs of the *torja* type, and he wanted to immerse the audience for

a few hours in only the delight of buffoonery, wordy duels and repartee laced with sexual innuendo. But Jharuprasad wanted to retain an element of protest in everything. He used to compose patriotic songs extempore and barge on to the stage to sing them. During this period, he once went for a performance to a village called Bindubashini and returned with a daughter-in-law of the village's Mukhopadhyay clan, whom he subsequently brought on stage to perform. After a mere evening's acquaintance, the woman left her home and family and came away with him. The name of this young woman – who had been abandoned by her husband – was Niyatirani. Some say the woman's name was Ashtabala and that the name Niyati was given by Jharuprasad. She was the daughter of a *kulin* brahmin family. She was naturally gifted with a sweet singing voice, and her innate virtuosity in singing songs against untouchability and exhorting patriotic awareness had entranced Jharuprasad. On her very first night on stage, she had donned the attire of Mother India and sung, 'Awaken, O children of India', and thrilled the audience. Niyatirani was an independent-minded woman. Although she was not literate, she could compose, extempore, songs against women's oppression. But it was because of Niyatirani that the group split. People were enraged at Jharuprasad for taking away the daughter-in-law of a brahmin family and making her perform the *khemta* dance on stage. He was beaten up and was subject to social boycott. (For a detailed account about this, the April 1993 issue of the magazine *Kandi Samachar* is noteworthy, although the name of the discussant is not given.) Notwithstanding all this, Jharuprasad remained obdurate. However, within a few days, Rakhari kicked him out of the group on grounds of misconduct. There had also been a complaint against him of coming for performances after excessive intake of alcohol. Meanwhile, Nidu ran away one night with Niyati. Some people said Nidu was not to blame, and that he had fallen into the clutches of the much older Niyatirani. (Source of the information: the previously cited issue of *Kandi Samachar* magazine.) No accurate information in this regard is available. But Jharuprasad gave up singing altogether, and for some time he worked as a lawyer's clerk under Gajendra Chandra Bhuiyan, and then as a ticket checker at Shree Radha Talkies.

4. His own group: Not finding any other occupation to his liking, he left all these jobs very soon, and in October–November of 1941, he set up his own group. He wrote the songs for the group. A schoolmaster by the name of Upen Das used to correct his songs, and he clearly forbade the adoption of an anti-British stance. But Jharuprasad did not stop singing anti-British songs, and it was for singing such songs that he received many medals. When he sang his famous 'Fifty-two cards, three aces', the performance was repeatedly attacked. Nidu and Niyati returned on hearing about his new group. He took them back affectionately, and thanks to the joint endeavours of all of them, the group became very popular. They were invited to various places in and outside Bengal. Their fame spread so wide that the police too kept tabs on them. Nevertheless, despite such conditions, he travelled with his group to places like Mymensingh, Jogbani, Champaganj, Kanthi, Baleshwar, Cuttack, Kalna, Ranchi, etc., and sang his patriotic songs everywhere.

5. There was another uproar regarding Niyatirani when the group was on a tour. She had left Nidu and started living

with Shakurchand, the sarangi player of the group. She made it very clear – 'Who I choose to stay with or not stay with is entirely my business. There's no need for anyone else to poke their noses into all that.' Jharuprasad tried a lot to resolve the problem, but it only got worse. Nidu came to blows with Shakurchand in public, during a performance. Within a few days, on the instigation of Niyatirani, Shakurchand seized the leadership of the group from Jharuprasad; he insulted him on the pretext of his drunken behaviour and kicked him out of the group. Niyatirani already had a sweet voice, now her face too seemed to have taken on a new kind of glow. Long queues of people thronged to see her perform. Thus, the group did not split even after Jharuprasad was driven out. Nidu, too, finally made peace with Shakurchand.

Disgraced, Jharuprasad travelled here and there for a while after being kicked out of his own group. During this time, he came in contact with the Bauls and received *diksha* from Shonkhomoni Baul. He became a full-fledged Baul after that, with an *ektara* in his hand and donning a saffron robe. A few years went by in this way. Meanwhile, not being able to get along with the group, Niyati too left and began searching for Jharuprasad. They met at the Kenduli mela one Makar Sankranti morning. That very night, she exchanged garlands with Jharuprasad. The two of them went from one place to the other, singing, and they spent some time in the veranda of an abandoned temple on the bank of the Ajoy river. When Niyatirani sang the song 'Love dwells in the house of lust…', the public crowded around her agape. In this phase, Niyatirani became so famous that a group of sahibs and memsahibs from America came and captured her on camera during a performance. (Source: Haradhan Chattopadhyay's essay cited earlier.) Because of his petulant nature, people did not like Jharuprasad very much. Since he did not have a good voice, his Baul performances did not get much attention either. All the attention of the common folk was directed at Niyatirani. She too regularly engaged in jest and banter with the audience. As a result, she gradually became distanced from Jharuprasad. He did not approve of all this, and he was always in an angry sulk. Around this time, a nephew of his arrived and began to stay with him. The foppish nephew's name was Taraprasad. One night, Jharuprasad saw Niyatirani in a compromising situation with Taraprasad and he thrashed his nephew badly. He also kept abusing Niyatirani in unspeakable terms. Niyatirani then assumed her real form and began beating Jharuprasad up. One of the bones of his leg broke as a result of the beating. Jharuprasad lay with his broken leg on the desolate bank of the Ajoy river. In front of his very eyes, Niyatirani exchanged garlands with Taraprasad and openly went around everywhere with him. Because Taraprasad was by no means a Baul, all this created a commotion in Baul circles. Jharuprasad sought out people and went around providing detailed accounts of Niyatirani's doings. She used to give two fistfuls of rice to the lame Jharuprasad to eat, but now, unable to bear people's taunts and full of anger and sorrow, Niyatirani vowed never to lay eyes on Jharuprasad again as long as he lived. Flinging away the saffron of the Bauls, Niyatirani walked out haughtily in front of everyone, with Taraprasad by her side.

Three

Philosophy of life

Any attempt to arrive at a firm conclusion regarding Jharuprasad's philosophy of life is fraught with risk. Various mutually contradictory religio-spiritual streams had come together and mingled within him. Some people have opined that, throughout his life, Jharupasad only searched for himself. But one clear aspect of his songs was the protest dimension. He did not have any apathy as regards any worldly matter. He drank heavily. Of course, he never conformed to any rules or customs of the land. And yet he composed songs about the corruption in the Kandi municipality and directly attacked the then chairman, Abirlal Roy, and the vice-chairman, Sanatan Choudhury. When this song was being performed in the village of Kamalkanda, the police arrived and stopped the performance. His song book was confiscated under the Defence of India Rules and he was freed only after signing a false confession. On the instructions of the chairman, his property was ordered to be confiscated, but no property to speak of was found. Sensing danger, Jharuprasad had made a *benami* transfer, in advance, of his share of his father's homestead. Before his death, notwithstanding his lame leg and heart ailment, he wanted to set up another group. In 1971, during the dark days of the reign of terror in West Bengal, he wrote an explosive song. Through the medium of song and dance, he unmasked the people's leaders in his own fashion –

> It's so easy to proclaim lofty things about Man – Hey!
> You kill boys in every neighbourhood, so what kind
> of leaders are you? Hey!

China comes to India bearing the message of revolution
With Mao Tse-tung as our leader, a new dawn's evolution!

Incensed by this daredevil song of Jharuprasad's, a squad of hoodlums pounced on the stage and stopped the performance at Balakuniya, Tiyada and Kalitala villages. For that matter, they even used country bombs. But Jharuprasad was not frightened, and he continued to perform the song on stage in a few other places as well.

Despite being short-lived, Jharuprasad's career as a Baul was full of various complications. He often advised 'wisdom in love'. He used to narrate with great zest a Guru-Ma's story to Niyatirani. Before her arrival on the scene, he had spent quite a few months in this Guru-Ma's *akhra*. The Guru-Ma apparently exchanged garlands with a person who had performed *sadhana* with his own mother as his *sadhana*-companion. Some people said that after hearing this unsocial tale again and again in all its juicy detail, Niyatirani became infuriated, and she then openly carried on her love play with the nephew. All this brought on the final blow to Niyatirani's life, and that was the beginning of her bitter experience regarding Baul *sadhana*. On the other hand, another researcher says that, although she had much regard for Baul *sadhana*, she was quite indifferent to actual Baul life. (The chapter on 'Baul Life' in *Folk Artist Jharuprasad* by Khetranarayan Choudhury is significant.) Jharuprasad had exchanged garlands with Niyatirani and yet, whenever he saw misconduct, he could not help protesting against it. He could discern the nature of a genuine *sadhika*, and he had also attained the heart of a true mystic. He was very fond of a song by Lalan on Baul life:

> How shall I realize the pure sadhana of Sahaja loving,
> When the stormy river of love trembles with longing.

Four

Although Jharuprasad could compose songs, he could not sing very well. So, he took recourse to various kinds of riddles and foolery in his performances. That was a fundamental aspect of his artistic endeavour. The riddle with which he began the performance, to get it going, was:

> A triangle with a hole in the middle of it
> Searching in that as if in a fit
> Success or no success
> The heart's in distress

He used to reveal the answer later, but meanwhile the audience went crazy sensing the hint at something sexual in the words of the riddle. The answer was 'push-net' – there was a cavity in the middle of the push-net that was fastened on three sides to bamboo sticks. The fish got caught inside the cavity or hole. So one had to put one's hand in and search for the fish.

Another favourite riddle of his was:

> The *elang* fish waggles its tail
> You'll get the fish at break of day
> The new lass's old groom
> Scolds her every noon

Jharuprasad used to present this ditty too, to the accompaniment of various gestures and comments. People used to listen to him eagerly, and try to find the meaning, each in his own way. But he never revealed the meaning of this one. In the way it was said, and with the cadence and rhythm of his words, there was a hint at something illicit. Perhaps he obtained all these riddles and ditties, which drew upon familial love in fisherman households, from family sources. (Source: the above-cited book by Khetranarayan Choudhury, page 21.)

Beginning his performances in this way, he then turned to other songs. Just as the songs he himself composed were of protest, similarly, there were also many other kinds of songs. 'In the songs relating to love, the primary melody of his life emerges clearly.' (Ref: the above-cited book by Khetranarayan Choudhury, page 36.)

Why did he charm me, O friend
When I'm not the wife he married
I'm only the other woman, O friend
I live in fear in another man's house
But he beckons me with his flute's melody, O friend

Or

O beautiful woman, I won't let you off easily
I'll take the kohl of scandal and wear it on my eyes

In these cases, Vaishnav *padabali* too seems to have somehow entered his songs.

Love's a labour and love's a gem, dear
Even better, love's a garland on the neck
It's the life of folks who love and perish
That's the most successful.

When Jharuprasad was at the peak of his fame, a kind of duet of his with Niyatirani was on every lip. Crowds of people from faraway villages, walking for as much as twenty miles, queued to watch him perform.

> The boy offered to pay three rupees, the dodderer counted out sixteen in cash
> Greedy for money, my dad agreed to marry me off to the old man.
> ... Why O why didn't this young woman die?
> The mother's after money and so is the dad, all the village folk are after money
> No one stopped her getting married to a doddering groom
> ... Why O why didn't this young woman die?
> Come evening, I combed my hair, made the bed and lay down beside the old man
> As he lay in bed, the old man could only cough, *khukur-khukur.*
> ... Why O why didn't this young woman die?

In the same style, another very popular song sung in two voices:

> Both voices: The two of us are a mirthful picture of lovely Bengal. (Repeat)
> Female voice: You're a farmer with a leaking roof
> Both voices: The two of us are a mirthful picture of lovely Bengal.
> Female: Instead of cooking for you
> I'll go away to Bombay
> Male voice: I'll grab you bitch on the Howrah Bridge
> It's not so easy for home and family to split
> Both voices: The two of us are a mirthful picture...

Again, during the famine of 1943, he had composed this song too:

How many people died starving
Couldn't get even rice foam all day
Golden Bengal was ravaged
By the British rulers, brothers, by the British rulers...

There is a song of his on the subject of setting up girls' schools:

Women's education
Knowledge and learning are the very foundation
Can't do without knowledge
In a free country.

When the country gained independence, he had sung out spontaneously:

The harvest shall be good now and all shall eat
That day is not far now
May farmers and workers be happy
That's what I want to see.

Again, in the last phase, the song to which he always returned and sang, perhaps it was the song of his own life:

Oh fate, what's your intent with this arrow on my chest
I came to steal but fell asleep, dear

'Most of the songs of Jharuprasad are unavailable in written form ... There are many versions of the lyrics as well. There are also doubts about whether all of them were at all written by him. The language sometimes gets a universal character, and sometimes through the admixture of Ghoti and Bangaal, it is dispersed in an extraordinary way. As far as possible, we have compared the versions while quoting the songs.' (Quoted from the preface of the above-cited book by Khetranarayan Choudhury.) Yes, a doubt always remains.

Five

Jharuprasad's profile and unique personality

1. Dancing style – It was a kind of eclectic comic dance, which was simultaneously a mixture of *alkap-gambhira-jhumur* and *khemta* dance. His performances included recitation of innuendo-laden riddles and ditties to the accompaniment of various bodily gestures and movements, through all of which he provided pleasurable entertainment. A telling example of his kind of humour – '*Paapa* never stays hidden, O brother...' one had to infer the meaning that '*paap*', or sin, could never be hidden.

2. Outstanding acting ability – He seemed to have an inborn talent to play multiple roles, simultaneously, ranging from British rulers to labouring folk. Even within very serious roles, he sometimes mixed buffoonery. In this respect, he may be said to be a predecessor of Utpal Dutt. (See the above-cited essay by Haradhan Chattopadhyay.)

3. Terrific courage – He never hesitated to compose songs that were explicitly of an attacking nature and present them in his performances. He was also beaten up for this many times.

4. Wide range of subjects – Contemporary events were at his fingertips. In the course of singing one kind of song, he could move with skilful ease to another kind of song. When Bulganin of Russia came to Calcutta around 1955, he included that too in his *gambhira* songs. He did not have to write and prepare these, it was as if they entered the songs by themselves. One can see the name of Mao Tse-tung, too, being used in the songs from his final years.

5. Acute social consciousness – He could not tolerate corruption and injustice. And he lashed out at it through his acting, his songs, mockery, banter and scathing criticism. The beginning of a *gambhira* song of his on the subject of Durga Puja was like this: 'Why do you come just once a year, dear – without Lakshmi the land's barren.' Whenever he saw injustice, he protested against it vehemently. But even if he was indulgent towards quite a few instances of impropriety in some spheres, especially in his own life, in his songs and acting he always remained vociferous against it.

6. Humour of life – Jharuprasad has been called a 'folk artist of the humour of life'. He used to quote a saying of Sri Ramakrishna quite frequently – 'Mother, keep me seated in delight.' He used to say – 'Life is wound in the swirls of a *jilipi*. It's all sweet liquid – you only need to know how to lick and consume it.' In the final phase of his life, he drank excessively. (Reference: the above-cited discussion in the magazine *Kandi Samachar*.)

7. Garb – Jharuprasad used to come on stage wearing dirty old clothes, a shirt that was patched but with a bunch of medals pinned to his chest, his eyes crusted with rheum and his mouth full of muri. The muri used to fly out of his mouth amidst laughter. Once in a while, he also used to come on stage in babu garb – he would wear a frilled dhuti-punjabi, with a zari-worked yellow dupatta wound like a shawl around his neck. Laughing heartily, he would say in folk dialect: 'I am here!' Fountains of laughter erupted from the audience at just that.

8. Appearance – He was never handsome to look at, he was short and extremely ordinary looking. What caught one's

attention was the mass of long and curly hair, and his bright and piercing eyes. When he walked, his paunch jutted out ahead of his head and hands. If not to his face, but behind his back, people called him 'Gopal Bhar', after the pot-bellied jester of yore. His mouth was always agape, a face fixed in a laugh with broken teeth. And so people found even his ordinary conversation hilarious.

Six

Jharuprasad received innumerable awards during his artistic career. These included a few cups and about eighty silver medals. In 1944, after performing in Purnea town, he received a gold medal weighing a tola and half. The song was:

> There's no match for Princess Vidyadhari's beauty
> A golden pot on the outside but full of poison within!

It is said that he had also done a programme once on All India Radio. Besides, a German scholar wanted to make a documentary film about him. It had been initiated but it is not known whether it was completed. (Source: the above-cited essay by Haradhan Chattopadhyay.) He was felicitated by the Lok Sanskriti Parishad of Murshidabad in 1956, and in 1963 by the organization Sabuj Sangha in the village of Sabalada. Jharuprasad was also felicitated during the Murshidabad district festival, organized by the People's Council in January 1972. It is believed that the writer Samaresh Basu had met him and had recorded many songs and conversations. (In order to collect first-hand information regarding Jharuprasad, I myself went to Kandi and went around a few villages. Sudhir Chandra Maal, MA, BT, the Bengali teacher in Bahadurpur High School, provided me with a lot of hitherto unknown information. I am indebted to him for his magnanimity.)

Seven

It was for bringing Niyatirani to the stage to sing that Jharuprasad faced the most castigation. Moreover, she was the daughter-in-law of a brahmin household, albeit deserted by her *kulin* husband, but a daughter-in-law nonetheless. It led to an ugly reaction in the form of public ire. Besides, this was also the principal reason why Jharuprasad severed ties with Rakhari Daam's group. In the eyes of the upper-caste Hindu society, the experiment that he undertook by bringing Niyatirani to the stage was an unforgivable offence. The IPTA of that time, too, did not view the matter positively. Even if they ignored the unrestrained humour and frolic in his song performances as his personal matter, they could not tolerate the matter pertaining to Niyatirani. The complaint against him that had arisen – that he had kidnapped a brahmin daughter-in-law – was completely false. Niyatirani had, of her own free will, forsaken everything that night – save for what she was wearing – and joined him. (For detailed information, the chapter 'Niyatirani in the Life of Jharuprasad' in the previously cited book by Khetranarayan Choudhury is worth referring to.)

Although Jharuprasad battled against poverty all his life, he appeared on stage whenever he was invited, always with a smile on his face. That was his nature until his dying day. Sometimes he was paid something, and sometimes he wasn't. He received grant assistance from the state administration once, from the allotment for folk artistes, and twice from the district administration. Around May 1972, he was found to be suffering from cardiac disease. He was unwell for quite some time, but no one went to visit him or even bothered to enquire about him. It was Niyatirani who, hearing about him from others, took him and had him admitted in Kandi Hospital. Neither his brothers nor nephews came to see him after receiving the news. He needed bypass surgery, but because of the negligence of the hospital authorities and governmental apathy, he did not receive proper treatment. With all her pleading with the doctors being futile, Niyatirani brought him by a rickshaw-van to her own house in the outskirts of Kandi town. Jharuprasad's nephew had left her long ago, she was getting on in years and she, too, was suffering from various health problems. She was then struggling to eke out a living through an independent means of livelihood, making bidis. Jharuprasad could not stand straight now because of his bad leg, and yet, a few days before his death he was busy trying to set up a new group with a few people. Nidu too returned to him after being called. He had by then married and become a householder, but he was not inclined towards family. Jharuprasad had no income then, he could not scrape together even a fistful of rice once a day. It was Niyatirani who looked after him; she used to provide him with a bit of rice, twice a day, from her own share. Despite these circumstances, he persisted with his attempts to get up, and he used to stay up nights composing new songs. He sang the stanzas that he composed to Niyatirani. Around this time, he was felicitated by the All India Cultural Council. The only thing he said in response to the felicitation (standing up, with the help of a staff) was: 'Now my belly can't be filled with flowers – now I need a bouquet of money.' On a winter's night, on 17 November

1972, having gone to perform while running a fever, he took ill. He was singing:

O chatoki flower, why does the bee come to you?
Why – why does the bee come to you?
O chatoki flower, why does the bee come to you?

Does the bee come for your colour, dear?
Or does its craving for honey make it come to you?
O chatoki flower, why does the bee come to you?

That was his final song, his final composition. On 19 November, a Wednesday, at 6.18 in the evening, Jharuprasad breathed his last while he was in his full senses, with his head resting on Niyatirani's lap.

Finally, the author's humble submission:

I do not know whether Jharuprasad really existed or not. I have neither the knowledge nor the erudition to find out about this. I merely copied, verbatim, the draft of a scholar's research paper. In that sense, I may be a plunderer but not a thief. And so I submit.

[Mohanirgronthiyo, 1998]

Journal: 1991

NO BLOOD FOR OIL

=

RYSZARD BUGAJSKI'S *INTERROGATION*

When human offspring become the offspring of dogs
Then it's not the dog
That wags the tail
But the tail that wags the dog

He saw a designer punjabi and hit-film-styled blouse-and-sari, he saw Calcutta of 1941, processions, uproars, thousands of protesting voices, voices united in protest, Presidency, Alipore and Dum Dum Central Jails, thick crowds of protesting folk in Kakdwip, Ahalya, a peasant's wife was killed, a fight for land, Telangana, Salil Chowdhury's song, the child that did not get its birth papers even after having gained the right to the light and air of this earth, the whole of Kakdwip protests this, why haven't any buds bloomed on any tree, no shoot emerged either, the more the butterfly became a silkworm another day, that night the whole of Kakdwip
After that, one day at the Park Street–Chowringhee crossing
A squad of rifle-bearing soldiers
Stood surrounding the Gandhi statue

Who had taken his copy of *Anti-Duhring* from the table, even after searching for three months the book was not available in any shop in Calcutta, it had personal markings in red ink, his proud possession, one time someone said this book will never be published again by Russia, if you find an old copy, do get that, Calcutta of 1970, mist of dawn, the boy is taken out of the police van and asked to walk away, he walks away, he was shot from behind, he fell on his face, the Maidan bloody with the red on the green of the dawn's grass, *Marxism is not sufficiently master of itself to be a science*, someone had been screaming that out from the nineteen fifties, if modernity is the cultural manifestation of high capitalism, one can see that the eyes of the rebellious Marxist young woman of Godard have been blindfolded, black cloth, every time they try to shoot and kill her she screams out the Mayakovsky poem, finally, exhausted, the commander roars *Fire*, volleys of bullets reduce her to lattice, the wind blows on the crooked-as-a-snake path, one can see Orwell screaming perpetually, *All pigs are equal but some are more equal than others*

At the Tangra abattoir
A relay satyagraha
By the All India Cow Protection Committee

In 1990, the year of *'Oye oye!'*, something or the other will take place that is congruent with their interests, which they'll embrace, like blind folk, as their own view, Ryszard Bugajski's *Interrogation*, how far can oppression take humanity, socialist autocracy, the Stalin myth, the face of protest in Estonia, asked to strip naked on the pretext of interrogation, you know, how effortlessly he tore out and threw away the load of the compromise called clothing, he was not naked, but signifying civilization and stripping it naked, the nakedness transcended every kind of bodiliness, this picture was taken seven or eight years ago, they did not let us see it, finding that film of his that begins with war

31 December 1990
Campaign for Pollution-Free Yamuna
Impure water was made pure
By pouring 200 litres of milk into the river

The earth is now shedding its slough her wombway spreads over the soil
Roots cling to the soil the roots make their entrance
Give birth to a new earth And after all, man is this soil's offspring
Accepting the roots on her body, the fatigued, unploughed land turns fertile anew
The winds of the new generation blow in, leaving everything trembling

When everyone enters
He will still remain outside Observing
No war at any cost, no riots, may the world's children grow in peace, the nation in the delirium of the journey to the land of implicit cognition, peace abounds, that cut-ball bodhi tree from every leaf of which hang the Third World's balls, that's good, the ugly steel barrel, something good, what has this incestuous civilization been able to create in all this time, losing faith in humanity is the original tale of loving humanity
When he organizes the entire argument
An entire earlier argument of his
Can be presented against that

And

Such comments bring whatever was said earlier

To a new dimension

NO BLOOD FOR OIL, after a few days, even this bit of peace, these faggots will get their due, what has this earth been reduced to by the combination of man's greed and his self-interest, so we want war and not peace, we want war, only war can stave war, not this beggarly peace, we want a peace that's as vast as the universe, which only war can deliver, the oil streams of the Gulf shall keep floating in, carried over from two hundred years, the bloody son of man, Saddam Hussein, performs magnificently this untimely January, posters come up in Chandni Chowk, *WE SALUTE THE LION OF THE ARAB NATION SADDAM HUSSEIN,* the roar of artillery on the soundtrack, and flashes of light go on rolling down, like date-treacle, the new recruits ask the captain, Are we allowed to shoot helpless people   You can do as you please   Can I eat in the shop and walk away, leave without paying   You can do as you please   How elated the two new recruits were then   Come, come just now, let's go to war, come, come, let's go to war, come, to war   They choose their sides and join the fight, carrying the ration of dreams he goes through an entire determined life, even after scouring the whole of Calcutta he didn't find a copy of *Anti-Duhring* in any shop, the earth sheds its slough, keeps spreading her wombway, clutching the roots she makes them enter her, her roots will give birth to a new earth, and humanity is after all this soil's offspring, accepting the roots on her body, the fatigued, unploughed land turns fertile, the winds of the new generation blow in and leave everything trembling

The one who searches for truth
Always loses to cautiousness
Truth is never safe

[Journal: 1991, 1991]

Love Story

He sees the washerwoman kill her son
and then wash soiled clothes.
When the work's done she'll bring her dead son
back to life again and take him home.
All these girls keep alive when needed,
and kill when needed.

Will you be able to come?
Perhaps no ... why do you ask?
Damn, if only you could understand without
it being spelt out...
Then do spell it out...
As if everything can be spelt out...
Saying so, she pinches his stomach and with
the smart of the pinch,
Love cooed, *Ooh, aah,* and rolled around.

The boy sat beneath a tree. He wore whitish trousers and a Hawaiian shirt. His hair was combed quite artfully. The girl was dressed in a salwar-kameez. Her shampooed hair blew in the breeze. She had a notebook on her lap. The boy's name was Kashinath, the girl secretly called him Love. The girl's name was Asha. She said to Love: 'Love, you're going to your village house during the holidays, aren't you?'

'Oh, don't talk about that, Asha – Baba's sent a couple of letters in the last few days. I just have to go. I thought I'd spend some time during these holidays with you...' Hearing Kashinath, Asha broke out in titters of laughter. And then she said, 'Love, so what if you're an engineering student, you're still just a village bumpkin.' Saying so, she put her hand on Love's lap. The sweet sunlight of a winter's evening. With her left hand, Asha pulled Love close and kissed him on the cheek. She laughed, *hee hee*. Kashinath sprang up: 'Hey, what the hell are you doing – there are people all around – can't you see...' Asha promptly feigned anger. 'Let there be people! I'm kissing my lover so what's anyone got to do with that ... Really, you're a ... you've remained a village bumpkin. It's best that you go home and look after your father's land and so on.' Kashinath laughed a bit and said, 'You know it, I feel somewhat inhibited unless it's in private. But just yesterday in the restaurant, for a long time we...' 'But that was only because I said so' – Asha said, snatching the words from his mouth. And as she said it, she pinched him hard on his elbow. With the smart of the pinch, Love cooed, *'Ooh, aah'*, and rolled around. It was Asha who then said; 'Listen, it's best that you go to the village during the holidays. I'm not going to be around.' 'Where are you going?' Asha now said: 'Why, didn't I tell you ... my uncle lives in Delhi. I'll spend a few days there. I love spending time with Parimal-da there. He's a very smart boy. When he's in jeans and a T-shirt and comes around on his bike – how can I tell you how handsome he looks! I'll spend a few wonderful days there.' Kashinath now turned very grim, he said: 'Who's Parimal-da, Asha?' 'Oh – I suppose I haven't told you ... Parimal-da is my cousin Kallol's friend. He's very interesting. He can go on talking for hours – one never gets bored. Very open-minded. He's good in his studies too – he's a star student of Delhi University.' Kashinath now gulped, after that he said: 'Oh...'

Love

I always saw only darkness inside my eyes. Perfect darkness. No one anywhere – I'm falling into a huge, black pit – I used to feel that way quite often. Everyone advised me to stop drinking and concentrate on my work, but all that talk never entered my head. I used to feel that I was standing beside a mountain. There was a deep abyss on one side, someone gave me a gentle nudge and pushed me down. As I fall, I turn blue in fear; even in my sleep I could surmise that if I ever fell down, there'd be no trace of even my bones. I used to scream out in my sleep. And just then I'd see Ma come towards me, as if floating through the air, she would stretch her two arms and take me to her bosom, a smile on her face. Asha looked exactly like Ma. And her face was so sad-looking that one spontaneously wept looking at her. Ma would hug me to her bosom and scold me, as she used to when I was small: 'I'm alone – terribly alone ... Why do you go the wrong way like this and sadden me!' People wouldn't believe me if I said it, but in my dream I could clearly see drops of water rolling down Ma's eyes and falling on my head and on my face. Ma would then hug me and kiss me. I would see an amazing dim light all around her face, in the dream Ma looked like a goddess, and then on the touch of a pair of fair-skinned hands I'd wake up, I'd see the light in the room burning, and Asha bending down over me, ruffling my hair and touching her lips to mine. Truly, at that time I had gone to ruin.

She pinched herself. Rubbed her eyes with both her hands. No, she was quite awake. It wasn't a dream. There was a faint smell in the room. The smell was a very familiar one. Her Love drank once in a while. There was Love standing in the middle of the room – he was looking at her and smiling away. And then he came running and hugged her. Little by little, he had lost himself. The door was shut. But then, how did this man come inside her room? She wanted to say: 'You shouldn't have come here. I'm married, I'm someone's wife.' With a smiling face the youth replied: 'No one other than you can see me.' As soon as he said it, her Love became invisible. Was she dreaming? The whole room was in semi-darkness. Only a zero-watt lamp burned. Once again, little by little, the youth emerged from the darkness and advanced towards her. 'Aren't you happy to see me?' He came closer. 'Why are you ruining my life?' 'What's my fault?' 'I have a husband, I have a family.' Love put his arms around her and hugged her. It was as if the bones and ribs of her chest were being pulverized. Could this be told to anyone? Her body was melting, just like a wax doll. She didn't stretch her arm. Didn't scream. Parimal was lying just beside her. Curled up small, he was sleeping peacefully. Call him? So who was in the room, who? Love? How did he come?

Many girls secretly giggled about him. He had come to college one day following the vacation. Suddenly someone called him from behind. He turned around. 'Excuse me, do you have PD's notes from yesterday?' He could gather that the girl wanted to get acquainted with him on this pretext. 'But I didn't come yesterday.' 'Someone or the other told me you had come yesterday. That you were sitting beside

Mahuya.' 'No' – he had turned grim. The girl promptly said: 'Why do you always make a bear-face like that!' A bear – he was astonished. The girl smiled from the corner of her lip: 'You're indeed a bear' – saying so, she walked away briskly. And just then, hearing Kashinath, Asha tittered in laughter, like a little girl. She said: 'Love, you're a jackass!' Saying so, giving him a gentle pinch and placing one hand on Kashinath's hand, she said: 'Love, there'll be nobody in our house tomorrow. So you can come there in the afternoon.' Kashinath asked: 'Why, where's everyone going?' Asha replied: 'Bapi's going with Ma to an aunt's house in Salt Lake. They'll only return at night, after dinner. And Dada's been away from Calcutta since the last two days. He's gone to Digha with his college friends. The house will be completely empty. I'll just give ten rupees to the servant and send him to the cinema...' Nowadays, she went twice or thrice a week to the joint that had come up on the sixteenth floor of a twenty-two storeyed high-rise on Camac Street. Common people did not come here. But one or two newly rich types did come once in a while. The girl said: 'Over here, you're my client. I'm your entertainer. Nothing more than that.' Stubbing the cigarette in her hand in the ashtray, she bent down and poured whisky into a glass. Then, after some time, the green zero-watt lamp in the room would light up, the girl would slowly pull down the trouser zip of the inebriated man, her father's age, and keep doing so. 'What's up, Uncle, how are you?' 'You've been here a long time, my dear, why haven't you ever visited?' Tea appeared very soon. Coughing a bit, the gentleman said: 'My dear, there's something I have to talk to you about.' 'Tell me, Uncle.' 'What more can I tell you, my dear, you are like my own son. My younger daughter will be taking the secondary school exam. If you could help her a bit, that would be really good. It was she who spoke about you. No, I won't take no for an answer, my dear.' Asha came to him the very next day to study. Books in her hand, a smile on her face. Standing at the door, she asked: '... May I come in?' 'Come in.' He lifted his head up and looked. He had never looked at a girl this way before. Because of his grim and shy manner, the girls and wives in the village avoided him. 'May I sit down?' Putting her books down on the desk, Asha sat down. She sat on a chair facing him. The desk lay in between. 'Are you taking the secondary exam this year?' 'Yes,' she said, with her head down. 'Which subject would you like me to take up?' 'Whatever you'd like to teach me.' He lifted his face up and looked her in the eye. Asha lowered her eyes. The boy brought his face close to mine and asked: 'If you don't mind, may I know your name?' At that very moment, forgetting all about Baba's severe scolding, I told him my name. 'Oh, you have a really beautiful name.' By then, I too had got back some courage. I asked him in return: 'But you didn't tell me your name.' The boy began to laugh. 'Did you ask me my name?' I said: 'But I did ask now.' The boy told her his name: 'It's Kashinath.' I said: 'God, what an old-fashioned name – it's not nice. Your name just doesn't match how you look. I'll call you Love – how's that?' Hearing me, Kashinath began to laugh. I too joined him in laughter. As he laughed, he said: 'You look exactly like my Ma when you laugh.' I was astonished. 'Why do you say that, Love?' Just then, Shankar came running and stood beside him. Looking out of the corner of his eye, he said: 'What's happening, boss, what's all this I hear?' 'What's up, Shankar, tell me.' He said, 'But you're a good guy. Don't mind me, I mean, don't do any hanky-panky with my lover,

I swear.' Turning grim, Kashinath said: 'But I can't understand anything, what's all this nonsense you're saying?' 'Look here, boss, don't pretend. You know very well what I want to say. I'm telling you clearly, boss, if you mess around with Asha, I won't tolerate that.' Kashinath was very angry now: 'What's all this you're saying – I teach her. I view her as my sister.' He didn't wait there any longer. He began walking away immediately. From behind him, Shankar kept shouting: 'Try to keep it that way, my friend. Or else...' While returning home alone over the last few days, I had observed a boy standing and staring at me at the spot where I wait for a bus every day. The boy was quite handsome to look at and appeared to be from a decent family. His eyes were lovely. Those eyes entranced me in a trice. I felt a kind of inner attraction. And so, when the boy looked at me and smiled, I smiled back too in response. I longed to talk to him. But the very next moment, I would remember Baba's severe scolding. As soon as he saw me, Baba asked: 'What's the matter, Asha, why have you come back so late?' I said at once: 'I went to the library after two o'clock. I got delayed making my notes there.' Baba said: 'Asha, you've grown up now. You've learnt about what's good and what's bad for you. I trust that you won't do anything that disgraces us.' I listened to Baba quietly, with my head bowed. When she came to study, she would become somewhat absent-minded every now and then. She had something on her mind. The day after he observed this, he directly asked Asha: 'What do you think about from time to time? You become absent-minded while studying.' 'Oh, it's nothing – please continue teaching.' Asha tried to appear normal. He thought that she was concealing something. He asked her again: 'You're concealing something, Asha. Tell me frankly.' At first, she was silent. After that, she said softly: 'Shankar-da is always after me. He stands on the road with a group. I'm afraid of them.' He turned grim. Without much thought, he blurted out: 'After we're done today, I'll accompany you.' 'No, no' – Asha cried out – 'I can go on my own. Shankar's friends are all frightful. They wouldn't hesitate to do anything untoward. To you too…' 'It's alright, but I can look after myself.' He tried to appear brave. After all that she had just said, it was impossible for her to continue coming. Then somewhat doubtfully, he said: 'Alright then, you needn't come here tomorrow. I'll come over to teach you.' Then, after some time, bringing his face to her ear, he said, almost in a whisper: 'Come on, Asha, let's go away somewhere together.' 'What's that – where shall we go?' 'The two of us will live together somewhere. We'll be a happy family.' 'Do you think that can happen – where shall I go leaving my husband and family behind?' 'Why, what's the problem – that man suspects you. Instead, just you and I shall start a new life together.' After a while, she said: 'In that case, whom shall I live with?' 'Why, here I am…' 'But that's only once in a while, secretly … If you had me fully, you'd get rid of me in two days. One doesn't like the same old thing every day. Don't I know you…' As she said it, she pinched his cheek. Quite hard. His cheek was smarting. That day it rained heavily the whole day, and there was a stormy wind too. I don't sleep well when it rains. I become depressed suddenly. It was almost twelve at night then. I was lying down silently, staring at the ceiling. I remembered Ma. After dinner, and before falling asleep, she used to read the *Kathamrita* of Sri Ramakrishna for a while. It was an old habit with her. But where was that Ma! Why, Asha has come in place of Ma – hasn't she? The next room was shut, completely still. Didn't meet any friends today. Who on earth would venture out on this disastrous night. The rain became fiercer as the night advanced. I was lying curled up under a thin sheet. Suddenly there was a knock on the door. The door knocker had not moved but still made a sound. I pricked up my ears. Again a sound. Who on earth could have come to call me on this disastrous night? Getting up from the bed, wrapping the sheet around me, I walked silently, and stood near the door. Once again there was the same knocking sound. I asked: 'Who is it?' From outside, a female voice whispered: 'It's me, open the door!' Asha – I clearly heard Asha's voice. Asha! So late at night! Before I could think anything, again came the whisper, which was nonetheless clearly audible, asking me to hurry up: 'Open the door quickly – I'm getting wet.' It was raining so heavily outside that it was impossible for anyone to hear her voice. She rushed into the room as soon as I opened the door. Draped in a raincoat from head to toe, a mysterious smile on her face. As soon as she entered, she said: 'Shut the door first, I'm cold.' I was vacillating. Looking me in the eye, she said: 'I said, shut the door first. I'm feeling very cold.' I shut the door and said to her: 'Coming to my room so late at night – like this...' She said: 'What terrible rain – I wasn't able to sleep all alone. He had night duty, so I thought I'd play ludo with you and while away the time. You have ludo and snakes and ladders, don't you? I love playing ludo and snakes and ladders.' After that, pausing awhile, she looked me clearly in the eye and said: 'You don't mind, do you?' Then Shankar shouted and called out to him: 'Hey, my friend, where've you gone?' Kashinath turned grim. He said: 'Shankar, whatever you're doing isn't right.' 'Hey, don't lecture me, boss. I know all about that. Being too friendly with Asha isn't right, pal. But I'll clear the way. Two or four days, that's all.' 'Alright, we'll see about that.' He put on a brave front and affected a boastful manner. And then he left the place as fast as he could. Once again, about a month later, he was returning home from college, tired. Shankar came and stood in front of him. There were three others with him. 'Hey pal, you got angry and left that day...' He was grim as usual. Yet, with an artificial smile, he said: 'All's well.' Suddenly, Shankar's friend, the boy who looked like a goonda, put his hand inside the open front of Kashinath's shirt and, scratching the hair on his chest, said, 'Hey boss, is it still brother-sister or have you reached Laila-Majnu?' Kashinath looked at him and turned his face away. A complete loafer. He was looking at him and smiling, exposing his teeth. Not getting any response, he muttered and said: 'Hey, get each of us a sister like that, I say.' Now he lost his cool. He turned around and landed a tight slap on the boy's face. As soon as he slapped him, he realized he'd made a mistake. No, he wasn't as brave as that, whatever he might have done hot-headedly, the truth was that he did not have the strength to stand up against Shankar's gang. They were ready too. By then, the boy had taken out a bicycle chain. Shankar sprang forward and held his arm, he turned around and spat out in abuse: 'You bastard, son-of-truth Yudhishthira...' 'You look as if you haven't eaten all day long ... would you like to eat something?' 'No, forget it. Alright, Love, can I ask you something?' 'What is it?' 'Can you strangle and kill me?' 'What the hell are you saying?' 'Tell me first whether you trust me or not.' 'But where are you?' 'I don't know.' 'Tell me truthfully, where are you?' 'I'm lost. What will I survive with?' 'With whatever you survived with so long.' 'But that's lost.' 'No, I don't believe that.' 'Don't be sad, Love, whatever had to happen happened. But you have to survive.' Darkness. Great darkness. He casts his eye and sees Asha lying down obscenely. Love picks up his sheet and covers all of Asha's body. He parks the scooter and rushes to Asha. 'Hello! Meeting you after a long time! I'm sure you're terribly busy with your husband and family. Tell me, how are you?' Surprisingly, there was no more hesitation in Love's voice. Although earlier, he used to falter when he spoke. Asha was astounded. She felt a strange sensation inside. Somehow or the other she managed to say: 'I'm fine.' She herself realized it wasn't her voice. For that matter, she even forgot to ask, 'How are you?' Love suddenly shifts to the second person intimate. 'You didn't ask how I am.' 'So tell me, how are you?' 'Can you tell me how I am – what do you think, looking at me?' As he said it, he looked her in the eye. Asha looked downwards. 'Yes, the funny thing is that, right now, a lot has really happened. Parimal had once come on a holiday together with Ashok.' Suddenly my head began to reel, I pressed her against the door and began to kiss her, and then, unseen by anyone, I lifted her up and entered the bathroom. Asha was shouting, but my body was full of an ogre's strength right then. Fortunately, I didn't latch the bathroom door from inside! After some time, the door opened, the people in the house entered and rescued Asha from my clutches. Pulling and dragging, they carried me and held my head down over the washbasin and opened the tap. Even after all that commotion, Parimal had dropped me to my house. I was in the rear seat, leaning my head back, my eyes shut. I vaguely remembered Ma's face. After dinner, Ma would sit down with the *Kathamrita*. I could hear them, everyone was worrying about me. Friends were repeatedly saying that I had supposedly gone astray soon after Ma's death. Later, I went to Asha's house and apologized. Seeing her looking at me with a smiling face, I was stunned – why do I keep mixing up Asha's face with Ma's? My head was spinning, I held the door to support myself. Asha took me by the hand and made me sit. She asked: 'Would you like to eat something? No, my dear, not at all. I didn't mind anything the other day.' The offer had come, to go over so he could have a look. The middle-aged managing director was terribly lonely. Had to give him company from time to time. Only then would the job materialize. A girl from the same neighbourhood had given her the lead casually. She had said: 'Take life easy, a lot of this is happening nowadays.' I had thought it would be rather simple, but it was just the opposite when it came down to brass tacks. On the specified day, dressed up and adorned, I turned up, together with the friend, at the man's flat. A well-decorated flat in a posh locality in central Calcutta. Going into the room, and after talking directly to the managing director, her dear friend brought her into the room and, before she left, she said – 'I'll be back after a while.' Her feminine awareness made her sense danger at once. After shedding stupid tears about his loneliness, and sometimes casting a spell with his words, when the man finally offered her a drink – even then she hadn't been worried much. Then the distance between them, dictated by decency, kept diminishing. Despite being in an air-conditioned room, her whole body was covered in perspiration. But she had to survive. She wouldn't ask anyone for help. For that matter, not even Love. In a theatrical voice, sitting with that managing director who was her father's age, stroking his neck, rubbing her lips against his, bringing her face near his ears, she had whispered: 'Hey – please, not today – today I have ... the coming Saturday will be for you – for you alone – okay?' But the man's desire was not quenched so easily, she had to sacrifice a bit, but nevertheless, she could more or less get away that day. Must survive, and again, decency had to be maintained. Another funny thing had taken place in Asha's own flat on her birthday. Someone had removed my lighter. Going to light a cigarette, I found I didn't have the lighter in my pocket. Asha was then cooking a special chicken dish. She was in the kitchen. I thought I'd certainly find matches in the kitchen. But I didn't find anyone in the kitchen. I looked around, everything looked kind of dishevelled. Suddenly, someone said from behind: 'May I know what's happening here?' Startled, I turned around and saw Asha with her friends beside her. Everyone was watching my antics silently. I said, 'I came to look for matches, I've lost my lighter.' 'To look for matches' – Asha said, her eyes flashing – 'and so you'll enter my bedroom without asking me? Don't you know you shouldn't go into a woman's bedroom without consent? Does one find matches in a bedroom?' I suddenly came to my senses. I realized I had entered the bedroom mistaking it for the kitchen. By then, many had begun to smile embarrassedly. Asha then took me aside and took out my lighter from her clenched fist and said to me: 'Here's your lighter. When you were having a drink, I took this out of your pocket, silly goat!' She pinched me gently on my cheek. I stared at her face in astonishment.

THE END

[Premer Golpo, 1992]

The Real Detective of the Mystery Beneath the Skin

He stands holding his reproductive organ and gazing at himself – *what part shall I play tomorrow?*

Ami[1] had developed a kind of bodily relation with the books, which was both gradual and incessant, and just after that, problems became manifest. They survive now by eating each other's flesh. Violets are blue, because another body emerges from the body and walks in front of silent Grushenka,[2] all along Khalasitola.[3] As it is, the girl was beautiful, her colleagues flattered her calling her a 'paragon of beauty', right from her college days she had observed only entrancement in men's eyes. Perhaps it was this girl who came to meet Ami. He happened to say: 'Come, come in, I was just thinking about you.' But the girl interpreted this in

---

1 'Ami' means 'I' in Bangla, and is also used here as a character's name.

2 The names Grushenka and the subsequently referred to Alyosha bring to mind Fyodor Dostoyevsky's *The Brothers Karamazov*. The name Theodore that also appears is the English version of the Russian Fyodor.

3 Khalasitola is a country liquor bar in central Calcutta, also known for its association with a section of intellectuals, poets, writers, film-makers, theatre persons, etc.

a different way, the eighth colour of the rainbow was about to be discovered. Girls were extremely possessive, for sure, but he was of the opinion that boys were even more possessive than girls. Now Ami says he is very tired, an infinitude of tiredness. He had been tired for all of the last three decades, which was even longer than he had been alive. And just then, after talking about this and that for about an hour, as she was leaving, he hugged Grushenka. She didn't resist, releasing herself slowly she says: 'You're a rogue.' He laughs: 'And you're a treasure trove.' 'You talk rubbish all the time' – Grushenka says – 'Tell me, why do you come so late – don't I worry?' *Good and evil are one, evil is merely the wrong choice at the moment of truth*. If the life I used to lead was a dream, then this is a nightmare, and the nightmare didn't end until it was transformed into complete insanity. Ami had just turned forty then. Double the girl's age. A face full of a red beard, two scrawny legs, a short, fat body. His female friends used to smirk, they said: 'He has the kind of appearance of someone who's eager to establish a physical relationship.' When he had no other work, he made models with bones. In the course of doing that, he had assembled a complete human skeleton. And in the same way, whatever he wrote, over an entire year, page after page – one night something got into his head and he tore everything into shreds and cast it to the wind. Even before an incident is prepared one ought to arrive at another incident, and from there to yet another incident, perhaps with a diametrically opposite thought, all of which would be created with another arrangement, unconnected, and as a result ambiguity is created, is bound to be. Because, perhaps, Ami, in a particular sense, just like some other writers, was a writer, the last-writer too. He began to lose touch with the external world, he was also steadily losing his mental balance. He stopped meeting his friends, he used to say that he didn't have clothes to go out in, didn't have shoes. But when he did get some money, he called all the people from the street and organized a grand feast of food and drink. Towards the end, Ami lived all alone in a one-and-a-half-room flat. His body had somehow come to resemble an old man's, although he was only forty his face bore the stamp of age. And when he was immersed in dreams in his spare time, he could see Theodore staring fixedly at him through the darkness. He had already sent killers. Theodore was passing off in his own name the pages of writing stolen from him. One day, he said that a maidservant had mixed a sleeping potion in his tea and stolen some pages from his new writing in order to sell it to Theodore. But the funny thing was that the man who was visible has reached the vicinity of the flyover by now. The boy consoles the girl, 'Just you wait and see – everything will be alright.' The car waits. The girl says: 'You must help me, I beg you, Alyosha, help me.' Ami leaves. The girl stands gazing at the door. And then she goes and lies down on the bed that's enveloped in darkness. The sound of a motorcycle starting and then going away can be heard. Who was it that said life was full of surprises – who said it, was it Theodore or Alyosha – or was it both of them? Grandma used to say that when I was a little boy, I apparently used to run around with my arms spread out like a bird's wings. People say that when you dream about flying it means you're growing up. But Ami used to fly even when he was awake and yet he could never grow up. Leaping off a mountain – flying over the ocean – Ami has such dreams even now. As if snatching his words, Theodore says: 'How amazing, I too was thinking of exactly the same thing at this moment.' At one time, there used to be a youth here, on this bed, whose name too was Theodore. Everyone used to call him Alyosha in jest. When he was asked, he used to say: 'I'm floating over clouds.' That was quite normal for those who had a problem in the head, after all as soon as they wished they could lie down next to the clouds. Many people ask questions about Ami being sent to the hospital and the subsequent incident. Was it at all necessary to send him to the hospital? Even if he was sent to the hospital once, was it correct to keep him there for the rest of his life? Erasing the difference between the self of the future and the self of the present, I reconstruct myself anew each day. How can I become what I have not yet become – all my hopes and desires are only a ceaseless endeavour towards this rearrangement. This circle will never be complete. My separation is eternal, Ami is insuperable like nothingness. There's always a distressed scream of nothingness within my existence, but this void is the kind of force, the force within one's existence – which makes man dream of ascending to a certain and well-knit future from an incompatible and uncertain condition. Many of Ami's friends used to declare that Ami did not behave like a lunatic at all. Yes, he was paranoid, but one often comes across people suffering from persecution mania who live with their families without causing any damage, leading regular lives. Maybe his neighbours had raised objections about him because he was not like other people. After all, ordinary people are bound to express their doubts about a man who only goes out at night, scribbles something all day long and then tears it up, who doesn't talk to anyone. It's love for people that makes Ami anti-human. Perhaps it was because of this that Ami exacted a great revenge on himself.

Conformity means death, only protest gives hope in life. Yes, Ami saw that a man practically gives him constant company, enriches him, sometimes more than a woman. Through this company, he creates a certain madness within me as well, because Ami too was a man. I had to ascertain whether Ami was really a man in various ways. I ascertain that by placing myself beside a man, and not just beside a woman. Through this, Ami understands his way of thinking too. Trying to know oneself without any sleight. But, being alone, continuously, and gradually becoming solitary, did not merit blame. After spending the night with Grushenka, the wild-mannered Ami – then, in those days – became endowed with some human qualities. In terms of thought and feeling, another dimension became manifest. And unlike in his youth, when he used to seduce many women, he constantly stayed beside the girl. In his earlier writings, a specific dimension of power, courage and madness was expressed, there was a wild exultation regarding man's aboriginal tendencies. After Grushenka's arrival, a lot of things in him became gentle. There was restraint regarding the perverted expression of flesh, a reflexivity entered his thinking. And the veiled melancholia in the latter phase attained a much higher level than in the former phase. Towards the end, Ami started living with the girl. That's why a melancholy countenance entered his final writings, shielding everything else. The two of them lived together then – Grushenka and Theodore. The gossip was that the girl bore his child in her womb, but that she had been completely unwilling to have an abortion. Changing her clothes and wearing a sari, Grushenka said: 'See how I look ... Come, where will you take me?' He suddenly held her face in his hands and said: 'Do you know something, Grushenka – do you know that...'

Notwithstanding her married life with her husband for so long, these words of the man who was her lover made Grushenka's whole being giddy, but she said: 'I'm not anything to rave about.' Ami looked at her and turned grave: 'If you were a man, you'd understand the fire – the fire you're playing with, Grushenka, standing between father and son.' The other level beyond this first level, where he had tried to reach, where there was no *compromise*, was sexuality. Here you can never be successful through pretence. That means you want to experience the sight of that level through your instincts. Your instincts tell you about your ordinary experiences which are outside the world of the mind, and through those you enter the world of the mind by means that are bestial or anything else like that – you see that. But, for that, every now and then you have to sleep with other girls too. You have to sleep with them both *actively* and *positively*. Only then will you know yourself. Actually I liked this too. I liked it with utmost honesty. I stayed back. I was trying to search for something, I'm still doing that now. In such matters, we either become mere slaves to our own pleasure or accept the girl's happiness as the final word. Both of these are a kind of lie. And lies do not lead to any investigation of truth. I am up to taking this risk. You can enter another secret world through the girl herself. 'Do you know how you are different from everyone else?' – Grushenka asks – 'You know how to listen. Men never listen to what women say. They only think about getting into bed. I don't mind getting into bed, but what's amazing is that you heard me all this while.' The truth can't be realized through words. It's correct to say that the moment of pure truth cannot be expressed in the language of any specific person, but it's also possible to create new kinds of signs, which are not used by people, through which the individual in the moment of pure truth can be defined. It is this that can be called, in Ami's view, the sign of oneself – meaning, one is one's own sign. Looked at in another way, one's own sign is signlessness – whose true nature cannot be expressed in any language in use. Perhaps the only part of our method of logical elaboration that is the real truth is what people cannot easily accept. He lay in bed, away from Calcutta, unwell. He muttered: 'I want to see the girl.' His wife was beside him – his wife of twenty-five years. Those who were near him said: 'There she is, right beside you.' He got annoyed: 'No, no! Not her, Grushenka. I want to see Grushenka.' Bad times have begun for me, brother, I was just recovering from kidney inflammation and now I'm writhing in spinal pain all day. For over a year now, I've been unable to sleep in bed. I sit with my back resting on a pillow all day and night, even the hour or two that I sleep is by resting on the pillow. At first a lung X-ray was taken but nothing was detected. It's been a week now since the spinal X-ray was done. A collapse of the third dorsal vertebra was detected. Ami comes and stands at the door. He stands with his head raised high, towards the darkening sky. Down below, the road going up and down the flank of the mountain recedes into the distance, keeps doing so. Dogs, apparently, eventually start looking like their masters. At one time, I used to think that this referred to a resemblance of nature or character. But later I realized it was not that – gradually the dogs began to look as ugly as their masters – the insides of the mouths of both were terribly filthy – a horrible, red, gaping mouth. And thus, Ami died one day. According to the hospital records, the cause of death was an apoplectic stroke. After Ami died, when his desk was opened, a large envelope bearing Dostoyevsky's name was found. But it was completely empty. Actually, Ami's case was different. He was merely a trapeze artist. Dressed in gleaming red satin, Ami floats around – swinging from one hand and then the other – from one end to the other end – even when he lets go, emptiness, he is held by an invisible bond. He was incapable of severing that tie, no one was capable of it. And as he floated in that momentary emptiness, he himself observed his own defeat. At some point, his writings came together and took over his life, it was the blown-away pages of the writing that determined how much of the writer was there or whether at all there was anyone called a writer. Or whether the term 'writer' was actually nothing but an imaginary notion, which had no existence in reality. *The unexamined life is not worth living*. The only way to deny everything that was *absurd* in the world was to lead one's life in an *absurd* way. With every new thought, Ami knows he has to attain death again and again.

[Twoker Niche Rohosyer, Ini-i Ashol Goyenda, 1993]

The 2,500-Kilometre-Long Ganga

or

The Picture of the Crowd Slipping Past a Man Who Ducked His Head and Took a Plunge

And all reality itself
Has to be realized from imagination

1. The death-line denizen

The blackish-red colour forming on the white sink immediately caught one's eyes. It was just like an abstract painting. The picture of the stomach's secret sickness rapidly exploded in deep colour over the white surface. Blowing whistles, they patrolled over the wall, which was some five feet above us. When they came near, we stopped our work of breaking the chain and were silent. But there was no need for such caution. Because it simply wasn't possible for the watchmen patrolling at that height to discern the presence of someone submerged neck deep in the water. The chains in the water continued to make a monotonous clinking-clanking sound. Concealing himself under the boat, he advanced and whispered something to me. There was the sound of water lapping the boat, the continuous sound of the water. Nothing that he said could be discerned. After a while, the ring holding the chain slipped off the fist and, pulled by the hidden current, the boat too left the shore and floated further and further away. Clutching the chain in my hand, I began swimming along with the tug of the floating boat. After that, both of us climbed in. The boat then drifted away from the bank and steadily made its way along the 2,500-kilometre-long Ganga. Knocking on the floorboards: two planks had to be removed; there may be a need for something to paddle with. Not worrying about the direction in which we were drifting, they just tried to ensure that the head of the boat was pointed towards the opposite bank. It was as if he understood our question, right then, as if a navigator's skill was his birthright. It seemed he wanted to wind the rope through the series of iron rings so that the boat would be fastened on all sides. Hopeless torment and the same detached despair. The use of the word 'guerrilla' makes a writer-worker a proletarian and definitely, substantially, accomplishes the extinction of the intellectual elite. Because he was of the view that violence, crime and destructive activities were all, in the current world, actually words that reinforced peace, orderliness and normalcy. Slowly, like this, he kept exposing civilization's pawnbroking and the accumulated hidden ploys, apparently...

In the middle of all this talk,
suddenly, as if materializing from thin air, a
teenage girl emerged. Clad in jeans and a T-shirt,
she looked like something one only saw in *Playboy*. He stared greedily. The country is India, it's Calcutta.

Tile-roofed slum hutments made up the entire area of Atabag Surkikal. They were so densely packed together that even daylight couldn't fully enter the neighbourhoods. Lane after lane, ever narrower lanes, a veritable maze of lanes.

Some fifteen females, elderly, young and children, were cramped together in an eight-by-nine-foot room enclosed with bamboo matting. They took turns to sleep at night. There wasn't space for everyone to sleep simultaneously. The old father and mother also lived in that very room, besides the two elder brothers and their wives and children. The younger son got married and entered the eight-by-nine-foot premises with his new bride. Babies were born, babies died. The children and youth set out at dawn in search of wages. One passed gambling, illicit liquor and drug dens every few minutes. They grew up in the climate of bomb and bullet battles, abductions and counter-abductions. Video parlours in lane after lane. Pornographic films were shown in broad daylight. Sometimes a scintillating two- to five-minute clip was added to a current Hindi film. Ten- to twelve-year-old boys too went in there to appease their curiosity. Sitting beside them were people their father's or uncle's age. Even before hair sprouted on their upper lip they became aware that it was very easy to earn through the trade. Delivering a few small packets of heroin from the main den to the small dens could fetch a crisp, large-denomination note. Wearing their school uniforms, and with the *patas* concealed within the pages of the schoolbooks, even the babus of the citizen's committee would hardly suspect them. The police wouldn't catch them, for all that was taken care of by the dealer through monthly payment arrangements. Lots of easy money lay ahead, as a smuggler, heroin peddler, supply man or *satta* penciller. To them, all this was part of life, no crime at all. Two brothers, ten or eleven years old – it was three at night then – were playing *teen patti* under the light of the lamp post at the head of the alley. Yes, gambling for money. And while gambling, one had no brothers. The one who won took all the money. Not a penny was spared because someone was a brother. He said: ‘Dada and Boudi are asleep now.’ When they woke up at dawn, he and his brother would get a place to sleep. They whiled away the night in this way, playing cards and so on. No, the police were afraid to enter this lane, so they had no fears on that score.

Firoz did not drink alcohol. However, he smoked ganja from morning to night. Under the banyan tree, immediately behind the workers’ quarters. He was always surrounded by the Class IV workers of the slaughterhouse. One of them, Chhote Lal, was Firoz’s right-hand man. From morning to night, a medium-sized jute bag was constantly in Firoz’s hand. The bag was filled up four times. Chhote Lal kept the accounts. He made bundles of the rupee notes. After that, the money reached Maqbool Mia’s meat shop outside the slaughterhouse. Everyone knew Firoz. The traffickers were also duly terrified of him. Someone in Basti no. 292 called me to the shadows and said: ‘Ganja Firoz is the local Sai Baba. The unofficial agent of the upper echelons. Even the babus make sure they don’t ever mess with him! We’re just supply-men. But his real babu – you’d never catch him even if you sat here and undertook penances! He lives in Burrabazar. Money flows by itself into his bag. Doesn’t have to ask for it. Firoz also has a side business. You’ll find out if you make just a few enquiries. But be very careful. I can’t tell you anything.’

'Where should I look?' 'Try to find "Daal Bhaat" under the bridge. He begs. A skinny boy.
You'll find out from
him. You'll have to spend a bit of money.' Daal Bhaat was found right under the Lohapul bridge. His actual name was was Nyara (Baldy). A twelve-year-old boy. He spoke Bangla
fluently. A restless look in his eyes. One could sense even at first sight that he was very intelligent. 'Hey, are you Daal Bhaat?'
'Cut that out ... just say which one you want.'
'Hmm' – 'Fucking idiot ... Hurry up!' 'But...'
'You want a *pata*, right?' 'Yes.' 'Are you new or what?'
'Yes, brother.' 'So that's why ... There are three types. For fifty-five, seventy-five and hundred rupees.
Since you're a newcomer, take the fifty-five-rupee one.' After buying the stuff, I looked this way and that, I gave a crisp twenty-rupee note to him as
baksheesh. Found out about a
lot of things. 'Pata' meant heroin. Firoz Sheikh had been running
this business in the Tangra area for the last few years.
The stuff came from Altaf,
in Garden Reach. The main sales hub was the slaughterhouse. Other than that,
Baldy, aka Daal Bhaat, was the medium for sale. I started to leave.
Suddenly Baldy held my right arm firmly,
looking helplessly at my face, he said:
'Babu, promise me, you won't tell
anyone else.' 'Why, brother?' 'That bastard, Firoz, will kill me. He'll thrash me and kick me out of the locality. He's very

powerful, Babu. A lot of big folks come in their cars to meet him.
He pays me fifteen rupees a day. That's what
my Ma and I survive on. He beats up
my Ma too. He forces himself into my Ma's bed at
night...' Yes, do you know, this country of ours, India,
became independent sixteen hours after the birth of Pakistan.
It was supposed to become independent on fourteenth August,
but
because the planetary configurations on that day were
not convenient, Indian leaders
decided upon independence at midnight.

I observed a lot of girls standing on the balconies of the houses and at the corners of the lanes. As we went by, a girl looked down from the window of a house and said: 'Oh young babu, I say, are you new here?' My husband communicated something to her in signs, I couldn't understand what exactly it was. After a while, he entered a house with me. A three-storey house. We climbed up a narrow staircase. A medium-sized room. Although it was still afternoon, a tube light was on. The window was shut, it was completely covered by a curtain. A fat, matronly woman sat on the cot, chewing paan. Seeing us, she stood up. Taking out a handkerchief from his pocket and wiping the perspiration around his neck, my husband said: 'Here's Middle Aunty. And this is Reba. She'll be working here in this place of ours from now on.' Chewing away on her paan, Middle Aunty replied indifferently: 'Alright.' After that, glancing at my husband and then looking at me, she said to me: 'You sit here for a while. I'll be back.' Middle Aunty left. Setting the fan speed to maximum, my husband said: 'You've legged it such a long way ever since morning, you must be very hungry. Just wait a bit, I'll be back with some food.' He went out of the room. Although the fan was on full speed, I still perspired. After about five minutes, Middle Aunty entered the room carrying a steel plate piled with food. 'Eat up, dear girl.' After setting down the food, Middle Aunty left the room again. To tell the truth, I was very hungry. I hadn't often seen so much food at once. At home, two bare meals of dry rotis and gourd curry. I devoured all the food on the plate. There were large sweetmeats, kachoris, a mutton chop. The size of the jalebis – pink in colour – dripping syrup! I licked and lapped up and finished everything. We had set out a long time ago, in the morning – travelled by train and bus – I hadn't really eaten anything. After a while, Middle Aunty entered the room with a glass of water. Offering me the glass, she said: 'Here.' After I'd drunk as much water as I wanted, she took the glass and plate. 'You rest here for a while now. There's work to be done.' Before I could ask her anything, Middle Aunty left the room and went away. I was all alone in the empty room. I wondered where my husband had gone. Would I get the job! As I was thinking about all this, suddenly Middle Aunty arrived, pulled the door shut, latched it from outside, and left. A strange fear seized me. I hoped I hadn't landed up in a bad place. I had come through so many narrow lanes, the whole place had seemed strange to me. Thinking along these lines, I wept. Then I began to knock on the door. 'Where are you – why did she shut the door – do open the door, Aunty ... oh Middle Aunty – where has he gone – open the door ... I fall at your feet.' I banged at the door. Finally, using both my hands, I pushed and shook the door. In a little while the door really opened. I saw a huge man standing in the doorway. Bushy hair on his head. A thick moustache.

Bare bodied. His chest was covered in black hair. He wore a short dhoti, tied like a loincloth. Looking at him, it seemed his body was made of steel. He pushed me and threw me on the bed. 'Why are you shouting?' he asked in Hindi. From his speech, I made out he was not Bengali. I began to cry, and said to him: 'Where is my husband? He brought me here saying there was a job vacancy in a company.' 'Oh yes ... So what if he brought you? Why don't you sit quietly?' I began to cry even louder, and pleaded: 'Let me go! I don't need anybody. I'll go by myself.' I got up from the bed. The non-Bengali man laughed and said: 'But you can't go away!' As soon as he said that, the man lifted me up, threw me down on the bed again, shut the door and latched it from inside. I trembled in fear. Even my tears dried up in the face of the fear of the worst. The non-Bengali man asked: 'What's your name?' I remained silent. 'Hey, why are you silent? Why don't you tell me your name?' Full of fear, I replied: 'Reba.' 'Tsk tsk, what a sweet name! Re-ba!' I broke into tears again and fell at his feet. 'Please let me go! I beg you, let me go!' The man began to laugh. He said: 'Let you go – oh no! This is Ali Baba's cave. It's not easy to reach here. And going away is also very difficult. Once you enter this place, you can't leave. Do you know what the name of this place is?' I shook my head. The man said: 'This is Sonagachi. Where women ... I mean...' Shocked, I mumbled: 'But my husband told me about a job in a medicine company...' As if he were robbing even my words, the man said: 'Yes, of course, this too is a medicine company. The babu who gets you will come to you, and you will keep that babu happy with medicine.'

A branch of a dead tree had been planted
on the stony earth of a

hill. A sanyasi
came everyday and watered the base of that dead
branch and prayed that
it came back to life. After a long time,
one day the dead tree did actually come back to life again,
living branches covered with leaves spread out
towards the sky. Tarkovsky tells us this fairy tale
at the beginning of his film, *The Sacrifice*.

On 26 July, a senior officer of the Reserve Bank of India, Mr Krishnatre, went to receive his son at half-past nine at night. He drove his car to Howrah Station and parked in the parking lane between platforms eight and nine. Almost at once, a black Ambassador car arrived beside it. Just as Krishnatre and his wife and daughter stepped out from their car and advanced a few steps, four youths sprang out of the Ambassador with daggers in their hands. Three of them pounced on the three family members, but they resisted and began shouting. The girl was struck by the dagger of one of them and wounded, but she hung on to the sleeve of his shirt. The wife, too, frantically resisted another man. To make sure that no one from nearby came forward to help them, the fourth person brandished his revolver, threatening anyone who dared. This incident went on for over twelve minutes. A crowd formed all around, but no one dared to come forward to help. Despite their utmost resistance, the gang took the mother's and daughter's valuables and left. The distance between the spot where the incident took place and the office of the railway police was fifteen to twenty yards. No policeman arrived there, even though there had been so much screaming and shouting, and over such a long spell of time. After the incident, Krishnatre ran to the police post and identified himself and said: 'They're running away! If they're chased they may well be caught!' The policeman there didn't pay any heed to that, and after questioning the family for half an hour, he finally snapped: 'Why do you set out wearing so much gold and ornaments? Theft and robbery is bound to happen.' On Tuesday, something fantastic happened on the first day of the law examination in Calcutta University. The examination was to start at noon. Around half-past ten, a bunch of students (both male and female) could be seen clambering up a drainpipe beside Ashutosh Building, making their way up to the first floor. Climbing up to the veranda, they would make their way to and enter the examination hall and occupy their preferred places in advance. They would tear up the pasted seat numbers and sit wherever they wanted. Boys and girls entering the examination hall clambering up a drainpipe – what's so great about that scene – you see a lot of that in films. Within a few minutes after the exam started, the gates of Ashutosh and Hardinge Buildings were closed and locked. There was a sizeable police deployment outside each gate. But from the direction of Medical College, and from across the street, books were supplied, one after another, via a rope line. Pedestrians stopped and gaped in astonishment at the scene. A crowd formed. Another group standing outside went about distributing the answers to the objective questions. The policemen on duty had their backs turned to the scene, they were busy kneading tobacco in the palms of their hands. A few examination candidates could be seen standing on the veranda and writing on their answer sheets. At the meeting of the University Syndicate, one member raised a question about the law examination. The spokesperson interrupted him and said: 'The exam took place quite peacefully. There was no trouble anywhere.'

The fourteen-year-old boy, wearing a checked shirt, looked quite intelligent and smart. It was evening and Teddy, sitting in his pad on Mirza Ghalib Street, introduced me to him, puffing on his long, imported cigarette. I wanted to know what he did. Without any hesitation on seeing a pajama-punjabi-clad Bengali babu, he answered in fluent Bangla. He said he ran a business. However, the business was a bit of a secret. He had with him whores of all ages and races. Of all ages from fifteen to thirty. He ran the business with them. When I asked to know what this business was like, at first he looked suspiciously at my pajama-punjabi. Then, finding reassurance in Teddy's eyes, he said, twirling an almost imaginary moustache: 'These aren't ordinary streetwalkers, Sir, they are all pedigreed females. Contacts are made with babus over the phone. I supply girls regularly to garden houses, parties, and even in offices.' Taking out a bulky envelope from his pocket, he continued: 'I have photos – do you want one? A college-educated, beautiful girl? With a sexy figure – can sing Rabindar Sangeet well. A person like you will really like her. Take her and go for a weekend to Diamond Harbour or Digha. Go and have fun. No diseases, Sir – no AIDS.'

2. The things that enrage me –
Whatever makes me sick

22 November 1988.
In the primary health centre
in Khatra 2 Block, of Bankura district,
the day Sriram Bauri's wife's newborn child
was eaten up by dogs...
What's the use of such momentarily enraged writing – after just a while
the anger will wane

Lay your arms on the two sides and lie down on the ground. Yes, on the ground, because ... because in this country, there's the touch of the soil in your advance. This fact has always to be explained to the people. Oh, how alluring the term 'touch of the soil' is! Everyone, from politics-wallahs to intellect-wallahs, is instantly captivated. Now you have to lie down and walk at the same time. That means raise your arse from your hips and as you bring it down again forcefully, keep raising it up. Ra-i-se. Observe how, in this country, to be in front, continuously, to attain the highest peak of progress, you can advance simply by lying down. Are you thinking about how to keep your image glowing? There's no point in thinking about that, the image shall be there, alright, once you've progressed. If there remains a nagging doubt in your mind, then just have the juice of raw turmeric every day, regularly, and on an empty stomach. From time to time, mix cucumber and lemon and smear it on your face and let it dry on its own. Scrub and wash your face, first with slightly warm water, and then with cold water. Observe how bright and radiant your darkened face has become. Gaze at the full moon that's risen today, it's so large. Late in the evening, the loud screams of a pig being slaughtered waft down from the sweepers' colony. For sure a red-hot poker is being inserted in the pig's anus right now. Dinu Thakur begins to clean Mother Kali's tongue, he uses oil paint. Kali Puja every Saturday – and Kali Puja is our public festival ... Where'll I find the *kerrysin* to light the lamp? What does the *gormin* provide? Utter two words and you're labelled a Naxalite. Yes, of course, it's been a long time since man went to the moon and brought back moon soil. Was displayed in this very Calcutta. Yes, Mr Editor, I feel repulsed by your mention of 'interview', it's like the daily piss and shit that I don't care a fuck about, about which bastard said what. Basically, I'm not a bhadralok, and the biggest tragedy is that I have to put on the appearance of a bhadralok all the time. To show my subjection to my wife, I wear rings with huge gemstones on my fingers, or else there's disharmony in the family every day. For me, the word 'India' is just another word – actually, I have no experience of its existence – and yet one has to express one's belief in an undivided India – otherwise the police will catch you, they'll make you forget your dad's name. And to tell the truth, you know what – this is what's called surviving like a fucking asshole. When Erendira's grandmother is murdered, you see a green tent floating away, g r e e n b l o o d ... I pressed the face down and then I landed a kick on the stomach. The person who was a writer had been frightened by the sudden assault. As soon as the kick landed on him, he was thrown on the street. A groaning sound emanated from his throat. The jhola bag on his shoulder had landed a few feet away. Books and papers scattered here and there. The pen in the pocket on his chest had also fallen away. The way it had been instructed – running my hand under his pajama, I squeezed it very hard. So hard that it burst and just after that...

3. Awaiting human relationship
The complexity of that relationship itself

Interrupting Avinash, Abhay Babu asked: 'Where's the lady now?' 'Not there.' 'What do you mean not there?' 'She's gone out, Sir.' 'Gone out?' 'Yes, she told Maheswar that she was going to the riverside for a stroll.' 'When did she go out?' 'Oh, that would have been at about a quarter to six or so. Because that's when Maheswar mops the veranda. She had told him before leaving.' 'What did the lady look like?' 'Oh, you could say she was quite beautiful. A slim figure. An intelligent look in the eyes and face.' 'What would be the lady's age?' 'You can't be sure with women – let's say twenty-four to twenty-five. She was wearing a brown-and-white, printed, silk sari. She looked nice in it. The most exceptional thing was the lady's hair. Although there was a faint line of sindur in her centre parting, the plait of her hair ... I mean, reaching past the buttocks ... not just long but also so neatly tied. When she was walking away, with her back to me...' 'Will you stop that! Don't you have anything else to say other than describing the lady's body, hair and buttocks?' 'But, Sir, you asked me...' 'Tell me what happened after that?' 'Oh, nothing much. In the evening, I spotted Harihar Babu and Titir Devi in front of a paan shop. Harihar Babu was buying a paan.' 'After that?' 'After that I didn't see anything to speak of. But at about ten at night, Arun came and informed me that the gentleman was apparently sitting at home and drinking. I told him not to blab about it. After all, anyone can drink, people do drink too nowadays, and so long as they don't engage in any drunken behaviour, there's nothing we can do. All these babus waste their money according to their whims and moods. Drinking itself is a status symbol now. It's best we don't bother ourselves with such trivial matters. Another thing, Sir, I was absolutely right. They didn't create any commotion. Rather, they had Arun get them some mutton curry at night.' 'That's enough, you don't have to jabber any more. Send Arun here now.' As soon as Arun entered the room, Abhay Babu shouted at him: 'Hey boy, how did you know the gentleman had shut the door and was drinking inside? You have a habit of eavesdropping, do you?' 'Oh no!

What do you say, Sir! It was I who fetched the soda and the potato crisps.' 'What was the lady doing there?' 'She was sitting on a chair and shaking her legs.' 'Do you know this lady, boy?' 'She's a frequent visitor when Boudi isn't around.' 'And?' 'And nothing else – when I brought the soda and crisps, the gentleman said, "Do shut the door when you go out." I don't know anything more than that.' 'What did you see in the morning, boy?' 'When Maheswar asked me to delay fetching tea, I didn't attach any significance to that. Because babus do guzzle booze and so on at night, they sleep like buffaloes until eight or nine in the morning. And as soon as they wake up, they say: "Get me a cup of strong coffee, will you."' 'Did I ask you about all that, boy?' 'No, Sir.' 'Then why do you jabber such nonsense? Tell me what you saw when you went into the flat in the morning.' 'As soon as I opened the door, I saw that the fan and light were on. And then my eyes fell on the bed.' As soon as their eyes met, she called the boy with a gesture of her hand. Sarala had gone to get milk. The door was open. The boy galloped up to the flat. 'What's the matter, Boudi?' She stared at him fixedly. Like Mithun, he too had a well-toned body. The boy felt shy. 'Boudi, were you saying something to us?' 'Oh ... yes ... I mean, would you please exchange my book from the library?' 'Why wouldn't I do that? Give it to me, I'll go and do it.' 'Come, come in.' She called the boy and took him inside. She made him sit right on the bed. In between appearing to look for this and that, she asked: 'What's your name? You didn't mind that I called you, did you?' 'What are you saying, Boudi – I'm an unemployed fellow – I while away the time chatting at the street corner in the neighbourhood. You'll get Siddhartha whenever you call.'

'And does that mean you're not supposed to come unless I call you?' 'No, I mean you are all alone the whole day, so for me to come out of the blue...' 'It's because I'm all alone that you should come. Time just doesn't seem to pass for me. Your dada leaves early in the morning and returns at ten at night. Besides exchanging books, you could also surely come to chat for a while.' 'Tell me, Ghosh Babu, did you hear any altercation or fighting or any kind of sound from the adjacent flat last night?' 'I did hear something.' Sitting up on his chair, Abhay Babu asked: 'What did you hear?' 'Quite a bit of noise, like a scuffle. But not too loud. Despite hearing it, I didn't pay any heed. There's bound to be some scuffling sound when a boy and a girl their age are in bed. When one's older...' 'What else did your mistress tell you in the morning?' 'She just said, "I'm going for a walk along the riverside. Last night your babu had a pain in the chest. He went to sleep very late. Don't bother him now. Give him tea at about nine. I'll definitely be back by then."' 'What was your mistress wearing?' 'Oh, a brown silk sari.' 'Carrying anything?' 'A bag, I mean a ladies handbag.' 'Okay. Do you suspect anything about the woman?' 'No, Sir, everything seemed to be alright. As always, her hair flowed down her back. Of course, our mistress's hair is something to see.' 'What else?' 'And how women adorn themselves. But she hadn't put on any *lipistick*.' It's lipstick, boy.' 'That's all, Sir. The man returned quite late on that ill-fated night.' Handing me the tea kettle he was holding, he folded up his umbrella and put it down. He shut the matted door of the shop carefully, took out two cups from inside, their handles were gone, and poured out tea and held the cups out towards me. 'Here, sip it while it's hot. There's no milk, I brought black tea with ginger. The wife made it, on a dung fire. There may be a slight smoky flavour. But don't worry about that. You're wet, you'll feel better.' He himself sipped a cup of tea first. Making an 'aah' sound, he said, 'The tea's really well made. Strong and sweet. It's hot. Here, take it, take a sip. It won't be nice if it's cold. Middle daughter came a few days ago. There was just a little bit of milk in the morning for my grandson. I said the milk was needed for tea. The wife said, "On a cloudy night like this, it's better to have strong black tea with ginger rather than tea with milk." So as soon as I learnt that's better, I brought you the black tea.' 'Mark today's date on the calendar. If we get married two or three months later, the baby will be born two to three months earlier. Don't suspect me then.' I said: 'Yes, Madam, I'll remember that.' Wrapping a towel of mine around herself, Titir went into the bathroom. But she didn't latch the door. There was the sound of the shower. Titir was humming a tune. After about half an hour or three-quarters of an hour, she emerged. She looked like a marble sculpture. The upper part of her impossibly fair-skinned breasts was wet. Changing into her clothes and swathing her wet hair in the towel, she came and sat beside me. She said: 'I'm terribly hungry. But I don't want anything hot or hard. Just a Thums Up.' I was about to get up to order that. Titir held my hand and drew me towards her. She said: 'Sit down. I need to talk to you.' 'Boudi! Oh Boudi!' Subodh entered the room, panting. She asked, 'What happened?' 'You don't love me any more like you used to.' 'Why? What gave you that idea?' 'Because earlier you used to address me with the intimate "you", but now you don't.' 'Oh, so it's that. But are you still a little boy like you were before? You've grown so much – why, after a few days you'll bring a colourful, sparkling bride home! Is it appropriate to use the intimate "you" now?' 'It is! If there's real love, the intimate "you" can be used.' 'Okay, okay ... now, tell mc, what news have you brought?' 'There's two things. The first is that Dung-lady is dead. And I'm leaving, taking a train tomorrow night.' 'Oh no! Dung-lady was such a nice person! She used to wander around gathering dung all day long, lost in herself, and when it got dark, she used to light a lamp and plaster dung on the wall till ten at night! Tell me, Subodh, the day I too suddenly die, what will you do?' 'Right ... but that's only if I let you go, isn't it? I'll hold you so tight that...' Saying so, Subodh wrapped his arms around Boudi and hugged her tight. 'What are you doing ... crazy boy ... Let me go ... it's hurting ... Tell me, where are you going on the night train?' 'To Tatanagar, as part of the office team, to play. I'll return after a week.' 'What will you bring me?' 'A load of iron!' 'Why's that? What'll I do with iron?' 'There's no alternative. Nothing's available there other than iron. Okay, I've got to go now ... A lot of packing to do.' 'Ma ... hey, Ma, see what Didi's given me to give to Anasuya Didi!' 'Where, let's see ... Oh, this is a very expensive sari!' 'That's what I said too. Didi said you don't have to worry about that ... Take it and go.' 'Alright, go, don't be late returning.' ... I miss Ma terribly today. From the day she first learnt about their love, she had explained so much. She'd say, nobody is happy after a love marriage. All the allure is only for a couple of days. Youthful attraction, pure and simple. Ma used to say clearly: 'That love shall not remain after you've been enjoyed for a few days. The very thing that you're now crazy about will seem to be your biggest mistake in the future.' And so it began. After that, for several months, like a seasoned actor, I went on acting with him. Ultimately, on the pretext of having some fun, I dragged Barun to a hotel in Sealdah. Before that, in conversation, I had tried to explain to him that I was glad Titir had left. I reasoned that she was jealous of this love between Barun and me. My succinct words, repeated day after day, had such an impact on Barun that on that very night, after drinking heavily, he couldn't control himself any longer. With consummate acting, I revealed more and more of the alluring feminine form to him. My skills of deception drove his excitement higher and higher. At the man's vital moment, drawing myself away, when I repeatedly asked about Titir, Barun, in his intoxicated state, blurted out a lot of things to me. Emptying the last dregs of the bottle in Barun's glass, I carried on my consummate acting. I pretended to drink from the same glass. Then I held out the glass to him. Barun badly wanted to have me close to him now. I pretended to get close to him. I went into his arms. It seemed Barun wanted just this all along. Trying to show manly recklessness with my body, he easily lost all control. I just gnashed my teeth and waited. A man like this, I mean those who usually drink once in a while, for pleasure – they can't be normal at all after consuming so much alcohol. I knew that. I quietly observed that Barun's limbs were gradually turning cold. His speech slurred. The acrid fumes of alcohol nauseated me. Yet I waited patiently to fulfil my objective. Within five minutes, he lay sprawled on the bed, snoring away noisily, like an animal. The drawstring of his pajama was very loose. I gather you have lots of questions. Take Burroughs's writing. It's composed of a kind of cut-up. What happens if I make that cut-up into my kind of cut-up? Again, even if I did the cut-up following the normal process of cut-up, where would things stand? How much of a difference is there between the two? No one is visible but the gate opens slowly. The inner circle and the innermost circle. The starter's gun explodes. In the flash of an eye, a group of three or four cross the first hurdle. He is not among them. He finds it extremely difficult to cross any of the hurdles. Even before crossing the thirtieth hurdle, I see that two or three people have finished the race.

[Aarai-Gonga Othoba Matha Nichu Kore Jhamp Deowa Ekjon Manusher Pashe Chhitke Jaowa Bhider Chhobi, 1997]

Oh Jesus, My Jesus – God's Lamb

From nothing was the best created, sin,
and the forsaken blood of a lamb
accomplished this astonishing feat

Who experiences the delight of creation after having waited for the first crop to fruit? Who cherishes the joy of producing an offspring after having brought her bedfellow to her father? They are now in unfettered bliss, effulgent. Do we understand why such gongs of joy sound in the genital country! Can we feel why the music of those who attain sin is so sweet and melodious! This is the melody of an unsocial love, the minstrel's ballad of sinners, where a woman achieves freedom in the form of a sister and spins round and round close to the reproductive staff, singing her minstrel songs. The walls surrounding God's city measure fifteen thousand miles. We can assume some things from this. What do these walls signal! From beginning to end, the wall is artfully adorned with gems – which is a symbol of celestial beauty and artistry; and for us it is all this that befits the grandeur to come as against the suffering of the present – but isn't this sinful earth's beauty and grace also comparable to heaven's artistry, beauty and radiance? Wherefore, during the mythic eras, those who got the opportunity of dwelling amidst such beauty were considered blessed? Death is the wages of sin. But what is the wages for – hissing like a flaming serpent, raising one's expanded hood to the heavens and then blazing suddenly to be extinguished in a spark of light? Orgasmic ejaculation. Two bodies in the hazy darkness of this tiny universe, belonging to Yama-Yami, sparkle as they find light and dissolve again into the darkness. Because there's no able body that does not seek, tenderly, that supremely human organ. But so long as the phallus is not obtained, there can be no ejaculation, there can be no pilgrimage. Foremost is worship of the phallus, and only then can one adopt the corpse posture of shavasana. And Yami does not know where that organ lies hidden. Some say that the queens of the day stole it and took it away at the moment of amorous passion, and some say that tender buds like blooming flowers are cut with it now. And it's the dirge of not-finding that's been sung here, in this story. Who do you look for, oh beautiful Vedic maiden!

What happened was that a snake lay on her bed

Walls surround the cave and the doors on the wall too are sensitive to touch, in keeping with custom. Each door is made of pearl, whose design delights the eye. On this subject, some commentators say that the pearl is nothing but a symbol of tears, because the pearl is formed of the tears of agony of the oyster. In the ultimate stage, these doors signal that only through the path of tears can the city of God be reached – the tears of guilt and all-consuming grief during the preparatory days. The doors would be opened wide and there would be a messenger waiting outside the door to welcome every intruder. It is only out of God's pleasure that the doors have been opened for us now. Although he will suffer and embrace death on behalf of all of us, nevertheless, the pearly gates will permit only those to enter who will really advance through the worldly gate that bears the name of sin, who will submit to his authority and follow him. Hey, look at the robot-navel crawling along slowly in the desolate wasteland, Yami fell asleep after having waited long and eagerly for Yama's naked body, there was no dimension on the soft delicate earth other than the rustling sound of the robot's eight hairy legs. The sun had set long ago, night had arrived, Yami was naked, she probed the darkness for her own sibling. At one time, it seemed that a band of people, far, far away, sprinkled womb-seed and disappeared, another time she saw someone standing silently beside the road, with a pink condom held in his teeth and his penis in his hand – the moment Yami approached, he dissolved into the darkness. Gazing at the row of stars in the celestial dome of sin, he sensed that Yami had arrived, now the story would grow, but the subsequent orgasm and seeing Yami absolutely clearly had not yet occurred to him. The phallus shooting semen close to Yami had only been hazily visualized by him, then, at that moment.

The story begins after that one day she came upon a peacock's feather

Waves rise in the field of barley as the southerly breeze blows, a bunch of vagabond parakeets fly around in a flock, daylight is about to vanish as the day comes to an end, the sky clear as a blue gemstone, with the furtive play of silver clouds on its bosom. After a hunt, Yama made his way towards human habitation, a grey-coloured wild boar slung on his shoulder. At the riverbank, where the road to the human habitation merged with the way to the forest of meditation, once again the two met – the girl was also returning home, she had just reached the road to the human habitation at the edge of the forest, with her a herd of cows – and two plump calves, one on each side of her, white in colour. Sometimes, lifting up their tails, they mooed imitating their mother, sometimes they raced ahead, sometimes behind; sometimes, stopping abruptly and gazing with their large, black-as-kohl eyes as if to say something. The next day, when Yama was again on his hunt in the forest, a female messenger came from the girl: she wanted to mate with her elder sibling, was ready to offer herself summarily, she was ovulating now, she desired a body, just the body, the body of her elder sibling. She had not discovered anything else. There wasn't any secretiveness in her either about surrendering herself, no sense of sin, she made it known that she wanted an offspring from her elder sibling's seed. Two fair-skinned infants should flank her and run around, babbling as they called their mother – that was all that the eighteen-year-old girl wanted. She spoke freely about her desire, her body was never afflicted by seeing any other young boy in the way it was when she saw her elder brother, Yama, double her age. After that, the eyes of the two fell on one another. It was noon then, Yama was thrilled to hear his own blood-sister voice her uninhibited invitation. Tired after spending the whole day in search of prey, as he advanced towards the cane grove at the riverbank hoping for rest – the girl stood blocking the path ahead: 'Accept me and fulfil my yearning, Lord. Give birth to a heroic son in my womb – a lovely tender bud like a plump ear of oat – put an end to my yearning.' Startled, Yama halted, speechless, he plainly saw his fate with his own eyes; he saw the still water of the river, the still leaves on the trees, all of creation still, the fragrance of this stillness everywhere, only a cool, ill wind blew in the green field of barley, swaying the stalks. He saw everything calmly, but he did not see anything at all, he suddenly came back to his senses at his sister's incestuous invitation, he looked fixedly into her eyes – the girl's thirsting face was turned towards him, she blocked his way. He remembered the tusked boar with a pointed face that he had hunted with great difficulty yesterday at the edge of the forest, leaping into the golden barley field. Till the very moment of its death, it, the creature, fought for survival and, although bloodied, it wanted to live. But now he would finally decide, he would surrender himself to Yami in order to become pure. Now he would be adorned with thorns, whose beauty was the fruit of scorn and shame, which he would henceforth carry with patience, humility and love for her very name. But wasn't this a normal matter where love reigns! After all, everyone endeavours to exhibit adequate love for the other. All heavenliness found fulfilment and exulted in this meekness and love of the Lord; the ordinary lives of sinners commanded to punishment were adorned with the long-awaited grace, and so it continued. The corpse sadhana began, Yami on the lap and the son of Goddess Saranyu, driven by fate, in darkness, in that tunnel-hole, deeper and deeper, the sadhana to initiate oneself. All along the slippery cave's wall, water has begun falling and splashing, a robot with eight arms and legs, trunk raised, advances, and yet does not go anywhere, motionless, tired, the robot, Yama; nothing can be seen in front, except – this sweet sound. Breaking through the blue darkness, Yama advanced, alone, through a solitary process, in his purificatory sadhana. Once something hit his foot and rolled away, Yama picked it up and saw it was the nape of a camel's neck. Dust-laden, grey, it lay in the middle of the path. Under the pressure of Yami's thigh, his ancient ribs were all crackling and breaking then. The thick roots of the tree descended along the crack on the mountain, Yami, in corpse asana, woke up with a start, as if her hands had touched a snake, cold, as if by the very touch she could hear its hissing sound. But why was everything so icy cold, why was the man so cold – did that mean Yama was unable to accept her with heart and soul, Yami wondered. All around, some folks kept whispering something, Yama heard it, indistinct; sometimes the apparition blazed into flame and then extinguished, once it seemed the stone wall was moving away speedily, making her completely free, again it advanced very slowly, it approached; very slowly, she sat, pressing down on his chest. From across the wall, someone's inarticulate lament, bloody, like weeping, complex particles of sound wafted by, or was it on this side – Yama could not exactly fathom. His feet were sinking in the quicksand of soft flesh, they kept sinking in without exertion, trying to gaze upwards yearningly he saw, very far away, the blue sky's opacity, only a hazy blue strip, an unbearable pink stone wall on all four sides. Slowly, very slowly, he felt time was slipping by, or that sometimes in life such a time came when nothing called time existed wasn't in existence, there was nothing, no path to advance on anywhere, or retreat, only the two of them sitting in their respective corpse asanas, boundless time in all directions, which, whether it was mobile or appeared to be still because of speed, it was beyond him to know. Making himself enter the dark well in the hope of becoming pure, Yama began groping everywhere for something in particular – no bottom, no top, there was once a pink stone on all four sides, there was a stone wall, now there wasn't even anything called four sides, only a delightfully soft mound of female flesh – lying abandoned, prostrate, knotted together, complex – the only existence.

Second death
the roaring lions run
the fleeing fawns run

There – there was the bottomless dark pit, which Yama saw on returning to his senses, where a fire burned endlessly, where he lacked the strength to retain any hope of obtaining solace, where it was impossible to sit, or lie down; and the walls were so terribly tilted that even looking at them made one suffocate. Nothing called light existed there, never existed, and everything there was immersed in darkness like human birth. Yama was not able to figure out how that happened. Even if there was no light, it was possible to see something, the things through which there was suffering, where souls were the broken relics of burning sins, who observed their carriers' misfortune with greedy eyes and kept alert watch so that all those journeying to death in the pit of fire, in an endless procession, never found peace under any circumstances. All suffering, if at all anything called suffering existed, or remained, came floating from them, all along the valley of birth. And God rarely waited to receive the unfortunate souls of sinners, the ones who were subject to death agonies. He was past his prime, he had prayed again and again to God so that he wouldn't give birth to the promised offspring through his own sister's womb. Year after year passed by, yet Yami was not granted any offspring. To outward appearances, merely brother and sister, no one could know that deep inside Yama a great struggle with God raged, an eternal surrender to protect faith, in which he had to remain resolute. His faith was celestial, shrouded in deep sorrow. And this was a struggle of faith. He had devoted himself to a permanent state of waiting, to partake of the next disappointment from God, to continue the struggle until he reached, anew, the station of believing. This secret life of his was wrapped in a vagabond existence, in hardship, waiting, in faith, and finally, in the devotion attained through faith, which had an influence on God himself too. But the kingdom of the dead too was earthly, a place of grief. All the sinners arrived at this place, and this happened in their lives when he descended to extraordinary misdeeds with them. They confronted different and nightmarish realities. He raised his hand, and said, 'You should rather fear the one who can destroy both soul and body in hell.'

Death, be alert
because it's He who's love

The sky and the air trembled ecstatically in the intoxication of stillness, exactly then, below the mountain, through the middle of the forest, went ten youths, flaming torches in each hand, the twenty torches of the ten men hissed and emitted spirals of smoke into the sky, and through the kiss of the glowing flames all the black darkness was rendered bright like day. The young woman was making them excited, emitting a shower of flowers of red light with her eyes, sharp as a razor, she said: 'Yama is unbearable, he's terribly cold, aloof and mournful, I shall hang my bridal garland on the neck of the one among you who can roast him. I want Yama to burn to death – like he has done to me, by keeping me alive – he kept doing that.' The girl was now a young woman, standing under the dark sky in the beautiful town, with tearful eyes she wept, sometimes in monstrous rage, she now wanted her desire to be fulfilled with this very band of entranced youth. Before they knew it, all light was extinguished, the youths ought to go to Yama's house that very night, there wasn't a moment to lose. Sloshed to the gills drinking soma, her hair dishevelled, the young woman kept saying: 'Yes, tonight, right now, tomorrow will be too late. I have seen the unmistakable shadow of death at Yama's doorway.' The youths' chests heaved, it was as if in front of their eyes the darkness was cloven and it opened, as if an ogress gaped from within that cleavage. They too were intoxicated with soma juice, they stared at one another, 'So then we have to burn Yama to death' – that was Yami's order, the order of a young woman in this forest of youths, who had no doubts whatsoever about giving herself away to them eventually. They did not have the strength to go against her order. They advanced. Accompanying them, Yami, in drunken guise, devoid of clothes, the dishevelled tresses touching her hip, in that state, her eyes, face, breasts and everything of hers was in darkness, she was soma-intoxicated, lurching. The fire was becoming more and more horrific now. In a moment, Yama saw the town swathed completely in darkness; it didn't take even a moment for him to recognize the woman. The darkness of light in all directions now, he understood what was about to happen, but despite knowing, he remained passive, not even a deep sigh escaped his chest, for he had a mind, he understood that he was a sinner, and he could not escape suffering for his sins. Yama prayed inwardly, 'Lord, oh God, protect this jewel of a woman, yes this jewel of a woman – who has no mind, who does not know what sin is.' He was tied up with a rope made from a bundle of grass, he made no protest. The shadow of the man wearing a crown of thorns fell on his eyes and face, the one who would be revealed in Jerusalem a few hundred thousand years later. 'Do you have anything to say, Yama' – a person looked at him in astonishment, he had never seen such a passive man in his life, but Yama only gazed in silence at the sky, whose colour had turned turbid to him long ago, the little that could be seen through the door – they stood gazing steadfastly at that side of the full sky – how far away – how far away, isn't it! From the very beginning, the youth was hesitant, he would not burn an innocent to death without instigation, he came running to free the bonds, but Yama did not move despite the efforts to free him. Yami screamed out: 'Don't free him, burn this impotent man to death, who doesn't heed pleasure even in his little finger!' He smiled wryly, where was fate taking him, he uttered clearly: 'I have to attain death, the punishment for discovering sin. But who are these people all around me, dispossessed of their senses from drinking soma, who can slay the body but can never slay the soul?' After that, he raised his head and looked at Yami, at her eyes: 'Rather, it's the one who destroys the soul and the body that I fear.' A moment's stillness. And then there was a soft sound of knocking, the oil lamps in the corner of the room came alight, after that the fire spread furiously through the house. Yami was startled momentarily: 'No, no – in truth, I did not want this...' Yama's whole body had then started burning, in front of her very eyes, in the fire she herself had instigated, blazing now; his body, genitals, knees, chest, the hair on his chest – he whose every confidence she knew, had known since she was born – which had remained mysterious to her, ever since she was born – that mysterious man, was burning, the one who could not be held captive, and yet was not uncaptured either. The young woman was weeping inconsolably, helpless, lost, for a moment she wanted to leap into the heart of Yama's fire and save him, disregarding everything, but the very next moment she controlled herself:

'What's the use – what's the use!' This man would never be her companion on the path to the fulfilment of her deepest desire. The fire's noose had then completely enwrapped Yama, the young woman thought she heard an indistinct moaning, she was waiting expectantly to hear that, perhaps there was still time, what if this wise man submits, this son of Goddess Saranyu, but no, there was nothing other than the popping and crackling sounds of the fire, there was no other cry, indicating life. And then from between her legs, like a spring flowing, a stream of blood sought to ooze out, it was oozing out, down her left leg, she was menstruating again in the middle of this very night, once again she was eager to give birth to an offspring. She could copulate with these youth for a few days, for sure, but would they be able to yield a healthy, sentient offspring, these callow boys – which only Yama, if he wished, could have given her? The young woman became dispirited, with a bitter taste in her mouth, Yama had burnt to nothing long ago, the remaining fistful or so of ashes lay near her feet. The young woman looked long at the dark interior of the human remains lying there. In front of her, with his body, Yama, once again, standing up now. There was no more animosity now, no more malice. He had made the requisite offering of his body for ascension to the world of sin from the world of man, the king of sin. At the moment of death, Dharmaputra's life became free of covering, she saw that. His coming together and life with God came to light. He was accorded the honour of being the father of sinners.[1]

[*Hey Jishu, Jishu Aamar – Ishworer Meshshabok, 1996*]

---

1 Yama-Yami (brother-sister) in the Rig Veda, and the Avesta too. He had not yet become the God of Death, an ordinary man, and Yami clearly desired and lusted for Yama, and…

Of the Right Size

Every real existence is completely determined by some other real existence

What an amazing thing a female is, Nachiketa – does she grant immortality? Before that, this story has a melodic composition and the story is of no avail without it. Because at this moment, the entire human society is merely a massive market. All other identities have been exhausted now. Your conscience does not lash you any more because by now your conscience is dead. You become more and more greedy, because greed is your supreme inspiration and your liberation, pleasure is your nirvana. A son says, if you're artful, you're bound to be successful. There'll come a time when those who're selfish will tell you, tell you again and again: 'Can I feed myself with those ideals, grandpa?'

So, there are accumulated stories behind the story too. A lively party is on in the Crystal Room of the Taj Bengal Hotel, a young business magnate with a glass of Scotch whisky in one hand and a telephone receiver in the other whispers: 'Hello darling, by now your husband must be in Mumbai, on the same bed as his beautiful secretary, so will you share this night with me, I am lonely and the night is young'; the answer from the other side, in a female voice, matched the question: 'Oh my God, I feel the same way too, I don't have any prejudices in such matters, I openly declare, what could be more boring than being in the same bed as a middle-aged man night after night – horrible – but excuse me – My driver's in the room – I had arranged that in advance – Oh, the size of his penis... – even my daughter swoons seeing it – Hello, if you don't mind, can't we do this tomorrow – tomorrow, I mean Saturday night – No, not at all, my husband won't mind at all, he's extremely liberal in such matters – he's with his secretary and I'm with my boyfriend, but we don't want to break up the marriage – my daughter's growing up, she'll think her parents are very selfish – Hello, okay, who's speaking – I don't even know your name – who's speaking, where are you calling from...' This story is a story of the top-seeded elite. The bidding rate is quite high. But let this story be. Hear a lower-middle-class story instead.

A wedding house, and that means loads and loads of females in my vicinity. Of every age and every kind. No one's to be outdone by anyone else in regard to dolling up. Each one vies with the other for attention. One rarely sees such a crowd of so many dolls other than at weddings. Sandipan calls it a whorehouse. Our *aantel* friend Sandipan. A Casanova No. 1. A revered guru in such matters. He had apparently even seen an old hag of over sixty orgasming.

I got a chance at the wedding of a distant female cousin. There were far more women than men there. A narrow, ancient staircase inside, it wasn't easy to go up or down. One had to bump into others. When I get a chance, I don't let the opportunity of making the most of it slip away. After all, I've known what a girl is from the age of eighteen. On the pretext of hurrying down the stairs, I bumped my chest against her breasts. I said sorry and pretended I had accidentally bumped into her. All were fucking practised babes, no one said a thing. A little smile, and then she moved on. Bandits strike and the village is desolate! A few girls stood at the foot of the stairs and giggled about something. I took the chance. On the pretext of going through the crowd in a hurry, I ran my hand on the fold of flesh on Boudi's waist and then moved it away. The babe was truly glamorous, just like Mamta Kulkarni. If one sets out to do such things, then one has to take a little bit of risk. Oh ... what folds – I'll die! I said: 'Why don't you move aside? Why are you blocking the way?' Boudi had quite a sense of humour, she was thoroughly modern. Looking me straight in the eye, she said: 'I suppose this is how you move people aside?' 'Oh – sorry, Boudi.' Actions speak louder than words. I had acted, and showed her. Don't ministers do it all the time: 'It's alright, we'll see about that later.' Boudi narrowed her eyes as if threatening me. With Boudi's indulgence, I was fearless for certain. Radiating the lustre of her breasts over which her *anchal* had slipped off, Boudi lifted up her sleeveless arm on the pretext of fixing her hair. After showing the forest she lowered the shutter quickly. So I hadn't done wrong by taking the risk. Calling her to a concealed spot, I said: 'If you don't move now, I'll have to press the horn and pass by.' Rolling her eyes, Boudi said: 'Beware, don't create a commotion at a wedding. The place is packed with people.' That meant, she didn't mind giving it to me. But not now, not in front of everyone. And then – to find out whether *zeher hai ke pyar hai tera chumma*, Akshay Kumar kissed Mamta Kulkarni three or four times, Dracula style, and created a bloody carnage. I visualized it clearly in front of my eyes. And so it went on like this. From time to time, I noticed that Mita was trying to stand beside me. She wanted to talk to me. She was dark-skinned, almost past marriageable age, yet no marriage was happening.

Her dad didn't have money either. She suddenly appeared with a garland of bel flowers and asked: 'Do you want a garland?' 'Give it.' Not wanting to disappoint her, I took it. I said: 'You look very beautiful today.' I knew that even if it wasn't true, it made girls happy to hear such things from men. Mita stared at me. Then she smiled mischievously as she looked at me. I knew the meaning of that smile. Even before this, whenever Mita happened to find me alone, she flashed me this smile. She had smiled yesterday too. A boy-snaring smile. She was getting on in years, and so she had become desperate. One can seduce such girls merely with eye gestures. But she was extremely dull looking. Her body was just not developed. Skinny. In that respect, she was nothing compared to Boudi. Married for about five years, but there had been no issue. She looked as if she would burst out of her clothes. Absolutely the real thing. Besides, I know from experience that the risk is less with married women. Especially those whose husbands are a bit old and spunkless. They swallow the bait in an instant when they see a shiny handsome boy. At first, they indulge you a bit and observe, but if you play along, she'll agree to everything without a word being spoken. Of course, it has to be done with some discretion, avoiding her husband and family. Won't disturb the home front, but want to have fun too. If seduced in the right way, no matter whether it's brother-in-law or father-in-law, they don't mind anything at all. So long as word doesn't get around. The fear of shame and scandal is there in full measure. Sandipan says: 'That's not entirely true either. The fear remains only until a certain stage. If need be, she becomes utterly desperate. Reckless.'

Everyone's in a terrible hurry in a wedding house. As I walked around here and there, I absent-mindedly pushed open the bathroom door and stepped inside. No, it wasn't locked from within, it was merely shut. As soon as I entered, I was jolted. Even a guileful guy like me had to bolt and get out. Mita had then just stood up and was setting her clothes right. I didn't quite understand what happened (I must ask Sandipan, the guru), there was a peculiar smile on Mita's face. As if nothing had happened. I said: 'Sorry, I hope you didn't mind.' For a brief moment, it seemed Mita was startled. After that, with a wavering gaze she smiled sweetly – 'No, not at all – what's there to mind? Something like this can well happen when one's in a hurry.' 'I hope you won't tell Boudi' – I wanted to see how far she wanted to go. 'Shush!' Mita stuck out her tongue – 'How can one tell anyone such things?'

I know Mita has an eye on me. I work in a bank, friends tell me I look like a ladykiller now. There was also Boudi's clear assent, because Mita was her cousin. Like any other simple and naive girl, she too had the notion that sooner or later the day would come when my attitude would change. That's why she had brought the bitch along. From afar, Boudi now raised an uproar. Swaying her hips, she came and asked her cousin, 'Why did you give the garland in his hand?' 'Why – what happened?' – she looked at her Didi in surprise. 'Does one ever give it in the hand … you should put it around his neck … you stupid girl!' 'Does it make you happy when your cousin puts a garland around my neck?' I asked her, standing woodenly and covertly pinching her butt. 'Of course it does' – Boudi replied, smiling slyly and rolling her eyes. As she made to walk away after that, she turned her back to Mita and admonished me in hushed tones, 'I'll take out your roguishness one day'. As I gazed at her swaying departure, my lips burst out humming: *Mere sapnon ki rani kab ayegi tu...*

Lunch Break

There was some prevarication about permitting the entry of an epistolary collection of an unparalleled writer in world literature into the country, the pretext was the usual one: obscenity. The funny thing was that the letters were not written by the writer to any girlfriend – James Joyce wrote them to his own wife. Quite a few letters in the collection could, in a one-sided view, be called bed conversation, but seen from another angle, it is definitely a treasure trove of language and literature, and also accidentally casts light on *Ulysses*. It helps one to understand James Joyce. One can also explain him in a new way. It's quite clear that it will take many more years for such things to penetrate our heads, it definitely will. Whereas the pavements in urban and semi-urban areas are flooded with sex magazines full of glossy, semi-nude pictures and all our sex fantasies. Soft-porn magazines are sold openly in every neighbourhood, and hardcore ones in concealment and undercover, yes, all this is now available in every neighbourhood, for that matter they've entered lanes and alleys too, perhaps you don't know that a couple have entered your home too. You didn't have a clue from the outside. But what do you know, your own eighteen-year-old son has by now already seen blue films with his friends, he studies in IIT doesn't he, you imagine the boy has a bit of fun once in a while, and that's quite normal at that age. But you know nothing. You've heard about ragging, but do you know what really happens? Whereas the sick, tired husband, who rested his head on his wife's shoulder in the taxi, had to atone for this sin by paying a fine of eight-hundred rupees. And then, right then, the superhit film song 'Muqabala...' reverberates. The bikini-clad heroine shows her bare butt, sorry, exposed buttocks, and dances like crazy. 'I have a right to hear praise of my figure – my plus point – what do you think?' she asks. *Athens* runs on Star TV. Every kind of sizzling sex on the ATN channel. MTV is now a vital part of the nightlife of the Bengali middle class. And why only ATN, on Star Plus, which is the status symbol of the Bengali middle class, soap operas play one after another, spreading foam, titillating. The screen constantly emits shrieks of animal emotions that electrify the body, like in *Riviera* or *The Bold and the Beautiful* or *Santa Barbara*. There's gratuitous nudity here, it's bold and beautiful too, which helps fulfil the suppressed desires and fantasies in the minds of our sanctimonious and hypocritical middle class. Father, mother, son and daughter of an enlightened family, all sit together and enjoy all that, and for later in the night, with some discretion, other stuff, on the video cassette player. What's the favourite national song throughout India now? Definitely '*Choli ke peechhe*', or otherwise '*Sexy sexy sexy mujhe log bole*'. No, there's no outraged objection on such matters either from any quarter, although it's a different matter with the orthodox types ... Look closely at the hero of this story, he doesn't drink much, but he has no sense organs except one. I've left out the issue of obscenity, this has been written with a view to exploring how far literature can be protected from aggressive porno-imperialism, audacity, with a view to seeing whether it can be protected, and whether at all that can be done, or whether the very idea is baseless, because literature is simply literature, and pornography can never become literature (although Sandipan Chatto has written,

'Superior pornography too transcends (like in the case of the Marquis de Sade) – at least it takes us in the direction of a healthy curiosity'), and together with that ... by now many, or perhaps some people, are growing restless, all these lectures have totally destroyed the story, Mister ... So it did, would I have written such linear stories of lacquered realism if I hadn't got an opportunity to deliver a lecture! Even if it's only for a moment, at least I did arrive at this genuine conviction. And isn't there a conflict involved even in such thinking? What does Sandipan, the master *aantel* of the story, the guru, have to say in this regard?[1]

It was late at night. I had been roaming around here and there, smiling toothily at a few people. And thus I whiled away a lot of time. After that, I ate with the last batch and stuffing a couple of paans in my mouth I arrived at the bridal chamber. My surmise had been correct. All the babes were sitting there, illuminating the room. All the honey was here. All were fucking Madhuri Dixits. One lovely was singing, I stared at her, transfixed, I just couldn't look away. Lightning flashed from her eyes, there was lightning in her blooming smile. '*Ankhiyan milaoon*' was just as ravishing to look at as her voice was captivating. The girl was truly beautiful, she was fair skinned, her face shaped like a paan leaf, large eyes, a slender waist, and below the waist, a large, tanpura-like, round, aristocratic butt. Brimming with health, she was indeed a delight to the eye, with man-slaying enchantment. My head reeled looking at the piece, it was as if I had been bowled just by looking at her. I had no desire to listen to

---

1 The word 'sati' does not have any masculine form. Only women become sati. But in the masculine form, 'sat' does not mean 'male sati' at all.

songs, I was only ogling the babe. I could intuit whatever there was to intuit from the contours of the sari. Not just plump, but kind of well-kneaded and crisp. Isn't there a slogan for potato crisps – '*Humko Binny's maangta!*' It would require skill to hook her – but that's what makes a He Man! '*Neeli neeli ankhein meri main kya karoon*' ITAL – I sat down at the gathering, pretending to hear the song. I saw that Mita too was sitting there, at a slight distance. Our eyes met. Mita smiled. I didn't pay her much attention. I didn't have the time now to bother about the Mitas of the world. I could only think about how I would pick up this babe. Fuck, I wasn't to be outdone either. I too had quite a reputation for being a ladykiller. Once they saw me, I too could make the heads of many virginal, saintly women spin. I had tasted all kinds of pieces, between the ages of fifteen and forty-five. Whatever I may be up to, after all one had to talk to someone or the other. I made friends with a pajama-punjabi clad, sweet-faced boy who looked like Lord Kartik. I knew the boy, but we hadn't been introduced. He must have been a few years younger than me. I addressed him respectfully: 'Do you know what film is running in Regal?' Fucking hell – so he's a regular too! With a wink he said, '*Reshma ki Jawani*. Ooh, God, Silk Smita!' 'Who's that,' I asked, with a simpleton's look on my face. 'Don't you know – she's a sex bomb. From the south. And it's a completely new print.' After that, rolling his eyes, he said: 'Let's snare a couple and go, let's do a noon show tomorrow.' Not revealing any enthusiasm, I asked: 'What's running in Bharati?' The boy immediately wilted: 'Rubbish ... family cinema. Tasteless. Who wants to see that.' The girl was still singing with full aplomb. Two boys too joined her in singing: '*Bholi-bhali ladki, khol teri dil ki, pyaar-wali khidki, – ho ho ho…*' There was lightning in her blooming smile then, lightning in her enunciation. One or another part of her was constantly speaking. As soon as the song was over, affecting a magnanimous tone, I shouted out: 'Beautiful … What a voice you have … Oh, I could die … Let's hear another one, Boudi.' This kind of flattery was common in the bridal chamber, some folks didn't mind. But the babe turned her neck and looked at me with narrowed eyes. Two splendid large eyes, which litterateurs call eyes that extend to the ears. Our eyes met. I could clearly see that she wanted to know what exactly my flattery meant. After that, surveying me out of the corner of her eye, she gave me a little smile. And seeing that smile, I was done for. I had been very intimate with women. I knew what each kind of smile meant. Her smile said, 'Hello handsome, I don't mind. If you're a man, advance.' And this at first sight! However much of a libertine I might be, I was a bit surprised. After all, she was a daughter-in-law of the family! And I had snared her in just five minutes! When my mind wandered to thinking about my future wife, I felt a thrill within me. I would marry someone or the other eventually. God forbid something like this happened to my wife. And now she began singing '*Choli ke peechhe…!*' There was a tumult. The bridal-chamber session had come into its own. I was advancing bit by bit, without really knowing it. I knew from experience that it was the man who had to make an advance, after all, no girl took it off by herself, however much she wanted it. One had to take it off. The risk had to be taken. And if it had to be taken, then it was best to do that for these kinds of whores only. And it was the married girls who had a bit of flesh on their bodies, who had acquired a good-sized tummy, which I liked. Oh, I could die! The skinny Mitas of the world ... damn ... they were useless bitches. Could get them for free. In the middle of the song, making sure no one noticed, I threw a rajnigandha bud at her. Perfect aim. It hit her breast and fell on her lap. Before rising at the end of the song, the married woman picked up the bud, smelt it once without touching it to her nose, and then slanting her neck she directly hurled lightning at me. Our eyes met. This time, the meeting of eyes was absolutely fatal. My gesture had been a clear invitation. The married woman smiled furtively from the corner of her lips. By slanting her neck, she had given her assent. I understood that the bitch was well and truly caught. One only had to wait for the time and opportunity now. '*Tere bin nahi guzre din, tere bin nahi guzre raat.*'[2]

The night advanced some more. There were more songs. Jokes were cracked, there were riddles. The bride twisted the groom's ear, on everyone's cajoling she made to kiss him without touching her lips. As happens in the bridal-chamber session, laughs, teasing, horsing around, mischief. And now it was time to go to bed. The groom and the bride were tired, they yawned. The groom was almost supine. He lay sprawled against some pillows. Many people had left. Only four or five of us remained. The married woman ... lightning-eyed ... I don't normally speak in such gentlemanly language ... was sitting apart. Once in a while, she was jocular with the groom. And glancing at me, she smiled

2 Long ago, Parshuram had written, 'Your own wife ought to be honourable, the other's wife ought to be shameless, that's what's most desirable to keep a man in good humour.' Seeing his own wife well-adorned, a man in his story had said, 'You look wonderful. Just like someone else's wife...'

furtively. As if we had known each other for long. Now, acting on the opportunity, I looked her in the eye and made a sign. I yawned. As if I was very sleepy. In words, I said: 'I think the attic has become a storage room now. I'll go there and lie down.'

The night was almost over. I looked at my watch and saw it was close to three. There were lots of things piled up in the attic. There were mountains of earthen cups, a stupa-like heap of paper glasses. I had hidden a bottle. I gulped down a lot of it, neat. After that, I pushed aside the things cluttered in a small part of the space, spread out the floor mat and lay down. It was Mita who had arranged for the floor mat in the evening. It was she who told me about sleeping in the attic: 'It's a wedding house – there's no room available, I'll make some space vacant in the attic. Spread out the floor mat and lie down for a while. No one really goes there late at night.' I felt sad for the girl. She was getting on in years, but she wasn't able to get married. She had become quite desperate of late. But let Mita be, would the married woman come! The bitch. After all, I did tell her where I'd be. I was indeed sleepy. I had shut the door. I was dozing off. I had been running around the whole day, I was worn out. Suddenly, something brushed my forehead, my sleep vanished. I was quite high, it took me a while to catch on. 'Who is it?' 'Me. Quiet.' A female voice, whispering. Warm breath fell on my face. A tuft of loose strands of hair fell on my forehead and eyes. Moving my hand to remove the hair, I touched a breast. I was electrified. I had long been familiar with this touch. I enclosed it in my right hand and squeezed. Of the right size. Soft and warm. But yet something seemed strange. She had looked different from the outside. And this one seemed bony. Although I was high, I could sense that alright. As soon as I began squeezing, fire began erupting from my head. 'Who are you?' There was no reply. 'Are you sure no one's seen anything?' I said that only because something had to be said. There was no sign or sound, she straightaway lowered herself into a more intimate position over my chest. No more talk. There was no need for any talk either. I wrapped my arms around her. Wherever I put my hands, she was warm. Almost singeing my hands. I was nice and high. The heroine clad in a red choli sang the song and, with her own hands, tore off the forlorn, hapless choli too, in order to show the black bra *choli ke peechhe*. No cry was emitted. Not even any moans or sighs. An absolutely seasoned babe. It seemed she was wise and well experienced, like a traveller of yore. She readily assented to everything. But yet she seemed somewhat bony. It hadn't looked anything like that from outside. I lowered one hand. I pulled loose her sari and petticoat. The breast was an angry red from the squeezing. Hot steam rose. I lowered my hand further. Down, down, below the navel. The pace of the breathing increased. Here's the door to the body, it was only if one could push the door and enter that … A married woman, yet I could see that she wasn't uninhibited, I myself had to spread her legs. After a while, she herself spread them wide, and so, unspoken consent to use the hand. At the very touch, I was startled. What's this – there was a raging flood. Sticky. This happens when one gets aroused. There wasn't the slightest difficulty. Half the world had been conquered long ago. All the girls here had been felled. Blood billowed through my whole body then. I did everything in wild intoxication. If one didn't say a few things at this time, it seemed rather vegetarian. 'You are much sweeter than your songs.' She was silent. Say something. No. Do you like it? Yes. Bitch! ... Son of a whore! I felt like swearing now. Slut-fuckers like us know sluts like you very well. But I said: 'What does your husband do?' She was silent. 'What does your husband look like?' 'Do whatever you're doing.' The voice appeared somewhat hoarse. As she said it, she held me tightly in her two arms. I too grabbed the vital spot, I clutched it in my hand. The maiden giggled in a hushed tone. 'Let me turn on the light.' 'Hey, no – no!' There was no talk after that. I turned her over. Climbed on top of her. There was deep, laboured breathing. Couldn't delay any longer. Without saying anything, I rose up on my knees. There was no difficulty in recognizing the dark spot. And yet she seemed somewhat wooden. Bony. I had cut my teeth at the age of eighteen. My younger aunt had taught me and instructed me in everything. Now I kept thrusting in the final moments of frenzy. Aah ... fulsome and eternal peace.

It was all over in about three minutes. I kept shooting and spilling out inside. With her thighs parted wide, she took it all in with utmost satisfaction. She wrapped her whole body around mine. Her bones rattled. Wasn't there any flesh on her body or what? Bones sticking out. Yet, what passion! Perhaps it was a long-accumulated hunger. Hadn't found it opportune or convenient to get someone. That's why the babe took such a risk and did the job.[3]

---

3 There's a story by Shibram Chakraborty according to which, at the time of her swayamvar ceremony, Damayanti had recognized Nala simply by observing customary male behaviour. In the myth, several gods, together with Indra, arrived at the swayamvar assembly, including some disguised as Nala, and also accompanied by Nala. Damayanti supposedly recognized the real Nala through the power of love and put the garland

After that, another five minutes or so passed. We lay wrapped around each other. Morning was still far away. Without saying a single word, she slowly let go of me and got up. I sensed that she was silently setting herself in order in the darkness. She speedily did the hooks of her blouse, brought down her petticoat and sari. I couldn't see anything, there was only the rustling sound of her sari. She opened the door slightly and slipped out. She was lost in the darkness, just as she had earlier emerged suddenly from the darkness. She didn't say anything at all when she left. As if neither of us knew the other. As if nothing had happened all this while ... What an amazing thing a female is, Sandipan, sorry, Nachiketa – does she take immortality?[4]

'Brother-in-law! Brother-in-law! ... The bride and groom are leaving, and you're still snoring and sleeping till so late in the morning ... Get up. Hey, what's this?' As soon as she said that, she bent down and picked up a silver hairpin from one side of the floor mat. The wild intoxication of last night had largely paled now. (*Saiyaan ne aise bowling ki,*

---

around his neck. But in his story, Shibram informs us that this wasn't what actually happened. Present together with Damayanti in the swayamvar gathering was Indra's wife, Sachidevi. Two exceptionally beautiful women had arrived at the assembly, and so quite naturally there was excitement among all the men present. The gods disguised as Nala feasted their eyes on Damayanti, but Nala, who loved Damayanti, was looking at another man's wife – Sachidevi. It was by observing this natural behaviour of the male that Damayanti recognized Nala. Shibram Chakraborty simply checkmates us here.

4 The word 'grant' used in the very first sentence of the story is replaced by the word 'take', and this word has to be accepted in exactly the same way.

that, God, I'm not able to get up.) But this is Mita's hair pin – how did this get here...! I get it. Boudi looked at me suspiciously. 'Mister Zero's turned Hero – or should it be Mr Hero's turned Zero!' The first thing in the morning and my eyes were glued to the folds of flesh on Boudi's waist once again. Oh, what curves – it was morning, and she had just emerged after her bath, her hair was wet – oh, I could die! I vaguely recalled that last night's babe had too many bones in her body. But this one's body was as soft as butter. I said: 'You didn't get anything. I'll explain it to you tonight, leave the door open.' Boudi looked me in the eye and fathomed whatever there was to fathom. As she rushed out, she gave me a small, loving pinch on my cheek: 'Even after this you're not satisfied, you rogue...' You fucking race of whores – I almost said that. Only know how to get fucked. Once they've got what they want, why, they don't even recognize you. But I couldn't say it. Sandipan, that guru of mine, has forbidden me from talking dirty. He says: 'My sideburns have turned grey with age, so you can believe what I say, nothing whatsoever comes of that...' So we've had enough, nothing more, and so I submit. It's the kind of stories that you like to read that are created for you, that get created. That's the convention. Because *jhoot bolna paap hai, nadi kinare saanp hai*. Because all of us were born of our mothers' wombs.

Story Quiz

Run your eyes over the story, and then answer the questions given below. Everyone who sends the correct answers within a week will receive a gift. Fair & Lovely. *Dil safed karne ke liye*. Hurry! Stocks limited.

Q 1: Who was the girl who came to his room in darkness – who was she...

Q 2: What is the surname of Sandipan, the guru – I mean, what could it be? For sure, this Sandipan is not *that* Sandipan, he's no praise-hounded Bankim-like creature (in the oblique sense), he's not of the right size either, which can be grasped in the hand – this guy spent his whole life simply *ghumaoing larkis* and eating *bhel-puri*, and drank away, leaving behind a (non)futile way of living, stiff turd, *teri nani mari to mai kya karoon*; yes, the guru, our *aantel* friend, Camus's calf (from Camay soap, because he truly loves the real Camay).

Q 3: Let us know in no more than twenty words, what lesson you derived from reading the story, or whether you derived any lesson at all?

The decision of the judges will be final and no correspondence in this regard will be entertained.

Corrigendum

In place of the word 'calf', there could be 'bastard', I didn't correct it, although my hand was itching to do that. And there should definitely be an 'Om Tat Sat' at the beginning of the story, in 36-point bold, which I forgot to write. And at the very end, after everything is concluded, there should be the phrase 'Experiment Solicited'. The font here would be simple, the same as the body-point, with just a dash on either side. Experiment Solicited: body-point.

[Sijer Jinish, 1997]

The Rainbow Serpent

Hark! The vanquished's skull, how supernaturally erotic!
– Kamalkumar Mazumdar

'The nation in which a ten- or twelve-year-old girl is the mother of a child, a fifteen-year-old boy murders his friend, a seventeen-year-old boy dies of AIDS, and an eighteen-year-old cannot read the diploma he receives – it's impossible to even hold that society and civilization together.'

– *Time* magazine, 21 November 1994

(Speech of the Speaker of the House of Representatives in the United States of America.)

⇌

Is decadence something to view with contempt? Critiquing the regal democracy in the United States of America, Octavio Paz had remarked: 'It is decadence that is the correct alternative as far as American society is concerned, a mixture of deep breaths and sweet smiles, painful sickness and tears of joy ... it is decadence that's stylized death, or to say it better, the art of living in the course of submission to death'. In order to know a civilization, it is necessary to understand the nature of its decadence too...

There's time, but again, the time has gone by too. Tridib is stubbing out a cigarette in the ashtray. And then, between a woman and fate is seated a golden-haired boy, the rainbow serpent. The commonplace image of the dead body keeps bobbing up. Did Rosie commit suicide or was she murdered bit by bit? If one strained one's ears, only the sound of water could be heard. It seems a call is wafting from across the river. What exactly was the relationship between Rosie and her father? Water too turns her away. Fire turns her away too. Only the scent of wild moss fills her hair, and heaven's blessing. Once again there's the sound of water outside. Her arms keep spreading, finally her arms break through the room's wall and emerge, now there are no bounds to the sky. Fifty-one-year-old Rosie has bought a blouse with a moon-cut pattern for herself for this Puja. She tries to move her fingers around again and again. When a watch becomes luminous in darkness, and stays luminous, it makes it more mysterious, ever more so.

□

From within the organic, realism now keeps assuming the form of longing, longing for the hegemonic form – *the will to realism*. An eternal female image, sitting on her knees, her hands clutching the burden of the earth upturned by the tractor. She looks agitated, the colour of earth on her hair, the wildness of earth. A mechanical groan crowds into the soundtrack, the rumbling sound of wheels. Mother India drowns in pleasure at the sound – *dharti mata, hum tere hi gun gaye,* Earth Mother, we sing only your praises ... In between that, a made-to-order sun splatters on the sky and ether over the swimming pool which is full of the unerring promise of an olive tan. And the common folk, the common folk all over India, sing the beloved song about the love-crazed brother-in-law's intentions, that's sung by his sister-in-law's sister, by singing it again and again they keep alive the reality of the story, they go on doing so...

□

I was sitting with Ma in the veranda. There was a mountain in front of us, with a Santhal village nestled in its bosom. Baba and Tridib-da were moving away rapidly, we were looking in their direction. Baba had mounted his own horse, while Tridib-da had mounted mine. I had forbidden him from mounting my horse, it hadn't been ridden for a long time and was steadily becoming awkward. But Tridib-da wouldn't listen to me. He said he'd bring the horse back to limber so that I could ride it whenever I wanted. They, Baba and Tridib-da, were rapidly advancing towards the invisibility of the sal forest, eventually they became one with the horizon. Ma said, 'Tridib will stay here for some days. He's taken leave.' She was very happy to have him here. Was it really happiness? I like Baba more than I do Tridib-da. Even before Baba returned to the bungalow, looking tired after the day's work in the colliery, I sat waiting for him. When Baba came home and hugged me, held me to his chest, kissed my face and eyes, how thrilled I felt. I too held him tight, I wrapped myself around him. I didn't feel like letting go. Ma came and looked aghast, she made some sign to Baba and told me, 'You're getting older too, darling – you've turned fourteen – what will people say?' Baba let go of me, I let go of Baba. But all evening, all night, through all my sleep, Baba's caress stayed with me. Tridib-da did not say a word all these days. I had rejected him straightaway. How simple Tridib-da was, and I was so cruel! Perhaps now I could keep my desires in check. God, please help me now so that I can love him even more.

□

The distance between the doll and the image is not much. It could be a god, of human descent, or a bird or animal, or anything whatsoever. The doll emerges from the image and in the throbbing-with-faith body of a female they are gods. Of all the toy dolls girls raise, not all are really toys. Ma Shashti's parturient abdomen is revealed, or sometimes the folds of the lower abdomen following childbirth. The lower part of some bodies is a solid mass, with no trace of sexuality. Only the coddled doll bears the signs of sexuality, the pubic hair and the triangle of the vulva are drawn with lines. The indication of reality is provided by spreading thick lines and curved lines.

□

From the very time the misunderstanding with Rosie began quite a few years ago, he had been observing how, among the people in his environment, the desire to possess ever more was rapidly growing. It was as if everyone was dying for more comfort, more luxury, more money. He wasn't exactly able to fathom this restlessness in people, their craze for happiness. His job was quite a high-profile one. Plenty of colourful temptations all around him. He couldn't give it up, nor could he reconcile with it. That was the beginning of a major difference of opinion. Rosie had changed somehow after coming to Calcutta. The inherent scent and flavour of water does not change no matter which utensil it may be poured into, even if that utensil's outward form was acquired. 'With all your idealism, you should go and live in a monastery. If you have to live with me, you have to give up this culture reeking of widowhood.' He had given it up, had given it up very soon, but in another way. In another dimension.

□

The Dagar girls said 'uncle' a lot while talking. Conjugal love had not evaporated, although the *henh henh* had become something like *hoon hoon hoon hoon tananana*. The personal assistant was beautiful, in various ways she had made it known that it was only after adopting protection against the possibility of motherhood that she had become a companion on his journey. Ghalib wrote, 'not a single beauty did my eyes spot yesterday, what's the matter, did I finally start getting older after three epochs...' A mild storm arose and the night became cool, he couldn't sleep.

□

Are we on the path of evolution? All evolution is beyond visibility, beyond thought, only an endeavour to adjust to the immediate sequence of events. So it is not always possible to predict the trajectory of evolution, applying reason. For his own purposes, man gradually adjusts to evolution, he does that constantly. It's not possible to either destroy or construct all this using reason. The ultimate fruit of all the work done by the European rationalists in the name of social justice was socialism. To explain the failure of socialism in terms of its practical failure would mean that, somewhere, reason's account-fudging remains. The failure of socialism is actually the failure of the theory relating to manufactured social development. Who can say whether a crisis similar to the crisis of the Soviet Union will not result if we seek to organize some society in the likeness of this theory? He finds his logic in Friedrich August von Hayek's writings. He keeps noting it down in his diary. Or is the matter entirely different? After a time, the logic finds him, its like-minded kin.

□

It was a terribly hot country, a net had to be cast to catch it, because there were golden anklets on its silvery paws. He used to return home late at night, his hair full of cockleburs, the smell of wild animals all over his body. After that began the journey along paths that crossed huge mountains. The desolation all around seemed to bring on a kind of unknown fear. The stillness was such that even the rustle of the cloak or the normal sound of deep breaths was inaudible. Grasping her shoulders, he asks her: 'Tell me, what is it that you think about so much!' She never replies. She only keeps revealing her own personal dreams. Shooting eagles with arrows, she climbs the highest mountain peaks, and standing on icebergs floating in the sea, she battles polar bears all night long. Is the girl a sorceress? Somewhere outside, a fox barks. The sound of someone's footsteps can be heard beneath the window. A pack of wolves, whining *choonh-choonh*, run along the edge of the mountain. The stench of fetid blood in their fangs. Rocks spread out everywhere on the vast and desolate field. He bumps into the pile of bones of abandoned corpses. He then keeps throwing stones in the direction of the cheap tombstone. He wants to break and crush the concrete. Yet heaps and heaps of coloured gemstones pour out from inside it. Leaping up, the tiger steps on his shoulder and goes away. In front of him, a python winds itself around a tree trunk, it darts its tongue in and out. He throws a stone. And with a whirring sound, that stone, all those blood-red stones boomerang and hit his own chest. Has some supernatural power possessed him? He thinks of returning home every day. But he never returns. Never. He only keeps losing his way.

□

What rationalists fail to understand is that no rationale is the last word. Within the evolutionary framework itself there resides an inner system for the correction of the framework. The system confronts the outside world in such a way that it results in the comprehensive development of the framework itself. Because the world outside matter is full of myriad possibilities, so, naturally, its inner framework too is bound to become full of infinite possibilities. The trajectory of its development cannot be cast in any predetermined mould through the observation of past events. There's no such thing as the last word in anything, and there's no such thing as the last word on the last word either. The development that takes place in the living world in the course of the evolutionary process follows the rule of spontaneity, and it is because it is spontaneous that rationalism cannot always explain it.

□

Just like how, by shutting one's eyes amidst darkness, one can reach another darkness inwardly, from within the silence between them Tridib transcended it and was experiencing an inner speechlessness. He wanted to say that, for about three decades, wagering his all, he had built a life, bit by bit, albeit only a single life – was it for this situation that he had wanted to build it? 'Why don't you understand, Rosie, there's a limit to how much even I can tolerate. And all around me are spread all the invisible bounds. The bounds of the mould. Going outside the boundaries means breaking the mould. I couldn't break it. I only carried on a mock show of life, a single life, according to the measure of the mould. A hundred times. A thousand times. Thousands and thousands of times. Perhaps that's my fate. But marriage is a social affair. The desire for freedom was within you from the very beginning. So then, is there anything else that remains to be recognized?'

□

I don't know what exactly is meant by love, but Ma says Tridib-da loves me. Perhaps it's him that I'll have to marry. That's what Ma wants. Ma wants the wedding to take place very soon. As we are Christians, Tridib-da is agreeable to a Christian wedding. He accompanies us to church on Sundays. But is such fidelity good? I was sitting on the sofa with my back to the door. I heard him come and enter the room. Tridib-da sat down next to me. He looked somewhat thoughtful. When he gazed at me with his pair of sad, black eyes, I felt his gaze pierce into me. I was very scared of that gaze. Would this youth remain faithful to me all his life! There was no conversation between us. The blazing sun, stillness. This stillness of nature ambled between the two of us. He didn't know what he'd do. I didn't know what I'd do. If he used force with me, that would have some meaning. But I knew he wouldn't do that. After some time, his hand touched my hand. I knew he would say something now. I slowly put my hand on his shoulder. He kissed me, for a long time. He hugged me to his chest. I placed my head on the chest, and my love. Nothing could be seen clearly in the room's hazy darkness. Perhaps outside, the long shadow of the devtaru tree was still swaying over the grass. After that, after a while, Baba arrived. Tridib-da held my hand and stood up. 'You've really made me happy today!' Saying so, right in front of Tridib-da, Baba began to caress me. I didn't realize when exactly Tridib-da left the room. To tell the truth, I was immersed in Baba. After some time, we saw him pacing up and down in the garden in the darkness, smoking one cigarette after another. His face was not visible, only his back, a beautiful manly back radiating good health. A bit of a stoop. In that pitch darkness, alone together in the room, Baba slowly held my hand, he drew me to his chest. Although I tried to resist, I could not. 'Hey, my dear – you're happy, aren't you?' I hugged Baba tight, for the life of me. How terribly weak I am!

□

She was quite slim earlier, but of late she was becoming fat, she seemed to have become heavier after the operation. Rosie had opened the cupboard and was selecting a sari. There was a row of them on clothes hangers – all expensive ones. Kanjivaram, Dhakai, Baluchari, Bomkai, Chanderi. Even before she could ask for something, he bought it for her. Tons of gifts. Who knew what he did with the PA girl. She had heard so many other things too. There was no end to drinking at night. If there was a party, then definitely so. How this man had turned out. He was far away from anything called morality. Nowadays, she only thought about Baba ... she was flooded with memories ... the colliery, the fields, the river, the clip-clop of the horse and the wild darkness of the sal forest. The darkness which her Baba brought back in his cupped palms, and then, when he flung it on her eyes and face it used to light up with fireflies, darkness, fistfuls of it, and fireflies...

□

'Eesh ... how obliging my man is! When did you ever ask me before doing anything that you ask me now?' 'So then tell me how it should be.' 'What do I know about that?

After all I'm your daughter, I'll do whatever you ask me to.' Stretching her arm, Ahalya put her hand in Tridib's hair, full of passion. He had selected the name Ahalya for his daughter after she was born, despite Rosie's fierce objection. Before he knew it, his daughter had grown up, got married and now she too had a daughter. She continued to ruffle her father's hair slowly. The five fingers of her hand slithered like snakes. They tickled him. It was a mixture of both passion and affection, and Tridib, embarrassed, stooped like someone haunted by ghosts. Inside the room now was the darkness of the colliery from thirty years ago, following the law of evolution. She remembered various other things, kept remembering, and eagerly brought down her lips, into the depths, to greater depths, clinging, her whole body. Rosie's father's shadow appeared on the door. Blood, there was only blood and more blood everywhere. She had murdered a person, her own daughter, blood dripped down her fingers all over the prehistoric darkness. After that, after some time, time rolled along and then stood still, light appeared, Rosie stood at the door, wearing the same moon-cut blouse, a candle in her hand, a strange smile on her face. Time stood still now. 'I have already seen every part of you. But I'm terribly scared,' said Ahalya, covering her face with her hands and trembling. 'But there are no buts. Lift your head up and look at me once. See whether there's any trace of sin anywhere. Sin, which man is capable of committing.'

□

The sexuality that is born right after a child's birth becomes even more complicated with the craving for synthetic satisfaction in sexual life arising from social failure. He has seen the value order created by this system in the sphere of economic life infiltrating into intimate sexual life too. On the one hand, it transforms sexual behavior into a synthetic and mechanical act, and on the other hand, slavery in the workplace is accepted, like impotence. The black magic of attaining satisfaction from sexual pleasure takes on a new dimension. Nowhere is there a healthy, strong arm, only a crowd of lustful masses all around, she is all alone in this forest of people, propelled by fate, bloody. After a long journey, she halts, extends her hand, perhaps she ought not to get lost like this. Every now and then it becomes cloudy. After all, untimely storms do occur. Ahalya had said that the other day. With her face in darkness, she had spoken about her husband. The girl dotes on her father. The father too loves his daughter beyond reason. Darkening the room, Ahalya goes on talking about all these things. She keeps gazing in the direction of my eyes, Ahalya, my own daughter, a strange smile on her face.

□

For whom am I earning money, Madam? Debraj touched Ahalya's shoulder. 'If you want to go to your father's house, then go. After all you are my better half, who else do I have but you!' 'Why are you spoiling my mood like this? I'm going to a joyful environment. Come on, get ready. It's already quite late...' 'Is there any booze, my dear?' 'Whatever you want – rum, whisky, gin, vodka, brandy. There was a bottle of champagne too. French. I had kept that aside for you. You were so late. It's finished.' Whenever he went to a party, he became a galloping horse. He made up for arriving late by downing a glass at once, and after guzzling three or four pegs, he began to reveal himself. He babbled loudly. Flailing his arms and legs animatedly, he danced, he exploded into guffaws without reason. On some days, he started singing too. Returning home late at night, he fondled his sleeping daughter. He kissed her until she woke up. He used to chat with his father-in-law about cyberporn, both of them swigging from the same bottle. No, in all this there was no perversion in him. Even now, he sat his daughter on his lap. He couldn't stop thinking of his darling even for a moment. He jabbered away with her and sipped vodka. Debraj had been raised in a completely different tradition. Clutching the wooden floorboard, Tridib wondered: Would he fall down, was he falling down!

□

Taking my hand in his, Tridib-da began examining the shrunken fingers, this way and that way. He said in a hushed tone: 'I know a terrific storm has blown over you.' I looked him in the eyes. After a while, Baba and Ma entered the room, 'Our darling has changed a lot' – Baba said, stroking my head. 'Yes, as soon as spring arrives, she'll be fit as a fiddle again.' Tridib began laughing in the very presence of Baba. And thus was the evening spent in conversation. Baba was sitting beside me, I was lying on the sofa. One hand of Baba's was held tight in my fist. Ma sat far away from us, crocheting lace. Just as it was about to be nine o'clock, she said: 'Now it's time to go to bed. It's very late.' 'But you won't be able to climb upstairs by yourself, darling' – Baba said. 'Why don't you see whether I can or not, Baba' – I said laughingly – 'after all it was only by holding your hand that I came down.' 'No, no, you can't do that – climbing up is much more difficult than getting down.' 'Let me try once and see what happens.' After that, I tried hard for a few minutes, but I couldn't stand up by myself, Baba was already prepared, he suddenly grasped me. 'You're crazy, my darling...' She was going to be sick again. 'It's alright, Tridib will take you to your room,' Ma said with a sombre face. Tridib had already lifted me up in his arms, as if I was a small doll. 'Put your hand on my shoulder' – he whispered, as he carried me in his arms. From his voice I intuited something else. I was tired, I had to rest my head on his shoulder. When I opened my eyes, I could not see anyone else other than Ma. She was looking at me and Mary was changing my clothes. Baba came after a while. 'Do you realize, my darling – you're still weak.' 'But I was able to come down in the morning holding your hand,' I protested at once. Baba was absent-minded, he kept looking out of the window. Perhaps he was looking at the fire burning in a Santhal village.

□

After spending the whole night in paradise, he returned tottering at dawn to his room. Does he recognize his room! He bent over the pillow to kiss his wife. On the pillow were two heads. Startled, he stepped back. Hey, do lunatics know they are mad! He wanted to erase his doubts by running his hand over the pillow. There was a man on the same bed as his wife. His wife's lover? The face looked familiar, but he couldn't recognize him clearly. Does he even recognize his own wife! As he turned around and stood, he saw her standing at the door jamb, with a lamp in hand, his wife! Showing him the light. On her silvery feet were golden anklets. They jingled. The day of the puja on the altar was fast approaching. It was as if everything alive was stirring in the stillness of the dead. With his nails, he tore away a thin piece of skin from the base of a nail. The smoke of his own cigarette was beneath his nose. The genie turned into vapour inside the water pot. When the fisherman opened the pot, it emerged like smoke, after that it took on its own appearance. Will he murder now! Should he murder now! But his hands – where were his hands! Who would he kill, and how? He had never been as hand-less as this before.

□

Whatever his problems were, they were all so far away, concealed under his thinking mind, or else, crossing the thinking mind, so close by that he couldn't express anything using language. He then began to retreat into himself, kept on retreating. And he thought that the system that was responsible for this plight of his was completely indifferent as far as he was concerned, and was unperturbed once he'd been banished to this silence. Again and again, silence appeared as the complement of speech, in the gaps within speech. And even when he spoke – was that always speech? Or was it merely the utterance of sounds, only meaningless beastly sounds? Small disagreements assumed gigantic proportions, and then it was as if the unspoken words themselves became a silent message. And the remaining part was speech astride speech, incoherent speech, as if it was never a sequence of words at all, never one word following another.

□

'Rubbish! What are you afraid of? I know the medicine to remove fear. I'll keep giving you a little bit of the medicine, and just see how your fears flee!' He laughed as he jested. But the young woman did not respond. She just gaped at him, as if in a confused state. He couldn't wait any longer.

He steeled his mind, whatever had to be done had to be done right now – at the very moment the girl was in doubt and indecision. Or else perhaps she would turn contrary ... And right then, Ahalya gave a gentle shove. The man was hea-vy. 'There, go to sleep now.'

□

Burglars were coming to the compound most nights nowadays, the day before yesterday they climbed up the rainwater pipe to the adjacent flat. Rosie shut the kitchen window and fastened it securely from the inside, using string. It had been ten years since she had moved into the flat, it had been whitewashed only once, that was four years ago. The house ought to be painted this winter itself. Should she put another foot or so of tiles in the kitchen? Could do that. Taking a gulp of water, she brought the jug down on the dressing table. She turned down the fan by two points. Kali Puja was over, it felt cold to have the fan on nowadays. Especially around dawn. How on earth did she start looking so drab? Holding one end of the ribbon in her teeth and taking a long time, she wound it round and round the base of her length of hair. That was an old habit. Or else loose hair would slip on the pillow.

□

Durga Puja, Christmas, New Year's Day – at these times, the father–daughter duo became gourmands too. Something new had to be cooked every day. If it was make-chocolate-cake one day, then it was fruitcake the next. If it was I-want-biryani one day, then the next day it was navratan pulao. Amidst all this, one day the principal actor's love was awakened, braving the thick crowd of New Year he went with his wife for an outing to Diamond Harbour. Such passion! How fine the Ganga looked in winter! Just see the wonderful colour of the sunlight falling on the water! As if it were just for them … But of course, all this had to be there, what's called *samsara dharma*.

□

Lying on her back on the bed, she was puffing a cigarette. He entered the room and shut the door behind him. 'Madam! Madam! There's some good news!' 'What's that?' 'Come next month, I'll have no more business with shared taxis. I'm getting a car from the company.' 'Really?' '*Yes!* Of course, it's not for me alone. Dutta from Accounts gets on at Gariahat, the two of us will travel together. But in the office, the car will be totally under my control.' 'Hmm…' 'Why are you hmm-ing – do you know what it means? My importance in the company is growing. There might be a hefty pay hike.'

□

'Shut all the windows. I need the warmth of your body. I feel as cold as ice inside. Come and sleep beside me. Give me warmth, not with your hand but with your body.' And then, at once, his body is prostrate.

□

A few eagles circled overhead. Someone's voice came floating from very far away. The lustre of lapis lazuli on the river water. Eyelids heavy with sleep. Sparkling teeth. Golden anklets on silvery feet. She came walking over the tallest mountain, to the sound of the anklets. She raised her head and looked, the face mummy-like, white. She asked:

'Where's he?' 'He's right here – in front of your eyes.' The mountain peaks had just awakened to the new light, the habitations below were still swathed in green shadow. The border steadily acquired clarity. Rows and rows of mountains visible, rising to the sky. The glowing chandeliers of Victoria Memorial could be spotted from afar. The water sprite. Pressing her temples and resting on her elbows, she kept looking fixedly at the reflection of her own face. The image of the colliery floated into her sight. Light fell between two mountains. Mackenna's Gold.

□

Tridib went to Mumbai for three days last week. His PA accompanied him. Ahalya spent the weekend with friends in Digha. Making an uproar. She was now in love with Bryan Adams. She always had the Walkman earphones on. She had to occupy herself somehow. She sat with fat English crime thrillers. On the front cover, a half-naked woman with a machine gun. A summary of the story on the back cover. Can't stop once you start it. Was she changing very fast? At the time of marriage, one heard a lot about such qualities of girls. Did one have to assume that all of it was true! All evening the throat burns, and sour burps.

□

'He's carrying on merrily with anyone and everyone. Apparently, the girl has huge desires. He doesn't give any money for the family, it's to that woman that he gives everything. It was because Ahalya-di went to Debraj-da's office that there was a commotion. And do you know who's helping Ahalya-di? That man who comes to their house ... Ahalya-di says he's her father. A bit elderly, but apparently, he's not really her father. It was going on from before she was married. Which man cares for his wife if the wife's lover comes to the house every day!'

□

The boundary of human society is only as far away as the crier's voice reaches, it was probably Aristotle who said that. In the communal or tribal era, perhaps society was as small as this. And it may also be true that society was directed on the basis of mutual assistance, and goodwill for one another was also the prime element of the feeling that was prevalent then among mankind. It was under the impulsion to protect one's line and expand one's line that man went beyond this small world of his and built an expanded society. If the desire to build an alternative system resides within man's very being, then there's no reason to accept that man will never achieve that. Man's own being itself would want to keep experimenting towards such a system, go on doing so, and it is through this experimentation that society will ascend to another system. But the question is whether that is an ascent? And exactly how far can human intellectual creativity go, exactly how much...

□

'You've become very bold, haven't you?' The young woman asked with a smirk. 'Of course, I will ... Didn't you notice when I started becoming bold!' Without letup, the lustrous body-sap spurted out. Oh, what pleasure. An inexpressible sense of joy suffused the whole being. As she wriggled, the young woman lowered her legs considerably. Within a short while, the inert body became vigorous again. Removed her sari, somewhat like closing a shutter. The girl appeared to be very excited. She kept heaving loudly. Felt ashamed at her own condition. Thank God, his own daughter was looking in front. Or else, the outspoken girl that she was, who knows how long she'd have gone on giggling. What's up now – once again the girl nodded invitingly. And at once she swooned. After that, controlling herself, she said, 'Mister, why are you just gaping ... haven't you ever seen a girl before!' 'No, it's just that you're my daughter's age.' Intoxication in her eyes, and bending towards him as she tittered in laughter, the girl retorted: 'So what?' In that case, what had he been doing all this while, and to whom! He kept gazing at his own face.

□

Countless tiny black ants were climbing up the wall. Carrying white specks, they were moving along, all of them. A well-disciplined, spectacular procession. The column of ants extended from the floor to the ceiling. Not exactly a thin line, not a bloodline either, it was as if the wall was hanging by a speckled black string. Quivering gently. Or alternatively, as if they, that is the ants, had suspended the ceiling, like in a geometric diagram...

□

A metallic sound rings from the bottle of rum and glasses. A mound of chanachur on a sheet of newspaper, and pistachios. 'Cheers' resound, and I pour it down my throat saying, 'Hey Ram,' and shutting my eyes. There's an elitism in my friends' drinking style, but I don't like to delay anything, I pour it down my throat nowadays in the manner of a peasant. And then I wipe my mouth with my arm. Everything in front of my eyes seems to be swaying now. The light from the battery-operated lamp becomes dimmer and dimmer. No more whooshing sound any longer from the casuarina forest. A wet mark under the tree ... I can clearly discern a leopard's paw. The conversation with the assembled beauties carries on in the presumed national language. I sing the song about the *deewana devar*. The girls keep laughing. They almost roll over laughing. That's how it is in soft porn. Everyone has fun. If it's hard core, say no more. I'm feeding clues into the computer. When required, I shall process all the special positions. A-n-y problem, old man?

□

'I'll get some pizza bread, please make some cheese pizza.' 'Oof, I feel so hot – will you make me some sherbet – hey, why are you making it with only cold water – add some ice cubes.' Has he murdered the one who didn't want to do the job? The two panels of the door keep going through the wall. From time to time, he reclines over the three-legged table and keeps gazing at his own body. Gradually his pace slackens, he turns towards the darkness, the girl wearing golden anklets on silvery feet hugs him once again, after that she becomes one with her own darkness.

□

'Hey, where's the mistress?' he asked the girl. The girl cast a sidelong glance towards him and smirked. Wriggling her body into a specific pose, she replied: 'The mistress is in the bedroom now. Her father's here.' Bare-chested Red Indians were roaming around in front of him then. A few tents here and there. The sentinel paced among a herd of horses, a spear in his hand. Colourful feathers stuck on their heads. Spread over the middle, nearly extinguished fires that never extinguish. A deep valley all around. Suddenly, hearing the sound of laughter, he turned around. On the roof-terrace of the house in front, a dark-skinned working-class woman was caressing the little boy on her bosom and laughing. Every now and then, she would suddenly begin tickling the child's bared tummy, the child would chortle in laughter. He did exist. His light in every lamp. And it was very late now. The late-night air was harmful to his body.

□

Reacting to his repression in the workplace, modern man tries to be creative in all those spheres where he is not a part of social labour. Outside of labour, man's right pertains to enjoyment and vices, where he is merely an individual. His repressed creativity keeps getting expressed as a yearning at the individual level – for food, sex and vices. The repression-based civilization that free men build upon the primitive world cannot distinguish between man and animal. Whether spontaneously or by attribution, this civilization rushes towards humane maturity, perhaps that's the last word on it. If the primeval text of theoretical construction is the hoodwinking primeval text narrated by August von Hayek, then all notions pertaining to the distance of the human world from the animal world, too, have to be seen to be the fruit of hoodwinking.

□

There is a cackle of hyenas in front of him, behind him a herd of deer. From his right side come the threatening grunts of wild boars, while along the left side, the rainbow serpent slithers around under the grass. But it is only the leopard, the picturesque leopard, that licks its chops, the stench of fetid blood in its mouth, its eyes fixed as it moves towards him, one step at a time, the picturesque leopard. Golden anklets on its silvery paws. The jingle of the anklets rings explosively in his heart. He shuts his eyes in the bliss of agony. Suddenly a rooster crows somewhere. Another rooster responds to that. One realizes dawn's approaching. The night is over. As soon as he opens his eyes he'll see, and unbeknown to him, in the sacred golden light of morning, the thirst for fresh blood inside him awakens. If he can, he'll murder someone just now. In this – this broad daylight, in the darkness of daylight. And then, putting the sun behind him, he keeps running, he alone has to go beyond his own shadow. And just then, with that, the film too comes to an end, the film is *Mother India*. Radha sees the likeness of her own husband in her son Ramu, she is really under the delusion that her son Ramu is her husband. The relationship of the mother with her two sons, unknown to the director, keeps assuming a multi-dimensional form, sometimes as younger sister, and sometimes a baby daughter, sometimes a wife. Gradually her behaviour with her younger son, Birju, steadily transgresses the zone of control, it heads towards an uncertain Oedipal framework. Radha shoots her son, throwing him off his horse. Riddles his associates with bullets, and the death process reaches a finale – from Shamu, the husband, and Sukhilal, the moneylender, to Birju, the son. After shooting him, the mother runs and hugs her son to her bosom and as she kisses him again and again, she begins screaming, blood from the bullet wound steadily drips from between her fingers, the blood is transformed into the water of an irrigation canal only in a literal sense. The hint of incest, that has given birth to passion and hatred in the same breast, itself explodes, it keeps exploding in the melodrama. The camera follows the fullness of the grain field, it stands still on the mother's breast. Indian films go exactly and only so far, neither a hair's breadth more nor less, and after that films are made, more and more films are made rapidly, Indian films, *Mother India*.

□

He can now extinguish with a single puff the most important wisdom of the greatest sage. He knows the poisonous vine now. He can sense the faint presence of the jet-black blood coursing under the skin. Looking through the modern means of concealment, he can see the entire female hip, which she actually wants to flaunt. Don't know why, but for some strange reason, every now and then he thinks that the characters are actually shadows, in darkness, of time; who do not have any fixed form, who can even become separate from the body if they want. Voluntary death has given him this gift. He can't give all this to anyone else. To no one at all. For that matter, not even to himself. Because he knows that once upon a time, it was with darkness itself that darkness was covered.

[Ramdhonu-Sorpo, 1997]

The Hand – Rough, Severe, Blazing with Resolve, Pliable, Clenched in a Fist, Surrendered, and Deceived Too

The external parts are arrayed in such a manner that, just as the entire environs of light are in deep shadow, detachment too does not get propriety, independent will is suspended. In this way, a specific historical event keeps rivalling even its own historical elements, their limited level…

The night was shrouded in darkness, in many places the path so narrow as to permit one to place only a single foot at a time. The soldiers numbered more than a thousand. I saw their arms and ammunition too. It was the same sad story! More than eight hundred guns were cracked and unusable, some were half broken and some a quarter broken. The rust inside and outside the barrels of the remaining muskets was almost half an inch thick. The gunpowder hole was obstructed in many barrels. And then there was the state of the ammunition. The gunpowder canisters hanging at their hips were almost empty – the gunpowder wouldn't last for more than two or four rounds. They had two or three lead shots on their belts, and at best some of them may have had some more in their paan pouches. There were no priming wicks hanging out from the butts of many soldiers' muskets. All the swords were rusty. The paiks said – 'Sir, there was no time to load the gunpowder because we were ordered to rush here.' The night was shrouded in darkness, in many places the path so narrow as to permit one to place only a single foot at a time. It was uneven, winding up and down, with the branches of the trees on both sides hanging over the path, and so nothing was visible. There was no sunlight ahead. If someone walked on such a path without a close watch, it would not at all be surprising if he stumbled and fell on his face. And who could cleave the impassibility of this dark night!

I hadn't slept a wink the night before. It had rained all night long. I was sitting on the veranda of Hotel Keonjhar. Mist and clouds were playing hide-and-seek on the blue mountains. One or two tiny villages in the valley below, settlements, green grassy tracts and mountains, and mountain streams, all like a picture. There was a memsahib in the adjacent room. She had come to collect local information about the Paik Rebellion. She taught in some university on the west coast of America. It was raining without let-up, pouring down in front of one's eyes. Three coffees already since morning. I heard that the whole of eastern Orissa, right from Baleswar and Baripada, was under the spell of a tropical depression. A waste of a trip.

The paiks were old and weak, half of them were afflicted with night blindness. No one was willing to volunteer for the king's cause. Those who were unfit for domestic chores were the ones first pushed to such tasks. And today the rebellion of the subjects had begun – it was impossible to guess who was a paik and who wasn't one, who supported whom and who collected vital information in disguise and supplied it to the enemy. The night was shrouded in darkness, in many places the path so narrow as to permit one to place only a single foot at a time. The subjects had rebelled and so now the order had come from the government to join the resistance using muskets and swords. War meant death – war meant pierced bodies – war meant a shroud of darkness – permitting only a single step. However many fiats were issued by the government, would capable, virile youths be the first to jump into the fray at once? So let the old and weak be the first ones to go, whose death would not add to the families' woes. Those who had stepped forward to mount the killer elephants had one foot in the grave. Wound over the heads of some of those old and infirm folks were tattered, dirty bits of cloth folded twice over, or else a faded, oil-stained gamcha. On their shoulders were the three-and-a-half-armlengths-long Munger muskets, weighing ten seers, there were swords dangling from their waists, staffs in their hands, and a sack of rice to last ten or fifteen days on their backs. A brass pot inside the sack of rice, and together with the pot, a bowl packed tightly inside the bundle. Clad in this brave garb, the paiks trudged along that dark path, knocking their staffs on the earth. The night was shrouded in darkness, in many places the path so narrow as to permit one to place only a single foot at a time. No sunlight ahead, one did not know who was a friend and who a foe, and especially on the faces and eyes of the young paiks who had come involuntarily was the shadow of something, dark like the night. Oh no – an aged paik in the middle stumbled and fell to the ground. The row of paiks behind him halted for a while until he rose up again. When the Maharaja's elephants advanced two hundred yards, the band of paiks fell behind by a hundred yards. But the elephants behind the paiks were not supposed to advance. From atop the elephant, the Maharaja's exhortations began: 'Soldiers! Advance – keep advancing!' Five or seven paik youths were deployed to drive the other paiks ahead. Within the space of the first two miles, the elephants had to halt four or five times. If they advanced in this fashion, could they ever cover the dark path – the path through the forest?

There was rain the next morning too. Braving the rain, we set out in the jeep that had been arranged the previous day. It was pointless to waste the whole day and be confined to the hotel. Christina too wanted to set out with us. Accompanying us was a Tamil family who were also staying in the hotel. The jeep made its way slowly up the mountain path. Once we crossed the rail line ahead, the open grassy tract met the mountain. A tunnel went through the mountain. Below that lay an Adivasi settlement. Since the passenger trains came only twice a day, the station was completely desolate. Christina took out a map, she looked this way and that way. She said: 'The paiks' main battle probably took place here, between these two mountains. But what needs to be found out is who exactly wanted to wage war.' Saying so, she looked at me and smiled. We had become acquainted last night. After a time, I saw that the road was concealed by the mist that enveloped us. I couldn't figure out whether it was mist or cloud. The vehicle crossed the gorge very slowly and began climbing up. Towards the end, the road was very bad. A few hundred feet below us, the muddy brown stream of water flowed frenziedly at a furious speed. Within a moment, crossing one mountain and arriving at the other, there was a plain, a vast expanse of pastureland. People's houses here and there. From Christina's conversation I gathered that she had come here before. She said: 'The paiks' cave is just ahead. It's said in the folklore of this region that they lost because they went into battle without first propitiating the deity of the cave.' She had also collected two or three alternative versions of the folklore in the local Oriya language. She had tape-recorded everything. She said we could hear it at night if we liked. We didn't show much interest. It would be better to visit the cave. Observing our enthusiasm, the driver looked at the sky a bit worriedly. Even though there was a pause in the rain, there was no sign of the foul weather abating. Actually, he agreed somewhat reluctantly to take us to the paiks' cave. But before that, halting the jeep, the afternoon meal was ordered at a tile-roofed shanty beside the road.

The driver said: 'We have to eat whatever they prepare. Won't get any other food anywhere else.'

The Maharaja took a decision: all the elephants would be at the rear, the row of paiks would be in front. And so was it arranged. The paiks were stooping under the weight of the heavy bundles on their backs, they began to walk slowly, moving at tortoise speed, all the way. So the elephants could not advance easily, even if the paiks at the rear prodded them a thousand times, it was impossible for them to advance any faster. The path permitted only a single file, so narrow as to permit one to place only a single foot at a time. If the man in front blocked the way, how could the man behind advance? In order to hasten the paiks at the rear, when the elephants behind were almost grazing against them, they ran hurriedly and fell on the paiks in front of them, and in the process several paiks tumbled and fell to the ground. This order of the Maharaja too turned out to be unsuitable from the point of view of moving ahead. He issued new orders. Finally, it was decided that the two elephants carrying the Maharaja and the chief minister would be in front. At the very rear would be the naib's elephant. The paiks in the front were issued specific orders to march closely behind His Highness' elephant. Keeping pace with the paiks at the rear came the naib's elephant, at the very end. This arrangement seemed to be more convenient than the previous one. There was no other alternative. The night was shrouded in darkness, in many places the path so narrow as to permit one to place only a single foot at a time, because the path was shrouded in darkness, the night, in many places the night...

One realized that the cave of the paiks was quite famous in this region. For the local folk, it was the abode of an ever-watchful god. Earlier, one had to enter with a flaming torch or a petromax lamp. Now, with sodium vapour lamps installed, it was made convenient for tourists to visit. The guide pointed out the stalactites and the stalagmites. The cave rock had taken the form of bees' honeycombs – images of gods and goddesses – birds and animals with unknown names. Cows, horses, elephants, bears. Everything of stone – everything here was of stone – and everything was worshipped. Coconuts and vermilion were the main puja offerings. The guide said: 'Long ago, there used to be human sacrifice here.' I saw yokes at the cave entrance. The dripping limestone water had assumed the form of chandeliers in some places, and ears of corn elsewhere. Some could be discerned clearly, again some had to be perceived using one's imagination. All this had been going on for age after age; when the liquified limestone drips down extremely slowly from the roof of the cave and descends, the drops of the liquified lime hang down from the roof and the water evaporates, with the excess liquid continuing to drip into the interior of the cave. Eventually, the evaporated limestone hardens. Images keep getting made on the floor. Perhaps in the course of several thousand years, about an inch forms. Often the images at the top and at the bottom become one, they form a pillar. Inside the cave, an unimaginable world along about a mile and a half. Defeating all of human imagination. Before one knew it, in fear and astonishment, one's breath came to a halt. As it is, in the interior, because of the scarcity of oxygen, one experienced breathing difficulty. One could also enter deep into the interior. A cold, moss-covered, slippery zone, devoid of light and air. A labyrinth of immaterial material. Even the slightest sound of speech produced unworldly echoes when it rebounded against the stone walls. The possibility of a new interpretation was in sight. There were arrangements for light till some way inside. But it was good to have a torch. One couldn't walk a single step without the guide, it wasn't advisable to do so either. In a few places, water gushed down from the roof of the cave. As I stood gazing at that, suddenly, I felt a stream of water beneath my feet, flowing from one end of the cave to the other. A whole river flowed along beneath one's feet. Perhaps many years ago, miraculous cascades of water used to course through the cave, one after another, with terrific fury. Water clung to the surface of the rock, the rock took on a soft appearance. All around were the final lamentations of those dried-up cascades. Rock accumulating on rock, forming rugged pebbles of rock. The guide said: 'Dishonest

Odia brahmins take away all these and pass them off as shaligram shilas.' Perhaps at some point in time, the water channel lost its speed, changed its current, leaving behind only abandoned ruins of the course, a river of dreams, in the cavity of a cave. The cave of the paiks.

Continuing the comic advance in this way, in the middle of the night we reached a forest dwellers' village beside the road. The stooped, devastated bodies were almost half dead. Most of the people were not up to walking a single step more. Eyes half shut, legs tottering, bodies bent double under the load on their backs and the muskets on their shoulders, they almost limped along haphazardly, not knowing in which direction they were going, merely following the man in front. These were the paiks, they were the warriors – the ones who would rescue us! And how were they to blame! With their fevered bodies, they had walked for twenty or forty miles to respond to the call to arms. They were corvée paiks. In the evening, after eating a stomach-full of rice, with the heavy packs tied to their backs, they walked along the unseen path, stumbling against rocks time and again. Many cut their toes and bloodied the path. After umpteen pleas and entreaties to the Maharaja, about half an hour's time was granted for rest. As soon as the order was conveyed, everyone just dropped down where they stood, without wasting even a moment. The pack on the back remained fastened, they only flung away the musket on the shoulder wherever they could. At their feet, clumps of thorny shrubs on the path that was knee-deep in slime – no one was in any condition to pay attention to all that. As soon as they dropped to the ground, everyone began snoring. I too had become terribly exhausted. I was sleepy, I could barely keep my eyes open; as soon as I dismounted from the elephant I lay down on the path. Oh Lord – this was uneven ground strewn with rocks, sticking out here and there like the blade of a sword. My condition was not unlike Bhisma's in his bed of arrows. The sharp edges of the stones jutting out cut the whole body. However exhausted I might be, could one sleep lying on such a bed of arrows? I tried to toss and turn two or four times, and after that, exasperated, I sat up. Wasn't there any level ground in this place? Nothing could be discerned in the darkness, from the sound of breathing I realized many people had fallen asleep on this. True, in response to our entreaties the Maharaja had granted half an hour's rest, but he had been completely unwilling to do that. The half hour went by in the blink of an eye. 'Come on – march ahead – we have to reach quickly' – the Maharaja's order came even before the alarm clocks could ring at the hour – 'No further delay, rise now – come on – hurry up!' Like the arrangement earlier, the elephants would be in front and at the rear, with the row of paiks in the middle. We thought, how dark it is, how distressing, how, moving through a night without end, we are entering even darker, even more distressing, unending nights. We don't know the way, we don't know the destination, simply walking on – unending, indeterminate walking. No one looked at anyone's face during the journey. No one heard anyone's voice. I didn't know who was in front of me, didn't know who was behind. Walking on, merely blindly following the man in front. Following blindly, because the night was shrouded in darkness, the path so narrow as to permit one to place only a single foot at a time. Because the path was shrouded in darkness, the night permitting only a single foot to be placed at a time.

We ate at the tile-roofed eating joint where we had ordered food in advance. Thick, red-grained rice, kolai daal, and as a special item, potato fritters. The five passengers in our jeep sat on the floor seats and ate the rice from lotus-leaf plates. Seeing the lotus-leaf plate, Christina got very excited; after mixing the daal with the rice she asked whether she could get some roasted chillies. The shopkeeper and his wife fed us with much care. On the way back, we halted to visit Keonjhar Park. Christina remained in the jeep, but the Tamil family was very keen. We went in too. A concrete gateway had been installed in front of the entrance by the forestry and forest protection department. Written on the tin board – Horticulture Nursery-cum-Training Centre, Keonjhar, Orissa. Entering the park, I saw it was an immense garden. There was research being undertaken regarding various species of plants. Several people were busy collecting data. The whole place was beautifully laid out. At one end, a picturesque pavilion. A concrete dinosaur for children to play on. Clinging plants had been cut and pruned in the shape of baby elephants. The sky once again took on a sullen appearance. There had been no sun, it looked as if it would rain in the evening once it turned dark. We didn't delay. Returning to the jeep, I saw Christina noting down something. The camera, notebook and tape recorder lay scattered around her. Seeing me, she smiled. Out of courtesy, I asked her what she was writing. But Christina was serious. Removing her spectacles, she said: 'I'll tell you something, please don't mind – the nationalism that you find in all these rebellions – and become all emotional about – actually it's not that. These were, in the main, driven by individual interests – a matter of a squabble. I understand your Third World sentiment. But not a single rebellion is any different – what you call patriotism is actually merely so many individual whims...' While trying to get into the jeep, my foot got stuck. I kept staring at Christina's face. The girl was terribly thin, she wasn't shapely either. But what exactly did Christina want to say! What exactly had she come all this way to do! However, we couldn't delay, the driver was hurrying us – 'Hurry up, there might be a storm and rain again in the evening!' As soon as we got into the jeep, its engine started noisily. Evening was descending all around us, it was windy.

Marching through the undifferentiated darkness, after a time, with the sound of musket fire and the people's uproar, the path kept quaking. The elephant I was mounted on was in the section facing the paiks, even the elephant was startled, it halted. I assumed that a large number of the rebel paiks were amassed between the row of mountains on the two sides, staring at the darkness. Later, I realized that the number of people I had assumed to be there, as well as the extent of musket fire, was actually not correct. I had been confounded by the gunshot sounds emanating from the cave in the mountain. If one musket was fired, it sounded like ten. My intention was to find an elevated place, covered with trees, where I could take the paiks and then try to defend myself. But when misfortune arrives, nothing at all is convenient. Actually, the path was full of trees and rocks, and so it was particularly suspicious as far as the enemy was concerned. There was no other option. I became completely devoid of hope. About a hundred muskets were ready, and gunpowder. The Maharaja ordered that the bullets be removed and empty rounds be fired. The hundred muskets sounded at that moment like a thousand. I realized my error.

[Rukkho Kothin Shopothdeepto Haat, Nomoniyo Haat, Mushtiboddho Haat, Somorpito Haat, Protarito Haat-O, 1996]

Memory Game

(Fifty years of Independence, the target an arbour on the island of Hawaii)

... It's great to hear the story of
Vidyasagar swimming across the Damodar...

EARTH TO EARTH
ASHES TO ASHES
DUST TO DUST

We had advanced a lot in the darkness of the night. Our ship was anchored in tranquil waters. The coast was covered by a grey forest. Every now and then, breaching that grey-coloured wall, yellow, sandy liberated zones of the lowland emerged, tall pine-like trees here and there – one or two in some places, and many of them elsewhere, touching each other. But there wasn't any variety of colour on the island, it was kind of melancholy. The bare rocky hills towered over the trees. The shape of one was weird, it just rose from all directions, but it was entirely flat at the crest, as if a platform had been made to place an idol, as if it was something nature itself had created. The *Mother India* was rocking gently on the sea waves. The thick poles for hoisting the sails seemed to be coming out of their anchoring; even with that, they were knocking against each other gently on one side and then another, with a creaking, groaning sound coming from all parts of the ship. I stood holding the railing firmly – the entire island seemed to be spilling out before my eyes. Perhaps this annoying rocking – perhaps the island's appearance, it's grey, melancholy forested land, bare triangular hills, the foamy waves crashing down on the flat beach – was making me feel melancholic too, notwithstanding the seagulls screeching all around as they plunged into the water and caught fish, notwithstanding the clean sand below the water, notwithstanding the warm sun in the resplendent sky. Someone said from inside: 'Don't be dejected, it's the hidden tide now, that's why the current's unreliable. It'll all be fine in time.' When the anchor was dropped with a splash, hundreds of birds screeched and began flying over the beach. The dense forest on the opposite side descended to the water's edge. The birds touched that forest in flight. They descended again in a little while. Once again, it was still everywhere. After that, slowly, that forest descended to the water's throat, the flat land of the shoreline and the crests of the hills seeming to surround it like a Greek amphitheatre. Small rivers nearby, marsh. Where two rivers met, the leaves of the vegetation all around were bright – so bright that one at once realized they were poisonous. The beach continuously emitted an odour of soggy leaves and rotting tree trunks, it pervaded the air. Tarzan used to lie all by himself on the seaside sand sometimes. He wasn't aware of it when a few guerrillas arrived on the island in a small dinghy and observed him closely. Coming upon him all of a sudden and seeing he was alone amidst the desolation, they began advancing towards him from all sides. From living for a long time in the forest like an animal, Tarzan had mastered the animal senses. He could easily hear the sound of any footsteps – however faint they were. Though Tarzan lay unaware of his surroundings, he rose when he heard the sound of many footsteps. The man who was ahead of all the others slumped down, following a single swipe of Tarzan's knife. The armed enemies retreated a bit in fear and stood blocking Tarzan's path to the forest. At first, because of the clayey soil and a kind of sticky weed, it was quite difficult for us to climb up. But as the hill steadily became steeper, rocky land emerged under our feet. The forest's appearance changed too, the trees had grown taller since they stood on more vacant spots. The place we were going through was the most beautiful spot on the island. There were so many kinds of fragrant flowers of strange colours and small plants spread all around that the grass was almost invisible. On another side were trees with thick trunks – the plants, flowers and leaves together created an amazing fragrance. Arriving at that gleaming, beautiful environment, all of us were very happy. Everyone in the band now laughed, leapt and shouted in glee and began to spread out in all directions. He and I were far behind. We moved ahead. But a rope was tied around my waist, he was pulling me along as he walked over the loose pebbles. From time to time, I moved forward to make it easier for him, or else he might have slipped and rolled down the hill. He was moving ahead with me in tow and I was helping him do that. The hillside was now steep and rocky. Suddenly a pile of pebbles rolled down with a clattering sound through the gap between the vegetation. In my condition, hands tied, I looked and saw something hazy jumping vigorously and going out of sight behind a tree trunk. I couldn't figure out whether it was a human or some animal. I only saw that the creature was fair skinned and its face customarily beautiful. The rope tied around my waist was tugged again and again. As soon as I started walking, I turned my head around and saw that the creature had emerged once again. But instead of concealing itself, it came all the way up and tried to block my advance. It was going out of sight as it ran from behind one tree trunk to behind another tree trunk. It was running exactly like a human, on two legs. But I had never seen such a beautiful wild human running like this. Looking closely, I became certain that the creature was human. It kept looking at my face. It wanted to tell me something. The rope at my waist was tugged just then, I began walking ahead unwillingly, leading the way. *a cloud of mist forms around him, like a ring around the moon. if the light is just right, the edges of this cloud, which is nothing more than the body's moisture, evaporating rapidly, shine in all the colours of the rainbow. violet, indigo, blue, green, yellow, orange and red. the rainbow gradually dissolves, colour by colour, each thing vanishing here corresponding to a stage of death, a death beyond the threshold of pain, orange-red visible at the end as it disappears. DEATH, a play of colour.* I looked out through a nearby niche. The embers of the bonfire had turned to ashes, they were standing in a circle in the middle of that. There was a flaming torch in one man's hand. One man was sitting on his knees, an unsheathed sword in his hand. The blade of the sword emitted flashes from the moonlight and the light from the torch. Everyone else bent down and eagerly observed the actions of the man with the sword. But I could clearly see; I saw that he had a sword in one hand and in the other hand was a book. I was astonished, how could two things that were so dissimilar be together in a man's hands? After a while, the man stood up and the entire band began to advance towards the *Mother India*. They were coming. I sat down quickly, grazing the wall like before. If they spotted me watching them, they would cut me to pieces at once. The door opened slowly. As soon as the band crossed the doorframe, they stopped and pushed someone like their leader to the front. If it had been some other time, I would have burst out laughing seeing the manner in which he moved ahead. The man was advancing slowly, hesitantly, helplessly. There was a long sword held high in his right hand, in his left hand a book. The tall man with blue eyes was directly in front of us now. Once all the goods were brought down, Jane said: 'Bring the people down now, one by one.' Someone objected to that. The mute man was then brought down. He was quite unconcerned, he went with whichever band called him and he carried their flag. After that, there was talk about bringing down the princess. But the princess said: 'My whole body has turned numb with lust on seeing Tarzan. I won't be able to get down by myself.' Brown said to Alexei: 'Please try to make your princess understand. If you waste time unnecessarily, we'll leave the two of you behind here and go away.' Alexei pulled out the pistol at his waist: 'Mind what you say!' Brown laughed: 'We won't say anything. You just follow our instructions.' After that, once the princess was brought down following a lot of convincing and reassuring, and the promise that she would be allowed to spend a night with Tarzan, Brown said to Teaboy: 'It's your turn now, Teaboy.' Teaboy replied: 'No, I'll get down from the tree by myself. You too have to come down with me in the same way.' Alexei asked in astonishment: 'But I'm human – how shall I come down then?' Glancing in the direction of the princess, Brown replied: 'You can either climb down the tree with us, or else remain here.' 'Give me a light, brother' – the boss said, and then, lighting his pipe and blowing out a mouthful of smoke, he said: 'Alright, that'll do. Put the torch under the pile of wood. Everyone else can lie down, there's no need to stand in his honour because it's we who are shooting him.' I didn't reply at all to all this talk. I was standing with my back leaning against the wall, looking the people in the eye. I must certainly have looked very brave, although inwardly I was despondent and overwhelmed. Not getting any reply, the boss sucked at his pipe silently for a while. After that, he coughed and cleared his throat and said: 'Now that you are among us, let me tell you what's on my mind. When I was young, I too looked like you – fierce, brave, reckless. I was involved in politics from a young age. I couldn't figure out what was right and what wasn't, I just kept my mouth shut and followed the orders of the leaders. Anyway, I'd like you to join us, and realize what's best for you. Don't go back to your old ways, and that way you'll be able to spend the rest of your life like other respectable gentlemen.' I heard him in silence. The boss was sucking at his pipe from time to time and blowing out smoke. 'Look, he was certainly a very good man, and there's no way one can deny that. But he was a stickler for rules and regulations. "Duty's duty" – he often said that. He had to give up his life to uphold the way of truth. It's terribly sad, but it's true. Anyway, the upshot is that you can't return to your own band again because of your way of thinking. Because they've started suspecting you. Of course, you can set up a band all by yourself, but you'll be terribly lonely. The band will not accept your independent thinking. If necessary, they might finish you off too.' Hearing the boss, I was somewhat relieved to hear the news that some of my friends were alive. There was no way I could disbelieve that all of them were furious about my decision to leave the band. Nonetheless, as long as there were people around, there could still be a band sometime or the other. 'Nor am I saying anything about the fact that you're in our custody now.' The boss chewed on his pipe and carried on speaking. 'Although you should know that we can kill you if we want. All it requires is a bullet. But we believe that no good ever comes out of frightening anyone. If you like our work, you can join us'. 'And if I don't like it?' 'Fine, you're free to say no. I don't think anyone will conduct themselves better than this as far as you are concerned.' My voice trembled, but I said emphatically: 'Do I have to answer?' I realized very well that death loomed over my head. 'Actually, you people want to know about the ship from me. About the *Mother India*. I'm telling you clearly that it was I who cut its anchor and it was I who then left the ship in such a place where it can never be found – not even by anyone from your band. You've killed a lot of people, killing one more person is nothing for you.' But I boosted up my courage and said in plain words – 'If you want to let me work as I wish, then tell me what really happened, why are you all here, and where are my friends from my band?' Seeing Annette's footprints, one could figure out that she had come up to this tree. No more footprints of hers were visible after that. She hadn't gone ahead and hadn't returned either. It seemed someone had lifted her up from there. But no one else's footprints were visible. She was certainly carried away from atop the tree. Brown became very repentant regarding Annette. Jane began to reassure him. After a while, everyone finished eating and set out on their journey. Fear, disbelief and suspicion had made them dejected. The earlier enthusiasm was no longer there. In particular, a sense of panic and terror regarding the mysterious enemy who had taken Annette away and fled overwhelmed them at every step. Only Jane's mental fortitude was intact. She walked ahead of all the others. After a while, finding Jane alone, Alexei said: 'Are you convinced now that I didn't murder Annette?' Jane replied: 'This is not exactly about murder, it's about a kidnapping. Perhaps it's an ape guerrilla. The indigenous people of the forest can't leap from tree to tree. Besides, they're not really good at climbing trees.' Alexei then said: 'In that case, you surely realize that I didn't murder my wife.' 'This incident has got nothing to do with that' – Jane responded – 'It's the courts that'll decide who killed your wife.' Around afternoon, Brown and Jane went into the forest and brought back a deer they had hunted. Teaboy cut its flesh and roasted it over a fire. Everyone ate in silence. No one was at peace. Everyone was heavy-hearted with the grief of losing one of their own. No one spoke while they ate. The first night, it was Teaboy's turn to keep watch. After that Brown, and then Teaboy again. At four in the morning, Alexei was woken up by Teaboy. He was feeling terribly cold. As soon as he reached the fire, he tossed in a lot of wood and made the fire fiercer. As he kept watch, he suddenly observed that the axe was lying close by. And just after that, his eyes fell upon Brown. He saw that Brown was sleeping now. He suddenly felt cruel and violent. It was only Brown who was his sworn enemy. Even if they reached the civilized world one day, there would be no release as far as he was concerned. It was Brown who had accused him of murder. Besides, if they were unable to find their way back to the civilized world, if they had to live their lives in the forest, then so long as Brown was around he could never get close to Jane. Because Jane liked Brown more. There was no one he would fear if Brown was no longer there. It was all the same whether Teaboy was around or not. He was a spineless man. And despite everything, Jane was a woman. If Brown wasn't there, he could make the proof of murder disappear. Alexei held the axe firmly in his hand. An enemy's death should never be deferred.

EARTH ASHES DUST TO EARTH ASHES DUST

Here's the compass – and there's the cape of Skeleton Island – it looks exactly like a tooth – let's see you align this skeleton and the tip of the cape with the compass needle ... The task began at once, exactly as he said. The male skeleton was laid down at a straight line from the island. It was observed that the compass needle was quivering, but it wasn't indicating any precise direction. 'It was exactly as I had thought' – he shouted out – 'his bullet-pierced skeleton was only an imprecise guide. There's only the North star before us – our final direction.' Seeing his bullet-pierced dead body, my blood too seemed to turn cold. The dead body was actually a joke. It was with death that he carried on his experiment with truth. Although he lived with a country of people, he was the only one who was all alone. Everyone had shot the man once and then dragged the corpse here and laid it down after matching it with the compass. They thought that only the dead body of this person could be matched with the compass. It seemed someone from the crowd shouted out: 'Why are you going on casting one-sided blame! Where did the pistol go? It's here for sure. The murderer wasn't someone who would unnecessarily shoot and kill a naked fakir. Besides, the wind doesn't consume a staff and spectacles.' 'That's right' – another person responded. An oldish man was inserting his hand inside the bones and searching. He kept searching among the remaining bones. He said in astonishment: 'There's absolutely nothing here. No souvenir, for that matter not even the pocket watch. The matter doesn't seem normal at all.' 'You're right, not to me either'. The tall man with blue eyes said. 'You're saying it's not normal, you don't like it either. But just think, if he was alive today, how dangerous the place would have become for us. After all he's just dead bones now. He's dead – yes, certainly – he did die, but his dissatisfied soul wanders around even today on this island. Oh – he really died a cruel death.' 'Yes, that's true' – the tall, blue-eyed man said – 'From a few days before his death, his disposition turned ugly. He was shouting angrily one moment, and praying to Ram the very next moment, and just after that he was perhaps humming his favourite song. After all, it was only that song that could be called his favourite one. To tell the truth, ever since then I find that song disgusting. It was very hot that day, the windows were open. I could clearly hear the song come wafting – nonetheless the man's killer was present by then.' 'Forget all this rubbish' – one person said to another impatiently – 'I do know that he's dead, and that he doesn't wander around either. At least he doesn't wander around during the day. Keep in mind that it was curiosity that killed the proverbial cat.' All of us began moving ahead. The sun was beating down overhead, there was sparkling light all around, but we were no longer advancing through the forest like before, all singing, however far away we were. Although there was no end to the differences between us, nonetheless all of us walked ahead slowly, holding hands dispassionately. We were all in a kind of stupor fearing the dead, incorporeal soul. It's not that the creation of discord between Hindus and Muslims was the upshot of British politics alone. Just as there was harmony between the two communities, so was disharmony present too. But greater provocation was being created wherever there was discord, and it was from this politics of fuelling discord that the mental preparation for partitioning India began. Mohandas Karamchand Gandhi was one of the towering leaders of the freedom struggle, using non-violence and truth as two novel weapons against the imperialist powers. Although Dr Hedgewar had participated in the anti-British national struggle from time to time, the Rashtriya Swayamsevak Sangh had usually distanced itself from the freedom struggle. On the question of Indian national consciousness, the Indian leaders were divided into two opposing camps. The preparations for the partition of India began in such a situation. The positions were like this: (a) Gandhi was against gaining independence at the cost of partition, but he later resorted to silence under pressure from the Congress leaders and stayed away from the festivities of independence, observing the day instead as one of mourning, by fasting in Calcutta; (b) Jinnah's demand was that the Muslim-majority northwest of India becomes Pakistan, and if after that, undivided Bengal remained independent, he had no objections, but in that case India would be divided into three; (c) Jawaharlal Nehru fiercely opposed the trifurcation of India, and his position was that India could at most be divided into two; (d) Prominent Bengali leaders, like Shyamaprasad Mukhopadhyay, the leader of the Hindu Mahasabha, Atulya Ghosh, the Congress leader from Bengal, and so on were against a united Bengal and in favour of the partition of Bengal. Fazlul Haq and a few others wanted to distance themselves from all these conspiracies, but their opinions weren't really accorded any significance. Gandhi was consistently against sacrificing the country to partition, but the wheel of events didn't follow his view. And after that there was only the darkness of the midnight of 15 August 1947. The flood of refugees began. There were communal slogans everywhere, arson, looting and murder. At a prayer meeting on 13 January 1948, Gandhi wanted to hear a song: *Jodi tor daak shune keu na ashe tobe ekla cholo re*. He was perturbed, his own beloved Sardar Vallabhbhai Patel had termed the Rashtriya Swayamsevak Sangh as patriots. What was patriotism? That India belonged only to those of the Hindu faith – did patriotism boil down to making such a demand? The roar of the three shots fired from a revolver began the dauntless campaign to institute Hindu Rashtra, or a Hindu state. Brown said: 'Who's going to be sentenced to death?' Jane said, 'This blood-stained axe was found on your bed, Tarzan. Everyone's seen it. You can look at it too.' Looking at Alexei, Tarzan replied: 'Was it you who secretly placed the axe on my bed? Your intention is to embroil me in this murder.' From across the wall, he said to Mudiro: 'Who are you? What do you want?' Mudiro replied: 'I'm the leader of the Waziris. We've been around forever. We've come in search of Tarzan now.' 'We don't want war. If you seek peace, then ten of you can enter the country, unarmed. We'll talk to you later.' Mudiro said: 'But warriors never lay down their weapons.' Udalo said: 'Alright, you can come with your weapons. But no more than ten people.' Mudiro said: 'We don't have more than ten people with us.' The gate was opened following the leader's instructions. As soon as Mudiro and the people in his band entered the country, the warriors surrounded them and took them towards the leader's house. When they reached there, the leader repeatedly said that there was no one called Tarzan, and that he didn't know about him. While they were speaking, the magician Opingu was boiling some plants in water and muttering spells. After that, the girls of the village began making arrangements for a feast in a clearing under the trees. Tarzan's small monkey, Nkima, was then sitting on a tree outside the village and waiting for the release of his lord. He thought that Tarzan was still captive in this very village. Meanwhile, after boiling the plants, Opingu poured the liquid into a pot made from the bole of a tree and took it to the site of the festivity. The girls were then pouring drinks into various chalices for serving during the feast. Opingu now secretly asked one of the attending girls to see to it that the juice of the boiled plants was mixed with the drinks for the guests. The leader now invited everyone to begin the feast. He had to have the same drink as the guests. The juice was mixed in his chalice too. But he didn't drink. He merely took the chalice to his lips and pretended to sip from it. However, Mudiro and all the people in his band drank it in good faith. Once the drinking course was over, various kinds of foods were brought. But Mudiro had begun to feel dizzy.

He was staggering. He wasn't able to eat anything. Mudiro figured out the matter now. He pulled out the long knife from the belt at his waist and screamed: 'Kill the enemies! They've fed us poison.' But almost before he could finish speaking, he fell down unconscious. All the people in his band also fell unconscious. Once they were all unconscious, a woman screamed: 'Kill them! They're thieves!' The leader said: 'Don't kill them now. Tie them all up and dump them in a room. It's a full moon tomorrow. Once the moon rises, there'll be dancing and festivities. I'll inform everyone nearby, they'll come to join the festivities too. All of us together will kill the enemies then and eat their fresh hearts.' Tarzan's small monkey, Nkima, was still sitting on the tree, he heard everything and smirked.

Diary Notes

> What's going on – what's all this! Is it just an attempt to create a concert by going on making a collage with one episode after another! No. The link between one and another isn't clear. Inserting it, mixing a punch – not with finesse, but just with broad strokes. Not creating characters but blurring them; not omitting conventional ways of thinking but attacking them. That's why the use of dynamite has become widespread as we approach the end of the twentieth century. The cold spells of the desert expedition have become inseparable from the tropical heat. There's only one question, who killed and left whom in this grove on the island of Hawaii – was it us who killed him, or he who killed us...

The sea lay behind me, the island beneath my feet. I could already hear the howl of the fierce wind blowing in from the sea. As if in exchange, a few gusts of wind, sometimes from the west and sometimes from the northeast, began blowing, accompanied by balls of mist. The dock just beside Skeleton Island lay exactly as still and silent as before. The shadow of the *Mother India* fell on the water which was as clear as a mirror. An entire Ashok Chakra flew across its mast. The patch of white stone was hazily visible through the jungle of shrubs. Bending over, and sometimes creeping ahead, after a lot of difficulty, I reached close to it. The darkness of dusk lay in all directions. Just below the stone, a small plot of green land lay concealed by dense underwood. There was a bit of a clearing in the middle, with a tattered, patched tent – a small tent, which could accommodate only one person, if that. After a lot of searching, I spotted a boat lying sideways beside the water. So it was this boat that everyone was talking about. He had made this entirely by himself, one, the only one. But could one get into the water in this boat, could one move out to sea? One could figure out in a single glance that it had been fashioned with his own hands. A frame had somehow been made with rough logs and rawhide had been stretched and fastened over that, with the hairs on the inside. One couldn't really call it a boat, it was impossibly small, even for a single person. One couldn't figure out how a grown person could get into it and set out on the sea. Tree trunks had been cut and placed crosswise, in front was a slightly wide part, there were two oars made of tender branches to paddle with. If I can get into the boat, if I can advance somehow through the eerie darkness, then I'll cut the anchor rope. The ship will then float away in any direction it likes. Some people wanted to raise the anchor and get away from the island. That could be stopped this way. A great bonfire was visible along the shore, the embers were smouldering, the people were sitting around it. Far away, there was a point of light at the top of the ship. The *Mother India* had turned around in the tide – its bow now faced the island – a pale yellowish light glowed from only a single cell. Some mist entering from the window reflected the light. The boat floated along wonderfully, carried by the light breeze, but it couldn't be steered in any direction. However much I tried, the current kept moving in the opposite direction of the breeze; after all, someone had admitted that if a person doesn't know the behaviour of the boat, it would be very difficult for him to row it. I didn't know all this. It kept turning and moving in every direction other than the one I wanted to go. I was floating diagonally towards the ship. Gradually something even blacker than the darkness was visible ahead, spreading out. I realized that it was the *Mother India*. In a little while, the masts came into sight, so I was advancing towards the ship! The more I advanced, the more the current gained speed. The current now pulled the boat so quickly that it seemed I reached the ship in moments. The anchor had been dropped from one side on a thick rope, I reached out and tried to grab the rope. But could such a thick rope be clutched in this way, with a single hand! It was as taut as a bowstring, the current of the tide was so strong that even the anchor fastened to the rope was pulled. All around the ship that blended into the darkness was the murmuring sound of water flowing, like mountain streams. If I could cut the rope now, the *Mother India* would float away rapidly, carried by the current of the tide. Everything was going fine so far. And then it occurred to me that cutting such a taut rope suddenly might be terribly dangerous. The rope would only shoot forward and hit me with great force. If I cut the rope now, both my one-man boat and I would be flung off the surface of the water. Who knows where we would be flung to! Nonetheless, I steeled my mind. There wasn't any other way either. Time was running out. I took out the folding knife, opened it with the help of my teeth, and began cutting through the rope.

EARTH TO EARTH
ASHES TO ASHES
DUST TO DUST

Just as evening was turning to dusk, Jane made a bow with a lot of effort, and also a few arrows. After that, she burnt the blades of the arrows in fire and made them hard. Taking them to Brown, she told him: 'Give me the knife. After all, we need to hunt something for our dinner.' Brown replied: 'So you're going out to hunt! I'll go with you too.' With a smile Jane said: 'You won't be able make it through the way I'll be going. If you can go a hundred yards with me, I swear I'll give you whatever you ask for.' Saying so, she climbed up to a branch of a tree and disappeared the next moment. Brown was left gazing despondently. Did the girl know magic! Annette said: 'She's gone off on her own. What if she falls into danger?' 'I thought Brown's going with her' – Alexei mumbled – 'If I knew he wasn't going, I'd have gone myself.' With all this talk, Brown got so agitated inwardly that he wasn't able to reply. Annette smiled out of the corner of her lips: 'Jane doesn't care a damn for a man's company in the desolation of the jungle.' Brown remarked: 'She climbed up to a tree branch in a trice and was gone. She didn't even give me a chance to say anything.' Teaboy nodded: 'Do you all think that she'll hunt only with her bow and arrow? She hunts differently.' Brown was most despondent: 'I think the girl's gone crazy.' Alexei was just waiting for a pretext; he was furious when he heard Brown: 'Just remember that Jane is an aristocratic lady. It's improper to refer to her as a "girl". Besides, who the hell are you to say something rude, like "she's lost her head"! Pretty-faced chaps always behave indecently like this.' 'Fine, I'm indecent, so what are you going to do about it?' – Brown retorted – 'I don't behave improperly with anyone unless I'm angry.' Annette stepped in between the two of them: 'The two of you have again begun fighting over a girl.' Alexei was boiling with rage by then, he rushed towards Brown: 'I'll teach him right now how to behave properly!' Annette grabbed his arm and stopped him: 'We're in danger now, we need to work with a cool head. You're about to come to blows over something as trivial as a girl. Come, Brown, let's make a roof for the shelter. Let's carry on with our work.' *the cracking and rumbling comes – it comes ever closer, like a thousand war chariots racing towards us across the sands of a battlefield. the pressure grows and grows, the ice beneath us begins to tremble, to lament in every conceivable voice, at first whistling like countless arrows, then screeching, ranging from the highest soprano to the lowest bass all at once – bellowing ever louder, it rises, bursts in concentric circles around the ship, rolling up the broken pieces of the floe. the terrifying rhythm of a throbbing howl precedes the greatest tension. then a loud crack follows, and several black lines scurry at random across the snow; these are new fissures very near us that can open into abysses at any moment.*

Diary Notes

Is the English that's used English at all! A foreign language! Or a part of my own thoughts! A part of

> my mother tongue! But I only know one language. All the languages of the world, all the mediums of expression become a part of my language. I write everything in my mother tongue.

Brown, with his axe, and Teaboy, with his empty pistol, left the camp. They walked in the direction from which the sound had been heard. Teaboy began shouting: 'Jane! Jane!' Brown too shouted loudly: 'Tell me where you are!' Jane emerged from the concealment of the forest. 'Come this way! I'm alright. There's nothing to fear.' They went there and saw that Jane was pulling out three arrows, one after the other, from a dead cheetah. A dead deer too lay beside it. Seeing them, Jane said with a smile: 'I killed the deer first. And then the cheetah appeared and stood in my way. It wanted to snatch the deer from me. And so I had to kill it too.' Gaping in amazement, Brown said: 'Do you always remove anyone who comes in your way? And so you shot the cheetah with an arrow!' Jane continued to smile like before: 'Do you think I bit it to death then?' Brown perspired: 'I was only congratulating you. Tell me, what do you want?' Jane replied mischievously: 'We'll see about that. For now, we need to carry the deer.' Teaboy said: 'I'm really amazed!' Brown enquired: 'So why not take the dead cheetah too back to the camp?' Jane smiled furtively: 'I hope the princess doesn't faint upon seeing it.' As soon as they reached the camp, Annette, wide-eyed in astonishment, remarked: 'So you've really managed to get us our dinner!' Without replying to that, Jane enquired about where the princess was. Annette now looked at Jane and smiled out of the corner of her mouth: 'As soon as Brown and Teaboy left to look for you, the princess went to bed with Tarzan.' It was close to dawn now. She saw that the ship, *Mother*

India, was still standing in the darkness at the mouth of the river. Tying the dinghy below the ship, she climbed aboard silently. She saw that everyone there was fast asleep. There was only one sailor who was reading a book with the light turned on. She knew the sailor. At one time, he had been their leader. He was the most cruel-natured among all of Rokofo's men. Seeing her, he was startled, as if he had seen a ghost: 'Who are you? – What have you come here for? – If Tarzan sees you, he'll kill you!' For the first time in her life, she bowed in submission, she whispered to the man: 'Speak softly, and listen to all I tell you. There's a huge amount of gold hidden inside this ship. No one but me knows where it is. I'm going to retrieve it, we need it for our revolutionary work. But before I take it away, I'll give half of it to you. You should help me, let me go in and take out the gold. I'll give half to you and take the other half and leave. No one will come to know. You'll come to no harm.' The man's eyes gleamed: 'I know there's gold in the ship. But I have no idea where it is. Tell me properly, how much will you give me?' 'Whatever I give you will be enough to keep you well for the rest of your life. You won't have to continue with this business of leadership, or being Tarzan's slave either.' The man thought for a while and said: 'Alright. I'll keep watch. You look for the gold and bring it. But beware, don't try to run away with the gold from the other side. In that case, you'll die.' The man began patrolling with his gun. She slowly went inside the ship. After that, she hurriedly removed all the gold from a secret cache and stuffed it inside an enormous pillowcase. Finally, she attached the time-bomb to the clock. And thus would the fate of the *Mother India* lie in her hands. And then with the pillowcase slung on her shoulder, she slowly emerged. The man was gaping greedily with the gun in his hand, he said: 'My gold!' She said: 'It's all in this. Half of this is yours.' In a flash, the man held the gun to her head and with a cruel laugh said: 'You can't leave with even a bit of gold. At first, I agreed to half of it, but if you want to live now, give me everything. You can run away to the forest, there's no need for gold and suchlike there. Or else I'll call Tarzan. His lion will eat you alive.' She looked and saw that the light of dawn had begun emerging all around. It would be dawn now. Tarzan and company would wake up. She silently handed over the heavy pillowcase to the man. And then she returned to her solitary dinghy. The class enemy, Tarzan, would be killed very soon when the ship was destroyed – that was her only consolation. But hadn't she been able to guess that things would take such a turn! Twisting her fingers, she smiled out of the corner of her lip. Meanwhile, Tarzan woke up and observed that the sky was very clear. The awaited red sun was rising. He instructed the sailors to leave the ship. They would first leave this island and go to some forested island far away. And from there to some harbour by the sea; where people looked favourably upon progressivism. He was startled by a sudden terrifying sound. He saw that the roof of a cabin in the ship had flown off in an explosion. A spiral of black smoke emerged from the cabin. From the way the smoke emerged, it seemed there might be yet another explosion. So one ought to leave the ship and escape without any further delay. His men did try to extinguish the fire with water, but the fire spread and consumed the entire ship. A boat was taken down, the men were lowered into that. As much as possible of the goods were taken along. By the time they reached the forested island, the entire ship, *Mother India*, was blown to smithereens with a terrific explosion. It's remains floated on the tranquil waters of the sea.

EARTH TO EARTH
ASHES TO ASHES
DUST TO DUST

'Alcohol?' – I asked – 'Great idea!' – 'So what would you like? – White or red?' 'I'd like red' – He said – 'Red liquor – just make sure it's strong, and that there's plenty of it.' 'Alright. – I'll get it. It won't take me very long to find it.' Descending the stairs at the rear, I first took off my shoes. And then I ran along the gallery in silence and went down the stairs and peeped into the space below the deck. I knew that the man wouldn't ever expect to find me there. But still, I stayed as alert as I could, and whatever happened was exactly as I had anticipated, my worst suspicions were proved to be true. The man was creeping and moving ahead slowly. His knees were definitely hurting – he let out a single indistinct moan, dragged himself on the floor and moved ahead below the deck and after that he pulled out a long knife from beside the coil of rope. The knife was bloody from base to tip. The stale blood had turned blackish. The man looked at the knife for a moment, he tested its sharpness on his palm; after that he hurriedly hid it in his pocket, quickly began crawling once again and returned to his former spot. I could see everything through the gaps between the array of rows of bottles of red-coloured liquor. And thus, I found out what I wanted to know. Although the man was wounded, he was able to creep ahead. He also had a weapon now. There could only be one meaning for the eagerness to get me out from the deck – I was the intended target of that knife. But what on earth would he do all by himself after he had killed all of us? Would he try to go to his friends at the marsh by crossing the island via the creek on the north! Or would he fire the cannon from the ship so that the couple of companions his friends had – would get the signal! The man's intentions weren't clear. But one could trust the man in one respect. Both of us were curious about where the *Mother India* would be. Both of us were keen that the ship reached the shore for now without any mishap. And that it went to a spot from where it could once again be set afloat easily in time without much effort or any risk. Therefore, I wouldn't be in any danger until the ship touched the shore safely. I was thinking about such things for sure, but my hand was busy. I picked up a bottle of red-coloured alcohol, entered the cabin, wore my shoes and climbed up to the deck again. He sat crouching with his back against the post exactly like before. His eyes were half shut, as if he couldn't tolerate light. Hearing my footsteps, he opened his eyes and stared at me. After that he snatched the bottle from my hand and snapped the cap off at once. It seemed that this task was a doddle for him. After that, looking me in the face he glugged a lot of the liquor. I observed that he didn't grimace at all. He shut his eyes and was silent for a long while. Then, blinking his eyes several times, he took out a half-smoked cigar from his pocket and asked me to light it: 'I don't have anything to light it with, and even if I did, I doubt whether I can light it – all my strength's exhausted. Ah … I think my time in this world is over.' I said: 'Alright, I have matches, I'll light it. But if I had been in your place and I thought my condition was so bad, I would have prayed to God to atone for my deeds.' 'Why?' – He tried to stand up straight – 'Tell me! – Why? What for?' I replied calmly: 'Why do you ask?

– Just a little while back you were asking about the people who died. You spent your life resorting to a great lie, your life's centred around a terrible act of murder. You shot a man while he was praying, the man who was the life of *Mother India*, upon whom the fortunes of *Mother India*, whether good or bad, depended. The man uttered "Hey Ram" after he was shot and then fell, his peaceful corpse is still lying upside-down on the deck, right near our feet. And yet you ask, "What for"!' He got excited and swallowed some more liquor, and after that he began speaking in a very sad voice: 'I wandered around one country after another all my life. I wandered across remote towns and villages of this country, I spent days on end in the *Mother India*. In all this while I've seen it all – good and bad, the best and the basest, storms and scorching sun, knifing and fighting, gun toting, what it's like to fast day after day. My experience is greater than anyone else's. I tell you, I've almost never seen good things happen to good people. The one who strikes first is the one who's the victor in this world. A dead man never bites.' 'But now you'll find out whether or not a dead one can bite.' – I blurted out. It wasn't as if I said that out of any conviction, I merely uttered it out of habit. Suddenly his tone changed: 'Forget about it, there's been enough of castigation – you listen to me now. The tide's coming in strong now, we'll be able to reach the shore very soon. Once that's done, our work's over for the time being. But the ship would have to be steered very carefully – not only because the harbour's narrow and shallow, but also because it's very long. If the ship has to be brought in, it needs to be steered very cautiously. I think you're very prudent and cool-headed as an assistant. The ship has to be steered skilfully, curving one way and another stealthily, avoiding all the barriers.' I thought for a moment and concluded that heeding him was the wise course to follow. I began working according to his instructions. Unless the ship docked, I wouldn't be free of them. As I approached the cape slowly, we came close to the land on the two sides. Like in all other harbours, there was jungle on both sides of the creek here as well. But the creek was extremely long and narrow. Straight ahead, at the end of the creek, I saw the remains of another ship. The ship had been a large one at some point of time. But having lain in this wrecked condition for long, it was entirely covered in seaweeds. A jungle of shrubs had grown on its deck, various kinds of flowers had bloomed on them too. I felt sad looking at the final plight of the ship, but one also realized that the harbour of the creek was definitely not safe. 'Look in front of you now' – he suddenly said – 'for an appropriate place to land.' It was completely flat land full of sand – with plants everywhere – there were beautiful flowers on them too. I asked, 'How will we set the ship afloat again once we ground it?' 'Why? – It's a very simple matter after all!' – He replied – 'When the water recedes at low tide, you've got to tie it with a rope to the base of some tree on the land, which has a thick trunk. Of course, the trunk has to be of the proper size. After that, if you pull the rope, wind it around the capstan to which the anchor is attached and pull it, the *Mother India* will at once slide into the water. Listen to me now, advance with caution. We're close to the bank. To the right a bit – slowly, to the left now, turn it slightly – slowly, slowly – so that it's imperceptible.' And so he began giving me instructions continuously, and I held my breath and followed them. He suddenly shouted: 'Stop now!' At once, as soon as the rudder was lifted, the *Mother India* speedily turned and advanced towards the wooded sandy bank below. Towards the end, in the excitement of steering the ship, I forgot to keep a watch over the *Mother India*. My eyes were agape to see how such a large ship docked in a narrow harbour. Forgetting all about the dangers looming, I bent down to observe how even in such shallow waters, the *Mother India* advanced, cutting through the water and rising waves. It advanced towards the harbour. *the completion of our task proved a brief dream. we painfully came to realize our misfortune would continue, and we succeeded only partially in maintaining our composure. the days grew ever shorter, each setting sun blazing more fiercely, encircled by red mists behind barriers of blue back ice, and as it set, each twilight grew dimmer. a dreary wasteland took us in, and we entered for we know not how long nor at what distance.* In order to frighten them even more, Tarzan then threw down the dead body from the tree. All the people then ran away, each to his own dwelling place. Their leader explained to them that this was a deed of the God who regularly ate the food they provided at the base of the tree. He told them that this God also took a lot of arrows from their homes. That some arrows in a quiver should also be left with the food henceforth. He wouldn't kill any of our folk then. Seeing all this, Tarzan returned to his lair, swinging from tree to tree. He observed that a short distance away, close to the seashore, a ship was moored on the tranquil waters, and a boat was tied beside. He observed that a few people were arguing agitatedly with a giant of a man. Suddenly a man pulled out a revolver and shot the man in his back, and the man raised his arms at once, screamed and fell to the ground. This was the first time Tarzan saw a revolver being used. He observed how a bullet shot out of that and killed someone. The people went and boarded the boat very soon, and reaching the ship, they climbed on to it. Many more people were moving around on the deck of the ship. Once all the people had boarded the ship, Tarzan descended from the tree and entered his lair. Suddenly, at some sound, he looked through the window, another boat was lowered from the ship and another group of people were lowered. Some among them were quite tall and muscular. Some of them had cropped beards. He saw a bespectacled, bare-bodied man with a staff in hand. From the crowd, a person said: 'That old fogey's an idiot, he doesn't know any more than us.' A youth said: 'Mind what you say! You kill our leader and pretend to be our leader. It's true we're under you today. But if you don't conduct yourself well with this old man, although I'm unarmed I'll punch your face and break your jaw! After all you're cowards, you aren't capable of shooting anyone from the front. That's why you shoot from behind.' Saying so, as soon as he turned around and walked a few steps, the man shot at him with his revolver. The youth was not struck by the bullet. Tarzan couldn't remain sitting on the tree any longer. He was seething with rage. When he saw that it wasn't possible to shoot an arrow through the thick foliage, he flung a spear with great force. The spear hit the man's neck, he fell down. A few people ran and tried to remove the spear from the man's neck. Blood gushed out. The girl screamed out. The youth said: 'This has to be Tarzan's doing. He's observing everything.' Saying that, he asked the people present there for a revolver. But the leader had only been wounded, he didn't die. He said: 'No, no one should give him a revolver.' The youth then picked up the bloody spear lying on the ground and walked away. Tarzan – to whom nothing in the massive forest was unknown, the forest whose every plant and creature was known to him – couldn't figure out how a man got lost in that forest, or why people feared the forest. Suddenly, hearing a sound from atop the tree, he was startled. He saw that the youth, Clayton, was standing tiredly, leaning against a tree, and not far from him, the cheetah called Sheeta was advancing stealthily towards him. As soon as Sheeta observed Clayton and was about to pounce upon him, from above the tree, the rescuer Tarzan roared out so terrifyingly that Sheeta slunk its tail between its legs and vanished into the clump.

Diary Notes

> Seeing all the violence, it seems that's what real life is. It's 'normalcy' that's a lie. The canal's to be deepened, the coolie-labourers who've come from Bankura dig earth that's measured in cubic feet. An infant sleeps on a mat. Rice boils in an earthen pot. His mother's gone to fetch water.

EARTH TO EARTH
ASHES TO ASHES
DUST TO DUST

Perhaps I wouldn't even have got the opportunity to undertake this battle if my trance hadn't been broken by a strange hush that suddenly descended. Perhaps I had heard a soft rustling sound, perhaps some breathing sound as well – waking up with a start, as soon as I turned my head, I saw the man running towards me, he had a bloody knife in his hand. Once our eyes met, both of us screamed out. A piercing, terrifying cry from my throat, and the man cried like a wild boar. And with that scream he leapt upon me.

But before that I moved forward, diagonally. The long rod used to manoeuvre the rudder was now within hand's reach. Because I gripped that firmly, I survived that journey. Almost as soon as my hands closed around it, it flew upwards and hit the man's chest. Screaming in pain, he fell on his knees right there. Before the man could get back on his feet, I ran out to the open deck. Once I was below the big mast, I took out the pistol from my pocket and aimed, cool-headedly. He had stood up by then, he came running at me. I shut my eyes and pressed the trigger. There was only some sound of friction and nothing else. No flash, no sound, no bullet. The gunpowder had lost its potency long ago. I ought to have tested the firearm earlier and loaded it with new gunpowder and cartridge. I was surprised that the man was still racing towards me despite being seriously wounded. His long, unkempt hair had fallen over his face, his whole face was blazing with anger. There was no time to load another cartridge in the pistol, I didn't want to either, because I was certain that all that had become irrelevant given the time in hand. But it was meaningless to run disorientedly ahead of the man. In that case, the man would chase me and in a few moments corner me like before. His bloody knife would be fully planted into my breast. All my nerves were tingling in excitement, I merely waited for him, standing firmly with my hands pressed against the mast. The man realized that I was ready to face him. He halted for a moment and then raised his arm and began twirling his knife. I began ducking by crouching and twisting myself and evaded his swipes each time. As if this was a cops-and-robbers game – I had played this game many times with my friends during my childhood. But I never felt the fear I now felt in that play. Nonetheless, as I kept eluding the man and avoiding his attacks, my courage too began to grow. For a moment there was an interruption in the game, we were then face to face, when suddenly the *Mother India* hit the bank at great speed and then rocked and shook and listed to the left side. The deck of the ship rose up as water gushed in through the portholes along the hull and one side was submerged. Both of us went somersaulting down together. And just then, suddenly, the dead body of the one who had been shot during a prayer meeting came tumbling down from behind. His arms were spread out on the two sides. The man's knee hit his head very hard, so hard that he moaned in pain and slumped. Without wasting a single moment, I aimed at him, but the water and the tilted deck made running impossible. As I was thinking about what I should do, I saw that the man had stood up again, he pushed away the dead body, and once again, there was the bloody knife in his hand. I steeled my mind, I jumped and grabbed the sail in front of me and hung from that. I climbed up the mast and thus reached the observation platform, and by steadying myself, I was able to climb atop that and sit down. The man's knife missed me by a few inches. I had to refill gunpowder in the pistol in a trice. The man realized what I was up to, he realized that the tables had turned. But he didn't stop; as he panted, he grabbed the sail and hung from that. Holding the knife between his teeth, he began climbing up the mast, higher and higher. It was clear that he was in pain, but he was as dogged as a wild boar, he had to finish me off. When he was halfway up, I realized that I would die at his hands unless I killed him. There could be no middle way. We had become mutual class enemies long ago. I screamed out as loudly as I could: 'If you advance one more step, I'll shoot and blow your head off! All of you'll know what the bite of a dead man is like.' He stopped. Observing his furrowed brow and face, I could see that he was thinking about something. Finally, he gulped a few times, and took the knife held between his teeth into his hand. And he immediately began speaking: 'Matters between us have come to such a pass that I think we need to come to an agreement between ourselves. There's a big enemy who's after us, they'll finish off both of us, they won't spare us.' Believing him in all simplicity, I heaved a sigh of relief, so I didn't have to commit a murder. I said: 'That's great, what kind of agreement do you want to arrive at?' Chewing his words, he continued: 'After all, both of us want to do good for people – isn't it?' Perhaps I had become a bit inattentive, and that's when it happened. No, because I wanted to believe him, it didn't occur to me to be prepared. In a flash, his right hand rose above his head and backwards, something came whistling through the air as it shot towards me. I felt a terrible pain in my shoulder, the man's bloody knife had impaled my shoulder to the mast. I was shocked, the man had just proposed a settlement to me. At that moment, in pain and endangered astonishment – I swear – I didn't aim at him intentionally or carefully – but my pistol roared with a great jolt and slipped out of my hand. The pistol was not the only thing that fell. Shot in the breast and howling, the man too fell downwards, headfirst, straight into the water. Because the ship was tilted, the masts were slanted over the water to a considerable length. I was sitting on the observation platform, and below me was the sea. Dreamy, blue water. Because the man was much lower, he was close to the water. He fell right beside the ship. A few moments after he fell, he floated up once, lifted up by a bloody and foamy wave, after that he sank forever in the dreamy blue water. Once the waves stopped, the water was tranquil again, I saw him lying in the ship's shadow, face down in the gleaming white sand. My body heaved in pain, I realized that the skin above my shoulder bone was tearing apart. I began to bleed more profusely, the knife thrown by the class enemy had gone through my shirt, pierced my flesh and stuck me against the mast. There wasn't much damage, I was only stuck to the mast, that's all. I was all alone on the ship now. Was there an even greater enemy behind me, who I couldn't spot? The current of the tide had just begun. The setting sun had descended to the horizon. The long shadows of the tall trees spread from one bank of the harbour to the other. Those shadows created amazing patterns as they fell upon the deck. The cool breeze of the evening had begun to blow. The sun set in a little while, and in the gathering darkness one began to hear the sound of the wind whistling as it blew through the trees. I was alone, it seemed there was no one around me now, neither enemy nor friend. *there can hardly be anything more exciting than the discovery of new lands. one's powers of deduction are constantly engaged by the visible configurations, and one's imagination is ready at once to create new ones. the excitement is diminished only by days on which one must journey across snowy wastes whose far shores lie at such distances that they do not change quickly enough to allow the traveller's imagination room in which to play.* Even if Mugambi didn't know everything about Tarzan, he had clearly realized that the person by the name of Rokofo was escaping after abducting Tarzan's wife, and that Tarzan was searching like a crazed soul for her. When Mugambi saw Rokofo come on a boat and board the ship, he realized clearly that, as soon as he was in the ship, he would let it go. The woman with a rifle in hand who had been keeping watch over the ship so long, and whom Rokofo had just a little while back threatened to shoot and frightened away, was Jane, Tarzan's wife. Seeing Rokofo boarding the ship, Mugambi was filled with terror. And so, a boat was needed right now, with which they could go and board the ship. After a lot of searching, a dinghy was finally found. The dinghy was right on the riverbank. But before the dinghy left with everyone, he heard a woman screaming. He realized that a young Adivasi woman had been lying on the floorboard all this while. As soon as an ape-guerrilla squeezed her neck, she had screamed out in terror. Mugambi pushed the guerrilla away and began talking to her in her own language. The girl's parents were taking her against her will to get her married to a man from another community. She had run away and hidden herself on the floorboard of the empty boat. She kept saying that she lived in the same place that Mugambi did. Hearing the girl's pleas, Mugambi took her along too. Meanwhile, shortly after Jane was captured by the sailors, Tarzan stealthily climbed on to the ship. As soon as he was in the ship, he saw that some sailors had pounced on a girl and were dragging her. Roaring in rage, he grabbed whoever he found by their hair and threw them into the sea. Jane immediately spotted Tarzan and screamed in joy: 'T-a-r-z-a-n!' Tarzan ran and lifted her to his chest. Suddenly Rokofo appeared with sailors and pointed his rifle at him. He aimed at his chest and fired. But he didn't know that Tarzan was immortal. Bullets couldn't pierce his chest. Just then, Mugambi arrived there accompanied by his band of animals. Four or five ape-guerrillas and Sheeta arrived and attacked Rokofo and his men. Seeing the big cat, he wanted to flee, but Sheeta didn't let him go. Jane realized that all these animals were Tarzan's acolytes. It would be difficult for

Rokofo to escape them. Terrified by Sheeta, he had thrown away his rifle and run to the farthest end of the ship. But Sheeta too ran behind him. Tarzan wanted to deliver the punishment for Jane's abduction with his own hands. But Sheeta didn't give him the chance to do that. It pounced on Rokofo and grabbed him by the throat. And then it clawed and bit and shredded his body to bits. Tarzan tried to stop it. He wanted to free Rokofo's bloody body from Sheeta's jaws. But it had now tasted human blood! Sheeta began to tear off pieces from the body of the still-alive Rokofo and eat. It was chewing living bones. Jane shuddered in fear. So Rokofo had wanted to ravish her. But did that mean ... She couldn't look into Tarzan's eyes then. She covered her face with her hands, tears streamed down her eyes. Jane silently wiped her tears.

EARTH TO EARTH
ASHES TO ASHES
DUST TO DUST

It seemed he was relieved to have accomplished this task. After that, he got up and laid a tricoloured national flag over the dead body with great reverence. Only the frame of the house remained standing, and in a corner, a fireplace made of flat stones and a rusty iron scuttle to keep wood! Before the house was built, the pit was concealed by trees. Seeing many tree stumps in the space in front of the fence and the sloping sides of the pit, one could see how a lovely jungle had been cruelly destroyed. Because there were no more trees, all the soil in the pit had been washed away by rain. Only in the part where a small stream from the mini-waterfall descended zigzaggedly, there was some green moss and some fern-like plants and shrubs on the sand on its two sides. Dense jungle began just a bit past the fence – only tall firs on the landward side, but there were evergreen oak trees too among the firs on the seaward side. Sand flew in through the gaps between the logs on the walls and the roof in the chilly evening wind. As if it was raining sand. Our eyes, the insides of our mouths and the dining table were all full of sand. The waterfall lay below the lake. A thick film of sand covered the ever-bubbling water there. There was no chimney to speak of in the house, there was merely a rectangular cavity in its place. Only a part of the smoke from the room was emitted through it, most of it was circling inside the room itself, we were exhausting ourselves coughing and rubbing our eyes. It was a large room. A seventeen- or eighteen-year-old youngster was sitting on one side, a new member of our band. His face was covered in a bandage, he had been struck by a knife on his cheek while he was fleeing from another gang. And lying curled up beside the wall was the cold corpse, covered by a tricoloured flag. 'The flag of peace' – I heard someone say that. The very next moment, oblivious to everything, he screamed out: 'The captain himself!' It was still dawn, bitterly cold, even one's bones were freezing in the cold. 'Who's there – Stop, or else I'll shoot you!' 'The flag of peace' – someone screamed out again. The tall man with blue eyes turned once again to look at the rebel youngster. 'What do you want to do with that flag of peace?' he asked loudly. 'We want to speak to you in favour of peace.' 'I don't have the slightest desire to talk to you,' the tall man replied. 'Nevertheless, you can come if you want to talk. If there's any treachery at all, it'll be from your side.' 'That's adequate' – the man replied in a tone of gaiety – 'We know that all of you are true gentlemen.' The tall man filled his pipe with tobacco and lit it. The other man looked carefully at everything. After that, he said: 'Since you've lit a pipe, let me light one too. Do you know – we're toiling folk – coolies and labourers. That's why we didn't realize how gentlemanly you gentlemen are, and for how long. You people talk about poor folk and we laugh. What I say is – please stop shooting at those people. And especially when they're asleep, don't attack them like thieves.' The man then went out and spat loudly in the water of the waterfall. 'Coming to make peace with us and then blustering at us' – the tall man roared out. The man stood up – 'We'll destroy this beloved house of yours today itself – so that you are left without any shelter' – saying that and muttering an obscenity he leapt out of the room and left. After trying a few times, the man with the peace flag somehow managed to take him across the fence. It had begun very innocuously. In 1883, one Raghubir Das, who claimed to be a mahant of Ram Janmasthan, submitted a petition to the deputy commissioner of Faizabad seeking to build a temple on a plot of land adjacent to the Babri Masjid. The petition was rejected. From 1949, a few mahants began a programme of continuous chanting and bhajans on the elevated platform of the mosque complex. One learns from a report of the Wakf board dated 10 December 1949 that the expense of this programme of continuous bhajan singing was borne by Mrs Shakuntala Nayyar, the wife of the district magistrate of Faizabad, K.K. Nayyar. It wasn't just the continuous chanting that was taking place; if anyone came to that mosque for namaz prayers, they were attacked by Hindus and Sikhs. On 22 December 1949, in the dead of night, someone or some people broke the lock of the mosque and planted a doll there. On 23 December, mikes were placed in the mosque complex and there were continuous announcements that Ram Lalla had revealed himself in the mosque. Nehru sent instructions to the chief minister of Uttar Pradesh to remove the doll from the mosque, but the district magistrate didn't do anything. He later joined the Jana Sangh and was elected to the Lok Sabha. Subsequently, a suit was filed. But because the verdict on the suit might go against them, they pondered over the matter. It was deemed necessary to build an organization in order to establish that religious faith overrides the decision of the court, and on 29 August 1964, the Vishwa Hindu Parishad was set up in Bombay, with much fanfare. The literary works of Kalidasa and Jayadeva found no place in their syllabus for the Sanskrit language, the main texts were the *Manusmriti* and Kautilya's *Arthashastra*. It was on the basis of these two texts that a Hindu Rashtra would be established. The main part of the programme of the religious propaganda department was distributing tiny idols of Ramachandra to Harijans to hang around their necks, pictures to hang on the walls in their homes, and idols to be installed in villages for regular puja. Only those who are Hindu by religion are the children of this country because one can't become a citizen of this country merely by being in this country's soil. On 6 April 1980, all those members of the Janata Party who were associated with the Rashtriya Swayamsevak Sangh established a new political party called the Bharatiya Janata Party. The Rashtriya Swayamsevak Sangh was originally an organization of upper-caste

Hindus. By focussing attention on Ramachandra, the Vishwa Hindu Parishad was transformed into an organization of all castes of Hindus. From as early as the end of the nineteen sixties, communal riots began to take place in various towns and cities of north and western India. The flames of communal riots blazed in places like Moradabad and Aligarh in Uttar Pradesh, Ahmedabad and Surat in Gujarat, and Bhiwandi and Jalgaon in Maharashtra. But more Muslims were killed by salaried security forces than the number who died at the hands of Hindu mobs. The message of the Vishwa Hindu Parishad was announced most powerfully through the rathyatra from Somnath to Ayodhya. What was referred to as the 'rath', i.e., chariot, was actually an indigenous-foreign version of Hindutva, a DCM Toyota van that had an air-conditioned rest room for Advani. But when that van reached urban areas or populous villages, Advani-ji would emerge from within and stand with his band at a spot behind the driver of the vehicle, and deliver speeches with a mike clutched in his fist. There were many lorries ahead of and behind the chariot, which were full of security forces and the Bajrang army, a Bajrang army on motorcycles too. 'Om' was inscribed on the front and four sides of the lorries, the BJP's electoral symbol, the lotus, was etched, and there were giant pictures of Ram, Lakshman and Hanuman. A few people dressed as Hanuman and Shiva roused people with catchy gestures, every now and then the inflamed public roared out. Womenfolk were entranced seeing live snakes wound around Shiva's head and neck. The public was certain that Ram had set out on a victory procession to claim his own kingdom after his exile; they were inspired to participate in the struggle to recover the lost throne of Ramachandra. In a turn of irony, the final words of the bullet-ridden Gandhi, 'Hey Ram', were revived by the inspired karsevaks' cries of 'Jai Shri Ram'.

Diary Notes

> It's true that the British lords handed over the reins of power of independent India to a class of aristocratic leaders. The poor peasants and workers didn't possess the awareness and organization needed to run the country, for that matter, they weren't even allowed to have that dream. When the peasants of Tebhaga or Telangana had just begun to shake themselves and were trying to stand up with their heads raised, political parties of every shade ganged up and directly or indirectly thwarted that effort of theirs. Why isn't there such a commentary in this piece of writing – after all, the subject is fifty years of Independence...

But Tarzan wasn't liking all this work any more. Because he didn't have any friends, he steadily began to feel an absence of some kind. It kept occurring to him that he was friendless, that there was no one he could call his own. The same Tarkoz who was once his work companion had now become his sworn enemy. That's why he wasn't liking the job of providing leadership to the band any more. His mind sought desolation and solitude. One day, he was trying to pick up fish from a small river. Hearing a sudden scream of terror, he was startled. Turning around, he saw Tarkoz holding an old female ape by her hair and hitting her. He figured out that Tarkoz was punishing her because she didn't want to part with some fruit. The female ape was sick and feeble, there was no way she could stand up to Tarkoz. At first, Tarzan warned Tarkoz, and then he attacked him. Tarkoz let go of the ape and jumped on him. The rage and hatred he had suppressed for long burst out at once. Tarzan didn't get any chance to use his knife. The two of them wrestled together for a long time. And then both of them fell to the earth and began rolling. Both of them were equally strong. Tarkoz had once been Tarzan's bosom friend, but Tarzan was cleverer, and when it came to strategy, he had foresight. After a while, Tarzan pressed down on Tarkoz's back and, taking him by surprise, he held his head in such a way that it seemed he could snap his neck if he so wished. But thinking about it, he realized that this would be futile. After all, he would have to leave at some point. If Tarkoz died, there wouldn't be any strong leader left in the band. And so, instead of killing Tarkoz, he merely demanded due respect and unwavering obedience from him. Gripping Tarkoz's head, he asked: 'Will you obey me?' Tarkoz replied in an indistinct voice: 'I will.' 'Do you accept that no one as strong as Tarzan was ever born in this world – can never be born?' Once again, Tarkoz replied indistinctly: 'I accept.' Tarzan then released him. Both of them brushed away the dirt from themselves and stood up, as if nothing had happened. Seeing them fighting, everyone in the band was astonished. The public was entranced by Tarzan's exceptional power and intelligence. They realized that Tarzan was an amazing leader. He could kill any enemy of his with ease, but he could also let them go when he held their life in his hands. After that, Tarzan stood in front of everyone with his chest swelled and asked: 'Are you convinced now that there's no one as strong as Tarzan in this world?' Everyone then replied in unison: 'Yes, we're convinced now.' Tarzan then laughed and said: 'From now on, all of you have to do as I say. What do you say – do you all agree?' Everyone replied in unison: 'We agree.' Laughing even louder now, Tarzan said: 'But after all, Tarzan is not an ape like you. He wants to return to his own folk. He oughtn't to stay here any more, because his work is done. Several new Tarzans will be born from among yourselves now. And you must strive to be your own Tarzan!' The public was jubilant, they voiced their opinion in unison: 'We'll certainly follow your instructions.'

Earth TO Earth
Ashes TO Ashes
Dust TO Dust

'They – all those lowly folk who landed up to occupy this house – have numbers on their side, there's no need to say that once again – but we'll hide and fight. I have no doubt that if you people help us, we'll definitely be able to thrash them and drive them out.' After saying that, the tall man with blue eyes turned this way and that and looked at everything. Observing that everything was in order, it seemed he was quite pleased. The wooden cabin with logs laid crosswise was not so wide, it had two openings on the sides and two openings in the front leading to a porch. But there were five openings in the rear. The total number of guns for the three of them was twenty. The fuelwood was laid like tables in the middle of the room, in four piles. There were four loaded guns and some dynamite on every table, so that anyone could get them simply by stretching their arms at the time of battle. Swords too were arranged separately in the middle of the room. A person took the metal container with the fire outside and extinguished the burning pieces of wood by burying them in the sand. About an hour went by in this way. After a few moments, one person picked up his gun, raised it and fired. Even before the sound of the gunshot echoed, the sound of gunfire began to be heard, one after another, from the four sides of the fence. Quite a few bullets pierced the wooden walls, but of course not a single one entered the cabin. Once the smoke cleared, one observed that it was as silent as before all around the fence. 'Did you manage to hit the man?' – the tall man asked someone. 'No, Sir' – he replied – 'I think it was because of the wind.' 'I can tell you exactly what happened' – a middle-aged man from across the room replied – 'Three shots were fired from this side. I saw three flashes of light coming from afar.' 'How many people were there on your side?' – the tall man asked a man with grey hair. 'At least seven shots were fired from the rear side – but it could have been eight or nine as well.' They didn't really have time to think about this. Leaping out of the jungle at the rear, a band of men emerged and, screaming loudly, they began running directly towards the cabin. Three men were hit by bullets and fell to the ground, one of them near the fence and the other two at some distance. Two were dead, while the other man, although hit, managed to get away limping, a few men were able to clear our protective fence, while at the rear, facing the jungle, seven or eight people kept firing at the cabin. The four men who had crossed the fence began running towards the cabin screaming. Quite a few rounds were fired from our side too, but because they were fired in a great hurry, not a single man was hit. Within a few moments, the lowly folk climbed up the mound and appeared in front of the cabin. The tall man began screaming – 'Kill them! Just kill them!' But our situation was steadily turning woeful. Just some moments ago, we were concealed and firing upon unprotected, exposed enemies. But now it was us who were steadily becoming unprotected, and for that matter, we weren't able to claim even a single man in return. They could blow up the cabin. 'Out! – Everyone get outside – Fight with them in the open space' – the tall man screamed out – 'Fight with swords!' All of us then came out, one by one, and turned towards the rear of the cabin. Bullets rained down on the cabin, and our beloved shelter was being riddled with holes. Without a second thought, I turned to the east, held my sword above my head and began running towards the cabin's rear. The very next moment, as if springing up from the earth, a terribly dark-skinned man came and stood before me, as if he were the Lord of Death, Yama, himself. As soon as he encountered me, he roared like a lion and raised his sword above his head. I clearly saw the shiny steel blade flashing in the sunlight. I didn't even have the time to be frightened. As soon as the sword in his hand began to descend, with a single jump I moved aside to the pit nearby. I fell at first on a pile of soft sand, I lost my footing and rolled down the slope. With my having jumped and moved away in a flash from the man's sword, he had stumbled and fallen. Before he could stand up again, a young man from our side, who leaped and came running from behind, brought his sword down on his neck. His head was separated from his body. Another man was hit by a bullet and fell to the earth at the very moment he was shooting into the cabin. 'Shoot! – Shoot!' – the tall, blue-eyed man was still screaming. His leg was smashed, he had lost an arm. But even in that plight, he was desperately trying to escape. A man appeared and shot him directly in his head. In all the rumpus, one couldn't figure out which side he belonged to. Everywhere there was the acrid smell of gunpowder and the distressed cries of men. I slowly gripped the sand and climbed up. There wasn't even a trace of the cabin. Someone said: 'Let's run – Our leader's been killed.' I saw him lying with his face buried in the green grass, a bullet had gone through his head. Blood gushed out from that bullet wound, his yellow brains lay splattered all around. Who knew how the dice of battle would suddenly turn...

Diary Notes

> If I were able to do everything that I want to, the creative output would turn colourless. There's cheating in the jingle of the in-visible princess's dancing bells. He doesn't see that – he gazes at the sun of the approaching century twinkling clearly. It is visible.

La then said to Tarzan for the final time: 'Oh Tarzan, my dear Tarzan, just tell me once that you love me. Tell me that you'll go across the sea with me, that you'll live there. No one can harm you then. I'm giving you a last chance.' Tarzan wasn't able to reply at once. A pyre had been made with logs of wood. The head priest was standing beside it with a flaming torch in his hand. La saw that Tarzan had been laid down on the pyre. Only her order was awaited. The man who was about to be burnt on the pyre today had one day entranced her. Tarzan was the first man whom she liked. If this Tarzan did not consent to her proposal, she would have to marry the misshapen priest. So be it, but if Tarzan didn't agree, he would surely burn to death. Observing Tarzan's silence, La fervently said: 'Tell me yes or no, Tarzan, give me a reply.' The very next moment, Tarzan emitted a scream that seemed to make the whole forest tremble. It seemed he had called out to some animal friend to rescue him. At once, an elephant could be heard trumpeting. Everyone there was startled. The sound of foliage being crushed could be heard from the north. Tarzan then said to La: 'I screamed to call this elephant. If it was any other time, it would have rescued me. But it's incensed now. This mad elephant could kill not just all of you but me as well. Look, La, I don't know why I couldn't fall in love with you, although you're beautiful. I won't be able to live beyond the sea, the jungle's fine for me. But even if I don't love you, I can't let you be trampled to death by a mad elephant. There's still time, cut the ropes tied to my hands and feet. I'll rescue you and take you away from here.' La could sense the imminent danger, she ordered: 'All of you run away wherever you can!' After that, she herself cut the ropes binding Tarzan with a knife. Seeing that, the priests exploded in rage. There was no way Tarzan could be freed like this. The head priest snarled and spat out: 'You traitor! You'll die for this! You've betrayed God by freeing the man who was to be sacrificed!' Saying so, he was about to strike her with a falchion. But the very next moment, Tarzan snatched away the falchion from his hand and lifted him up with both his hands and hurled him to the edge of the jungle. The roaring mad elephant arrived there. Tarzan lifted La and climbed up a big tree. Encountering one of the priest's men, the elephant wound its trunk around him and flung him away. It picked up two more men and trampled them to death. The others ran in terror in whichever direction they could. Once everyone had fled, not finding anyone there, it looked in the direction of Tarzan. He was then sitting with La on the highest branch of the tree. But the elephant wasn't going to let him off. It began to push the tree with all its strength. After being pushed continuously, the tree began to wobble. Its base came loose. Finally, it seemed the tree would be uprooted. Tarzan then leapt with La to the branch of another tree. The elephant realized that and began to push that tree too. Before the tree could be uprooted, Tarzan leapt once again to another tree. And then to another one. In this way, Tarzan swung and leapt with ease from one branch to another, like a monkey. La held on to his neck with her eyes shut. *waiting. days. weeks. waiting. months. years. waiting to the heart's despair. the trap would not open. ever again. on the twelfth day from the nation, the frozen sea pushes in on the MOTHER INDIA from all sides. no open water anywhere. the MOTHER INDIA is no longer a ship, only a hut wedged in among ice floes, a refuge, a prison, the steam engine mere ballast, the wheel an absurdity.* That's what he did then, he sat in the cockpit of the plane and turned the ignition on. After ascending a few thousand feet, it began to fly around the island. On this side, Tarzan jumped out of the aeroplane and parachuted down into an arbour on this island of ours, Hawaii. Just then, a man pointed to the dead body lying there and began a diatribe: 'This man's responsible for everything. This is the man who cast a magic spell on everyone and made them break their oath. The man knows magic. Kill him first.' And just then – Tarzan arrived. The pilotless airborne aeroplane exploded loudly on the temple issue. And because of that, a fire broke out at once. Addressing everyone, Tarzan began to speak: 'Let all of us leave this place safely.' Perforce, everyone agreed. Because they knew that Tarzan was never an ordinary man. He alone was king in the arbour of the island of Hawaii. They hesitantly began to look for a way out of the temple issue. The whole temple-mosque was then smothered in smoke. In just a little while, the sky would be alight with blazing flames. Then, one of them, the tall man with blue eyes, said: 'I know there's a tunnel that leads out of here.' There was a lot of searching then. They looked this way and that. But no shortcut exit was found. A situation was created such that no matter which way they went, everyone had to emerge through some temple or the other, through some mosque or the other. On the other side, the fire had begun to turn into a blaze, it spread across the whole country. Tarzan then firmly held the bare-bodied man with a staff and said: 'Show us the way out of here, or else I'll take your life!' He suddenly smiled: 'Aren't you Tarzan – the eternal Hanuman of four epochs?' Astonished, Tarzan said: 'Are you the person who was shot to death!' The man smiled again, he smiled benignly: 'Politics has at least taught us to say that "he" is responsible for all failings, "their" party is responsible, not me, not our party.' He said: 'The branches can never touch the roots, however high they might reach.' The fire had spread across the entire country by then, the entire country had started burning. But even if the country was burnt down, they didn't care about all that. Tarzan knew well that the fire couldn't scorch him, no riot could take his life. Arriving at the edge of the forest outside the village, all of them gathered together once again. Brown, Jane, Mudiro, Teaboy, Kima, Alexei, Sheeta. For that matter, even the tall man with blue eyes. Although I pretended to know him, he couldn't be identified throughout the writing. Tarzan placed Buira in Mudiro's hands. Once again, he went from tree to tree and returned to the exact place he had set out from. To the east point. After that, with a fixed gaze, he began sniffing the air in order to figure out where the people of the subcontinent were going, and by which way. He tried to figure out what they wanted, what their thinking was. He would definitely reach everyone to the arbour on the island of Hawaii. Your sins too shall be buried in the womb of the earth with your skeleton. And then some people carried him to the top of a tree and escaped from the treetop itself. He would be used again, in a new way. How one ought to think, how the public ought to be handled, all that would be taught too. After all, it was absolutely necessary to create the arbour on the island of Hawaii. And after all it was they who were sacrificed in all that work. He and them.

A Final Note, from the Diary

I'm middle-class, and centrist in my thinking as well. I'm not one to take any kind of risk, I don't want to get entangled in any bother of clearly supporting or refusing anything. I only frolic around in my imagination with the breezy air of the arbour on the island of Hawaii blowing on my skin, I love to do that, and several Tarzans lie nurtured in my heart. That's why I can neither swallow such a death nor vomit it out. Only the sun keeps getting stuck in my throat. Do I support his being shot to death in that way? I can't say 'yes' and I hesitate to say 'no' too. Is his fearless devotion to truth acceptable to me? I don't really know that either. I haven't thought about it. This is all I can do, this is the only way I can, only half-burnt belches, only self-justification all the time.

EARTH TO EARTH
ASHES TO ASHES
DUST TO DUST

[Memory Game, 2001]

Swaramelakalanidhi – The Treasured Art of Vocal Harmony

'You couldn't keep the water of love
In your unfired pot'

> In this *jhumur*, two gandhars and two nikhads in particular are employed. In some parts, the use of *komal* (flat) dhaibat endows greater sweetness. The voice emerges momentarily and is never prolonged. Here, in the stable part, hold the *komal* dhaibat on the 'kaa' of the word *kaancha* (unfired) and then release it at once. Only when pure rekhab is accepted as *komal* is the objective of such use manifest.

And taking me through my soul to a great mountain, he showed me the pure city there, descended from heaven. He showed me a river of the water of life, which was bright as crystal; it emerged from the throne of God and of the Lamb and flowed through the middle of the street. Then the soul and the girl said: 'Come. Let whoever hears also speak. And let whoever is thirsty come, let whoever wishes to do so partake of the water of life.' All the people then heard thunder, lightning, a battle horn being blown, they saw a smoke-covered mountain, and the people were terrified. They said unto their respective souls: 'Talk to us, we shall listen. It does not matter if God does not speak to us.' The soul said: 'Do not fear, because he is coming to test you and to show you your own terrifying nature from the sins you commit.' According to the discourse, in the shadow of the material world's transformation there exists a great respite. Self-expression throbs, eternally, without cause, purposelessly, the eternal state of bliss, because in all these acts of nature there is no master. Ama attains fullness in cooperation with creation, and in the present narrative, everywhere, at all times, there are songs in praise of Ama (the new moon). When Ama (the black dot) sits on the moon it's the full moon (ঁ, the symbol for vowel nasalization, the sign of the name of God or for a departed one), the new moon and Kama-Gayatri (the highest of all mantras), sixteen lettered, within which lies the art of nirvana, the foremost art of nirvana, and the symbol denoting the spirant (◌ঃ) – just these three-and-a-half, four, four-and-a-half components. The symbol of the spirant is born from the outward motion of the dot, and from the symbol's inward motion is the dot created. In destruction, the material's fundamental existence is secured in Ama's dot, and Ama then assumes the form of Chhinnamasta (She of Severed Head), blood coloured, she drinks her own blood. The region below her waist is spread out like a sacrificial yoke, the face agape to receive, Chhinnamasta agape. He stands face to face with an indeterminable time that is submerged in sea rocks. The flowing river *versus* the lascivious sadhu. Can writing emerge without scorching one's fingers? Now there'll be the sound of a pistol, and a heap of hungry words. The presently restless volcano shall come to life again and again.

***

An abundance of streams of water everywhere, and Charon, the ferryman on the river Acheron, ferries dead souls across. Hell, Dante's vast expansion of darkness, a secret land; earth's centre of gravity at its head and tunnels stretching from Italy to Assyria. The expanse of the tunnels of hell. And

Inferno is the real hell, Purgatory, which remains opposite Jerusalem. There are streams of water here, Charon is the ferryman on the river Acheron. He has been commanded, he transports dead souls across the river. The ones who live there are people who have lost everything, those who cannot even hope for death. Virgil and Dante are living souls, so he does not agree to take them to the land of the dead. They, the two ignoramuses, see the reptilian demon, Minos, with its coiled tail, sitting across the river, straddling the gates of Hell, it judges sins through the number of coils. The name of the first circle of Hell is Limbo, those who do not know God but have also not committed any other sin (not knowing God is also a sin) live there. When Virgil and Dante reach Purgatory, Virgil keeps showing Dante the shadows at the rear. The Lord, with a sword in hand, and many, many more behind him. Before everyone stands Homer, and after him, one after another, Horace, Ovid and one more person. Yes, there was one more person then. 'It's the wise one who searches.'

***

It was almost a quarter past eleven at night then. Suddenly, in the headlight of our jeep, I saw a girl come running from the direction of the border. Dishevelled in appearance. Stray bits of hair over her face. As she screamed, a strange moan emanated from her throat. I was then in the driver's seat. I stopped the jeep at once and jumped out on to the road, the others too followed me. I wanted to know what exactly had happened. The first thing I did was to grab hold of the girl. There was terror in her eyes and face. She was only wearing a petticoat. Her sari had fallen off somewhere, at some point. Her blouse was in tatters, as if someone had cut it to shreds with a sharp blade. The part around her breasts was almost completely torn and hanging out in front. That did not protect her modesty. 'I wanted to know about the incident and not a description of the girl. Had you ever seen her before?' 'No, Sir. It's likely that a women-trafficking gang had kidnapped her and brought her from Bangladesh.' 'Would you be able to recognize her if you saw her again?' 'I can't really say, Sir. But I thought she looked very young. Maybe fourteen or fifteen.' 'Did she speak to you?' 'No, Sir, she only screamed, "Help me, save me from their clutches!"' 'Would you be able to recognize her voice if you heard it again?' He said in a dejected tone: 'No, Sir, I don't think so. Someone was chasing her.' 'All of you saw his shadow, isn't it?' 'Yes, only the shadow, Sir. Can one see anything clearly at night? Everything was in darkness then. I won't be able to tell you whether he looked like a military man.' 'There's been no rain there for the last three days...' 'It's foolish to try to look for footprints. Dew fell as dawn approached. And so, even if there had been any footprints, they would surely have been concealed by the dew.'

***

A girl was murdered on Monday and her body was thrown into a well in Notunpalli, in the Purba Putiary locality under Regent Park Police Station. The girl's name was Rita Pal. She was about ten years old. The police and fire brigade personnel recovered the body using hooks. Rita's clothes lay beside the well. Her family members said that she had been raped before being murdered. The police stated that Rita's clothes had been found lying beside the well, torn to shreds. A short distance away, there was fresh blood on the grass. Going to the spot, one saw that there were bloodstains in the abandoned hut as well, where Rita was killed. Because the hut had not been used for a long time, grass had sprung up on the floor. Blackish blood had accumulated on it. There were clear signs to indicate that, after the murder, the body had been taken out through the window of the room, dragged to the well and then thrown in. The police stated that there were marks of Rita having been hit with something heavy on her back. There were also strangulation marks on her neck. Rita's mother said that the girl used to wake up at five in the morning and then go to the toilet outside. After that, she bought bread from the shop in the neighbourhood, and then made tea, that was her daily routine. On this day too, when Rita went out to the toilet, her mother came into the room. But when Rita hadn't returned until six-thirty, her anxiety began to mount. She couldn't be found in the nearby tea shop and at Rita's uncle's house either. At about seven, another one of Rita's uncles came to wash his face at the tap near their house. He was the one who first heard that a girl had been found murdered on the opposite side of the road. He ran there and saw a girl's frock lying beside the abandoned hut. It was his niece's frock. He ran towards another abandoned hut that was about fifty feet away. Although there was no one near the well beside this hut, there were blood marks and strands of hair from her head on the grass. The residents' complaint – there were gambling and liquor dens in the three abandoned huts, every kind of anti-social activity took place there, in front of everyone's eyes. No one says anything or wants to say anything.

***

And God said, let us make man in our image, let him have dominion over the fish of the sea, over the birds in the sky, over the creatures on earth and above all, over all the reptiles that move along the ground. God created man in His own image, He created them as man and woman, He created Adam from the dust of the ground, and breathed into his nostrils the breath of life, and the man became a living being. He planted a garden in the east, in Eden, and there He put the man He had formed. In the middle of the garden were the tree of life and the tree of the knowledge of good and evil – He had both these trees grown. He then took Adam and put him there to protect the garden. And He instructed him, 'You are free to eat from any tree in this garden, but you must not eat from the tree of the knowledge of good and evil, for when you eat it you will certainly die.' He then thought, 'It is not good for the man to be alone; I will make a helper suitable for him.' God caused Adam to fall into deep slumber, took out one of his ribs and then closed up the place with flesh. From the rib taken out from Adam, He made a woman and brought her to Adam. Then Adam said, 'This is now bone of my bones and flesh of my flesh, she shall be called woman, for she was taken out of man.' That is why a man leaves his father and mother and is united to his woman and they become one flesh. Let it be said that at this time, both the man and the woman were naked because until then the sense of shame had not been born. Until then, man was sinless.

***

Perhaps life and death are one and the same. There were thirty or forty letters in the bundle. The letters were tied together with a ribbon. All love letters. Unless I had seen the letters, I wouldn't have believed that such fervent declarations of love to a man over sixty could have been made by a girl his daughter's age. In some parts, a few subtle marks of sexuality too could be discerned in the letters. So, was the girl still alive? I became terribly eager. Then, with a mysterious smile on her face, she gave me four photo albums. The pictures were of a very ordinary kind. The first three albums were full of family pictures. As soon as I opened the fourth album, I shuddered. Could any bhadramahila stand before the camera and have such pictures taken! I felt disgusted even to turn the pages of the album. Below every picture, the place and date had also been mentioned. The lady was forty years old. Looking at her, one could see that even at this age she had been able to retain the attractiveness and physical beauty of her youth. Most beautiful of all were her ever-smiling, blue eyes. One could then recognize the girl who had come from Bangladesh. Three shadowy figures kept moving around the door of the living room. All three wore khaki clothes. The man in the middle was a sergeant. He tried to catch our attention. The bloodthirsty tiger's lust for blood erupts anew now. This time it wants to hunt very large prey.

***

Now the serpent was the craftiest of all the creatures made by God. He said to the woman: 'Did God really say, "You must not eat from any tree in the garden"?' The woman said to the serpent: 'We may eat fruit from the trees in the garden, but it was only the fruit of the tree that is in the middle of the garden that God asked us not to eat or touch, for if we did that, we would die at once.' Smiling slyly, the serpent said: 'You will certainly not die; because you are man, when you eat from it your eyes will be opened, and you will be like God, knowing good and evil.' When the woman saw that the fruit of the tree was good for food and pleasing to the eye, and also desirable for gaining wisdom, she plucked its fruit and ate it. And she also gave some to her male companion. Then both their eyes were opened, and they realized that they were naked. The day had arrived to sew fig leaves together to make coverings for themselves.

***

Dhaka, 23 November 2000 – A Hindu woman in Bangladesh sacrificed both her children to Mother Kali, who had appeared in her dream. The woman, Shibanirani, a resident of a village close to the border in Sirajganj district, told the police that she killed her five-year-old son, Avinash Chandra, and seven-year-old daughter, Swapna, with a sharp weapon after she was commanded by Kali in her dream. The neighbours saw Avinash and Swapna lying dead in the temple. Shibanirani was nearby, her sari bloody, praying to the goddess. After her arrest, Shibanirani said: 'Whatever I did was only on the Goddess's command. This fast, this sadhana, was only to please the Goddess.'

***

It had almost stopped snowing, the wind too was slowing down, it did look as if the visibility on all sides had improved. Observing the rows of stars in the sky, I wanted to stick to the eastern side and advance a bit towards the north. 'Okay, get up there now.' 'Get up there?' The girl turned towards me. I couldn't see her face because the searchlight was not on. But I discerned the tone of surprise in her voice: 'How shall I get up there?' I said sternly: 'Why, in just the way you did earlier.' I couldn't suppress my anger: 'Jump and get up there.' Astonished, she stared at me, and then she said, almost in a whisper: 'What – what are you saying?' 'Jump quickly – jump and get up there,' I said again in a commanding tone. The girl then turned around and tried to jump up with all her might. But her fingers couldn't get to even within two inches. She tried again, once again it had the same result. The third time, I pushed her up a bit, her hands touched the edge, for a few moments the girl hung in the void. Then she fell to the ground with a thud. She looked at me in a strange way. A really wonderful trick! 'I can't do it,' she said in a frightened voice. 'What do you want to do to me, what do you want from me!' Seeing that I didn't want to reply, she began appealing in whispers: 'Let me go, please let me go.' Right then I caught hold of her hand with a jerk. 'Did I go through all the hardship so that I would let you go?' After that, perhaps the final wall too fell down. I said: 'Please open your blouse and show me the place where you've got a cut on your back, show it to me now.' The girl slowly cast her gaze over the horizon, then looked at me with steady eyes: 'Is this why you've brought me here?' 'Where – show me!' I didn't reply to her, I said in a metallic tone: 'I don't know…' She moved back a few steps. I didn't reply, I held her hand firmly now. Darkness all around, and a live woman in front of me. Blood rushed into my hands then, and, in truth, blue-coloured strings.

***

'Kissing is no more natural than wearing clothes,' says Vaughn Bryant, professor of anthropology at Texas A & M University in College Station. This may come as a shock to those sitting in the back row of a cinema, but kissing is largely a cultural thing you can't blame on your genes. Even if our primate ancestors did it, kissing is by no means universal in human cultures. People living on the island of Mangia in the South Pacific, for example, were passionate lovers but knew nothing of kissing until Europeans arrived there in the 1700s.

Theories abound as to the origins of kissing. Some think it dates back millions of years, and started when women chewed up pieces of food and passed them directly from their lips to their babies' mouths. Kissing might have signalled affection between mother and child after these food exchanges ended. But this can't be the whole story, because Papuan mothers of New Guinea and the San women of South West Africa still wean their infants by feeding chewed food mouth-to-mouth, yet neither of these people kissed until it was introduced to them by Europeans, says Bryant. If our ancient human ancestors did kiss, they were coy about depicting it in their art and writing. One of the earliest references comes from India and dates from around 1,500 BC when the Vedic Sanskrit texts were written down from oral history. These describe the custom of rubbing and pressing noses together, says Bryant. He believes that this could have been the precursor to lip kissing. By the sixth century AD, the Indian erotic text, the *Kamasutra*, was full of references to kissing. It describes three 'primary' kinds of lip kisses between lovers, and even dictates what the response by the person being kissed ought to be.

The custom seems to have spread across Indo-European culture, with the Greeks being the first Europeans to take it up. But the prize for bringing tonsil-hockey to the masses has to go to the Romans. Those lusty Latins even had separate words for different types of kisses. The osculum was the peck-on-the-cheek greeting, the basium a more amorous lip-to-lip affair, and the savilum was a passionate tongue kiss. Kissing soon became central to European life, but by the late Middle Ages, the Catholic church decided that it was getting out of hand. The church decreed that kissing in reverence of God was acceptable, but kissing done with intent to fornicate was a mortal sin and kissing for carnal delight a venial sin.

Smell is actually the body's phenotype (observable characteristic) for your immune system, says Rachel Herz, a psychology professor at Brown University in Rhode Island. Women subconsciously prefer the smell of men whose genes for a class of immune system proteins called the MHC are very different from their own.

If a man in ancient Rome passionately kissed a high-ranking woman in public, she could legally press for marriage. And until the 1400s at least, a kiss under the mistletoe was a serious commitment. From the first peck, kissing has grown to mean many things – kiss of passion, kiss of life and kiss of death. These days, it won't land you in wedlock, but you might end up with more than you bargained for. About 278 colonies of bacteria, for one thing. So before you accost the object of your desire at a New Year's party, remember, a kiss is not just a kiss.

– Clare Ainsworth (*New Scientist*, London)

***

The dead body just lay in the middle. T h e d e a d b o d y. The mob surrounded the dead body and kept on expressing their ire. When the police arrived, they became incensed. The body was taken inside the premises of a local youth association. The mob began throwing stones and bricks at the police when they tried to take it away by force. A few police personnel suffered injuries while trying to take away the dead body. Senior police officers rushed to the spot as soon as they received word of the commotion. After that, the mob and the police fought a pitched battle, with the dead body lying in the middle. A group attacked from one direction and another came running from the opposite direction. Tear-gas shells exploded. Smoke everywhere, the battlefield was enveloped in smoke, no one could see clearly any more. The dead body lay in the middle. The dead body. All of us went together this Holi to a forest bungalow near Hesadi. The full moon could be seen through the clearing between the trees in the sal forest. The forested hill seemed to be floating in the moonlight. Suddenly drumbeats erupted from across the hills, fires lit up near and far. I heard that the Holi festival had begun in the villages of the Mundas. The watchman encouraged us: 'You should go, go around the Munda hamlet. You'll get A-class mahua.' After that, he said something smilingly, and when I asked him the meaning – 'You may get girls too. Their flavour's altogether different, not at all watery. Big babus from the city come here for some variety.' Without further delay, I ate the chicken curry and rice and set out quickly. The forest had been cleared. There were a few sal and mahua trees here and there. There aren't any wild animals there any more, but they used to be there earlier. Through the middle was a road for shiny cars. I didn't have to go very far; after walking for fifteen minutes, the village emerged in the clearing between the trees. The Munda girls, as one, sang as they danced, a few men accompanied them. Mahua flowed freely, and seeing us, a dark-skinned, curly-haired youth came forward. He wore a pair of jeans with eight pockets, and a colourful Hawaii shirt. A cigarette dangled from his fingers. Taking me towards the darkness, he straightaway asked whether we wanted women. Young ones, haven't had children yet, they're still girls, you'll have great pleasure, he said all that. There were five of us, all of us became enthusiastic, and after some bargaining it was settled at three hundred rupees. Only Vivek began to quibble, about whether they had venereal diseases, and so on. We didn't pay him any heed. We had had quite a bit to drink, we were in no condition to listen to him. They were all standing here and there in the darkness, some had lamps in their hands so that one could see their face and get an idea about the curves of the body. Black shiny bodies, each one wore a blouse and it was also clear that some had brassieres on. I was a bit surprised, but as there wasn't much time, I selected two tender ones. The pimp convinced us that the two of them were sufficient for skinny, callow youths like us, the two of them could handle five men. They were practiced in all that. And you'll see that neither of them has hair smelling of castor oil, all that's gone, they use soap and shampoo now, they use perfumed hair oils, they regularly apply Fair & Lovely on their faces in order to become fair complexioned. After that, he said, 'You are all city babus, let me know if you want to use condoms, I have foreign stuff, but it's a bit expensive.' Once again, we were surprised. I spotted some trouser-and-shirt-clad bhadralok here and there, possibly customers too. The boy was happy to get the money; after concluding the matter quickly, he offered us cigarettes, he began to explain that all these babus came frequently; people also came by car nowadays, they came in groups and had fun. They leave the young girls in such a state that they're unable to stand up for the next two or three days. We didn't like hearing all that. Ordering a few bottles of mahua and holding the two girls in my arms, I entered the room. One of the girls said laughingly in fluent Bangla: 'We'll make you happy, Bengali babus, but you must give a baksheesh.' The singing and dancing outside would carry on all night long, and the hunting festival would begin at dawn. The dead body just lay in the middle of all this. T h e d e a d b o d y. The mob surrounded the dead body and expressed their ire. They became incensed on seeing the police. The dead body was kept in the premises of a local youth association. The mob began throwing stones and bricks on the police when they tried to take it away by force. A few police personnel were injured while trying to take away the body. Senior police officers rushed to the spot as soon as they received word of the commotion. After that, the mob and the police fought a pitched battle, with the dead body lying in the middle. A group attacked from one direction. Another group came running from the opposite direction. Tear-gas shells exploded. Smoke everywhere, the battlefield was enveloped in smoke, no one could see clearly any more. The dead body lay in the middle. The dead body.

***

In this age of commercialization, on the question of whether it is morality or immorality that is worthy of support – just as it is difficult to overcome the desire for generalization on that subject, it is as difficult to gather sufficient facts and evidence appropriate to establishing one's position. Again, in another way, being able to gather these facts and evidence is also the easiest task.

***

Whatever happens in such a situation is what transpired – inevitably, everyone's gaze fell upon an innocent man. Everyone's intention and desire was to be free from the nervous excitation, suspicion and deviation brought about by applying one's mind to an apparently trivial matter. This situation brought that great opportunity. Never in my life had I seen such a wonderful mentally ill person. I was observing whether the oil stove was burning properly, I turned around when he suddenly started speaking. He called me behind the canvas screen. 'There's a terribly funny thing happening on our earth – come and see it at once!' I wanted to see. Faraway, in the northeast corner, far above the horizon, donning a huge form, a bunch of garlands of light had turned bright. The light seemed to want to spread very far in the dome-like sky's darkness. It was as if, at every moment, with the increase and decrease, there was a rise and fall. At first, the whole sky was filled with light – the next moment, a specific form, form after form, the play of multiple colours began. 'But this was only one screen – after just a while you'll see, so many kinds of rays, lines, luminousness, rainbows – and so much more! And this is what's most beautiful. Of course, you'll find that once you're accustomed to seeing it time and again, you won't want to gaze at it any more.'

***

A prohibited area bounded on all sides. Only a white line had been drawn. On each side stood two persons carrying automatic pistols. There were orders to shoot at sight. If anyone so much as put a foot across, he would not be warned. The final command was that, as soon as the light began to fade, everyone had to get inside. The permission to go out would be granted only if a special situation arose. This was not possible without long planning and training. A woman clad in black came forward, she said: 'I have some questions. Whatever is happening here is all done through signs, and it's being done by practised people. Can we assume that this is human trafficking?' Just a few steps ahead, a mound of mist stood unmoving. A massive shadow of a ship appeared on the wall. It was time for the tide to come in. A ship as big as this could not be sent back in such a short time. In the opinion of the first group, the top of the ship was so high that it would surely collide with the bridge when it passed under. In the view of the opposing group, the former view was completely without basis. The ship had perhaps passed beneath it many times.

***

There was a rich man who was dressed in purple and fine linen and lived in luxury every day. At his gate lay a beggar named Lazarus, whose body stank from sores, full of blood and pus, and who longed to eat what fell from the rich man's table. Dogs used to come and lick the cuts and sores on his numb body, they used to lick the blood and pus and the beggar used to moan in agony. The time came when the man died and the angels carried him to Abraham's side. The rich man also died and was buried. In hell, where he was in torment, he looked up and saw Abraham far away, with Lazarus by his side. So he called out to him: 'Father Abraham, have pity on me, send Lazarus to dip the tip of his finger in water and cool my tongue, it has become dry as wood with thirst, and I am in agony in this fire.' Smiling wryly, Abraham replied: 'Son, remember that in your lifetime, you received your good things while Lazarus got only grief and pain all his life; now it's his turn to know joy. And besides all this, between you and us a great chasm has been set in place, so that those who want to go from here to you, from heaven to hell, cannot, nor can anyone cross over from there to us. Between you and us lies a great chasm, immense and unbridgeable.'

***

A family. Comprising a mother and her son. One day, the son told his mother: 'I want to go to foreign lands.' Mother said: 'That's wonderful. My son's going to foreign lands.' Mother was very happy. She called her son and said to him, 'I bless you. May you be well. May you be successful, but son, let me tell you something. You should not travel to foreign lands all alone. That's why I've brought this crab. Take it along with you.' The son was taken aback hearing his mother's words. He asked his mother: 'What's the use of taking the crab along? Besides, where would I keep it?' Mother said, 'Do something, son. There's a camphor box in your bundle. Keep this crab companion in that.' The son did as his mother said. The next day, as soon as the sun rose, he touched his mother's feet in pranam and left for foreign lands. He walked a great distance. By noon, the sun became fierce. Walking along the road in the sun, the boy became very tired. There were rows of trees beside the road. He sat down under the shade of one of the large trees. He rested. A cool breeze wafted in the shade of the tree. His body felt cool. Gradually, he fell asleep. But there was danger lurking. While the boy was fast asleep, unknown to him, a big snake emerged from somewhere. Expanding its hood, the snake made its way towards the boy. As it neared the bundle, it got the scent of camphor. Snakes love the smell of camphor. It was attracted to the smell. The snake then removed the camphor box from the bundle. It began to strike the box on the ground. It wanted to open the box and eat the camphor. After repeated striking, the box came open, and a crab emerged from inside the box. The same crab that the boy's mother had given him. The crab emerged and squeezed the snake's neck with its big, fat claws. How would the snake escape now! The snake could no longer move. The poor snake slowly became unconscious and died. The boy slept through it all. He was fast asleep. He woke up after some time. It had turned into evening then. He got up briskly to resume his journey. As he went to lift the bundle, he saw the camphor box lying open. And beside it were the dead snake and the crab. He then understood what had happened. He thanked the crab inwardly. And he thought to himself: 'If Mother hadn't given me the crab, I would have perished right here today.'

***

Not encountering any hindrance, he advanced at great speed towards the face of the slope, and we were left behind. At first it seemed he was driving it properly, but the very next moment I realized that I was wrong, he did not have the capability to do such things any more. The massive steel body weighing four or five tons came crashing down, spun around on the slippery bosom of ice and rolled down the slope at great speed. I could not believe how it advanced along the straight, narrow path avoiding the crevices – the speed steadily increased, and all the while there was only a loud metallic sound that shattered to smithereens the silence in the heart. I don't know how exactly I managed to stay alive. Like a lunatic, I ran behind, every now and then, I leaped and shot across – as if pulled by an unseen hand, one slip of the foot meant certain, inevitable death. Suddenly, after colliding with something massive at the curve and rolling around a few times, it fell with great force, tail end first – and the very next moment, it broke into pieces. The wall of the crevice was closing, it was deathly cold; it advanced bit by bit. As soon as I climbed up, I saw the wall had moved another two inches. Transferring his weight somehow or the other on to his hands and legs, he was gazing, stunned and incredulous, at the harsh walls on the two sides that were slowly closing in, he wanted to keep gazing. Holding on with great care, I walked the distance between the two of us. They themselves would blast it out of the water. A shooting pain near the shoulder. Later, I heard that we had fought like lunatics for four or five minutes. And there's only me in the gap. Only me.

***

I've not travelled that much in India, but I've travelled quite a bit in West Bengal. Towards the end of the nineties, I once again began setting out for trips on a whim, carrying only a shoulder bag. I travelled to the Diamond

Harbour–Kakdwip–Namkhana region almost every week, sometimes going to the district and subdivision towns as well. In Siliguri, Burdwan, Malda, Krishnanagar and also Tarakeshwar, right up to the Champadali crossing in North 24 Parganas – everywhere I learnt about the honey trade operating in broad daylight. Recently, I travelled around Tamluk and its adjoining areas. The whole country seems to have become a red-light area. In the various important places in Tamluk subdivision, on the roadside, in the bus stand, in some hotels near the rail station – the flesh trade thrives now. A section of school- and college-going students have, willingly or unwillingly, become associated with this; they are falling into its net. The trade begins from Mecheda rail station. On one side, as one goes along Nandakumar High Road, on National Highway 41, on the road to Digha; and on the other side, all the way to Haldia – that's the spread of the racket. Different kinds of and different classes of educated, semi-educated and illiterate groups of women from various parts of the state regularly cast their net, standing in various places beside the road, soliciting customers. From a girl of fifteen to middle-aged women – every kind of female can be found here. They can always be seen in the Mecheda rail station, the bus stand and some nearby shops. Their pimps bargain openly with customers. Some khalasis and workers on private buses are also linked to them. Street intersections beside cinema halls, in Durgachak and Kapastraria, are where the trade flourishes the most. Lured by the prospect of quick money, quite a few girls from the adjoining region are getting enmeshed in this trade. Even girls from ordinary farming families. Not just that, some girls from various schools and colleges have fallen into the net. At the same time, sex workers from Kolkata and its environs are coming to this locality, drawn by the livelihood imperative. Some take up permanent residence in a hotel or lodge. Most of the school and college girls who bunk classes come purely out of curiosity or to have fun, with a friend or fellow student, and they go to various hotels or lodges. Some of them visit these hotels and lodges frequently and become familiar with the manager and workers, through whom they then start catching unknown customers. Luring them with the prospect of earning quick money in the thousands, the agents associated with the hotels and lodges draw them into this trade. Sometimes they threaten them. They compel them to join the honey trade. Gradually, the girls become associated with this trade. They don't do it regularly; they only do business when they find wealthy customers. Perhaps the folks at home don't know anything, or they believe she works in a nursing home or something like that. The business is presently booming in a hotel on Nandakumar High Road at the Maniktala crossing in Tamluk, and in quite a few hotels and lodges in the vicinity of Kapastraria and Mecheda station. Just as the people of the locality know about the places where the trade takes place, similarly, the police too know who the high priests of the trade are. One can also find rooms here to rent for temporary stay. Girls who come from outside rent these rooms, or book rooms in hotels for a week or so. They ply their trade for a week there. They go home for two or three days. And then they return to the seven-day routine. Among them are full-time sex workers from Bongaon, Baguiati, Kalyani and even Park Street in Kolkata. Someone is known as Minu, and someone is called Chitra. Some have up-to-date names. Needless to say, all the names are fake. Many of them are educated. There are also a few who have completed their higher education. In Kapastraria, there are twenty or twenty-five girls at all times, every day. The owners or managers of some of the hotels here are the high priests of the trade. Their pimps are spread out everywhere. It is they who function as spokes of the operation. In Nandakumar, somewhat wealthy customers can be found. In Kapastraria and Mecheda, the trade caters to the pockets of all classes. So the latter two places are more crowded. Looking at the Meena–Minu–Nishas, one would never think that they are linked to this trade. They behave just like a well-educated and respectable woman or daughter-in-law. Even their gait. Among the customers too, one does not observe any distinction between high and low. Students and youth, government employees, officers and engineers are all on the list of regular customers. Of course, there are people from the underworld. Everywhere one sees the quick-money trade.

***

Then I saw a great white throne, and He who was seated on it; the earth and the heavens fled from His presence, and there was no place for them. And I saw the dead, small and great, standing before God's throne, and books were opened and the dead were judged on those things which were written in the books, according to their deeds. And the sea gave up the dead who were in it. And they were judged, every man, according to what they had done. Then death and hell were thrown into the lake of fire. That lake of fire was the second death. Anyone whose name was not found in the book of life was thrown into the lake of fire. Then I saw a new heaven and a new earth, for the first heaven and the first earth had passed away and the sea was no more.

***

On Sunday morning, a local brahmin priest in Behala was arrested on the charge of raping a child. Some people offered resistance when locals went to thrash the priest. In their opinion, no matter what might have happened, one could not raise one's hand against a brahmin priest. The incident happened at about eight-thirty in the morning. The priest, whose name was Parshuram, lived in a house on Santrapara Road. A child named Nisha lived next door. Parshuram performed puja twice a day at the local Shani temple. Besides the local folk, all the traders of the locality respected him for his divine wisdom. In their view, the sadhak, Parshuram, could never have done something like that. According to police sources, the three-and-a-half-year-old child often went to the priest's house to eat nakuldana. On this day too, the child went to his house. The elderly man of sixty-five then shut the door and raped the child. People nearby rushed there hearing the child's screams and cries. The child was then bleeding and writhing. The brahmin priest was caught red-handed.

***

The precise reason for the dull bloodstains that I had seen in the cabin was finally known. 'Where did you find them?' I wanted to know. He mentioned a place from the symbolic map. The entire procedure paralleled the preceding events. At first, they were kept imprisoned in a deserted, desolate hut. But there was no shortage of food or drink. Each person was also given a blanket. After that, one morning, the prisoner woke up and saw that all the armed guards had become invisible. There was silence for a brief while, and then the creator's resounding, grave voice was heard: 'Where will you go this evening, Caroline?' 'I'll go to the bhadralok's world, we've been invited there. Both Eve and I. He has invited us to sit in the honeycomb.' Again the unnerving silence. Once again for a very long time. Then, the creator said: 'Only forty hours more, Caroline. Yes, Annabelle, I do remember. Someone or the other simply has to pay for that.'

***

Adam and Eve then heard God calling them as He was walking in the garden in the evening, and they hid from God among the trees in the garden. But God called Adam: 'Where are you?' Adam said: 'I heard You in the garden and I was afraid because I was naked, so I hid.' And He said: Who told you that you are naked? Have you eaten from the tree that I commanded you not to eat from?' Adam said: 'The woman you put here with me persuaded me to eat the fruit, I did not eat it willingly but only after being compelled to do so.' Then God said to the woman: 'What is this you have done?' The woman said: 'The serpent deceived me, and I ate and made him eat it too.' So, God cursed the serpent: 'Because you have done this, cursed are you above all creatures, you shall crawl on your belly and you shall eat dust all the days of your life. And I will put enmity between you and woman, and between your offspring and hers, he will crush your head, and you will strike his heel.' To the woman he said: 'I shall make your pains in childbearing very severe, you will give birth to children with painful labour, and you will desire your man, and he will rule over you. That is my curse.' To Adam he said: 'Because you listened to your wife and ate fruit from the tree that I commanded you not to eat from, you are cursed; no matter what you do, your whole life will be spent in distress, you will never be free of woman's evil counsel. Both of you will go on encouraging each other in sinful deeds, until the day you return to the earth. Because that's where you were taken from, you are only a grain of dust and it is to dust that you will finally return.'

***

Two local youths were arrested by the police on the charge of raping a married woman who had gone to Digha from Kolkata for a holiday. The accused are associated with the fish trade. The rape occurred on the sea beach in Digha last Sunday. Police stated that a newly married couple, residents of Bhowanipur, went for a holiday to Digha last Saturday. They were accompanied by two of their friends. On Sunday evening, they headed towards Mohona. There, three youths threatened them with a cleaver and blocked their way. Two of them forcibly took the woman away towards Shankarpur on a motorcycle. The other person held the woman's husband and his two friends there, threatening them with the cleaver. The two youths took the woman first to the sea beach in Shankarpur and then to a hotel. The two of them raped her on the beach. Later, their other friends arrived and they raped her too, one after another. They then took the woman to a hotel and they raped her once again. The local fisheries development committee did not accept this accusation by the police. According to them, the police had only a superficial view, whereas there was a well-planned sex racket behind it. The wife had an excellent rapport with those who had been charged with rape. As it happened, the four persons coming from Kolkata on that day had been invited to the warehouse of those who were accused. After lunch, everyone was drinking together. The woman too. The woman was giving company to her husband and the two youths inside the room. For that matter, they had also called over the accused persons to their hotel. All of them together carried on their fun all night long, everyone merrily watched a rented blue film. Late at night, the woman passed out after drinking. There were no clothes on her body. The bellboy in the hotel had seen all this. The accusation of rape was entirely motivated and pre-planned. The woman wanted to blackmail the two local youths who were in the fish trade. Actually, it was a ploy to extort money. The detailed report has not yet been obtained from the police.

***

On Wednesday morning, there was a commotion in a girl's school in north Kolkata, the commotion was caused by three monkeys. The monkeys kept pulling the students' saris, they tore their blouses to shreds. Some of them got together and snatched the tiffin from students and began eating that openly. They entered classrooms and vandalized a light-post. Weird sores on their fingers. There are some large trees in the school on Duff Street. On Wednesday, the monkeys were initially hidden in the trees. After that, their red-black faces came into view. Come Thursday, they began jumping into the verandas too. A few students went and enticed them with food and drew them near. And again a few also wanted to drive them away by a show of force. They made faces at them. Just after that, a male monkey began attacking the girls defiantly. It began making vulgar gestures. A yoke like splayed knees, it becomes a symbol. On Thursday too, a monkey was seen sitting under the table of a girl who was wearing shorts. An atomic cyclone took shape then, all the lights in the girls' school began going off one after another. The bell rings in the blind school.

***

Overwhelmed by deep thought, he advanced slowly towards the other end of the bridge with his hands thrust into his trouser pockets. Across the bridge lay freedom. Every now and then, he beheld the natural beauty of the surroundings. Barely visible in the distance was the peak of the golden hillock. The coastal part. A belt. Stepping down, he pretended to bend down and look outside, he gently pulled the green rope tied to his hands. It was hanging loosely then. 'What are you doing here?' Startled at hearing a female voice, he turned his head and looked. After that, he kept loosening the red thread: on one side lay beautiful nature, and on the other the extremely beautiful woman – Tell me, in which direction should he look! 'I say, I don't suppose anyone praised your beauty so openly – so shamelessly!' 'No, a few have definitely done so...' As soon as the girl began pulling the green rope slowly with her soft hands, he held her hand firmly, he asked her not to pull such things in that manner. Letting go of the rope and looking all around once, the mysterious woman said: 'Can you tell me what's happening?' 'Nothing at all, I'm fishing in murky waters.' 'I can see that. But doing this under these circumstances is not so commendable. Because a woman in flesh and blood is standing in front of you.' She ran her soft hand over his manly fingers, and then suddenly, stooping down, the woman looked for and picked up the blue string, after that she gave it a sharp tug, the man at once began to feel dizzy and numb: 'I've heard that those who catch fish, I mean those who can catch fish, can also tell great tales. Don't you know any tale like that?' 'Of course I do.' 'Then why don't you tell me?' The man stared at the woman for a few moments. There was a tug on his blue string then. He said:

'You are very beautiful, will you believe my story?' Her face became radiant with a smile, the woman said: 'Do you really mean it, that I'm beautiful?' 'Yes, I mean it.' 'In that case, I have to be a disbeliever.' She tittered in laughter. After that, taking the man's extended hand in her own hand, she said: 'Those who fish in murky waters can also tell tales about the murky waters. My dear man, I want to hear you tell the tale about becoming a disbeliever.'

***

I am the true vine and my Father is the farmer. He cuts and throws away every branch in me that does not bear fruit, and he tends every branch that bears fruit, so that it may bring forth more fruit. Now you are cleansed through the words I have spoken to you. Abide in me, and I shall abide in you, as the branch cannot bear fruit of itself unless it abides in the vine, no more can you unless you abide in me. I am the vine; you are branches, who dwell in me and in whom I abide. If a man abides not in me, then, like a branch, he is cast forth and is withered and men gather them and cast them into the fire and they are burnt. Abide in my love. If you keep my commandments, you shall abide in my love, even as I have kept my Father's commandments and I abide in his love. These things have I spoken unto you that my joy might remain in you and that your joy might be full. This is my commandment, that you love one another, as if I am loving you. These things I command you, that you love one another. I am a vine and my Father is the farmer.

***

Bhubaneswar, 22 November – A female convict sentenced to death for murdering a child had got married. And at this moment, she is pregnant. The judicial system has been thrown into a dilemma regarding whether, on humanitarian grounds, her death sentence should at all be carried out. The matter is unprecedented and quite complicated. Kalpana Majumdar is a female prisoner in Koraput district jail, charged with kidnapping and sacrificing an infant in the Malkangiri region of Orissa. She is now two months pregnant. On 30 April 1997, she had picked up a four-year-old child and sacrificed him at the feet of the goddess. There were two accomplices with her. After the police lodged a case against Kalpana and her accomplices, the Additional Sessions Judge in Malkangiri sentenced the accused to death on 7 July 1999. The case was later transferred to the Orissa High Court. In between, Kalpana was released on bail and got married within a day. Now she is two months pregnant. Many people believe the whole thing was neatly planned. Kalpana's father informed the Division Bench of the High Court that, in the month of September of the current year, a person by the name of Suren Mondal had married Kalpana, voluntarily and after knowing everything. Suren was twenty-two years younger than Kalpana. But their respective ages could not present a legal hurdle to their marriage. The High Court asked the jailer to submit an affidavit on the matter of Kalpana's release on bail, and her subsequent marriage and pregnancy. The jailer informed the court that, in spite of trying to obtain accurate information about the marriage and pregnancy, they had failed to do so. The woman repeatedly said to the jailer, her chest puffed out in pride: 'I am pregnant, how can the law hang me! If I am killed, the child in my womb will also die. But my child has done no wrong. By which law will my child be killed?

Which magistrate will sentence the innocent child in my womb to death?'

***

The mouth drawn by Magritte is steadily transformed into an unprotected vulva, it keeps getting transformed. Garcin tells the woman to take it easy, but the woman likes to stay alone sometimes. There are three principal characters in the play; there is also a valet. There are no windows in the room, and so no light from outside can get in. There's only a single bulb inside, and light, whose brightness can't be increased, it's not possible, it never becomes bright, it doesn't get extinguished either. There are planks for sitting, but they are immobile, it's just not possible to move them from their positions. Garcin says that he has developed a sadistic kind of nature, that liquor and women have become part of the scent of his body, and that he derives pleasure by taking vengeance on them. No one has suspected him as yet. Inèz, who is also a lesbian at times, says she used to have an affair with the wife of a sibling, a desperate one. No one found out. Hearing everything, Estelle keeps saying that she had thrown her own infant into the water merely for love, to satisfy the desires of the body. No one suspected her. At the very end of this sinful play, in order to make a final settlement, Estelle takes out her knife and keeps chasing Inèz, and Inèz says: 'Oh my dear woman, my dear man – your stupidity abounds! Who are you going to kill – who – are we at all alive! And we have to be like this eternally, in this in-betweenness of wanting to die and not being alive.'

[Swaramelakalanidhi, 2001]

Translator's note

The Bengali title of this anti-story, 'Swaramelakalanidhi', is the title of a famous musicological treatise of sixteenth-century Vijayanagara. Authored by Ramamatya in the year 1550, the work is counted among the nine gems of the theory of Carnatic music. The original text comprised thirty-two sections. One of the sections appears four times, once in 'standard' Bangla and thrice more in different (made-up) 'dialects'. In the translation, it appears only once. One section was about gender in Bengali grammar and Bengali vocabulary, which does not appear here. The section taken from *New Scientist* appeared in English in the original text. Finally, several sections are from the Bible. The author had translated it into Bangla in his own style. In the translation, the English text from standard versions of the Bible has been reproduced, while retaining the author's touch.

You'll Dance, Miss Snub Nose

At the back of the human body, there's a particular region where no hand can reach. Neither the right nor the left, no hand can in any way reach all those spots.

1.

On Saturday, for much of the night, there was a different kind of rain in the Kalipur locality of Madaritala. The colour of the rain was green. Seeing the green rain, terror spread everywhere. Thick, slimy, sticky drops began raining down around midnight. Close to dawn, it rained again. The same green rain. There was an ancient Kali temple in the locality. The temple compound was covered with dense clumps and bushes, and no puja was ever performed there. An eyewitness said that the rain began inside the compound of the Kali temple. It then spread across the nearby areas. When phone calls were made to the police station to ask for more information, they were told: 'We too have received reports about green rain. A section of people has started getting out of hand because of this. We have received reports about that too. But if the public becomes crazy, tell me, what can we do? After all, we can't fire upon the unarmed masses. That would be against the Constitution.' After this, when asked about the green rain, the Alipore meteorological office responded that they did not know of any such reports. Nothing could be said until tests had been conducted. However, if a mixture of copper and chromium was present in the air, the colour of the rainwater could be green. In their view, if this incident had really occurred, then an in-depth investigation was definitely called for. Going to Kalipur, one saw all the houses had turned green. The impact of green colour splashes. As if green colour had been sprayed there. The marks were so sticky that they couldn't be washed away with water. A science teacher in the local school said: 'The more water you add, the greener it becomes. Look to the west, the colour of ogres and evil spirits is also green. All the ogres in those countries are green. This calls for in-depth investigation. And if it wasn't something supernatural, then why would the rain centre around the Kali temple? We believe in science, but there are many things which science cannot explain.'

2.

Bratindranath was seated on a chair, leaning back a bit, his two hands clasped behind his head. His elder son hesitatingly called him: 'Baba!' At once Bratindranath looked at his son. Ajoy said: 'Everyone wants ... I mean, today, all of us...' Bratindranath remained in the same posture, he said: 'Tell me clearly.' 'I mean, we want to have a party, that's all.' 'That's great, but one doesn't get good *bhang* nowadays ... At one time, in front of Tiwari's ship in Burrabazar...' 'No, I mean everyone thought ... I mean everyone wants to drink beer...' 'Beer!' Bratindranath seemed to be taken aback a bit. 'So who all are going to be there?' 'Everyone, three sons, three daughters-in-law, two sons-in-law, and four grandchildren.' 'Grandchildren will drink beer … they're thirteen-fourteen years old…' the words burst out of his mouth! 'So what of that … all of them study in English-medium schools. They move around with boys and girls from good families. And in the West, no one thinks of beer as alcohol. They drink it instead of water.' Notwithstanding his age, Bratindranath had his wits about him. He understood all there was to understand. 'So there are about fourteen of you. Where will you get so much beer now!' 'No, no … we won't need more than fifty bottles. I can arrange for that in a jiffy … You don't know anything. A lot of middle-class families stock alcohol nowadays. Phone them and they send it across. They charge a higher price, but at least one can get it at any time. And as it's Holi, not only whisky and beer, you can get any kind of booze you want. It is Holi today, Baba, so all of us, brothers, sisters, sons and daughters, want to get together and forget about everything and simply have fun. If anyone passes out, so be it, but we'll all be at home after all. You have done so much for us, and borne so much hardship to raise us well, we won't do anything without your knowledge, Baba, we'll drink only after letting you know and getting your blessings. We want to have a day of fun – and relax, that's all – so please don't say no. You don't have to take the trouble of coming upstairs. Bhojua will bring you the milk and bread at the appropriate time. You can eat right here and then go to bed. You could listen to the radio. There should be nice *kirtans* as it's Holi.

3.

A resident in the women's hostel on Dilkusha Street fell ill, and centring around this, there was a public disturbance and a lot of tension. The residents complained that the matron of the hostel had locked it from outside and left. She did so every day. When the girl suddenly fell ill, it was not possible to call a doctor for her. Her condition progressively deteriorated. One person was thoughtful enough to phone the police station. But there was no clear response from the police station. The bold girl then scaled the rear wall of the hostel and went out, broke the lock on the front door and sent sick Ameena to a nursing home. When the lock was being broken, the old wall of the hostel, on the Dilkusha Street side, began to collapse. Wooden supports had to be placed there. The girl was the only one who voiced a protest: they were locked in like this every evening. If any male family member came for some important purpose, he was not permitted to meet the resident. They were told to come in the morning, during visiting hours. All the other girls stood by silently, they did not utter a word. The matron, Gulshan Ara, announced that it was only for the girls' safety that they were locked in. When the student by the name of Ameena Khatoon fell ill, she had left to call the doctor, and meanwhile the watchman had gone home to eat. So they were in no way at fault in this regard. Gulshan Ara stated that Ameena's illness was nothing too serious. She had not done anything wrong by locking the girls in. It was better that the girls did not go out after dusk. Otherwise, their character would be spoilt.

4.

On the pretext of getting her a job, an uncle of the young woman sold her in Sonagachi two years ago. Before that, they had stayed as husband and wife for a few days in a hotel in Sealdah. She was not permitted to leave her room in Sonagachi. Even if she so much as stepped out to the veranda, the madam thrashed her. She had to sleep with customers from noon till four or five the next morning. On some days the number of customers exceeded twenty. And no one could be turned away. One day, at dawn, the girl somehow managed to escape and hid in the veranda of a local youth association. Come morning, after people heard about everything, she was handed over to the Burtolla police station. Later, the police presented her at the court. The court sent her to the government home for women in Liluah and issued instructions for her family's whereabouts to be ascertained. Even after a lot of search and enquiries, the police were unable to find any trace of her family members at the address provided by the girl. Later, seeing the incessant wailing of the girl, they went a second time, and searched out and found her parents. At first, they did not want to be identified as the girl's parents. Later, the police identified them with the help of neighbours. Both of them, the father and the mother, said in a single voice: We can't take the girl back. Her chastity has been destroyed.

5.

Twelve policemen, including the officer in charge of the police station, were beaten up by the local people when the police went to demolish an illicit liquor den. The incident occurred on Saturday night, at Dihi Bhurshut. A sub-inspector, who was seriously injured when the villagers attacked the police, was taken to the S.S.K.M. Hospital in Calcutta. Police patrols were deployed because of the tension in the area. The illicit alcohol trade flourishes in Dihi Bhurshut, which is near the border of the Howrah and Hooghly districts. An illicit alcohol market runs openly during the day. Vendors come from far-flung areas to buy the booze. On the day in question, around evening, twenty-two plainclothes policemen, led by the officer in charge, carried out an operation to destroy the illicit alcohol den. They left their police jeeps at the bus stand and entered the village. Some villagers attacked them when they were taking an illicit alcohol seller with his jerrycan to the police station. They got together and fell upon the policemen and began raining slaps, punches and blows on them. They screamed obscenities at the officer in charge and beat him too. In the process, they managed to seize a sub-inspector. At first, he was dragged and taken into a shop, and then his hands and feet were tied and he was given a sound thrashing. After some time, a huge police contingent arrived, surrounded the village and began combing operations. They picked up and took away many young and middle-aged men. The villagers were now seething with rage. Their complaint was that the police repeatedly let off the real culprits and oppressed ordinary people. The culprits were informed about the police operation in advance, and they escaped. The police arrived and began arresting innocent youths. None of those who were taken into custody that day were present at the spot, they had got off the bus after returning from their jobs in Calcutta and were walking home. They were arrested midway.

6.

'Marilyn Forever!' 'Immortal Marilyn!' 'Remember Marilyn!' 'Dying to kiss Marilyn all over!' 'Love you Marilyn' – all these were the names of various fan clubs. All were devotees of Hollywood's entrancing blonde-haired star, Marilyn Monroe. Even though it was forty years since the mysterious death of the beloved star, all of them gathered at a particular place to commemorate 5 August. Specially made life-size mannequins were also sold in these places, for some secret purpose. Not ordinary mannequins, mind you. The breasts were formed artfully, the butt as well, there was a hole in the vaginal region, and the pubic hair was also put in place skilfully. Nowadays nothing was secret any more, they replied, without the slightest qualm, we badly need the mannequin in bed. Especially married men unhappy with their sex lives. This year too, a few thousand devotees arrived at Marilyn's crypt. They had come from many faraway countries. Their contention: they wanted 5 August, the day Marilyn passed away, to be declared as 'Love Making Day'. They appealed to all the heads of state in the world to accept the demand. Otherwise, they would launch a large-scale movement. And women supported this.

7.

The next Saturday too, there was green rain in Kalipur at noon and at night. Experts from the Pollution Control Board went there to investigate the cause of the green rain. Green rain fell in front of their very eyes. They collected samples, but could not provide any clear scientific explanation. The colour of the rain that night was dark green. The preliminary response of the experts was: 'Such incidents are rare. We have pored through the scientific literature. But we could not find any information.' Soon after, word of the green rain spread and queues of people formed in Kalipur. They dug out and carried away soil with the green splashes. They took away roof tiles from houses. Swarms of people in all directions. Queues of people – spotting an opportunity, some people mixed green colour in water and merrily sold it off as green rain. People paid fat sums of money and bought it. Ordinary people, for sure, but officials from the government also arrived for inspection. Many bought the leaves of trees which bore the stamp of green rain. For them, it was a divine substance in this Kali Yuga. Science could not explain it. Puja commenced in the ruins of the Kali temple. A minister, who had come with his wife by car, stood afar and out of sight from everyone, paid obeisance to Mother Kali by knocking his knuckles on his forehead, and also got his driver to buy a glass bottle filled with green rain. Meanwhile, the experts investigating the phenomenon suspected that this could have been caused by some fuel substance used in the brick kilns. They went to some of the brick kilns nearby. But when they went there, they found that the wind there blew in the opposite direction. The experts were of the view that some such fuel was being burnt in the vicinity, which caused this kind of rain. Finally, they split into two or three groups and went on providing their own explanations.

8.

From our own correspondent, Kanthi – Villagers beat up a schoolteacher for allegedly sexually abusing a female student; they thrashed him and smashed his testicles. The incident occurred at the Betua High School in Betua village on Saturday. A female student of Class 6 complained that on finding her alone in the school premises, the teacher sexually abused her, and destroyed her virginity. The school had half-day on Saturday, and so school hours were over and nobody was there. The girl went crying and informed the boys in a local youth association. The boys from the association and the villagers created a commotion and got together, entered the school, caught the teacher and blindly rained punches, slaps and blows on him. The girl's father picked up a whole brick and smashed the teacher's testicles with it. He was admitted to the nearest hospital in a severely injured condition. When he regained consciousness after about a week, he spoke in detail about the incident. He tutored the girl, Gitali, in English. He did not want to teach her any more because she had failed in and repeated every class. The other boys and girls in the tutorial home were also going astray on account of the girl. 'I asked her to stop coming. The same night, her father came and right away proposed that I marry Gitali. He said: "She has loved you for a long time, but she wasn't able to say it."' When he immediately turned down the proposal to marry the student, her father was enraged: 'You made a mistake, teacher'. Within a month, this incident occurred.

9.

Every day, at least two or three hundred drug addicts rushed to Dakshindari. Just as there were school and college students among them, there were also people who were well established in society. Some people came by car, parked it at a distance, and then walked. This was a marketplace for smack. Daily labourers, workers, rickshawwallahs, rag pickers, and even mendicants, everyone was equal here. Twenty-five rupees for a pinch. Good stuff for a good price. People came from Diamond Harbour, Burdwan and Hooghly – for that matter, people came here even from as far away as Assam, just to buy smack. Both retail and wholesale markets operated together. Going to Dakshindari on Monday, I saw pinch-quantities of smack being sold openly, albeit somewhat out of sight. All this happens with the knowledge of the police, they regularly receive the collections. Not exactly like a market, but people came, bought and left. A crowd under an abandoned tin-roofed shed, behind a lathe-machine factory. Some were sitting there and smoking the stuff. There were raids of a window-dressing nature from time to time, the stuff was removed in time. Yet, unless two or four persons were taken into custody and charged, the police couldn't uphold their dignity. Two or three small fry, who ran away when they saw the police jeep, were caught in possession. Bapi from Metiabruz, Mohammad Ismael and Shankar from Rajabazar, and Bhola from Dum Dum. A sixteen- or seventeen-year-old, jeans-clad girl from a decent home was also caught at the same time. The girl pleaded fervently: 'Please release me, my father is a minister's PA.' 'Why do you take this stuff?' 'I can't live without having it. Many boys and girls from my college have it, boys and girls from decent homes, like me.' Hearing she was the daughter of a minister's PA, she was scolded a bit and then released. Her boyfriend was standing not so far away. Bapi makes tea crates, age twenty-four. Ismael said that for the last two years he was compelled to rush here, pulled by the drug. He had to get three pinches every day. Bhola sold *sattu*. He was Ismael's friend. And eleven-year-old Khasti was a rag picker.

Sometimes he begged for a living. He also stole whatever he could whenever he got an opportunity. He broke down in tears: 'I have to steal to get money for smack. I'm not a thief, Sir. When I feel the need – I just don't know what I do ... I lose my senses. I steal anything I can.'

10.

The name of the arrested youth was Shankhu Mukherjee, age thirty-four. Shankhu Babu lived near a cinema hall in New Alipore. The youth belonged to an educated family, and he too had been a good student. He had graduated from IIT-Kharagpur with a first-class first. After he was arrested from his home on Monday night, he was taken to court on Wednesday and released on bail. For quite some time, the officer in charge of the New Alipore police station had been receiving a strange kind of complaint. Women walking in front of the cinema hall or on the pavement on the opposite side had suddenly experienced a stinging sensation, either on their back, or their exposed waist, or even near their breasts. They looked to find the spot bleeding. Going to a doctor, it was found that an air-gun pellet was lodged there. After repeatedly receiving such complaints, the police got down to investigating the matter. But they were simply unable to find the source of the air-gun pellets. On the basis of information from an anonymous source, on Tuesday evening, the police raided Shankhu Mukherjee's house. It was a close friend of his who had telephoned the police station and disclosed everything. An air gun, together with forty or forty-five pellets, was found in his possession. He said he had never intentionally aimed and fired at any woman. His hands did such things against his will, and continued to do so. His hands never aimed at any male, but as soon as he saw any exposed part of a female body, his hands became fidgety. He became restless. The hands fired upon the exposed backs, waists, and also on the visible, half-exposed region of the breasts. He had no control over his hands. He also admitted that he had become attached to the gun ever since he had been gifted an air gun for his thread ceremony in his childhood.

11.

Question: I am forty years old. About a year ago, I fell in love with a young woman. I am a musician in a band. She used to sing in the same band. But people in my family did not like the girl at all. They were of the view that this could never be a happy marriage. That a meeting of minds between the girl and me was extremely unlikely. Anyway, we got married. Very soon, I realized that, in truth, in many aspects of my life, I could not be one with Subarna. First of all, she had innumerable former lovers. She flirted with other men night and day. On some days, I returned from work to find her with a male friend behind closed doors. Nor did she have any remorse about all this. She did everything with my full knowledge. For many days, I tried to bring her around. But I'm unable to. I don't have as many lovers or friends. On the other hand, it's not as if she doesn't love me. Even after all this, she makes love to me all night. I just don't know what I should do. Answer: Girls usually become somewhat restless after marriage. Win her over a little bit. Perhaps there's some laxity or looseness of some kind in your personality. Because of which it's difficult to sustain the attraction. Do something, sleep with the first girl you find. Do it right in front of your wife. When you have sex with her, make such amorous sounds that your wife can guess that you are in a state of supreme bliss with the girl, that you are enjoying the whole thing tremendously. Sleep with the girl every day and make her pregnant. After that, call the girl over and pay her a lump sum as compensation, take her yourself and get an abortion done. You can get such girls nowadays, who're willing to do anything in exchange for money, who're willing to get anything done. They have made this akin to a profession. But do everything with the full knowledge of your wife, do it without the slightest qualm. One has to learn how to keep one's wife in control. It's possible to get nuts-and-bolts training for that. Practical training is imparted on how to give supreme satisfaction to your partner, and on what you should do to achieve that. The advertisements for these things are published openly, perhaps with some beating around the bush, phrased in some clever words. You just have to keep your eyes and ears open, and stay that way.

12.

The images are lifted from the altar, carried on the bosom, and then arranged on wooden boards. One group pushes from the rear, and another group pulls and hauls up from the front. Most of the time, one finds that Balaram and Subhadra can be hauled up to the chariot without any difficulty, but all the hassle is with Lord Jagannath. Moving him is not at all easy. Everyone is worried sick lest he stand up athwart. At first, calmly pronounced Vedic mantras are recited. If that does not work, recitation is begun in worldly language. The assembled *pandas* chant the mantras with gusto. If even that doesn't work, the session of enticing the Lord with sweetmeats is begun. Rows and rows of huge lumps of the choicest sweetmeats are brought and arranged in front of Jagannath, so that he is lured to move by the khaja, goja, nadu and other assorted sweetmeats, and stand straight. If that does not work either, the limits of patience are crossed. Some people, some senior *pandas*, let loose a stream of vulgar ditties, one has to shut one's ears if one hears that. All that foul language does not reach the ears of the masses in the distance. If that does not work either, a senior *panda* then strikes a few blows with the stick in his hand, even as he sings the vulgar ditties. The stick rains down, there's a flow of invective and vulgar ditties, and Jagannath finally begins to move and rise. The masses in the distance can't really guess anything, they pull the ropes as if their lives depend on it. The god begins to move. The excited masses scream out: *Jai Jagannatha Ki Jai!* The devotees now have the ropes of the chariot in their hands. At an unseen signal, the ropes start being pulled. With a roaring sound, the chariot advances along the principal thoroughfare, carrying the armless, maimed Jagannath, the People's God.

13.

After lots of inspections and tests, scientists realized that the green rain was actually shit – bee's shit. The minister made a speech about this and forbade the people from being directed by superstitions. He said the experts had examined and tested the green rain and not found any trace of harmful chemicals in it. Only pollen from parthenium, coconuts, mangoes and common flowers and grasses had been found in the green rain. There need be no apprehension about any serious damage from all that. And of course, there was no apprehension whatsoever of the end of days. People were getting scared for no reason. As soon as they saw reports about green rain in the newspapers, the minister instructed experts to conduct an on-the-spot investigation and submit a report. The experts had got into a car and rushed to Kalipur. They were there when the green rain fell. The car's windscreen was plastered with the green rain. They busied themselves collecting samples. After conducting tests, four kinds of pollen were found in the green rain. And it was only bees that consumed such large quantities of pollen. The green rain was only the shit of airborne bees.

14.

A cutout of clouds in the sky. On the maths teacher's blackboard, water just keeps leaking from the sly hole in the reservoir, simply keeps leaking, it fills up very little.

[Nachbi Khendi, 2002]

Holding Capacity Even in Intimate Entry

The farthest I can be

Standing in front of the mirror, the two of us look at one another and laugh like jackasses and put on our clothes, and Arko says once again: 'Maem, I don't feel like going home, why don't we do it once more.' I say: 'No, my dear, there's no use trying to be so bold.' Kolkata flows along on the two sides. Here, look at the Divine Mother, a picture of the Panchachulli peaks. Two pairs of legs, and what a terrifyingly beautiful, dark vortex hole. It glows. It extinguishes. We used to say love fresh off the chafing dish and a stroll on Lovers' Lane. Whether boy or girl, everyone is proceeding by turning the steering wheel towards their target, they just keep doing so. Without holding back anything, Sulagna hugs Arko, she tells him unambiguously: 'Ice has to be broken in December, not in March. We believe in parallel culture.' They keep breaking ice, in public, laying it in front of each other. After overcoming the initial hesitation, they begin to move in time to the same drumbeat, every now and then they change their posture, they keep doing so, just keep doing it. A village road, in Khudropola. The falling observer will never really understand that he is crossing the horizon of the black hole. Making use of the opportunity, Ruma declares – 'As if I'll let you go unless you show me!' Whatever was in the north earlier has all now turned to the south. East and west have exchanged directions by now. Pressing the pillow to his ear, he tries to go back to sleep. Beneath one's feet, the river flows along, spilling over the two banks. After that lie tidal flats. A patch of yellow light keeps descending. Well-bricked walls, but a tin roof. Only infants in underpants were around in the courtyard. A queue of pots, pitchers and buckets at the municipal standpipe, awaiting water-supply time, red, blue and green buckets. It was not exactly a basti, yet still a basti. He observed television antennae sticking out above quite a few bamboo-lath windows; cable television wires too were visible in a few places. There were cheap curtains, albeit dirty, hanging in a few houses. Runa asked: 'What did you want to know?' Poroma laughed and replied: 'I wanted to know whether Tarun understands all this and whether or not he responds to all this.' 'Who knows where the refugees of development from beside the Tolly Nala are.' Runa laughed, and said, 'You lot are real peasants. In our place, even schoolgirls take the pill regularly. Can anyone ever say when, or where, or under what circumstances, something might happen? No one takes a risk, after all everyone has done it at least once by the time they are thirteen or fourteen.' I put the teacup down. Surama was sitting cross-legged. Sitting comfortably on the sofa, she watched the bloody battle of lions hunting zebras on the National Geographic channel every now and then, she watched an average amount of sex. Any excess in life was not good. Life had taught her that lesson. The sun advanced some more. Birds called. People of her age had saccharine instead of sugar. Gave up salt. Woke up at five in the morning and religiously went for a walk. An immense hand of cracked concrete on the reddish granite platform: a clenched fist. One's eyes kept gazing at it. A flaming torch held in the fist. The fist was so inappropriate that it looked as if the torch had been stuffed from outside. A fist of concrete, now it had become black with dirt and grime. And the heights to which it could have ascended weren't reached either. After all, space pierces the sky and races away. The great void. A picture of the Milky Way. And just at the bottom, continents after continents, and racing storm clouds pass them by. Every now and then, a particle of moving light, like a slender lifeline. *The sky's the limit* – so she knew this too. 'You had once told me that you'd take me to Digha, that you'd show me the sea, but you didn't take me. You said, after all, the rest of life is there for the sea. But there's only examinations now. Work hard at first, and then there's pleasure. But does pleasure come later? Even if it does, can we recognize pleasure, can we identify it, and accept it as one's own?' 'What did the man say, Didi?' 'Oh, whatever he keeps saying ... that he felt dizzy when he saw me ... that he had never seen anyone as beautiful as me before ... but he doesn't want to cheat me ... He loves me ... I have to go on Saturday when his wife goes out to perform puja ... He wanted to give me an advance ... In such matters, the rule is that the amount of money should be increased as much as possible, by putting pressure ... You can't say it now ... but only then ... at the time of the real thing ... he'll agree to whatever you ask ... When you arouse a guy he loses control ... you have to extract everything just before he puts it in...' If the black hole is like any other hot thing, then heat from that ought to be radiated and the stationed observer ought to be able to see that radiation.

That means the dark well is not entirely dark – is that possible?

In that case, has the horizon of the black hole remained very close to us – in the middle of our Milky Way, right in the middle! As instructed by Sunil, Manasi went to her room and said: 'You lie down on the bed and I'll spread the mat on the floor for myself.' After a while Sourav arrived. The door of the room was open, he went in straightaway. Bimal couldn't restrain himself from saying: 'You don't stop at saying anything, Boudi, do you, and what do you finally do, you point me to your own widowed aunt.' Thick lips and thin lips – the way to apply lipstick on the two kinds of lips is different. Ascertain first whether it is the upper lip or the lower lip that is thicker, and then make it thinner using a lip liner. A thin look has to be given to the curving points as well. Actually the excessive part of the thick lip has to be concealed using foundation, so that men don't discern anything. If you apply a dark coloured lipstick, even a thick lip looks thin, but keep in mind, only a lipstick with a matt finish makes a thick lip kissable. On 10 May 2001, in the German parliament, the Green Party accepted all the demands of sex workers and announced its complete support in favour of enacting a law. The flesh trade was not sinful, not immoral either, it was an economic enterprise just like any other business. A long-standing demand of sex workers was that if the flesh trade was legalized, they would pay tax to the government, and once they paid tax the enterprise would be legal. With that, sex workers would no longer be looked down upon by society; similarly, they would get benefits from the government, they would get the facility of health insurance. On account of paying tax, they would also receive pension in the future. The government's rationale – so they are in the flesh trade, but why should they be deprived of basic citizen rights on that account? The

Speaker of the German parliament said: 'We want to build a society that is more tolerant, democratic, humane and flexible.' It is Germany that is now the foremost country in the whole world as regards human rights. The government has already supported same-sex marriages and enacted a law to that effect. Men can marry men here, and women can marry women. Male prostitutes have been recognized, and they too have been granted licenses. There's no other option in the economic culture of the global marketplace. The generation here has a global outlook. Needless to say, future generations too. To them, business is merely business, it has no ethics or morality. The flesh trade is also an enterprise, it is required for bodily needs; besides, the business is also of a personal nature. If it is done with a person picked up from the street, in exchange for money, it's not as if that's some epic disaster, it is entirely an economic enterprise. Immediately after the collapse of communism, girls in Moscow and St Petersburg were asked: 'What will you do now that the earlier system has fallen flat on its face?' The reply of most of the girls was: 'So what of that, *sex is a good weapon to earn marks and dollars. And we do like to do it at all times, anywhere.*' Possibly, in something written by Dipak Majumdar, there's an observation, something along the lines of: 'In the language of ancient Greece, technique and artistry create a kind of synonymity, they had created that.' Of late, in quite a few Muslim states, the 'hudood' ordinance has been introduced. According to this ordinance, in case of rape, no complaints by any woman will be accepted. Under the ordinance, in the case of 'jina' (i.e. unauthorised sexual relations before or after marriage), it is the woman who has to prove that she has been raped. However many complaints are made, the man is not considered guilty until guilt is established, he is not considered responsible. If the woman cannot prove the use of force, it is she who will be severely punished, while the man will be deemed innocent and freed. Earlier, in some instances, judgements took place relying on forensic and other evidence. Now everything depends on the eyewitnesses. In other words, there must be a witness at the time of rape. And this witness cannot be a non-Muslim. Unless a witness who is a Muslim testifies, it is not possible to prove that rape has been committed. Human rights lawyer Hina Jilani has said: 'According to a report by Human Rights Watch, a large number of women have been compelled to go to prison almost without trial. They are becoming victims of various kinds of mental and physical oppression there. Becoming victims of various kinds of perverted and inhuman sexual abuse too. But proper information is not available, it is not made available.' On Monday afternoon, in the Baribasa locality, under the Bhaktinagar police station in Jalpaiguri district, a woman named Seeta Haluwa sold her own infant son to a contractor for seventy rupees. The buyer, Kalu Ghosh, had the donation papers in this regard prepared, and obtained Seeta Devi's thumb impression on that. It is believed that after Seeta Devi sold her one-and-a-half-year-old son, she ran away with her brother-in-law's son. His house is in the Thakurganj area of Bihar. Police from Bhaktinagar and Siliguri police stations began investigations on this day and confirmed the facts. The residents of Damgram said: 'Officers from the police and the administration are coming time and again. They are making enquiries. But no one has the least interest in finding out where the woman has gone. They say animatedly: "If the woman is apprehended and handed over to us, we ourselves can take the necessary action."' Sin cannot be comprehended or detected the way the matter of crime can be. # Is sin something heavenly then? # Not so, there are various kinds of dimensions to crime, and there is punishment, but man does not exactly know whether or not there's punishment for sin. In Mexico and elsewhere, if a woman becomes pregnant, she is thrown out of her job. They have to go regularly to a doctor and obtain a certificate to the effect that they are not pregnant. Almost till the age of fifty or fifty-five, a very indecent and objectionable kind of watch is also maintained by the government to see whether regular menstruation takes place. Again, in some places, on the pretext that there weren't enough women doctors, men themselves gang up to strip women naked and examine them. I had seen through the institution composed of husband, wife, son and daughter a long time ago. I chew my food well so that it can be digested properly. I fall asleep as soon as I shut my eyes, and before sleeping, I take possession of my wife's body. Both mind and body stay healthy. And thanks to that, there's no difficulty at all in applying one's mind to daily chores after waking up in the morning. One feels quite fresh the whole day. When there's a need for any fundamental transformation, I try to find a way to do a patch-up job, and howsoever serious the problem is, I find a piecemeal solution. I hear so much talk of revolution everywhere, but no one talks about a revolution in thinking. Only the odour of burnt diesel is emitted from buses and mini-buses. # Keeps on being emitted. 'Do it then, Babu ... It hurts when I put my finger in ... Tell me how I should lie down...' As each day goes by, the number of development refugees too keeps growing. River dam projects coming up one after another, even the bit of homestead land of the Adivasis of the area is lost to the push of development. Runa laughed and said: 'Don't pretend, my dear ... Poroma wants to see, show her ... If there's no rain even a snake's poison increases ... After all, you saw both of ours ... we are going to see yours now ... if you don't show us, we'll see forcibly...' The son came once in two years to visit his father. He got married in that country itself. A girl from Bangalore. A microbiologist. 'Any kids?' 'None of their own. They have adopted a baby from Kerala.' It was cold. Night had fallen. The stars in the sky lacklustre in the mist. 'Have your daughter and son-in-law separated now? Hadn't heard about that. Not directly, I think.' Who did I set out to burn and who was it that got burnt? I had said that no one should remember me after I die. Or shed any tears of attachment. I don't have the slightest desire to be immortal. And don't suffer unnecessarily. People come. People go. That's the law. Life itself, like one's other life, rests on a big lie. Again, I've also seen the kind of people who place fruits on the tree for birds to eat ... 'When do we see each other again, darling?' I said: 'I'll phone and call you when the time is convenient ... It can only be when my daughter is in school, or when my husband returns late from office ... be a bit patient ... you'll get all you want. There's another public holiday this very month, so one can take a day off after Sunday and ... make arrangements to go somewhere, some place nearby ... I'll talk to my husband and manage it alright...' The subject of a picture by Mary Casatt, a young woman in a theatre watches the stage through opera glasses, and from another row, in the same way, a man watches her. Because of a shortage of beds in the hospital, the eight-year-old girl was being treated even as she lay on the floor. The doctor in charge stated that six stitches had been made to close the wound. But the bleeding continued. The girl had not said a word, she lay on one side and just sobbed. The grandmother seated beside her said: 'We were cutting grass. Suddenly her younger sister came and said – "Didi is covered in blood, it's bleeding profusely from where she pees." I ran there and saw that she had rolled up her frock and pressed it to the mouth of her vagina. The whole garment was dripping with blood.' The underage girl's father, Naseeruddin Sheikh, stated: 'Our younger brother, Jabbar, did this to my eight-year-old girl. Jabbar called my daughter to his house at around ten at night that day on the pretext of watching television. He's my brother, after all, so I didn't stop her. I later heard that a blue film was playing then on the video cassette player. The beastly outrage was done to her as he watched that, and in the name of giving her new clothes.' Later Jabbar Ali came up with a proposal for settling the matter. Jabbar straightaway declared: 'I wanted to close the matter by offering even as much as fifty thousand rupees. Allah has given me two hands. Why did he give them to me? Considering he's my own elder brother, as a final offer, I wanted to transfer ten katthas of paddy land in his name. After all, nowadays such incidents happen frequently. No one makes such a hue and cry. It's true, I was a bit out of control that day, so it's understandable that I struck the wrong target. But Naseeruddin disregarded my offer and suddenly lodged a complaint on the incitement of the party dadas. I have already spoken to the panchayat pradhan. After all, as they say, if you can't get what you want through fair means, then you have to adopt foul ones. Let him do whatever he can. Our women's association investigated every thing and they have submitted a report: "This was an incident of normal bleeding. It happens to all girls. Some a bit earlier, and some a bit later."' In reply to a query, a local bigwig said: 'We don't know anything about all this. It's their personal matter, they will deal with it.' Mrinalini Devi was married on 9 December 1883, at less than ten years of age, to a twenty-two-year-old groom. She was a mother by the time she was twelve. The groom completed his fatherly duty of fathering the first child in 1886, and then in succession, the fifth in 1894. Besides sexual intercourse, did he, Gurudev Rabindranath Thakur, think about the child-bride's body-health capability, the elixir of dense substance? What do you think, Babu – will that little girl too be able to do it ... Of course, she'll be able to ... by that age, a lot has been learnt ... Winding the end of the dupatta around the finger, and then freeing it. A load of oil in her hair. Tied tightly in a ponytail. A hair band on that. There's no need to worry about uninviting lips, divert the man's attention with a bit of outward artifice, prop up your breasts in such a way that your boyfriend's eyes are glued to your nipples. So that he thinks the two of them wink at his manhood from time to time. You have thick eyebrows, with which you can convey a lot of things that can't be said, you have two slanting eyes, entice your boyfriend to plant his lips there and kiss you gently. Keep in mind, your biggest weapon is your pair of plump and prominent breasts. If your breasts are not big, there are a thousand means nowadays to make them appear large artificially.

Whenever you are in front of your boyfriend
Draw his eyes off your lips and keep them
Glued to your jutting-out nipples

See, the earth's trembling. Just conceal it a little, reveal a little, hold it up from time to time. Always wear a blouse that reveals three-fourths of the dangerous cleavage, the cut of the blouse should leave the back almost entirely bare, so that, on various pretexts, his hand can stroke all that. Just observe, your boyfriend will become excited, where does he have the time to observe your thin lips! 'Wait, let me get into position first ... fold your legs ... you mustn't cry at all' # 'What are you doing, I'm telling you I'll get up' # 'Look if I don't do it like this, it'll slip out ... Being the first time it will be a little ... Here, put your arms around my neck ... hold me properly ... don't let go ... You'll feel pleasure very soon ... Then you'll feel as if the whole world is trembling wildly...' A storm blows over the universe ... Their house was near the top of the Madankuri mountain ... the intoxicating fragrance of polash blossoms in the month of Choitro ... The horizon used to be tinged with crimson ... 'God, what'll I do with so much meat and rotis' ... 'You'll need it for sure, you'll feel hungry then...' 'My parents would be informed that I've been invited to Sulagna's house. I've informed Sulagna too. After all, you finish quickly. At most an hour and a half. We'll be bored after that. No one will mind if I return home by nine at night.' The gape of the mouth of some girls is big, this is a flaw of the lips. In such cases, first apply foundation on the excessive part of the lip to make the mouth look small, and then apply lipstick with a lip liner. A big gape, with the tongue lolling out, looks terribly ominous, men don't like all that. However, by enticing and cajoling him, if you can just get him aroused, they won't have the time to look at whether it's a big gape or a small gape, so long as they can get a hole, whether small or big, a black hole, a dark pit. I visited a renowned specialist in Kolkata after having a bad pain in my lower abdomen. He examined me and told me that I had pelvic inflammatory disease. Besides, there was also a tumour. After conducting some tests at first, he operated on me. I was on saline drip for a week. I had been told earlier that normal food would be provided after the operation. I was surprised when that didn't happen. Later, I found out that I did not have a tumour. The operation had been done in error. And as a result of that, it was like trying to remove a postage stamp from an envelope. The rectum had torn. But there was no cause for worry, this could always happen, and as long as the saline drip continued, the wound would gradually heal. I told the doctor: 'Some blackish substance is continuously being discharged from my vagina.' He said: 'Don't worry about it, all that will come out for a few days.' He prescribed a strong dose of antibiotics and advised rest. Going to the toilet after two days, I saw faeces being discharged from both the rectum and the vagina. I was taken to a nursing home in that condition, and after examining me, the doctor said: 'You have a recto-vaginal fistula.' He prescribed medicines, and giving me an instrument looking like a large pair of scissors, he said: 'You must use this, with cotton wool, to clean the stool from the vagina, and then apply betadine lotion.' As soon as I asked whether I could be admitted in his nursing home, he said: 'That's not at all necessary. It's not such a serious matter. Such things can always happen. Everything can be done at home.' That afternoon, my elder daughter did in fact do whatever the doctor had advised. But because she couldn't bear the stench, she returned to her in-laws' house that very evening on the pretext of having left her husband and family behind. I was dejected. At nine at night, as soon as I tried to stand up, shit began dropping. The bed was covered in shit. I was taken to the doctor once again. I was then in a half-dead state. The doctor performed a colostomy operation; he fixed me up so that the stool could collect in a pouch. Now he said: 'After two or three months, once the recto-vaginal fistula is cut and repaired, a new operation has to be performed for transverse colostomy repair.' The gentleman paused for a few moments and then he asked: 'Do you believe in planchette?' 'Planchette! I can't say I believe in something which I haven't seen with my own eyes.' 'But Arthur Conan Doyle, Rabindranath and several more sages not only believed in planchette, they were also active in propagating it. What's called research. But planchette is not what you think.' Considering everything, it seems man has accepted this condition of his ... has accepted it altogether. Why would you use only lipstick to make your lips entrancing, you have a great weapon, lip gloss, the ultimate weapon, the Brahmastra, to vanquish all men. If you can use it appropriately, your boyfriend will be floored. Keep in mind that as far as a gorgeous look is concerned, lip gloss is incomparable. If you have to go to the nightclub, only a lip gloss can give you the perfect look. Nothing but the tiny brush of the lip gloss can really make your lips a work of art, so that the lips never look unbecoming. Once you do the lip-colouring course, you will never want to gloss all of your lips. The trick is that the gloss must be applied to the centre of the upper lip, the middle of the lower lip and the two corners, so as to highlight them. The man will definitely be in your control. From time to time, he will want to pull you towards a dark corner. Sulagna laughed and said: 'But I have boyfriends there, they suck me regularly. And how can I tell you what else they do!

I can't tell you in words what a pleasure it is ... Of course, all that is my personal affair. Can't talk about that anywhere and everywhere.' On account of being associated with the Pulse Polio programme, I had the opportunity to visit border villages too in West Bengal. In my experience, I have seen that, in appearance and bearing, the ones who create the most hindrances were a class of bigwigs of the minority community. The children of any house would be hidden away in a neighbour's cattle shed and they would say: 'There are no children at all in our house.' After making enquiries, when we peeped into the cattle shed next door, we were then told to come after an hour as the children were playing hide-and-seek. We went after an hour: 'Come after some time, they have just gone to the pond to bathe.' Not to be deterred, when we went to the house after a while, we were told: 'Why did you come so late? All the children have just left together for their aunt's house.' In this way, our game of hide-and-seek too continued. Finally, a kind of leader-type emerged, exasperated: 'You don't provide the midday meal to the children when they go to the madrasa, and you come now to give polio drops! Go and tell the government, no, we shall not give our infants this poisonous medicine. The children are certain to become hijras when they grow up if they have it, there's no way they will be able to continue the family line.' After almost an hour of trying to explain and convince, finally, when we were leaving dejectedly without success, stones began raining down on us from the direction of the mango orchard. Swarms of stones came flying towards us from the branches of the trees. One person was hit on the shoulder, another on the waist. And one landed right in the middle of Sandhya-di's head. Sandhya Bauri had come to give polio drops and had fallen, her head split open. After some jerking movements, the body became stiff, the eyes became still, and yellowish brain matter and blackish blood began to gush out from the split-open head. Nonetheless, I put my fingers in repeatedly and made it a bit wider. I put three fingers in together. There was a decorative clay mango on the almirah, exactly like a real mango. Red and blue cranes of glass. Looks very beautiful in the sunlight. Select a lipstick according to your complexion and remember a few important things. There are four kinds of complexion. Whitish, wheatish, pinkish and yellowish. If you have a whitish complexion, any lipstick of a red shade goes well. But those possessing this complexion should never think that the fair colour comprises ninety per cent of your beauty. A lot of *secret treatment* is required. Bear in mind that, with this complexion, beauty expresses itself only a little. And in such cases, if the lips are not made up carefully, you'll look *flat-faced*. Coming to the wheatish complexion, light brown, peach colour, maroon, or a new colour from mixing pink and red may be applied. In case of a pinkish complexion, the lipstick should be of any of the various shades of pink, or just light pink. Besides, purple shades can also be used. For a fair yellow and yellowish complexion, if peach or golden lipstick is applied, your colour will express itself more, you'll easily be able to catch a man. Various methods of seducing men are available nowadays, all very secret things, call us on 24017717 and contact us. For a nominal fee.

Besides we can also provide you chemicals to mend cracks.

Men can also call, almost eight dozen kinds of lipsticks for you are available now. Besides, there's always special aromatherapy. You're sure to catch girls. Money returned in case of failure. Keep in mind, it's not pretty looks or stormy passion, men are today won over by slender waists. The sex appeal of a slender waist is absolutely unfailing. A tiny tattoo near the exposed navel, a broad and silver-coloured belt – that's today's fashion. Cowboy belts too are the rage. Let the wave of solicitation begin from just below the navel. So that the panty inside, at the border of visibility and invisibility, sends a thrilling signal. Keep in mind Britney Spears, Madonna, Shakira and Alisha Chinai – all of them wear their jeans half an inch above their sex. Curves. Sets the whole world atremble. So why shouldn't you be able to do it? Be brave, advance with a steadfast gaze. Arko-da hugged me close and kissed me, he fondled me. Running his hand over the pad, he told me: 'Serves you right, you can't eat bananas for three days and three nights.' The two of us laughed. Arko-da did not let go of me. I too didn't want to move away from him. How nicely he was fondling me. When we thought tea must be ready, the two of us came out of the room. A country liquor distillery located at Indrapuri Studio. A queue there from early in the morning. Crowds of people in places. People lurching over one another as they talked. Exactly then, the stranger arrives. He looks this way and that. In a muted tone he asks Pronami: 'Where is he?' Pronami points towards Devdas. Devdas is stone drunk. The stranger goes near and says: 'There's something I wanted to talk to you about. Please conceal yourself!' Devdas asks annoyedly, 'Why?' The stranger asks in whispers: 'Did you go yesterday to the border with the jeep?' Devdas waves his hand and says, 'I don't know anything.' The stranger says, 'A tourist was taking pictures from your jeep. A girl. I want to know where she is.' Devdas says: 'What the hell – so many people come and go every day. Who will I keep track of?' The stranger now holds out a hundred-rupee note. Devdas promptly puts it into his pocket and looks this way and that. After that, he whispers: 'A beautiful girl was sitting on the side seat of the jeep. Quite young, she was wearing tight jeans. She was clicking away with her camera. If you laid eyes on her, you wouldn't be able to take them away from her. That's it, only so much for one hundred rupees. No more than that. For the rest, be prepared and come to Eve's bar. I'll be there around ten at night.' 'He proposed straightaway. But he's not a bad person. He asks for it from time to time. He's willing to pay whatever amount I ask for...' 'That's what everyone says, find out how much he'll pay.' 'He gave me his phone number too. But I'm afraid...' 'What's there to be afraid of, girl, take advantage of the opportunity. Come, let's phone him.' 'Will that be proper?' 'Who's telling anyone? Uncle and all will never know ... Come, give me the number. Here, speak...' 'Hello, is that you, Uncle? This is Reeta speaking ... what you said ... I mean, I'm willing. Yes, not more than that ... A day or two during the week, depending on time and situation ... approximately half an hour. How can I tell you how much you should pay ... after all, you know our situation ... consider everything ... Alright, yes, good, that will be fine ... If you say so, I can come this evening ... yes, yes, I'll come ... Alright, I'm hanging up now...' 'The postures, signs and gestures of women standing in the street are their own personal matter, their fundamental right' – says Sulagna – 'by what right then does the police want to pick them up and take them away from there! Amazing audacity on the part of the police! They'll pick up anyone who they think is a prostitute. And how can they figure out that it's a prostitute? Or is it by observing "postures", "signs" and "gestures"?' John Denver keeps playing, Hea-ven-ly Lu-vv ... I said, 'Keep doing it for as long as you can, but don't come. It tickles me for long...' Both of us were silent for a while. The road became slopey. The rickshaw was bouncing up every now and then. We had come quite a distance from the rail line, yet the sound of a passing train floated by. Seeing his condition, I too couldn't hold on any longer. I said to him: 'Come, be in the sitting position and hurry up and come.' Cracks are visible on the bridge even before the inauguration. 'You're an uncivilized brute, bend down, am I that tall...' The stranger was looking for a brave boy for a special job. He had to go to the border. He had to go there and bring back pictures of mating scenes of the black panther. From as close as possible. 'The male panther's penis should be vividly visible. A middle-aged memsahib has ordered it. She'll pay well.' 'Because it's the first time, it'll be quite painful for a day, after that everything will be fine. And then, it's only pleasure and more pleasure. The same thing happened to me too. Happens to all girls. You turned thirteen last month, after all you know everything. If you can keep the babu aroused, then there won't be any more deprivation in the family.' 'As if boys need to be snared! Take you, for instance, did I snare you? You snared yourself!' Saying Bipin-da was calling him, he was forcibly taken away from his house. After that, sand was stuffed in his mouth and his eyes were gouged out with a knife, and finally his testicles were chopped off with a single stroke of a cleaver. As soon as a couple of people were told about the incident, they kept saying: 'This is Bipin Babu's affair, we have nothing to do with it.' 'Yes, dear babu, how much will you pay...' 'Listen, your daughter will stay in the babu's flat, he'll pay, of course, but if the babu can be made happy, you won't be hard up for anything. His wife's dead, but he has pots of money, his only daughter studies in college, she leaves around nine or ten in the morning and only returns in the evening.' 'Listen, do you remember all the things I taught you and showed you in the morning? You must never say "no" to anything. Or else the man will get nasty…' 'He squeezed me so hard three or four times that I got wet…' 'None of the boys in our party are involved in cases of rape, that's the handiwork of the other party. Actually, they are the ones who lie. They commit rape themselves and put the blame on us.' # 'All this talk is not correct, the character of every member of our party is as clear as pure water – scrutinize all their résumés – no one has a record of being involved in rape ever since they were born' # 'Actually, they are terribly cunning, and faction ridden, and so internal feuds keep happening. There are a number of groups within the party. There are fights, internally, and rapes, and then they turn around and lay the blame on us.' The sun gently spread its rays over the Gourishankar range. One scene after another, from the blood-red snow-covered peak, through shades of purple, till it assumes the whiteness of snow, the scene changing at every moment … 'And what about girls? The attractiveness of girls is, after all, all over the body, sometimes here, sometimes there, but that they have something called a mind, have an independent existence, when will we ever think about all that…' Paula said, with great embarrassment: 'Really, Runu-di, you've become very bad … you don't stop short of saying anything at all.' Runu laughed and pinched her cheek, and she said: 'Let me get it done first, I'll tell you everything after that…' After that, giggling loudly, she collapsed on Paula: 'Listen, when older men marry fresh little girls like you, they can't control themselves, and do you know...' In the face of controversy and protest, finally, *Encyclopedia Britannica* was compelled to remove the name of one of the two books on Ramakrishna from their bibliography. The two books were *Kali's Child: The Mystical and the Erotic in the Life and Teachings of Ramakrishna*, by Jeffrey John Kripal, associate professor in the Department of Comparative Religion at the University of Pennsylvania; and, *Ramakrishna Revisited: A New Biography*, by Narsingha P. Sil, a professor of History in West Oregon University. A criticism had arisen on the grounds that indecent and tasteless opinions had been expressed regarding Ramakrishna's life, philosophy and daily behaviour in these two works of scholarship. The complaint of obscenity was also made. Stating the reasons for deleting references to the book, *Britannica* made a preliminary announcement that, following protests from the Ramakrishna Mission, the Government of India and devotees of Ramakrishna and Swami Vivekananda, references to Narsingha P. Sil's book were being removed. Besides, it was difficult for them to retain in their bibliography the names of any controversial books that directly hurt any beliefs. I went to Santiniketan during the spring festival this year. Indeed an abode of peace. After all, the girls there don't wear noodle-strap tops. But among the shadows, and furtively, everything happens, love play. I've seen a condom too in the hostel bathroom. Paula, her face flushed red with embarrassment, said angrily: 'That's not possible ... you're talking nonsense, Runu-di...' The practice of nailing advertisements to the trunks and branches of trees has come into currency nowadays. Banyan, ashwath, mango, jamun, shirish, krishnachura or sonajhuri trees, the ones that are commonly seen on the streets, are entirely covered with advertisements on tin plates. One does not see any tree on the roadside in the city or in the village which has not been assailed by hammering in iron nails. If the use of plastic and loudspeakers can be banned in mountains and forests, then why can't advertisements nailed to the trunks of trees be banned? 'I'm seventeen years old. I've finished school and entered college. I fall in love whenever I see a girl. I want to have physical relations. I get terribly aroused. My hands itch to do something desperate. I swear on Mother Kali!' Laloo Prasad's party recently purchased one thousand maunds of bamboo. Staffs would be made from the poles of bamboo. An equal quantity of mustard oil has also been purchased to season the staffs in oil. Next Saturday, Laloo's supporters will publicly observe the swing-the-staffs-and-make-them-drink-oil programme with five million staffs. They will observe a day of swinging-the-staff-and-saving-the-nation with these seasoned staffs, they will congregate in the Gandhi Maidan, in Patna, so named in memory of Mahatma Gandhi, they will expose the government in New Delhi. Laloo Prasad has appealed to people across India to make the swing-the-staff-and-save-the-nation programme a success. Have a carrying license for illicit liquor In our patriarchal social system, having forcible sex with women is almost eternal, it's been happening from ancient times. In front of a hall full of people, right in front of the eyes of revered gurus, Draupadi was being stripped naked and all of us remained sitting with our arms folded. That's the Mahabharata. Please, Didi, don't tell aunty about this ... I'll do whatever you say ... I swear on Mother Kali '... Books? What's the use of reading books – books are after all dead knowledge – they've gone out of fashion.' 'I'm a second-year student. I'm head over heels in love with a girl. It was love at first sight. I can't live without her. I let her know about this through a friend. What I like most are her rolling hips, and the huge valley below her navel. And the bit of plateau too. Everything's digitally beautiful. Oh, I could die. But the girl didn't pay any attention. She said straightaway that she does not have time for love. What shall I do?' Descending the staircase, I saw that the lights had come on everywhere. Dim lights meant unhindered romance. Illuminated trees, illuminated leaves, illuminated branches, illuminated birds. Bits of light were circling the very sky. It was as if, nowadays, there was light flashing every now and then. Never in my life have I seen such awful use of light. And henceforth, even if one wants to get away from all this light and suchlike, one can't. After all, there are portable lights too now. You can carry the light wherever you like, however you like. Soon after, Kajli says: 'It's best to be safe, let me go and close the door.' Aunty became angry and said: 'I'll give you a tight slap ...' John Denver plays on the cassette ... Love Song ... Paula was restless: 'Let me go, just let me go. Not a moment longer. If you don't let me go, I'll really scream now.' Devika Rani, of *Achhut Kanya*, flies away holding the hand of the Russian sculptor, Roerich. Kamala says once again: 'Poroma loves the press of your elbows and hands, she told me the other day. And that you apparently fondled Moumita's thigh and made her panty wet.' A wet face. The fragrance of glycerine soap. Aunty said: 'What are you ashamed of?' # 'If you get angry...' # Aunty said impatiently: 'My dear – I won't be angry ... won't tell anyone either ... so tell me now...' 'A match for Kamala has been found. The boy's not bad looking. But a bit squint in the left eye.'

Middle Aunty said: 'Oh my, don't you know, when boys are like that, it's called Goddess Lakshmi's squint. Extremely lucky.' 'He's graduated in engineering and just joined a private firm. Gets money under the table too. His father's demands are a bit excessive.' As I was walking, I saw Poroma Didimoni standing right in front of the entrance of the market. I went near her on my bike. 'Inu-da, I'm scared of the dark...' 'Come, let's go and sit in that empty auto-rickshaw...' Lowering her head in embarrassment, Poroma said: 'After all, you'll get everything tomorrow ... you can't hold on today, isn't it?' 'Then give it to me ... *Ghabrao mat ... hoga, sab hoga ... Abhi Poroma Didimoni ki baari hai...*' With the doors on all sides closed, a confined area was created. Take a look, ivory-coloured foundation has been applied on the model Bubu Sinha's square face. Her cheeks have been shaded with tan beige. After that, a layer of ivory compact. Soft-pink eyeshadow on the eyelids and on the edges of the eyes, a special kind of homemade kohl. It would be good to do a course with some kohl specialist, they will teach you all this very well. Now, draw a faint line of the cake eyeliner all along the eyelids. Apply black mascara. A touch of dark pink and brown blusher in the region under the cheekbones. Smear soft pink-cream lipstick all over your lips. A thousand varieties of this shade are available in shops, and you have to select one very carefully, considering what kinds of shadow are available at any point of time. The slightest mistake and the whole objective is defeated, your boyfriend won't be dying to kiss you. Always remember, if you have a square face, never keep your hair tied tight, and make your face up in such a way that your jawline is concealed. Look at yourself now, there's a whole new dimension to your appearance, your lover wants to touch you, wants to do plenty of other things. As soon as the hand descended, Poroma said: 'You're an uncivilized brute ... Does anyone do all this in an auto!' Perhaps Kamala was annoyed, she said: 'No, I won't give you ... Don't be a brute, I tell you ... My dear, you'll get it in Digha tomorrow, won't you...' When the fever persists, I change the antibiotic. 'I'm dying to kiss you ... There's only the two of us here, inside this auto ... I'm going to kiss you...' If it takes so much time for the movement of commodities, the magnitude of the transaction loss is most worrying ... 'Inu-da, please ... no more ... Who knows who might see us ... Please keep your word ... I'll let you do everything tomorrow ... Ple-ase...' In the middle of a conflict, always, so many more other conflicts lie in wait ... An auto going towards the riverside. 'Why don't you come at night?' The same path every day. Yet every day it is a new one. There's nothing allotted besides this path, on this path is the expedition to the Antarctic, and on this very path, the journey with Kalpana Chawla, leaving behind current space and journeying to another space. A young woman has to protect herself very skillfully every day in a crowded bus. But the path of her peregrination outside this skill is her own, even if it's via a rod. India drowns in the crashing light on the fair-skinned, smooth back visible between the gaps in the straps of Madhuri's breast cloth: *Didi tera dewar diwana*

Won't go with wares
To this marketplace of love

The girl was young. Her mother too worked as a maidservant. She knows how to light the gas stove. She knows that if she can catch the babu's younger son's eye, she can earn a bit of extra money. How did she learn to handle fire at such an early age? Returning from the water tap, Nayan asked: 'Aunty, why did Budo-da come so late at night? You had got back from his place just in the evening.' Without getting annoyed in any way, Aunty replied: 'Do you know, he wants you.' 'What do you mean, "wants me"?' 'Wants you means wants you. As if you don't understand anything! Why do you pretend? At your age, I was already carrying Ponchu. And here are you lot, flying around in frocks!' 'Eight hours, that's only talk, but we have to work for ten to twelve hours every day. The contractor keeps us off for one or two days in the week, if young women workers can catch his eye, they get work seven days a week, it's thirty to thirty-five rupees a day. There are also some who are paid as little as twenty rupees. But they make us sign for a hundred rupees. By way of recreation, furtively drinking country liquor. It's not been decided who these brick-kiln folk will vote for.' 'Why not?' A leader-like person provided the answer. He said: 'The contractor has not yet told us whom to vote for.' Nayan asked: 'What?' Aunty smiled, and she said: 'There'll be no one at home tomorrow. He wanted you for breakfast.' Nayan acted a bit coy: 'What does breakfast mean, Aunty?' 'You don't know what breakfast is. He'll fondle you and so on for a little while! Lay hands on you. But going too far is forbidden. I've explained it all to him, down to the last detail. Hear me, all you women, be careful when you do something. And just what do you lose? If a boy of his age touches you, your body won't get wasted. You'll get ten or twenty rupees right away. Besides, won't you be able to skillfully extract a soap today, a shampoo tomorrow, and a churidar-kameez the day after tomorrow? Does anyone let go of such an opportunity nowadays!' Harried by the nuisance caused by the growing number of cats, the Writers' Building will see the initiation of a cat-catching programme on Friday. Cruelty to animals is illegal. The cats shall remain in the Writers' Building. However, they will be caught and caged. Why this programme against cats? Well fed from eating leftovers of fish and meat, by the time office hours start, these cats begin stalking through the office chambers. They roam unhindered through the gaps and niches between tables and chairs. As soon as they spot an empty chair, they jump on to it, shut their eyes and sleep peacefully. It has been observed that their numbers are not so negligible. Vexed at this situation, last year, Writers' Building undertook a similar major cat-catching programme. But only about a hundred cats were caught then. However, the correct figure could not be ascertained. Their ears were pierced so that they could be identified, if necessary, and then they were released. All the cats could not be caught during this major programme because many jumped up to the window parapets and set off towards safe places, they seemed to have sensed danger in advance. Some were absolute kittens. On the logic that the enemy ought not to be eliminated, they too were caught and caged. The current programme will be even more comprehensive, it is unlikely to be completed in a single day. Last year, lots of people had left their work and gathered to watch the cat-catching. The corridors of Writers' Building were packed with crowds. Journalists too had come running when they got the news. This time, the slogan 'Do it Now' has been issued, addressed to the government employees. It is hoped that, this time, people will not leave their work and run to watch the cat-catching. If you are middle-class, then bear in mind that your days are over. Either ascend to the upper class, or else descend to the lower class and sink.

Hurt me, broke me
Proved you're Bengali

Close to men and women's coupling, loads of nature and grasshoppers. The people of golden lustre sit with yellow roses in their hands, men and women, even the illumination of light is meagre. The body keeps getting liquified until it almost assumes a symbolic character, from time to time it symbolizes just the boastfulness of life. Just the melancholy. Something more than symbolic suggestion. Shireen Jeejeebhoy, a research scholar, writes of her own experience: 'In India's border regions, there are also villages where, by the time girls are ten years old, they are married off and the newly married girls there don't really know anything about sexual life and relations, and its leading to pregnancy. They view the coming of an offspring in the womb as an entirely miraculous event, dependent upon God.' Fearing social boycott, Raju's mother bunks her part-time maidservant's duties, and she goes with a flag in hand to add to the crowd in the public meeting. She had been called to the party office and told that if she did not attend the public meeting, she would not be allowed to live in the neighbourhood, her ration card would be confiscated, she would be socially boycotted, etcetera, etcetera.

A fierce battle
Between two lovers
Regarding the heroine

Me? I'm only a player in the defeated team. Sometimes I think there's decay accumulated in my blood, it keeps accumulating, a self-instituted death oblation. A winding path over the Bhitarshila mountain. Towards the interior, even more interior, because *she walks in beauty*. And right then, the little girl gestures with her hand and sings for her baby brother, the old canary steps out of the cage and then returns again. It had then lifted its foot to take the last step. The second foot was still outside, suspended. She had wrapped something like a dupatta around her shoulders, looped around her neck. Amidst innumerable people, disregarding the groping of lustful hands, not paying any attention to creatures and commodification, the foremost woman prepares a piece of land to stand on. In the course of using the red-brown bag like a shield, she then found an entire rod. So what if the rod was long, slippery-smooth, but it was still a rod, a prop. The soles of her feet were getting wet with perspiration. Now she feels she is indeed foremost. Because, perhaps a person meets, or could meet, another person only once in a lifetime. Only visuals are born then, that keeps happening, one after another, unseparated. # 27 February 2002. Godhra-Gujarat-India # According to the government, eight hundred and twenty-two dead # Number of houses set on fire, ten thousand two hundred and four # Burnt shops ten thousand, four hundred and twenty-nine # Houses looted, one thousand two hundred and seventy-eight # Only visuals are born. Through the entrancing blue light, Paro keeps running, and through the whole hall, 'Devdas', 'Devdas' echoes – which man doesn't want the same for himself too, a listless, eager, wide-eyed maiden coming running like that. If it isn't her one battles for, then for whom does one do that? And then, one after another, doors come flying to the front. Light enters, light is extinguished. I go on stroking with my hand. # There's no opportunity to gaze in any direction #

A reader's opinion
Who read the text in manuscript form

Is this a story at all? The piece ends and yet it's not clear what exactly the problem is. The characters remain static in their own situations. The link between one character and another, between one incident and another, seemed to me to be extremely artificial. Can the present generation be won over with all the sexuality one wishes? It's difficult. I can't see any objective on the part of the author other than performing a stunt act ... *Ab tera kya hoga, Kaliya.*

EVentUally HOpeful

The whiteness of paper causes the amplification of light

Om Tat Sat

(A lot of the information in the text has been taken from *Beauty: A Comparative Analysis,* [Ed.] Kaul & Krishnan. And lots of information and reports have also been obtained from *No Paradise Yet: The World's Women Face the New Century*, [Ed.] Judith Mirsky and Marty Radlett. I turned news reports in English into Bangla, and in a couple of instances, I directly used the Bangla text too. Twisting, wrenching and mixing everything into one, taking information out of news reports, in my own way, wringing them, that is to say, the way Godard had taught.)

[Nikot Probishto Somporkeo Dharonkhomota, 2003]

Madankatkati – Crunchy-Crispy Passion

A team of cricket illiterates from Champaner suddenly learnt the game and defeated adept rivals.

There's nothing to be shy about, it's only between you and me

There you go again with your rubbish early in the morning ... no! It's better not to, besides, I can't sin

It's not a bad idea if a husband and wife jointly run an enterprise, do you understand ... no one ever has too much money ... good food, fine jewellery ... every girl wishes for that, doesn't she ... look Maya, I'm simply telling you the truth, if you go around the neighbourhood, you'll realize ... there'll definitely be a case or two

I don't know, dear, I don't go around the neighbourhood, so how would I know

A lot of people do all this, I know it, those who're the quiet types are the ones who're most cunning ... alright, don't men gape at you, tell me my dearest

Of course they gape, and how they gape

Do you know, a bhadralok lives in our neighbourhood, I've heard he's a military man, he isn't married either, he's tall and stocky in appearance, you'd be scared looking at him, I'm acquainted with a relative of his, the man's sent messages through him several times

Right ... when I went past his house last month, he had called out to me, oh baba, I got so scared ... the gentleman lives all alone in a rented flat

Eesh, does anyone squander such a wonderful opportunity, be a bit clever, Maya, people starve to death unless they're clever, tell me, why did you run away, you could have heard him out, heard what he has to say, what he wants to say

Peeping through the hole, I saw they were exchanging fire with the police

As if I don't know, he'll ask me to sleep with him, what else would a man have to say

You made a terrible mistake, Maya, you could have spent half an hour or an hour with him, he wouldn't do it just like that, it would definitely have been for money, any other girl would have simply

Alright, please tell me the truth, are you trying to test me

Not at all, there's nothing to test, I'm telling you the plain truth, if ten out of ten girls in society are bad, how long will you stay good, perhaps inwardly you want me to stop you, but that's what leads to turmoil, if you have your husband in hand, then there's nothing whatsoever to worry about

I got that, let's say I bring someone home, where'll you be

Why, don't we have two rooms, I'll be in one and the two of you'll be in the other one, just get rid of your inhibitions and then everyone'll be happy

What do you mean everyone'll be happy

The historic crematorium in Nimtala will be beautified to resemble the Gandhi Ghat in Delhi

You're right Maya, that's not correct, however wealthy women might be, if they don't get proper satisfaction down below

Whatever you might say, since you want to hear it, I'll talk, all these years of being married to you was quite alright, but now I feel there's nothing inside, my darling

So tell me that I'm lying

Look, if you're willing

But I've already told you

As long as you don't create any domestic turmoil about this, there's no need to get the military man, there are so many rich guys here, the half-old man in the provisions store devours me with his eyes, if I just give him a hint … besides, that contractor fellow has a lot of cash

The senior students had stripped him naked and poured hot liquid wax in his anus

How much will he pay … that's the problem … nowadays you can get girls on the streets, men don't want to spend much, but if you've got what it takes and can appraise the situation and strike accordingly, then, if not five hundred, he'll definitely give two hundred

Let's see how it goes, but I know there'll be no shortage of men for me

If you can squeeze out money

Just you watch, now that you've put me into the business, I'll conduct myself accordingly ... get up now and start cooking, let me go to the market

Alright, go ... I have evening duty ... tell me, how will I know

Why, when you see the door bolted from within you'll know someone's in there, the food'll be kept in the other room, eat quietly and spread out the floor mat

Alright

I warn you, don't try to peep or anything, the man who spends money and comes for satisfaction mustn't be annoyed

Binodini ascends from the waters of the Ganga and comes directly towards Bihari

Hello Boudi, it's been a long time, do tell me what you need

I need a lot of things, but where'll I get the money

What do you want to say, Boudi, please tell me frankly ... if it's money you need

We're needy folk, if we don't need it then tell me who does

How much do you need, tell me

I'll do that, but how will I repay you

Pay me when you can

Why don't you come to our house at night, nowadays my husband has night duty, we can chat for a while, I'm all alone and don't have anyone to talk to

You say

I'll tell you then how much I need

I too wanted

Do come, I'll make you forget all your sorrows

Really, Boudi

A deaf-mute girl was stripped naked and branded on her genitals with a red-hot skewer on the accusation of stealing a bulb

Do come from time to time, no one will mind

But your husband

He won't say anything

The neighbours ... the neighbourhood

Makes no difference whether they're there or not, it's just a half-domestic neighbourhood, in fact people come in the afternoon to the house next door

Amazing, I didn't know about that

So much happens inside the basti houses, do outsiders know about all that

Alright then, but I hope I won't end up getting thrashed

Oh no, my husband and I will take care of that, but I need five hundred

Immediately after word of the murder got around, the incensed mob began to damage and vandalize the neighbouring locality

You're asking too much, Boudi, if it's about two hundred that'll be okay

Not two hundred, make it three hundred, once a week, four times a month, at the same rate

You're very clever

Did I ask for too much

It's alright, but I can't pay you now, come at night and take it, when I'm closing the office

Alright, when will you come ... I wonder when the old man from the provisions store will come

The language of love was the language of his protest

Uncle, when will you come

After I close the shop

Alright

Will there be something then ... I can't spend the whole night, at most till eleven at night

Okay, I'll cook and keep food ready

Oh no, there's no need to cook, there'll be a commotion at home if I eat outside, I can't stay away at night, can't eat outside

When you come, how'll you recognize my house

I know it well, I've been observing it for a long time

I hope you can remember it

The leader of the People's War Group has been arrested in the jungles of Goaltor

Dada, could you please give me a couple of things quickly

What's the hurry, you've come after a long time ... hey, you rascal, get a nice cup of tea, tell him to make it a special one, tell me, what do you need

Oh, I need lots of things but I can't get the things I need, like oil and soap

Is that all, chhee-chhee, when I'm there

No, no

I'll give you the whole month's provisions, later, when you have the money

Oh, how can that be, where'll I get such a lot of money all at once, I know you'll give the stuff, but unless one repays on time, does anyone give anything, tell me

I like you, that's why

Exhibiting the male body is the latest fad now

I like you too, Uncle

But the matter of liking is of a different kind, I'm sure you understand, I won't let you lack for anything

I know

When I'm with you, all deprivation will fly away

But all this is sinful, besides I'm scared, I've not thought about the husband aspect, and there are neighbours and the neighbourhood

Don't talk about neighbours, as if neighbours matter in such neighbourhoods, if you're without food would anyone come to feed you … listen, do something, go home, I'll send all the stuff in a rickshaw, my shop's closed tomorrow

Alright, but do think about my situation

Patriarchy does not depend merely on the individual bearing the father's name, it creeps into every possible level of the man–woman relationship, at home and outside

What's up, how far have you gone with the cooking ... what's in the pan ... oh, only some vegetables ... listen, please cut this fish

I can't cut such a big fish, why didn't you have it cut

We've got to eat, haven't we

Why did you get such a big fish, won't we need oil

You don't have to worry about all that, how much oil do you require, make some tea first, a rickshaw full of stuff is on its way ... now that you've given your consent, just you see what I do, and how ... look at these two crisp hundred-rupee notes, and there's a rickshaw full of goods, that's from the provision store

How will you pay back so much money

Don't I have the capital ... why aren't you cutting the fish ... the contractor won't stay the whole night today, only till ten, and tomorrow's the old man from the provisions store, each one comes once a week, you can keep watch if necessary ... we don't need anything more ... can you go outside and look, I think I can hear the rickshaw horn

A woman phones the fire brigade in the middle of the night: there's a fire in my heart, please come and douse it

Yes, my dear Maya, a rickshaw full of goods

Go, go and get the stuff ... bring it carefully

As if I ever create any trouble

No one looked at them, everyone arrived happy and content

Baba! Where'll I keep so much rice and daal

Put everything under the cot, I'll arrange everything tomorrow morning ... did you pay the rickshaw now

He didn't accept it

Why's that

Look Maya, the receipt is for four hundred and twenty rupees ... really Maya, in just a single day you've managed to organize this

Henceforth, you just keep quiet ... arrange all the things properly ... quite a good amount in cash, and then there's the regular liaison

But that would mean a lot of hardship

You idiot, the hardship won't be every day, just for a day, and then everything becomes familiar ... here's the cut fish

The kidnapped businessman returned after the payment of a huge ransom

Those who appreciate a fine body know how to pay the price

Try to arrange the things on the shelf if you can, instead of talking ... let me fry the pieces of fish, and then I'll make the gravy, just enough for the two of us

Here, take a look, is it done

It's okay, but there's more stuff in the bag

There's so much stuff here, every kind of spice, he's sent all the household requirements

Go and have your bath, won't you go to work

Let it be, I think I won't go today

What on earth do you think, you'll eat and go to work like everyone else, you're not going to live off the money earned by your wife, I'm telling you, you have to go to work every day, bear in mind, I can get along even if you're not there ... taste it and see

What can I say, have I learnt cooking

Learn to cook too, those who'll spend the whole night with me will extract full value for their money

Howrah's starving workers now want to take revenge through the ballot

They pay for the quality they see

How's the fish, do you like the gravy

The taste of fresh fish is something else altogether, I'm eating a big fish after a very long time

Baba! My stomach's really full, when you return from work today, remember to buy condoms, the last packet is still there ... who knows what diseases people have, got to be careful

Alright, baba, one burden's gone, let me get the cycle ... so I'm off, but do be careful

Yes, my dear, go now

Then Rohini Hattangadi looks for and picks up a stone, and meditating on Shiva, begins to perform puja

Hello, Boudi, I'm sure you were waiting for me

Yes, do come in, sit in this room, let me shut the door, it's a small room, no cot or anything, you won't be very comfortable, Uncle

I will be, for sure I will be, keep this relationship in good shape, and why only a cot, you'll get so many things ... do you know Maya, when a son comes of age it's very dangerous ... I can't sleep with your boudi any more, but of course your boudi has no more sex ... where are you, come to me

I want to sit on your lap

Come, let's do that ... if you sit you'll understand

I don't allow that, if they're squeezed too hard they'll begin to sag ... yes, like that, use your hand

Maya, can you ever forget me

I'll try, Uncle, we can chat later, but finish the business first

I don't have the patience to sit any more, fold your legs

On Children's Day, we vow that we will not let children be deprived of the full development of all their inner capabilities – Department of Women & Child Development, Government of India

No, don't do that ... where's it, put it in ... why do you delay, how much longer, Uncle

I don't know

Why're you acting like a teenager

Don't I get aroused

Take it, will it run away this time too, not like that

Believe me, Maya

What

No great damage was done by that, why are you getting up, lie down beside me for some more time

A time-bomb has been placed on the rail line in order to blow up the Rajdhani Express

Where do I keep it

You don't have to get up, who's stopping you

Would you like to eat fried fish

Is there any

Baba, why wouldn't there be any, the taste of fresh fish is something else altogether, do you get that, let me make tea, fried fish and tea

You're stupid, fried fish goes well with booze ... I drink now and then

But the taste of fresh fish is something else altogether

No, not today, next week, around nine, the shop's closed on that day, you see I have to keep up the home front as well as the external front

Whatever you wish

In Burdwan, a sick child was given another child's injection

Hey my dear, this is the first time I've earned, but if you don't like to see that

I'm all aflutter inside, you know, I feel at peace, you know what you want

So what if there's some hardship, there's greater happiness besides the hardship

That's what it'll be, Maya, I hope your wishes are fulfilled

How many more days before next week

It won't do to be so crazy ... hey, it's ten-thirty, tell me what I should bring for you

Will you make a list and give it in the market, after all, you've already given all the stuff from the provisions store

I have to get up now ... stuff to do at home ... this door's open

Oh baba, at least he didn't enter the room ... don't be standing at the door, who knows who'll

I'll see you around

Yes

You ... you'll live long, I thought you were sleeping inside

What on earth ... no one came

But you said he'd stay all night, I'm sure you lied

No, my dear, not a lie, you see he has a grown-up son at home, it's not possible for him to stay all night, he left just fifteen minutes ago ... here, take off your shirt and trousers, I'm terribly hungry, have a wash while I serve the rice

Globalization and patriarchy – it's because of this nexus that in the forthcoming World Social Forum of 2004, one of the ten key subjects for discussion is patriarchy

How many times

At first twice in succession, and then once more before leaving

Is that all

Just the three times made me forget my dad's name … what're you doing … has the strength of an ogre, hey, please massage my body, just see how it's swollen from squeezing

Baba, it's really swollen … will I get something

You'll get it, my dear, but massage my body first

You just carry on, Maya, just carry on, there's nothing to fear, if required I'll opt for the night shift, I'll do all the household chores as soon as I wake up in the morning

That you have to do, my dear, I'm earning now, look here, it's in my interest to give peace to those who come, isn't it, they'll give me baksheesh

That must be extracted

If you're at home, I'll be panicky … fear in the mind

Alright, as soon as I can I'll take the night shift

A complaint was made against a promoter for deploying hijras to evict a tenant

What happened, why did you get up

I have no clue about what you did when

You're lying

You're terribly naughty, hey, I'm sleepy now, let me go to sleep, when you wake up in the morning, wash the cooking utensils, sweep the rooms, make tea and then wake me up

Alright, let me sleep now

The ballot papers were torn in the booth itself and the box was dumped in the water

Hey, Maya, wake up, it's nine, don't you want tea

What time is it

It's nine

Nine ... have you done all the work, have you filled water ... where's the tea, give it to me, I'll lie down in bed and have tea, I can't get up before I have tea ... do you know, I slept so well, my whole body feels light ... light the stove, I'll have a bath and then cook today, God, what an ache, dear

Is it bad ... listen, it'll relieve you if I give you a hot compress

The seven-year-old girl, Rinku, searches among the ashes of the burnt hut for her textbook

It'll be great if I can get some

You'll get it, but go to the toilet now, you've been farting away all this while, take your bath and come out

I've lit the stove, let me sweep the other room

We should get some good mosquito nets, pillows and quilts now

There's money in hand, so we can buy it

Do you think I'll buy it with my money, are you out of your mind, it's the people who come who soil our bed linen, and it's they who'll buy it

Hey, can you hear me, where are you, please give me the towel, what a lovely fragrance the soap has, what soap is this dear, what's it called ... this is the way, Maya, as long as you're young, just grab it

Come out, let me take a bath ... I have to sleep a while after eating

Nowadays, in private parties, women openly hire male dancers and make them strip naked

Boudi, are you at home

Who is it

It's me

Oh, it's you, it's so dark outside, what time is it, just wait, the light's not turned on, how on earth did I sleep so long, it's seven, if you hadn't called me ... come, come in, believe me, it's terrible, I've never slept so long

Is that so, what did you dream about

A lot of stuff, please sit down, let me just go to the washroom, God, I badly need to pee

A boy died leaping from the roof, imitating Spiderman

Would you like to have some tea

Yes please make it ... hey, silly girl, I have a family too, I know all that's needed in a family, just maintain the relationship with me and you'll never know deprivation ... listen, your nightie's in the cloth bag

Here's the tea, but there aren't any biscuits

Take it out and see

Alright, I'll wear it and come

Why, wear it in front of me

Okay ... it's nice ... do you like it

Hearing about the death due to a wrong injection, the superintendent said – But he would have died anyway

Not in this room, come to the other room … I've prepared everything for today

Whatever you wish, take me wherever you want … oh, such a lovely room, absolutely secluded … is your husband alright

Yes of course, why shouldn't he be alright … I say, weren't you supposed to come at nine o' clock

I just came along

Whatever you think's right … so where shall I sit, on your lap

That's right … you're even younger than my daughter

Look here, love doesn't heed age

Buchanan and company won't allow Sourav to recover from his injury

I'm struck by the enchantment of your face

Oh baba, what have I sat on dear

How on earth did your husband manage to get you

I don't know … maybe it's so … where's your thing

Right … let me look at you

You can't make out the colour in this light

A manly woman has been arrested for posing as a man and marrying an eighteen-year-old girl

So you've snared me

What do you mean

There's nothing to fear, there may be a little bit of hardship … hey take a look, I hope there's no piss anywhere, I don't like it

I've put on some scent for that reason, go ahead, don't worry

I won't hurt you

Not like that

In today's world, dreaming of surviving as a gay person is a purely personal matter

So that's what makes the guys happy, they get pleasure when they inflict pain

But there's no other worry, you stay this way and you won't ever have to worry about difficulties

Go to sleep now … what happened, do you feel like it

Can you take a risk regarding whatever concerns your home

I'll give you more

There's no point giving you unnecessary trouble … lift up your head and look, gaze at me, keep gazing

Take my love, don't get lost

What are you saying, Maya, my head will go in

Try to put your head in and see … I'm not lying

What does that mean?

It means nothing

It seemed a baby was being delivered

[Madankotkoti, 2003]

Lenin's Lenin, Notwithstanding Syphilis

(The bus isn't going to start just because you bang its sides)

> Two brainless eyes on a fine body. Red and blue angular lights on one side, and on the other side a sexual angle on camera. The heroine is having to get wet, take her clothes off, smear artificial excitement on her body and do everything possible, as much as possible, with the hero. Or else the audience won't lap it up. The film has to be a box office hit. Because of the global market and competition. And Lenin is a commodity, a very exorbitant commodity, in this World Trade Centre.

It was a stormy year, a rainstorm straddled
The entire country. The clouds were scattered,
And the storm descended upon us, followed by hail and lightning.
The wounds lay gaping in farms and villages following repeated attacks.
Lightning began flashing and the flashes turned violent and mad.
The heat burned ruthlessly, lungs suffocated.
And the light from the fire lit up
The silent darkness of the starless night.
All of creation and humanity at large were devastated

An eerie anxiety beset everyone's hearts
Breasts began to pant in agony
All the dry mouths were closed tightly shut.
The cold breath of dew descended. The leaves turned colourless and dropped
Whirling around in a dance of death as they stuck in the breeze
Autumn arrived, in dusty alleys came autumn
Drenched in rain's tears, submerged in black slime
Life became hateful to humanity,
Life and death – were both equally unbearable to them.
Anger and pain scraped and ate them up endlessly.
Their hearts turned cold, empty and melancholy like their houses.
And then suddenly there was spring. Spring right in the middle of the rotten autumn.

Just after crossing the bend, the garland of tales kept flowing speedily on both sides. A steep red hill rose up like a wall from the road. With bushes and shrubs. The river lay far below, windows of coloured glass, stones embedded in the walls, and marble floors. One could still see the frame of a foreign car from Lenin's time in the garden turned jungle. The sound of dew falling. Time stood still, past-future-imagination-reality all mixed up and becoming one. In front was the quarry lake of Handikhola, brimming with water, and the forest smells of the Tadoba Andhari reserve. Only herbivores came to lick the salt at odd times. New silt bars on the banks of the river. Almost becoming part of the land. Scanty shrubs in some places, cultivated land in others. Patches of castor oil plants, gum trees and thorny shrubs here and there in the cultivated land. Some of them had rickety huts covered with grass used by farmers to guard their crops at night. Winter had just started making its presence felt. The shoots of wheat had just sprouted from the soil. This was the time when wild boar, seasonal wild boar, came at night. They pranced around the farms, eating some of the crop but destroying most of it. The farmers stayed awake all night to chase them away. Guarding their crops. They brought quilts and pillows when it was bitterly cold in January. They burnt bunches of dry hay to keep themselves warm. The old men still smoked hookahs in this region and coughed while doing so. The youth of course smoked bidis and cigarettes, the bidis stuffed with marijuana. There was a walking path at the entrance of the village. It joined the gravelled road in the distance. It was gravel only in name, because apart from a red hue there wasn't a single piece of gravel in the road. The road had become indistinct, but it could still be recognized. The encrusted mud from the wheels of bullock carts lined both sides of the road. Monty encountered Kusumi as soon as he arrived at the road in the morning: 'Hey, I'd asked you to come yesterday, so why didn't you?' He stood on one side, avoiding the slime. 'Have you got a new fuckmate? I sat the whole afternoon holding my dick, looking out through the window.' 'No Kaku, it's nothing like that.' Kusumi stopped in her tracks, a trifle afraid. 'I got caught up with some work and so I couldn't come.' 'Oh, so you've become very arrogant now – getting smarter by the day.' 'No Kaku, it's not that, I swear on my Ma, it's something else.' 'Let's hear that, what is it?' Monty asked. 'I'll tell you later … I'm already late today … If I don't start cooking on time, the mistress will get late for school … she'll give me a mouthful. Let me go now.' Saying so, Kusumi began to walk away.

Monty instantly caught her elbow and threatened her in a muted voice: 'Be sure to come! In the afternoon ... like before ... I'll keep the door open.' 'Alright.' Kusumi walked away briskly into the lane with the ship-like building. Guarding crop fields in this way had been going on for generations. These weren't ordinary boars, they were of a different pedigree, with different wiles. Very shrewd. Some called them boar-ghosts. They walked past humans so silently that their hooves didn't make the slightest sound in the silent darkness. When they heard the bubbling sound of the farmers smoking their hookahs, they blended into the shadows on the fence and waited silently. Then when the night became darker, they cautiously jumped over the fence and entered the farms. They could be heard crunching and chomping as they ate the crop. When they were chased after that, they ran like horses and jumped over the fence. If they were in danger of getting caught, they bared their teeth and bit their chasers. So many people had been bitten by boars. These boars chomped bones and flesh with their teeth. They could eat up an entire human. Leaving only a few bones in the desolate fields. Belonging to protesting humans. Catching these boars wasn't at all easy. No one ever tried to catch them on their own. When a farmer heard the sound of crops being eaten, he rushed out of his hut and alerted his neighbour: 'The boars have come, O sons of farmers – take care of your lives and honour – beware, beware!' Pishi came and said: 'Hey Monty, what do you do all night that you need to sleep till ten in the morning. I finished making luchi-begunbhaja for you long back. It's all gone cold. Get up and have your tiffin.' A bottle of pickle had been placed on a mat in the sun in the veranda. A few freshly prepared boris on one side. Still wet. Some large, and also some flower-boris.

Across the courtyard, a tulsi shrub on its brick pedestal. He got up and stretched himself. He hadn't been able to see anything properly till he arrived late at night. His body was still aching from the bus ride. There was a clump of marigold flowers next to the ashsheora wattle fence. Large yellow marigold flowers. On the other side was the patch of purple-coloured bonkolmi water-spinach in bloom. Juicy gourds were coming to fruit on the asbestos-sheet roof. After finishing my toilet and freshening up, I sat down for breakfast. Having spent her whole life in towns, Pishi finally came and settled down in this remote forested village. She laid two more luchis on my plate, and then began: 'Have these. I've just fried them. They're hot. This place won't remain remote and forested for long. Hordes of people are coming here. Just step out and you'll see houses coming up in the paddy fields. Electric poles have already been erected. There'll be electricity very soon. But we don't have a concrete roof yet, only asbestos sheets. It's very cold at night.' I had realized that in a single night. The meeting had been convened in the shed in the old community ground of Chongarbonmahatari village. Buildings were gradually being constructed here and there, and farmland was being taken over. There was a patch of elevated fallow land in the middle. With a very old banyan tree. And a brick pedestal. Actually, the main trunk had been devoured long ago by termites and the tree was now propped up by its aerial roots. Beside it, a tiled, eight-roofed hut with a low ceiling, whose unseasoned bamboo poles had withered and were riddled with borer insects. Some of the roof supports had also been infested with borers and were hanging down. The pale borings of the insects were all over the floor. The men sat on one side of the shed and the women on the other. A lantern that was a few centuries old, with a broken glass, hung from a rope in the middle of the room. Many had brought lanterns with them. Those were beside them. The single hanging lantern, patched up, as usually happens, by a sal leaf, swayed slightly in the breeze from time to time. Its light and darkness too swayed over the faces of the people. Food would come towards the end, it was a tea break, and at such a time Gita-di came and shouted, 'Bishu-da.' We had met last night and introduced ourselves. They lived a few houses away, the three sisters – Gita, Mita. The youngest sister, Nita wasn't there then. None of the sisters were married. I was a semi-urban guy, a scoundrel of the first order, so I did scratch myself a little. In the light of day, I saw that she was quite old, a wooden body, but there was a great effort to hide her age that was manifest all over her body. Pishi said: 'Come here, they're eating.' Bishu and I were eating on the veranda. Gita looked at me from the corner of her eye and shifted her gaze: 'Bishuda, why don't the two of you come to our house in the evening, we can go for a stroll. And as she said that, she directed another sly glance at me and went away. It wasn't as if I hadn't got the hint, but I pretended not to understand. I saw Bishu had lowered his face and was smirking to himself. It was the end of October. Winter had just begun to set in for the year. Most farmers had harvested their crops. Even those who had a few plots left to harvest had come to hear the deliberations. Regardless of the kind of matter to be discussed, nowadays people never gathered in such numbers. But the matter today was an entirely new one for this region. Women often got beaten up by their husbands – this had been happening since time immemorial. Some women then sat with their hands and feet helter-skelter and screamed and wept. Some took their youngest child and went off to their fathers' houses for a few days. The neighbours too got together and sat the two sides down and arrived at a reconciliation. That was the traditional custom. The room was just near the entry to the village. Bamboo goal posts had been erected on a large field on the right where football was played. There were bamboo clumps on both sides of the field. The village began a little further away. Tall, thorny bamboos had almost enclosed the room, which was made of brick and cement, with an asbestos-sheet roof. Monty was sitting in the outer room with the door shut. It wasn't easy to figure out that there was someone inside. Kusumi arrived in the silent afternoon. The door of the room wasn't bolted. After casting a cautious eye towards the road, she quickly slipped inside and hurriedly bolted the door. A cigarette in his right hand, and his left hand inside his lungi scratching his groin, Monty said loudly: 'Why are you so late?' 'What can I do, I had to say at home that I was going to meet the seamstress Didi, and so I had to spend some time talking with her before coming here so as not to get caught. We have to think of everything, how will you understand our troubles!' Kusumi looked meaningfully at Monty's hand while speaking. So far, no woman had ever demanded to know why she should be beaten in this way – what right the husband had to beat her – and sought justice. Some folks were saying that the woman had been put up to it, especially by Chinu Aunty. Some were whispering among themselves that actually the woman wasn't a good sort. Lame Gure was hardly ever at home. It was a poor family. He had to go far away in search of work. A tall man would then come at night. He would knock on the door like a thief. And now, incited by others, the woman was trying to frame Gurupada. Be that as it may, Kusumi had not made any complaint herself. Chinu Aunty had been going around complaining on her behalf. And a few wayward boys from the youth association were saying that if someone was at fault then it had to be deliberated upon. Why had someone raised his hands against a woman for no reason? But this complaint angered the menfolk. They were completely unwilling to accept that a wife could openly complain against her husband in the village council meeting. It was evening by the time we had finished our lunch. I was getting ready to go out after resting a bit, when Bishu said: 'You go, I need to go to irrigate the rice field.' He smiled slyly and slipped off along the path by the pond that headed towards the rice fields. I had then treaded very slowly and just gone past the palm trees and reached the house when I saw the slut standing there, dolled up like a babe, in a Madhuri Dixit pose. The receding tide of age on her body. At this age, girls who failed to get married became desperate. Simulating a most girlish voice full of gaiety, she said: 'I've been waiting for so long. Everyone at home has gone to a feast today, but it's always better to be careful, come to the other side.' There were only a series of gardens in the direction she pointed towards. I was surprised, she hadn't enquired even once about why Bishu hadn't come. The people were seated in a haphazard manner. On one side, with his head inclined, was the village leader, Naren Pallye, smoking his bubbling hookah. Everyone in these parts knew him. He was reputed for always saying the right things. His decisions were accepted without much ado in the panchayat meetings too. So much had changed in the villages and the country, but he had not given up his habit of smoking the hookah. He didn't get the same satisfaction from smoking bidis and cigarettes. He was now stoking the fire in the clay bowl of the hookah from time to time. An elderly man with a head of crewcut white hair, white eyebrows – that bore the stamp of many years and much experience. The skin on his cheeks hung down with age. He wore a very old shawl from his grandfather's times, with its worn out zari-worked border flashing from time to time in the light of the lantern. Monty puffed deeply on his cigarette a few times, and then crushing the stub under his slipper, he said: 'You seem to have become too clever. So why does your mistress suspect you?' 'I don't know, but she has a very suspicious nature. If she sees me talking and smiling with some boy, I've had it. She scolds me no end. The way she interrogates her husband!' 'So you could have told her.' 'Yes, and lose my cooking job, that's all! Come now, do whatever's to be done quickly. The mistress's husband is supposed to return today. He'll come in the evening. I have to go and knead the flour dough, make parotas and crisp-fried potatoes ... He likes that very much.' 'Wait girl, you've found time after so many days ... you can't talk of going as soon as you arrive. Do you think all the soap, scent and powder I buy you every now and then are for free? Won't I claim my dues? You will have to repay with interest. I want to do the business at a leisurely pace today. Is it any fun otherwise?'

The forces of darkness were hidden in the shadows,
They were sliding on their chests in the dust and hissing, they were lying in wait.
Suddenly they sank their teeth and knives
Into the backs and legs of the bravehearts.
A serpent gaze was at the ready in the darkness.
Ghastly murders, communal oppression and unleashing of slander

Are proclaimed as love of the nation,
The gang of black ghosts celebrate
In unrestrained derision,
They are smeared with the blood of their known and unknown prey –
Those who fell prey to vengeance,
Those who for no reason were mercilessly
Killed in the treacherous attack

The land was slightly sloping, secluded by shrubs and bushes, nothing could be seen from afar. We went and sat under a big jackfruit tree. After I sat down, she sat down brushing against my body. I got the hint. I wear a bhadralok mask, so how would this lot be able to vie with me in roguery. She had seated herself so close to me that if I didn't engage in some banter she'd feel uncomfortable, she'd feel ashamed. I knew from experience that in such matters it is men who must take the lead. I was thinking about how to start when Gita raised her head and looked around and then shamelessly placed her right hand on my pajama. I didn't hold myself back after that. I can match you at every step and do one better. I'm not going to be seduced by you so easily. This is how it's been since time immemorial. Today everyone had teamed up to catch the boars. Red bandanas around their heads and blue gamchhas around their waists. When they reached the edge of the field, they halted a bit. They cast a glance at the juicy ears of paddy on the farmlands, and then in small groups of five or six, they jumped into the field. They were determined to catch the boars today. Wild boars. A hazy moonlight covered the tranquil green fields. Dew had started falling. There was no dreamy haze in the eyes of the men any more. Set chins and fiery eyes. They descended. It was as if they were getting lost in the darkness. Quite some time elapsed in silence. And then there was a huge uproar across the fields. The crashing sound of fences breaking from all around, the sound of darting through shrubs. The blue, pink, black and white boars leaped wildly in the dreamy moonlight. They didn't look like boars at all then. Only the beating and the thuds. Accompanied by people shouting. All in all, a grand celebration of boar hunting across the fields. I looked her straight in the eye and asked innocently: 'When did you have your periods?' She was embarrassed at first, she seemed a bit bashful. She couldn't imagine that in such a desolate setting a young man could ask a young woman such a dirty question in such a straightforward manner. She had expected a nice romantic dialogue about love. Instead of that, what kind of a question was this! Since I had decided to be a libertine, there was no point in being ashamed. I descended into hard reality again: 'Tell me when you had it.' Trying to be smart, Gita-di now said in a dry voice: 'I don't remember, probably eighteen or nineteen days ago.' As if imparting wisdom, I said in a serious tone: 'From sixteen to seventeen days after the periods to about three to four days before the next period, even if girls go up and down ten or twenty times a day there's no possibility of getting pregnant. A totally safe period.' I thought she smiled fleetingly. Or was I the one who had made a mistake! Touching her, I realized that if any bastard married her, the fucker would be a terrible loser. Everything seemed to have vanished from her body, as if by magic. Next to the village leader sat the panchayat member Nitai Gantait. His house was just behind the field. He had sharp eyes and a thick, fancy moustache over his lips. Wearing a half-sleeve shirt over trousers, he was kneeling down, intent on breaking a boil on his feet, and from time to time, he raised his head to gauge the character of the gathering. He didn't smoke bidis or cigarettes, he knew all that caused cancer. He was keen on buying a Hero Honda motorcycle soon. There were a few other village leaders nearby – Lakhiram Kuiri, Sekendar Ali and Tilak Mahato. On the right, sitting pressed together in a crowd, were the common toiling folk, some with only a piece of cloth around their bodies, others wearing soiled vests. One or two people with very old, faded khadi shawls too. A few new, coloured shawls were also visible in the crowd. I got up from the bed and stretched myself. Pishi had served me tea and puffed rice. The biscuits had finished. The shop was a little distance away, so it couldn't be fetched right away. Bishu and I were eating, I asked him, 'Can't we get date-palm juice here?' 'Yes, we can ... But not today ... I'll get some for you tomorrow ... Tastes like nectar. Right now, the other juice is available ... Toddy ... Want some?' I said, 'I don't have a distaste for anything. Do you get moonshine?' We were conversing when a thirteen- or fourteen-year-old girl arrived, and after glancing at me, she turned towards Bishu. 'My sister's calling you, she asked you to hurry.' I gathered that this was the youngest sister, meaning Nita. I was a bit surprised. Yesterday evening the eldest sister had invited me, and today it was the middle sister. So let's see which way the water flows. After all, I wasn't exactly inexperienced, I had fucked many girls of that age in the arse. 'There, there they go! Catch them! Throw the lasso, man, throw it!' What kind of boars were these, they were tearing through the lassos in an instant and jumping over the fences and escaping. Easily crossing through deep ponds. 'Hit them with lathis on their legs, bring them down to the ground, make sure they can't get up. Cover the right side, that's where the bastards run away from.' The voices of the men running through the field chasing the herd of boars could be heard. Various kinds of opinions. Some boars were caught, in ones and twos. The moon had floated to the middle of the sky. The shadows of trees and shrubs lengthened. Awakened by the sudden commotion, birds left their trees and flew to other perches. The boars that were caught were dragged to one spot. They lay on the earth with their four feet tied. How colourful they were. Pink, blue, green and white. While some of them were of amazing mixed colours. It was difficult to pinpoint clearly. As they lay on the ground, they continuously tried to break the ropes binding them in an attempt to run away. After the men, the women sat down at a little distance from them. They were wearing ordinary clothes, most of them had ghomtas drawn over their faces. One of them was an elderly woman – with the bright line of sindoor on the parting of her hair visible through the gap of her broad-bordered ghomta – she had white shell bangles on her hands. Behind her were the relatively younger women. Some of them wore cheap saris in deep colours with their arms covered with coloured glass bangles. The rustling sound of the movement of the young women was blending with the clinking of their bangles. A crowd of small boys and girls was standing around the meeting place. They were all from the village. They hadn't been able to sit because they were kids. They were standing in a circle and watching the proceedings. Even in this cold, some of them didn't have anything to wear on their bodies. Of course, some had come with their fathers' shawls wound around them, which hung down to their ankles. Many had wound their mothers' old saris around themselves, hung with a knot at the neck. As Monty opened her frock, he said:

'Do you know, Kusumi, your body's simply growing by the day ... It's not safe to wear just a frock any more. If the boys at the roak get their hands on you, they'll eat you alive.' 'Why don't you buy me a salwar-kameez, Kaku ... And who was it that made me so – you! The other day, Kakima almost caught me!' Kusumi burst out in fake anger. Monty laughed. 'Just admit that you get restless and itchy if you don't get rammed.' Monty kept fondling her. 'What a body you have, the very sight makes my dick lose control.' Kusumi put her hand under the bed and brought out a packet of condoms. 'That's also your doing, Kaku. If you arouse me like this...'

In drunken stupor, their fists clenched and mouthing swear words
The gang of scums holding vodka bottles
Ran like a pack of animals
With the money of treachery rustling in their pockets,
They were dancing the dance of bandits.
The gloomy laughter of owls in the darkness of night
Raises echoes as it proclaims
The death of happiness and freedom,
A cruel winter brings an icy storm
From the kingdom of eternal ice
And covers the continent
With a shroud of thick white snow.
Here and there, the small black church spires
Of the dreary villages buried in the snow
Are visible like muddy black slime.
Hunger accompanied by devastation and sunless winter,
Have dug themselves deep in all the polluted homes.
Across the endless snowy fields
And the endless and immeasurable steppes –

Where the burning winds of summer bring fiery heat –
The evil icy gusts come and go like white vultures.
Those gusts of snow that tear bonds growl and whistle,
As their immense talons endlessly hurl snow with countless fists.
They sing the hymns of death
As they did in centuries gone by.
The storm roars like a hairy wild animal,
Pouncing on anyone with even an iota of life,
And flies like a terrifying giant snake with flapping wings
To wipe out all signs of life from the earth.

As Monty fondled her, he changed the subject. 'So your mistress's husband ... what's his name ... the one who corners you at every opportunity – is his one better or mine?' Kusumi laughed inwardly thinking of the comparison! The mistress's husband gifted money and other things without letting the mistress know ... And besides, there was a sizeable baksheesh every month ... Whenever she asked for ten or twenty rupees on some pretext or the other, she got it ... Of course, he recovered all that at once, with interest ... and he looked like a wild elephant. Full of power and stamina. Nevertheless, so as not to make Monty angry, she cleverly said: 'No, how can he match you! He becomes tired very soon ... after all, he's getting old.' Monty was pleased to hear such praise and thought of himself as a fucker par excellence. A plump man from the crowd shouted out: 'Come on, Dada, start the meeting. It's getting late. A wayward youth from the other side retorted: 'Where's it late, it's just the beginning of the apocalyptic evening.' 'Yes, yes, here...' – the leader, Naren Pallye, gave his hookah to an old man nearby, coughed once or twice and cleared his throat: 'Everybody's here, isn't it – so let's begin. Hey Kusumi – please stand up, dear – tell us what's your complaint.' I got acquainted with Nita in the course of visiting their house. She studied in a school in the village itself, in Class 8. The teachers were very bad. They failed her in every class and made her repeat. They were simply unwilling to give her pass marks. I had no difficulty in figuring out that even at this young age, the girl had matured considerably. She said that she had to go to the video hall in the adjacent hamlet at least once a week. Or else she couldn't digest her food. When I asked her name, she turned flippant and said, 'Find out from my sister.' Bishu said: 'Is Pintu your brother-in-law that you're not telling him your name?' She laughed and said, 'That could well be. After all, our families are known to each other.' I was surprised at how far their imagination had gone in the space of two days. Perhaps village girls can do all that too. Their house was on the other side of a pond, a few tiled roofs, some thatch roofs too, and a cowshed. There was a barn on the right over a filled-up pond. The village ambience was still to be found here. Asking Bishu and me to sit, Nita went in search of her middle sister. My jaw dropped as soon as Mita entered. I hadn't seen her properly at night, the eldest sister was after all a dry piece of wood but this one was a stunner. She seemed to be oozing juice out of her whole body. I was just an ordinary chap, even sages would have ejaculated seeing her figure. I was floored. Bishu smiled slyly and then he gave a silly excuse and left. 'You sit and talk. I have some work to do.' Kusumi was sitting behind Chinu Aunty, resting her chin on her folded knees and looking down. Nineteen- or twenty-years-old, dark-skinned, but with a pretty face. You would think she was younger if you weren't told. Seeing her, you wouldn't think that she was a mother of two. Two sharp eyes on her plump face, hassled looks – a head of unkempt dry hair – the line of vermilion was lost in that – a closer look revealed inflamed welts on the sides of her temples. Despite not liking it, she veiled her face when she stepped out, the scoundrel Gurupada had told her many times after their marriage, 'Keep yourself veiled always when you're in front of babus, that's the custom here. Their gaze isn't decent, they eat women up with their eyes.' She had got a job of washing dishes and clothes in the panchayat pradhan's house, but Gurupada hadn't consented. Thinking of all this, Kusumi had veiled her face today as well, who knows, someone might object otherwise. She would do whatever Adari Boudi had tutored her about before coming to the meeting, she wouldn't open her mouth regardless of what others asked, she would merely sit with her head bowed. Let's see whether the danger recedes or not. On hearing the leader's call, she raised her right hand to pull her veil down some more and kept sitting with her face down. Thinking that she would get up, the leader was silent for a while, and then he again said in a calm voice: 'Kusumi get up, tell us what's your complaint.' The boars too had realized the danger today. They weren't entering the crop fields. They stood quietly in the shadows of the trees and shrubs. Only when the men reached close to them did they run helter-skelter. All the men had long lassos today. As soon as they spied a boar, they flung the lassos around their heads. The more the boars ran, the more the lassos tightened around their necks. As the noose tightened, they were forced to come to a halt. The other men immediately came running, shouting, 'Kill, kill the bastard sons of boars, every day you come and eat our sprouting paddy, if you've had your way for ten days, then today belongs to us farmers.' They beat the boars with lathis and brought them down to the ground, but it wasn't so easy to tame such boars. It turned into a battleground. As time went by, the men became more and more violent. With hair awry on their heads, red bandanas around their foreheads, lathis held aloft in their hands, the angry men tramped around the fields, caught the boars and beat them. Beat them up and caught the boars. Seeing me gaping at her like a bokachoda, Mita laughed. 'What are you staring at like that ... you cad!' And as soon as she said that, she stuck her tongue out, affecting shame. 'Oh no, I addressed you with a tone of familiarity. I hope you don't mind?' I thought, why should I mind, you slut, just seeing you has driven me crazy. I said: 'It's alright, it's no great calamity to address someone you like with familiarity.' 'How did you know I like you?' 'If you didn't like me, you wouldn't have asked me to come urgently like this!' Nita served tea and biscuits while we were talking. Some large-size coconut sweets on a steel plate, and water in a brass tumbler. 'Have the tea first, brother-in-law, or else it'll get cold, and have the other things after that.' Nita left the room, smiling and swaying her hips, she was a ripe plum even at this young age. I wasn't very surprised at their behaviour, but I hadn't expected things to move so fast. Feigning innocence, I asked: 'Who's the girl?' 'Oh dear, you haven't been introduced yet ... She's my younger sister Nita.' 'She referred to me as her brother-in-law. I hope you didn't mind.' I had deliberately provoked her. Mita showed no signs of shyness. 'If you don't mind anything, then I too won't.' At one spot, a multicoloured boar had been lassoed. But men couldn't vie with the power of these boars. The youth holding the lasso had fallen to the ground, but he didn't let go of the rope. He was holding on to the rope with all his strength, the boar was running and the youth was being dragged along the ground behind it. His lungi had come undone and got stuck in a large clump of thorny wild jujube. That was also being dragged along. 'Help! Help! I'll be killed!'– screamed the youth as he was being dragged along. But before people could come to his aid, the boar jumped through the gap between two wood apple trees. The youth somehow managed to get his body stuck against the roots of the trees. I didn't know whether to be happy or to display anger. The eldest sister was drying up by the day and this slut was overflowing with it. I said: 'Shall I say something, Mita?' She wasn't surprised at all, and just smiled and said: 'How did you know my name?' A suitable dialogue from Bengali films came to my lips: 'It doesn't take long to find out the name of someone you like.' She smiled even more: 'You're a great conversationalist!' I smirked inwardly, if I didn't speak well, how would I net a babe like you! I'm just waiting to lay my hands on you. I said: 'I liked you the moment I saw you, darling.' But the girl was very clever, she wasn't going to be wooed so easily. This girl was definitely going to get an explicit commitment from me, she said: 'In what way do you like me, is it just liking or is there love as well?' The way the conversation was progressing, it looked like I'd be able to get down to business just now. The slut was already wooed. She just wanted me to say it out loud. Kusumi's body seemed to move a bit at the call, but she didn't get up. She pulled the veil a little more, and lowered her face a little more, and kept sitting. Everyone was waiting eagerly to hear her speak. Seeing that she had failed to get up despite two calls, everyone turned to look at her. The leader called her once again: 'Kusumi…' Suddenly

Chinu Aunty rose from beside and stood concealing her. A middle-aged widow, she used to work as a nurse in the district hospital earlier, and now she was allegedly inciting the younger women to form a women's committee. She knitted her brows and looked around, and then said in a shrill voice: 'What will that young woman say amidst this gathering of men! This will also be a matter for discussion later. The whole village will be agog. Ask that man what he has done.' She said that and went one step ahead and in the image of a woman warrior shouted at the scoundrel, Gurupada: 'Bastard – murderer – first tie his hands behind him – we'll deliberate after that.' My hands were desperate. I started. 'I love you' – I said it in the way it ought to be said in such situations, in that lover-like tone, and kissed her lightly. She didn't resist the least bit. My hand moved in. It was partially inside her panty in search of the cleft of her buttocks. I was thinking whether to go further or not, but my hesitation wasn't leaving me. There was probably no one there in the house other than the younger sister. Maybe she had called me over like this because of that. Anyway, I didn't stop my handiwork. I realised that she was gradually getting aroused. She was writhing and moaning: 'I can't wait any more, give me peace, darling. I won't survive without you. Love me more, pull me close.' I thought, what the hell, she's carrying on like a bitch in heat. She seemed to have learnt her dialogues well from watching films. I don't deny that I'm a scoundrel. But this girl has gone way past me. She's even fallen in love. And mouthing love dialogues in the heat of passion.

The storm bends the trees, mows down the forest,

Piling up mountains of snow.
The animals have fled to their caves,
The paths have vanished, no sign of wayfarers.
The skeletal famished wolves come running,
Roaming at the tail of the storm,
Maddened, they violently snatch at the prey,
Raising their snouts to the moon they howl,
And all that is alive trembles in fear.
The owl smiles, wild monkeys clap.
Drunk black monsters whirl in a vortex
And their greedy jaws growl:
They have smelled killings,
They await the bloody signs
Everything is covered with ice; death is everywhere, all of creation is frozen cold.
As if there's no trace of any life,
As if the whole world is the pit of a grave.
There's no sign of free and enlightened life.
But the fruit of this flower has taken refuge in Mother Earth.
The bowels of the mother have that amazing spark
It has kept itself alive, away from sight, wrapped in mystery
The soil will nourish it, it will receive heat under the soil,
After that it will be born once again in a new life.

Not being able to restrain my excitement, I took her to the bed. Mita quickly began to undo her salwar when Nita pushed the door and entered the room. Seeing our situation, she stuck out her tongue and covered her eyes with her hands. But actually, she took in everything through the cracks between the fingers. She put on a peculiar act and laughed, 'Hey Didi, you got down to business with brother-in-law on the very first day – I'm going, close the door properly from inside.' She went away swinging her hips. Wow – who was hitting on whom! Will all three sisters queue up or what! So what if she was such a small girl, I can vouch that if I lay my hands on her, she'll definitely not say anything, rather she'll be happy. I saw that Mita jumped up and bolted the door. After that she started undoing her salwar quickly. It seemed as if she wasn't prepared to waste a single second. The boar was tugging shrubs along jerkily and running. The abrasion of the coiled rope had bruised the hip of the youth with a deep wound. Four or five people came running and lifted him up. Blood flowed from his bruised elbows. Gurupada pressed his hands on the wound. But the blood would not stop. 'Lift him carefully. We'll have to take him to Jatin doctor.' Another man said: 'Wait, man, wait. Don't shout. Our farmer bodies don't yield so easily. Tear a handful of durva grass and bring it here.' Three or four people ran and brought some fresh grass. He chewed the grass, spat it out with saliva, and applied all of that on the bruised elbow. After that, looking this way and that, he asked, 'Does anyone have a rag?' Someone said, 'Tear the lungi he's wearing.' 'That won't do, it's completely soaked with slime.' 'Okay, wait, I'll give it to you,' said Haru Thakur and tore a piece from the gamchha on his shoulder. He then tightly bandaged the elbow. I then told Bishu everything. Including the fact that Mita had mysteriously asked me to visit again at night. Bishu was astounded. 'What have you done! You've arrived in this remote rural area and you've already hooked up with two women!' 'The elder sister couldn't get married – but after all, age doesn't wait – she's become desperate. She's latching on to whoever she finds. The middle one too is a shrewd customer, she's got down to finding a husband on her own. But can one get a groom without dowry in these rural parts? Their parents aren't around either, so there's no one to search on their behalf. And the brother is in deep waters supporting his own family. I feel pity for them these days.' Bishu promised to help me too once he heard everything. Everyone was astounded by Chinu Aunty's sudden burst of shouting. The whole assembly of people gazed blankly. But Chinu Aunty didn't sit down. She stood with her head held high as before. The panchayat member, Nitai, had been intent on breaking the boil on his foot ever since the meeting began. Seeing the state of the meeting, he slowly stood up. He cleared his throat and said: 'Be quiet now for a while, Aunty. Let's understand the matter. Let the complainant speak in front of everybody.' I went to bed early after dinner. But I just couldn't fall asleep. Mita's figure kept floating before my eyes. When would I get my hands on the babe? Stroking it with my hand, I said, 'Sweetie, be quiet now, I'll grease you tonight.' Eleven o'clock rang on the wall clock. That was dead of night in these rural areas. Nothing stirred, not a sound anywhere. A jackal seemed to cry out in the distant bamboo clump. Jackals were still around in the country! I gently opened the door bolt and stepped out. I could hear bats flapping their wings. A sharp chirping sound. A large-canopied tamarind tree lay in front. That's probably where the sound was coming from. Once his face was fanned, the youth slowly returned to his senses. Gurupada brought him to a clean place and laid him there. He said: 'Thakur, you sit with him. Let me go and see what's happening over there. The boars are dangerous after all.' Haru Thakur immediately said: 'Yes, go. I'm very tired. I can't run in the fields any more.' Saying so, he sat down next to the youth. He had really become tired. His eyes were sunken and the shawl on his shoulder was caked with mud. One of the men joked as he went by: 'Thakur, where are your rubber slippers?' 'Oh my slippers! I left them under a tree in the pandemonium to catch the boars.' Some of them entered the field once again. They wanted to catch a few more boars while it was dark. Once the morning star rose, they would go back to their respective homes. Because boars had to be caught in the dead of night. 'Why? Will it be a great calamity if she doesn't speak?' Chinu Aunty said in her rasping voice, cutting Nitai short. 'How many times must a helpless young woman have to relate her ordeal! She's already said what she had to say. Why did this owl-faced devil of a scoundrel beat her up? You people have to give her justice. After all, he has to feed and clothe the wife he married. Or else she has to make her own arrangements. What will the two kids eat?' 'Ahh – Aunty, stop, stop – let me speak.' The seriousness of his tone shocked Aunty. Nitai Gantait said: 'He certainly beat her up. But why? What happened? No one beats up anyone for no reason. Something must have happened.'

Authoritarian rule,
Nationalism,
Obscurantism,
Have irrefutably proven their characteristics,
They have killed us, killed us, killed us in the name of these,
They have sucked the very bone marrow of the farmers,
They have broken their teeth,
They have chained people and buried them in jails,
They have looted, they have murdered...
According to the law, for our well-being,
For the glory of the Tsar, for the honour of the empire.
Oh soldiers, drown your sorrows
In a glass of vodka!

Oh bravehearts, shoot at women and children!
Kill your brothers as much as possible,
So that your Godfather can be happy!
And if your own father is shot down
Then let him drown in his own blood,
In the blood spilled – by 'Cain'!
Drink the Tsar's liquor and become an animal
And kill your own mother mercilessly!
What are you afraid of?
Those in front of you aren't Japanese.
They're only your neighbours, your acquaintances,
And they're completely unarmed.
You've been given orders, O servants of the Tsar.
Don't speak! Just execute,
Cut throats, shoot people, crush them under the hooves of your horses.
You'll get medals and crosses as rewards for your dastardly deeds...
But for century after century you'll be cursed, you gang of Judases!
Oh masses, give up your last garments,
Hurry, hurry! Take your clothes off!
Spend your last penny and drink liquor!
Grind yourself into dust and die for the glory of the Tsar!
Become like the draught animals you were, you eternal slaves,
Dry your tears with the edges of your clothes
And bang your heads on the earth!

Monty shook his legs in glee, 'Didn't I tell you to set me up with your next-door girl Juthika, what happened to that?' 'I couldn't speak to her. She doesn't like me speaking to you.

I think she's guessed; she turns her face away from me, she avoids me. If she gets angry when I tell her and complains to my Ma, then I'll be done for.' Monty didn't stop her. 'I got it, you want more money. That's why you aren't making an effort. Tell me how much money you want. But I must get Juthika in exchange for that. Let's see how clever the girl is!' Kusumi said: 'That's not it, Kaku, it's not about money. Actually, I'm afraid of broaching the subject with her. She's a different kind of girl. She wants to study. She's not like us.' 'That's why I want her even more. I've laid quite a few girls of her age! I've seen a lot of saints and virgins. But all of them tilt in one direction. You just introduce me to her properly once. I'll do what I have to after that.' 'What could have happened?' – Auntie shouted once again – 'She's stopped feeding the bastard. If he doesn't get to eat, then this is what he'll do.' 'Ah Aunty, will you stop or not?' Sekendar Ali admonished her in a stentorian voice. Even though he was young, he too was a leader in the village. He was a member of a political party. Waving his hand, he said: 'If you won't let others speak, then why have you called the meeting? Enough is enough, please sit down quietly now. Let Kusumi say what has happened. When a meeting has been convened, she must state her complaint herself. Then we'll hear what Lame Gure has to say. And then we'll decide. That has to happen, or else how can we come to a decision? Both people have to tell us their complaints themselves. We'll hear them both. After all, you can't clap with one hand.' As if it were a matter of fun, a callow youth from the crowd shouted out. 'That's right. Let's hear them both.' At once, the voices of some more people from the sides could be heard. The others nodded their heads in agreement. Meanwhile, Raja's mother went near the young women and started joking while leaning against the tree trunk: 'The men will eat us alive this afternoon. They've spent the whole night chasing boars. They came back and had rice kanji with roasted chillies and are sleeping now. They'll get up from their sleep, and after bathing and eating, they'll take revenge for the night on you. Go home and cook something and feed them. You know the saying, "A sunburnt farmer and a heated coulter. The pen of a usurer and the abuse of a young sex-worker."' Kusumi pretended to be innocent and asked: 'What does a heated coulter mean, Aunty?' 'Do you want to hear? Don't waste time. Go home. Calm your husband first. Keep some rice for me.' 'Of course – who are you to me – I'll feed you well.' Kusumi did a turn with her lip upturned. A middle-aged man looked approvingly at Kusumi doing the turn and nudged his friend's hip: 'Just look at the cow's udders, see how full they are. If you fucking milk them, you'll get a bucketful.' Madan Mistry went to the city every now and then to work as a mason. He winked as he stroked his moustache: 'Spot on. She's very saucy at this age, isn't she?' Then he whispered: 'The husband, Lame Gure, is a complete country bumpkin. A ghost. On the other hand, the wife looks invitingly at all men. She's always standing at the door. It's quite obvious that her body has desires. Will you make a try!' I raised my head and tried to see whether the light from Mita's house was visible or not. Even from a distance, there was a sign of hazy light coming from the crack in one of the windows. So, was the girl lying awake waiting for me? Theirs was an old, two-storeyed mud house. Mita had said in the course of conversation that they were very poor, their parents had passed away. The brother was an ordinary electrician. The three sisters lived on the ground floor. The brother, his wife and two children on the first floor. The jackal seemed to cry out again from afar. I pushed Bishu and saw that he was fast asleep. Here was I, restless with desire and he was snoring peacefully. Let it be, let him sleep. I got down from the bed and tied the lungi tight. Then I shut the door and tiptoed out of the room.

Endless oppression!
Police whips!
Sudden conviction by the tribunal
Like a volley of bullets from a machine gun!
Punishment and the spray of bullets,
The terrifying forest of gallows,
To punish you for your rebellion!
The prisons are full,
Exiles oppressed by endless grief,
The volley of bullets tear the night to shreds.
The vultures have lost their appetite from eating too much.
Pain and sorrow
Have spread over the motherland.
There is not a single family
That is not devastated by loss.
Oh despot, carry on your bloody celebratory feast
With your executioners,
Oh bloodsucker, set your greedy dogs
To tear out and eat the flesh of the masses!
Oh despot, knit a fire!
Drink our blood, you ogre!
And exact your revenge, punish us
Oppress us one last time!

Aunty had been trying to assess the mood of the people all this while. Now she took a step forward, waved her hand and said: 'I agree she was a bit at fault. She's an outgoing girl. But that doesn't mean that she should be beaten up like this. There should be some pity in people's hearts. Just see how she's been beaten up.' And before anyone could realize anything, she turned around and yanked Kusumi's hand to make her stand up in front of everybody. This sudden pull led to the ghomta sliding from Kusumi's head and the anchal of her sari falling away from her bosom – the inflamed welts from the beating on her chubby body were visible in the flickering light of the lantern. The disconcerted Kusumi moved away and sat down on the ground on her haunches. She covered her face with her two hands. Chinu Aunty went on grumbling: 'Regardless of her transgressions, she's a wife. A mother of two. How can she be beaten up like this?' I was scared too. My escapade would turn sour if someone spotted me. People would beat me black and blue, all my womanizing would end. I've heard that rural people are anyway conservative. Whatever's there in my destiny – I prayed to Ma Kali and picked up courage to walk along the pond. A narrow walking path with thorny bushes on both sides. The sky was starless, and the darkness had settled down on all sides. I passed the palm trees and finally arrived near the window. I cleared my throat slowly. Immediately one of the windows opened slightly. I heard a whisper: 'It's open, come inside.' The door opened as I pushed it. As I slid in, a woman's hand bolted the door. After increasing the light in the darkened lantern, she came and stood before me. I almost had a heart attack on seeing her. This was Gita instead of Mita – the elder sister! 'Stop, stop, Aunty – don't shout any more. Quiet! Sit down. Don't say another word!' A few people rushed up to her and forced her to sit down. The sudden turn of events had quietened the whole meeting. Even if it was only for a fleeting moment, some people had seen the inflamed welts on Kusumi's body. After forcing Chinu Aunty to sit, Nitai came back to his own place and shouted at Gurupada: 'Tell me what happened! Why did you beat up your wife like this? Did you witness anything with your own eyes?' Gurupada was seated among the men in one corner, with his head bowed. He remained seated that way, without moving, even after the panchayat member asked him a question. The whole gathering was looking towards him quietly. Nitai shouted even louder: 'Hey Lame Gure, did you hear me – stand up! Tell us what your wife's fault was, that made you beat her up.' I gaped wide-eyed, my head began to spin. She was wearing a bit of a panty and a brassiere. Below her hips were two dark-skinned thighs like the trunks of palm trees. If she held me with those thighs, that would be the end of any sexual urge. My eyes moved away from her thighs for a moment. Oh God! What an immense paunch. And there were folds after folds. My experienced eyes told me that was definitely a tummy that had had an abortion, or else it couldn't be like that. However much she tried to hide her age, she was definitely above forty. Even though she had taken care of her appearance, the creases on her face betrayed her as a hag. A wooden body with a big paunch. Because she had been wearing a nightie the other evening, I couldn't discern anything. Realizing that my mind was elsewhere, she said: 'I've sent Mita and Nita to a friend's house to sleep. So that I can get you alone for myself. I hope you don't mind!' Given her desire, I wouldn't have to do anything, this girl would catch me and rape me. Her eyes and face had turned red with excitement, and she was perspiring. She was breathing heavily. Even through the tight brassiere, it was obvious that her breasts had sagged with age. She was biting her lips frequently. There was a slight brown moustache over the lips, with beads of sweat on it. Gita had, by then, gripped me in her arms and was moaning while caressing me with her right hand: 'This body of mine is only to make you happy, my loved one. I gave my all to you from the moment I set my eyes on you. In the temple of my mind, you are my Lord from today.' What a predicament, the slut had given me her all the moment she saw me. But that was exactly what Mita had also said. Nothing had happened yet, and she said she had given her all to me. What a predicament indeed. All the doors and windows were closed. No longer afraid, I increased the light of the lantern. What if I play another kind of game now? Let me gaze leisurely at her body and whatever happens after that will happen. I couldn't understand what was happening within my head! Was I changing my position, because I could clearly see my hand pulling down her panty with a single tug. Then, a dark-skinned man of about forty with a harried look and a towel over his shoulders stood up from among the men. Short in stature and already looking old. People call him Lame Gure because he limped a bit. From all sides, pairs of eyes turned towards him. Everybody was looking expectantly at him to hear what he had to say, and how he answered the allegations against him. The lantern hanging above was swaying slightly. Gurupada had now stood up and was murmuring something to himself amidst the larger silence. Nobody was able to hear anything, only his lips were moving. Gita was probably dumbstruck by what I was doing. She would be. Instead of doing the real thing, setting aside everything, if a chap was just looking at her private parts, without getting excited, without jumping on her, for that matter, without even touching her – she couldn't imagine that. Becoming alarmed, she began to shake me by my shoulders: 'What's happened to you? What are you doing? What are you looking at like that?' I began looking at her naked body with the same scrutiny that I had exercised as a kid to examine a two-rupee note in order to win a bet by finding some hidden feature. I saw the pee hole just above the opening. The outer lips seemed like the sides of a deep pond, seen in childhood, unfathomably deep, where there were no shores. Red like a lotus in the middle, covered with golden fur. As if an island had woken up in an unknown silt bar, the clitoris. Pulsating with arousal. I kept looking at her. Just looking at her. Similar to the idol of a mother deity. Eyes afire, lips smiling, a beautiful synthesis of the tender and the hard. The path from the gate to the sanctum sanctorum lay outstretched...

Countless people will lose their lives
In an unequal battle!
Nevertheless, let us move forward
Towards the much desired freedom!
Come, let us chase the mice away from their holes!
Onward to battle, oh destitute folk!
Down with the whips and gallows!
The struggle of free humans, break the barriers and emerge.
Oh Liberty, give us
The world and freedom.

> (Lenin's poem has been cut here and there. It has been cut but it has not been distorted, not even the commas and full stops. The poem has been translated by Arun Mitra, from the French. Source: *Swadhinata*, 1947.)

[Syphilis Holeo Lenin Lenin-i, 2004]

The Rippling Waters

At some point, I crossed the limit and entered
The universe. The light of fire was emerging
From the dark constellations now. After this
We would reach the centre of heat.
We were jostling against each other
So wonderfully now, and as we jostled we took birth,
Were born. The birth of life. The steamer was moving along its own path, but it had no maps of its own. Whichever direction it moved in became its watercourse. Small fishing boats were floating nearby as well as far away. In some places, fishermen were fishing with their nets spread out. Sometimes I saw floating houses of thatch. Seeing a house of thatch like that, I asked Ma: 'Where's the house of thatch going along the river to?' Ma said: 'Actually it's a boat carrying thatch. Hay traders are carrying it to the city.' I suddenly spied a small glass door. The entrance door to the steamer was massive, there was no glass on it. For some reason, I ran towards the glass door. Behind me, Ma, Baba and Didi all shouted: 'Where are you running to – wait, wait, don't go there – there's a huge river there.' Paying no heed to anyone, I kept running. As I ran, I saw that on the door it was written: Pilot Cabin. I warily stepped inside. A man was turning a wheel inside. He kept turning it. Once to the left, and then to the right. I went and stood beside him. I

had heard from Didi that steamers were piloted by boatswains. Seeing me, the man gravely turning the wheel said: 'What do you want?' At once I asked him: 'How much further do we have to go?' He ran his hands on his salt-and-pepper beard and spoke: 'Perhaps a bit further. But it may be much further too. After all, there are tides on the river, one has to go over water and that takes time. Come and sit quietly next to me. Look at the water. The mass of water.' Clad in multicoloured jeans and T-shirts, sporting wristbands and chewing paan-masala, they were bursting aloud continuously in Hindi and incorrect English. After talking among themselves for a while, their attention turned towards a sari-clad young woman. She appeared to be a college student. She was standing, holding on somehow to the handrail. Just as she was about to alight at Titagarh station, they sang a couple of lines of a Hindi film song, and then looking directly at her they began discussing the vital statistics of a popular film star. Not satisfied with that either, the three of them feigned falling from the jostling of the crowd and pressed down on the girl from three sides. One of them from behind, while another openly reached out and fell upon the girl's breast. The other passengers in that crowded compartment were busy with themselves. Some people turned to look out of the window and gazed at the scenery outside, while some pretended to be counting the holding-straps hanging from the ceiling. I know the girl, I see her getting aboard the 9.30 train. When I found her alone one day and asked her, she hesitantly said: 'Tell me, what can I do? I have to commute every day. Who'll protect me? If I go to the police to complain, I'll get even more humiliated. Not only do the police not register a complaint, on the contrary, they ask me all kinds of indecent questions.'

Gurumata Vajrayogini instructed: 'Get me the fruit of the tree of life from Yogadya. There's nothing more I desire.' He had no idea about the tree of life or its fruit. Nevertheless, assigning the highest priority to Vajrayogini's command, he set out in search of the fruit of the tree of life. As he walked along, he reached a large pond. The name of the pond was Payomukham. Through the gaps between the trees, he glimpsed a strange sight. Men were filling pots of water from the Payomukham pond and carrying them on their heads, while women dressed smartly in military attire kept watch all around the pond. Beholding this sight, he was astonished. Why did women in this land have authority over men? Not being able to overcome his curiosity, he asked one of the men carrying a water pot, who at once got frightened and signalled him to be quiet. He was even more astonished. And then suddenly, from both sides of the road, loud knocks rang out, bugles began to emit sombre sounds. Perhaps some eminent person was walking on the road. He moved away from the thoroughfare. The very next moment, he saw a woman from a respectable family, smartly dressed in military attire, moving along Payomukham on horseback. Rows of men on both sides were waving fly whisks. He came out of his trance at an elderly woman's touch. He hadn't noticed her coming and standing beside him. 'Are you coming from Vajrayogini?' – the elderly woman asked, and smiled softly – 'I knew you would come. Follow me, it'll be good for you.' Still in the stupor of astonishment, he began walking behind the elderly woman. If one went to the village surrounded by forest, one would see that everyone, from children as young as two or two-and-a-half to infirm adults as old as eighty, ninety and a hundred was busy collecting sal leaves and making bundles of them. No one in this neighbourhood had even a chhatak of land to speak of. If I collect leaves from the forest and sell them, I get to eat. If it rains, the leaves aren't dry. Are we to starve to death if there's no work? There are eight bellies to feed including the children. That's why we have to go to the babus to ask for loans. The babus give ten or twenty rupees and say: 'I'm giving you a loan in bad times, but after all, you won't be able to repay me very soon. So work on my land for two days in exchange.' From there, we directly followed the course of the river. The river in these parts was tranquil and sombre, even when one walked along the bank there was no sound at all. As if some great force was silently lurking inside. The scenery on the north was blocked by a mountain, only the door on the south was visible. At dawn, everything was cold, but soon after the sun rose, the air turned hot. There were loo winds in the afternoon. I walked along the riverbank – there was no road, in fact there was no sign of anyone there. I walked for a while, and then I halted, and walked again. The dry run was on, the technicals. Madhura was rehearsing on the ramp. She stepped forward to the rhythm of the music, she swung her hips animatedly, paused, stood in position, and then returned. A mock session, providing answers to all the made-up questions. And finally returning to her own position. Her steps, her way of answering, looking, bursting into laughter – everything was measured, the way the experts had taught her. Not the slightest bit more, or less. In that event, everything would be ruined. The main pageant was in the evening. Madhura was about to participate in the biggest and most reputed beauty contest in India. A forty-five-year-old, skinny housewife said: 'The doctor said to take the X-ray again. But where will I get the money! Sometimes I get a handful of rice once a day, and sometimes not even that. But I did manage to get an X-ray done once after a lot of difficulty. The doctor also asks me to eat well and have milk, fish, fruits and so on. Or else, he says, I won't be rid of the TB. May the faces of such doctors be scorched! I've realized it's all my fate. If there's death in my destiny, who can stop it, Doctor Babu?' Meanwhile, *Hiroshima Mon Amour* began playing. France was under German occupation during the Second World War. In that harsh time, the French girl in the film fell head over heels in love with a German soldier. Those golden days were spent in bliss. After a time, the youthful lover died in her very arms. All night long, the girl felt her lover's warm body turn colder, the body of love. A long time passed. Time sped by, the world was transformed. After a long time, the French girl went to Hiroshima in connection with an anti-war film, and while there, at a particular moment, she told her life story for the first time to a Japanese youth. And as she told him, she was startled, were the images of all those days fading in her mind? The golden hue of those memories was her lifeblood! How terrifying all this meaningless existence was then, the attempt to stay alive! Four or five aged women almost dragged a girl to Vajrayogini. She was dark-complexioned and plump-faced, she wasn't older than twenty or twenty-one. She was screaming like a lunatic, flailing her limbs. As she screamed, she tugged at the only sari she possessed and pulled it open, and with her long hair spread out in front of her she shook it agitatedly. Vajrayogini stood still for a while, observing her, and then she moved forward and drew a circle with the long bone in her hand. First, three arrows of proven size lying in the middle of the expansive courtyard were planted in three corners of a small triangle. After that, the three sticks were brought together and tied with a red string, and slowly taking out a skull smeared with sindoor from the shoulder-bag, muttering mantras all the while, it was hung above the arrows with the help of another piece of red string. The girl continued to scream and flail her limbs like before. The yogini tied her hands and feet firmly. Her eyes were almost shut now, drool was oozing out of her mouth, she seemed to be becoming lifeless. Vajrayogini now chanted mantras loudly and began circling around the girl. From time to time she screamed out in a theatrical way, as if she was battling against some unknown soul. There seemed to be the style of an invocation and prayer in the initial part of the mantra chanting, and by and by it assumed the form of a powerful dance of destruction. Dancing around the girl in this way, the yogini was covered in perspiration but there was no respite for her. She went on screaming and chanting mantras. Afternoon turned to evening, and after that, in time, daylight too came to an end. And at that time, at the turning point of light and darkness, the skull hanging over the three arrows suddenly began to move. As if some invisible hand was moving it. The skull was swinging wildly now. Many of the onlookers let out terrified screams and began running away at that. Looking at the situation then, it seemed the public had been waiting patiently since afternoon just to see this sight. Fear and anxiety were writ large on their faces, all of them ran to a safe distance and craned their necks to look. Some people were knocking their heads with their folded hands. The skull now swung wildly a few times and then fell to the ground. The sick girl screamed out at once and then fainted. Vajrayogini now took sindoor from the skull and smeared it on the girl's forehead, and bending down to the girl's ear, she began chanting mantras inaudibly. After a while, the fastening on the girl's hands and feet were removed, it seemed she was slowly coming back to her senses. She suddenly sat up with a start when she realized she was no longer tied. She was fully conscious now and observing her condition, she tried to conceal her shame with her hands. An elderly woman standing near her threw a shawl in her direction. Piyasa had just turned ten. She studied in an English-medium school, of course, and she stood first in class. She attended drawing classes, and went swimming too. And she also loved watching films. Obviously Hindi and English movies. She almost turned feverish the moment Bangla cinema was mentioned. Rabindranath Tagore might be a world poet, but Rabindra Sangeet sounded like a dirge to her. Her Ma was a teacher of Bangla, so she forced her to watch Bangla films. Whenever *Hirak Rajar Deshe* or *Feluda* were playing on TV, Piyasa had to watch, and in exchange she was allowed to watch a Hindi film of her choice. Her Ma wanted her to watch *Bombaiyer Bombete* now. She thought her daughter would enjoy it, and besides she would realize that Bangla cinema was also enjoyable. Piyasa's body language changed on hearing her Ma. After that, she came to a compromise with her Ma. The condition: she was agreeable to watching this Bengali movie, but she had to be taken to INOX afterwards. After watching Harry Potter there, Piyasa decided that henceforth she wouldn't watch films in any sundry cinema hall. While walking along the bank of the river in the afternoon, I suddenly heard the chortling sound of laughter. I thought it was village girls making merry. As soon as I advanced a few steps, I saw that ten or twelve small boys and girls had all jumped naked into the river to bathe. There were a few older boys and girls as well among them.

The water was so cold that when people like us got into the river, our limbs turned numb. While they swam underwater from this bank to the other. They seemed not to care a whit that the river current was strong. They didn't demur in any way at the appearance of a stranger there. All of them began agitating the water. After having walked for a long time along the directionless river, I suddenly came upon a walkable path. So what if it was only good for walking, at least it was a path! I had to follow this path because the river took a bend at a massive hill that suddenly rose from the water. There was no way to move ahead, however much one wanted to. I began descending along the path on the western side. That was a path that had formed from the footsteps of people walking on the hill. That was the only road here. It curved left around the hill, turned right again and then once again became a path on the left bank of the river. The passengers in the ladies' compartment threw a twelve-year-old 'male' bhutta vendor out of a running train. That day, Niraj Prasad had tried to enter the vendors' compartment with the sack of bhuttas on his shoulder. But since the train began moving, he wasn't able to get into that compartment. When the ladies' compartment appeared before him, he hopped in there. Some lady passengers raised a commotion at once. Although Niraj Prasad pleaded and implored that he be allowed to get off at the next station, no one paid him any heed. As soon as the train left Kuntighat station, he was pushed and thrown out. Looking at the riverbank, I surmised that this was a cremation ground, there were human bones lying all around, skulls, arms and legs, and for that matter, half-burnt backbones as well. I had not seen this cremation ground before. I had never even imagined such a cremation ground. Where on earth had Guru Mata brought me! Paying close attention, the yogini was examining all the bones, one by one. She picked them up and explained to me which one was an elderly man's jaw, which one a part of a middle-aged woman's hip and which one a young man's rib. The right side of this bone's been eaten, a dog did it. That means it's very soft, it probably belonged to a small girl. Of course, an entire skeleton was essential for a tantra-sadhana, but besides that, two more parts were much needed. The skull and the knee bone. If the bone belonged to a menstruating virgin, that was the best. And if it was a degenerate daughter of a brahmin – there was nothing more one could ask for. That bone would veritably speak. I was studying in college then. A bunch of us were returning home after watching the matinee show at Globe Cinema, window shopping on the way. My eyes were riveted to the show windows at the Grand Hotel arcade. Shoes of such wonderful design, such beautiful names! And such a variety – stilettos, sneakers, boots! But what were the prices? I pressed my nose to the glass and began to look at the prices. The beige-coloured ones were Rs 1,000, the black ones Rs 1,200, and the burgundy ones were only Rs 25,000. Baap re, what were these shoes made of! Abhi quipped: 'With girls' skin!' He had to turn around at once. All the blows landed on his head and back. Even after all that beating, Abhi bared his teeth and smiled: 'I say it again, it's made of the skin of girls…' The guide sat on a small plank sticking out near the top of the mast, he had binoculars in his hand, his eyes were alert. Every now and then, he raised his binoculars and looked at something faraway and then shouted to alert the men: '*Thik hai, sab kuchh thik hai* – move ahead, move ahead!' This arrangement was to look out for any sudden danger. The guide was sitting high, near the top of the mast, his body was firmly belted to the post so that he wouldn't fall. However much the ship swayed in a storm, he wouldn't fall, rather, from high up on the mast he would be able to see everyone and everything. Everything was going along smoothly. Suddenly the guide raised his loudspeaker: 'Attention! Attention! Stay awake! Keep everyone awake! The coast guard says a storm's approaching, those of you who're on the deck, please make sure you fasten yourself with the belts at the ship's railing, those who are worried about seasickness are requested to go down to the cabins below, the ship might begin to pitch and roll at any time.' All of a sudden then, the ship rolled to the left, and the very next moment, in a volte-face, it began to roll precipitously to the right. The sailors were running hither and thither. A miracle had begun to occur at the rope of the sail. With great dexterity, the oarsmen hurriedly lowered the sails, in exactly the same way as a circus tent is brought down. Without the sails, the ship looked kind of bald. The engine was started right then. The fearsome dance of the ship against the waves had begun. The captain was trying to keep the ship in the direction of the waves. The bow of the ship would pitch up, and the very next moment, it was the turn of the stern to pitch up, while the bow fell below. A massive wave rose up and submerged everything. I wasn't at all prepared for all this. A woman's face emerged from the deck: 'We've had enough – let's go back – don't go any further!' The ever-vigilant guide responded via megaphone: 'Don't be afraid, our ship is under control, we're used to sea storms like this. The firm hands of our esteemed captain are at the helm. Trust in him. The storm will pass very soon and the morning sun will rise.' Going to the school and returning home, with a heavy bag on the shoulder. When the exam results came out, Mummy–Bapi wore dejected looks. After all, everyone got a high first division nowadays, but could one move ahead without four- or five-star marks? The classroom hummed, the teacher was gravely writing an arithmetical problem on the blackboard. All the faces were turned attentively in that direction. They figured out the problem, they tried to figure it out. He, only he, gave up and turned his attention to his geometry set. One could engrave one's name very well on the high bench with the spike of the compass. I sat beside him quietly for a while. After that, I asked: 'Doesn't the river ever end?' The boatswain said: 'Water flows down the river to the sea.' I asked again: 'Where does the sea end?' Without any annoyance at my query, he began speaking, as if to himself: 'I don't know all that, my boy. The river ends at the sea, but there's no end to the sea.' After saying so much all at once, he looked me in the eyes once, after that he stuffed his hand in his pocket, took out two lozenges and gave me his hand: 'Have these lozenges, we'll probably reach by the time you finish.' I had just put one lozenge into my mouth when Didi tugged my shirt from behind: 'Come, we've reached.' The hooter sounded and the steamer slowly began anchoring at the jetty. All of us climbed down the wooden stairs. I saw people climbing down hurriedly and running over the sand. It seemed everyone was in a hurry. Although it was beside the water, the sand was hot under the fierce sun. Many people had bare feet; they could get blistered. I asked Ma: 'Why is everyone running like that?' Ma replied: 'How strange! Don't people have to reach their destinations? People are running to catch the bus, if they're late they might not get a place to sit.' If the river was offered the blood of human sacrifice, deluge would be averted – having received such an instruction via a dream, Sheonarayan had sacrificed his eighty-year-old father and offered the blood of that sacrifice to the Phulhar river. Using the bonti used to cut hay, he severed his sleeping father's head from the torso. The old man slept through it all. Bringing the warm blood in a clay pot, he made an offering of it to the Phulhar river, he did puja with flowers and bel leaves, and then, after he finished bathing, his mind free of anxiety, he went to his room and fell asleep. Even though the people in the village were shocked about the whole affair, Sheonarayan said impassively: 'I received the instruction through a dream that the Phulhari river was thirsty for human blood. And so, accordingly, choosing an auspicious time, at midnight on the dark new-moon night, I sacrificed my father. I offered my own father for an auspicious purpose, so what can anyone say about that! There won't be any more deluges. Mahanandatola Binaimari will be saved. By the blessings of the River Mother, we'll get back the lands of ours that were washed away.' Taking him along, the old lady arrived at a magical city. Rows of men were entering the city carrying pots of water, while another group were going with empty pots to fetch the water from Payomukham. Arriving here, in a trice, the old lady assumed the form of a young woman. Of an apsara. Without paying him any attention, the young woman began playing 'catch' with the celestial spheres of the magical city. The spheres were not ordinary ones, the sun and moon had been brought down from the sky. He was astonished and bewildered. Observing his plight, the woman laughed uncontrollably: 'My name is Dahika, I possess the knowledge of yoga, all this is child's play for me.' And then, putting her hand on his back, she said: 'You've set out to eat the fruit of the tree of life, your Guru Mata, Vajrayogini, has sent you, isn't it? But it's no easy matter to eat the fruit of the tree of life. Your life may be at risk in that event. You're just an ordinary man, how do you expect to do this?' After a pause of silence, she began speaking again: 'But there's a way. Don't go for the fruit of the tree of life and suchlike. This is the kingdom of Promila. If you have to be rescued from here, you must play the cosmology game with some woman. You'll be released only if you're successful in the game. You'll be able to set out on the search for the fruit of the tree of life.' After saying so much all at once, Dahika took a bit of time. Observing his hesitation, she smiled softly: 'The moment I saw you, I knew you were an ordinary man. A simple, easy-going man. You're not capable of eating the fruit of the tree of life for your Guru Mata. It's clear that you're not eager to either. It's better that you do something. Drink the water of Payomukham and stay back with me. You'll see that you feel no more hunger or thirst. An unending thirst will be created within you, a thirst for the water of Payomukham. The more you drink, the more thirsty you'll be. That thirst of yours will never be quenched as long as you live. You'll merely fetch the water of Payomukham by water pot, carry it and drink it, fetch it again and then drink it again. But the water will be guarded by womenfolk, this is the kingdom of Promila. For as long as you live, you'll have to live with the thirst for the water of Payomukham. An unending thirst.' It seemed a rupee coin had knocked on the windowpane of the car stopped at the traffic signal. Through the glass that was full of condensation from the air conditioner running full blast, a face, but it wasn't really visible. An emaciated baby in the crook of an arm, a scrawny body draped in a sari that looked like a torn rag, a pair of imperilled eyes. She seemed to want to convey something to blissful people like us by waving her hand. I was about to roll the glass down fully, but Madhura forbade me. 'It's all play-acting. Haven't you read in the papers that these people rent babies and come to beg. This isn't her own baby. They fool people and earn a lot of money by the end of the day. Actually, it's their livelihood to make a fool of men like you.' I just kept looking. There was only the thick glass of a temperature-controlled car in between. Perhaps poverty was now only a habit of theirs. The traffic signal changed from red to amber, and from amber to green. The car moved forward. The face with the baby in the crook of the arm was left behind, two floating eyes. An emaciated baby on rent. What percentage of society did they comprise – was it ten or twenty or thirty or was it sixty, seventy! Or was it even more than that! Damn! Why should one think about all that! After all, the government was there to take care of them. There were political leaders. And there was fate. There was God too. Would be nice to light a cigarette. My throat had been dry for long. 'Do you want to climb up? If you climb to the top of the mast, you'll be able to see the whole world. We've made arrangements for that. There are planks along the mast. Of course, you've got to see everything through the binoculars once you climb there. It's forbidden to look with bare eyes.' Hearing him, I gazed at the top of the tallest mast. Why not see what it looks like through the binoculars from there! Taking recourse to courage, I stepped on to the rope ladder. The guide hauled me up: 'Wait, take the binoculars. Look closely in all directions with that, you'll enjoy it. But tie the safety belt around your waist first. One never knows when there might be some danger.' I climbed up the rope ladder slowly and reached the top of the mast. There was a platform made of a plank. One could sit there with one's legs dangling. There was also a pouch to keep the binoculars. By the time I got settled there, I thought I was feeling giddy. I shook myself vigorously and first tied myself around the waist with the safety belt, I looked around to see whether everything was alright. It took some time to steady myself. I had climbed to the top of the ship's mast and was sitting there, the very thought seemed to make my head spin. The plank was below my feet, I was standing up alongside the mast, all by myself, with the binoculars in my hands. And all around me was water and more water, one had to bend down in order to have somewhere to plant one's feet. The ship was pitching, the mast was pitching too, I was coming down close to the water and then suddenly rising up high. Suddenly the loudspeaker blared from near my feet: 'Are you okay? You're not in any difficulty, are you?' I said: 'I'm in the sky, I'm floating, I can't see anything at all.' 'Look in the distance using the binoculars' – the voice in the loudspeaker wafted up – 'See how the sky becomes one with the sea, look at the beautiful and captivating scenery that's created. How beautiful life and being alive are – isn't it!' There was silence for a while, and then the voice wafted up again: 'Don't try to look to the left or right, just keep looking in front. Adjust the setting on the binoculars, look at the beautiful red sunrise.' I then adjusted the setting on the binoculars and began looking, and kept looking. I couldn't see anything clearly. Nothing was visible. I twirled the focus knob this way and that, and then looked. Everything was hazy like before. Had I gone blind! Where was the captivating, beautiful scenery! Something occurred to me, I threw away the binoculars. Although not so distinct, there was the sound of a splash. Did I hear that sound! I was looking through my naked eyes now. The water nearby, the water far away, the water even further away. The water accumulated and formed one burning screen after another. Lo and behold – an invisible universe floating on the water! I screamed: 'I found it! I found it! I'm beginning to see it!' I could see it all with my naked eyes. All those invisible worlds. Waves collapsed in the sea, creating water, and as the water stilled itself, it turned to fire, fire melted down as water. Because nothing emerges from anything, nothing remains unchanged. There was only an infinitude of emptiness in all directions. A gaping emptiness. Nothing that entered it ever returned. Not even our beloved light. And then

Watching Shefali Jariwala dancing and prancing in the song

Kaanta Laga

Twenty-first century India explodes. Her body shakes to the rhythm of the song

Her vital stats swell up. Everything inside's visible

Just that bit of

An off-shoulder shirt that hangs on her breasts, and an expanse below the navel

The thong panty inside her jeans

Is prominently exposed, all twisted like a smooth snake

Her body and her flesh tremble and slither like

A snake in coition with its mate: '*Kabhi aar kabhi paar...*'

A couch potato shakes himself and sits up: 'Oh fuck! Look at the size of those!'

Turning his head around, he hurls his commentary:

'Mister, you deserve to be kicked, you're obsolete

You have the habit of finding flaws in everything –

How would the boys and girls of today come of age

Unless they go to nightclubs!' On another channel

Zidane has the ball at his feet and there's a helpless goalkeeper in front of him.
And after that? A go-o-o-o-o-al! The air
Turns heated in an instant, blood curdles. The famous Mexican wave
Spreads across the stadium. There's nothing anywhere, only Zidane
Running along the sideline with his arms raised ... Running ... Running along.

[Jolchholchhol, 2004]

Nappy Change

(Yes, for Tapasi Mallick, institutionally murdered
at the behest of debased power mired in political absolutism,
power junkies, their geriatric bones creak and yet
they carry on like dogs in heat...)

She was a young girl, just eighteen or nineteen years old; it was dawn, and while it was still dark – perhaps it was this moment that was referred to as 'brahmamuhurta' in the Upanishads – she had gone to the fields just like she did every day, before the civilized world woke up. She came here every day at exactly this time, to defecate, before any light had emerged, she could not imagine that today a few members of the human species were stealthily lying in wait for her, men, her own fellow citizens, intending to grab her and burn her alive, because of a single fault of hers – she used to protest, she had learnt to protest, even in this system. Not wasting a single moment, since daylight would begin to peep out anytime, the men straightaway pounced upon the girl who had just squatted down to shit, she was defecating with her eyes shut. She was grabbed and thrown right there on the field, without even letting her finish shitting, they had to extract whatever bodily pleasure could be had before burning her – she was a fresh, juicy babe, just looking at her made them randy, could one let her go when she was in their clutches – the meagre clothing was ripped off, the ancient sari and blouse, dirty and faded, were torn to shreds, there was nothing underneath to protect her modesty, she was completely naked under the unceasing assault, and then, pressing her down and shutting her mouth, one person lifted up his lungi and began to rape her, the entire rape was smeared with excreta, but they did not bother about anything, they kept thrusting into her, piston-like, raping her continuously, one person after another kept raping her. Suddenly, following the physical assault just described, as the girl was being raped, as she was shrivelling in pain, she fell unconscious. A thin stream of blood from her vagina began to trickle down to the earth, to the all-enduring soil. As soon as they had sated their lust, they rose, one after the other, they lowered their lungis in keeping with the laws of civilization, and now the phase of actually executing the instructions had to be started, at this very moment, before the public awakening. All of them together lifted up the half-unconscious body, she was laid into a specific pit. One person, seeing the girl in this condition and not being able to bear it – perhaps she was the same age as his daughter – picked up her crumpled-up sari and blouse and threw them over her. A large tin of kerosene had already been brought earlier, a person ran to fetch it, daylight had just begun to peep out now, inverting the tin, kerosene was poured all over her body, the body that just a little while ago had given them manly pleasure, sexual pleasure. They did not waste a moment, with no delay at all, they carried out the task exactly as instructed, a matchstick was lit and thrown on the body so that all evidence was destroyed before daylight. The body blazed furiously, it kept burning, turning to ashes. Nobody knew anything then – no one saw anything.

The *asli khel* began just after this

The ruling party said: We believe in democracy, we believe in people, it is humanism that is the core belief of our party. Our people can never commit an act like this. This could only have been done by the opposition, by the people of the opposition party. Having done the deed, they want to cast the blame on us. The public will not tolerate all this. We will call a Bengal Bandh on this issue. The opposition party said: We believe in democracy, we believe in people, it is humanism that is the core belief of our party. Our people can never commit an act like this. This could only have been done by the ruling party, by the people of the ruling party. Having done the deed, they want to cast the blame on us. The public will not tolerate all this. We will call a Bengal Bandh on this issue.

Was this then the handiwork of ghosts?
Raping her, pouring kerosene over her body and burning her
In order to destroy all evidence!
Indian democracy
Inevitably inflammable
Scratches her arse and shrieks
Could well have been a ghost, because when it has not been legally proven
Under the justice system, that some person committed the act...
But there's something to consider
After all, the girl had learnt to protest...

It's been less than a week since I took up the job. It's in the vicinity of Pune, not really on the fringes and not really in the city either. I was walking along the pavement one morning, there was a breeze fluttering all around. A woman sat on the pavement, under an ancient banyan, the heavy silver bajus of olden design on her wrists gleamed, a huge round gold ring on her nose. There were lots of bunches of fresh, green grass in front of her. A cow stood tethered nearby, actually it was a bull. A few steps away, the well-decorated Hanuman mandir. The marble Hanuman-ji, adorned with sindoor, wielding his mace, was clearly visible even from outside. One could not help being startled by the sight of the thick garlands of marigold swinging from his neck and the beautification of the sparkling white figure of Hanuman with the yellow-saffron of the marigolds and the yellow-saffron of the sindoor. I stopped there out of curiosity. First came a woman of about nineteen or twenty, a modern girl clad in the latest cut of jeans who had almost shorn off all her hair, who bought two bunches of grass and held it to the bull's mouth. As if the bull had been waiting for just that, it pounced on the bunch of green grass and began to gulp it down. After that, when she bent to touch the feet of the bull for ashirvad, the lower edge of her top rose very high and the maroon-coloured panty under the jeans became dangerously exposed. The girl knew I was gaping at her body, but she did not bother about it, she strutted on her high heels, crossed the road and walked away. After that, a middle-aged man got out from an Ambassador car, who looked like someone belonging to the upper rung, well-established in life, smartly attired in a suit and tie. He laid a few bunches of grass in front of the bull and bent down to touch its hoof to offer pranam, and then without looking at anything, he hurried into the car. The car started at once. Just after that, I observed a student of Class 7 or Class 8, dressed in his school uniform, a schoolbag on his shoulders, who too bought a bundle of grass, offered it to the bull, knocked his head in pranam and went away. After that came another four or five people, one after another. Among them was someone like a minister, who arrived in a Scorpio car, that's what I surmised seeing the pilot cars in front and behind, and the accompanying police and security guards. Later, I asked a colleague from the locality about it and got an explanation. It's a long story. All to do with faith. They consider the temple to be the abode of God. The bovine too is a part of God. Feeding it grass is a form of service to God.

Mahasveta Devi

No government can unshackle people's minds. If it could, then things like female foeticide, the dowry system, dowry deaths and the extensive rape–trafficking–sale of women would not be happening even today, throughout the country. For generations upon end, we have been nurturing all these crimes. Child labour exists as does the bonded labour system. It's been proved now that although many laws have been made – and are still being made, will continue to be made – we have failed to translate the laws into practice. Millions of rights have been proclaimed through the medium of panchayats, but those have not been realized. The 'Right to Information Act' has in fact been a complete failure in my state. The greatest failure has been on the part of the political parties. They could not show the way. Think, for instance, about the real face of the Left Front government in West Bengal. The record of the Left Front over thirty years in wasting, weakening and crippling the country's independence is incomparable. But the cultivation of good-for-nothings proceeds at a furious pace. The guilt for failure is a collective one. Is the cultivation of fundamentalism any less widespread? What happened in Gujarat in 2002 must definitely be condemned. But what if, just the other day, Taslima Nasreen had been severely injured or even murdered in Hyderabad? Fundamentalism too is like the fabled poison tree, which can never be destroyed. 'Freedom' could not be achieved in full measure. We did not allow that to happen. It could be said that we have made the word into a caricature of itself. That I can say these things is also a result of freedom. Are we really free in the sense in which Vidyasagar or Rammohan were free, with no difference between their thinking, beliefs and practice? The funny thing is that in their time, the country was enslaved. And we have been free for sixty years.

CUTOUT

Ranajit Guha

The people of the lower classes have definitely made demands, and continue to do so. But we frequently see that even without any prior thinking, these demands hurtle, impelled imperceptibly, towards the sphere of protest. And if protest too does not work, then that grows into resistance. I think that in the course of this extension, or you could say, this 'metonymy' – going from demand to protest, and from protest to resistance – one can sense a new kind of power, which is not at all synonymous with civic rights. Although it is something associated with citizenship, in the intersection of the 'set' of civic rights and the 'set' of the bases of other kinds of power of which I spoke, civic rights consciousness undergoes a qualitative transformation, in terms of density and reach. However, this power, which is a precondition of transformation, is as human as civic rights. There is no divine inspiration or external agency involved.

All the transnational corporations rushing to set up industries
Get the Third World's
Water, earth, air and labour – all almost
Free of cost –
That's why they come running –
Running, running,
They want to come;
They act as if they are gushing over with care
For the Third World –
For the famished people of the Third World

Although the notion of rights aroused by this power – the primeval power of which I am speaking – is human, however, in comparison to modernity, in comparison to the state apparatus of the modern era, state perspectives and ideals, it is something much older, it is as old as humanity itself. For as long as humanity, using its collective energy and faculty of speech, has made the world its own, for so long too has this power been manifest as the fundamental constituent of humanity. The world that was once purely inanimate became human through the force of this power. That's why this power, which is the source of the consciousness of rights, has to be seen as belonging to a different category than the comparatively modern notion of civic rights. That is why, for me, this power is a primeval expression of man's inner power. I think it is the mother of the primeval sense of rights informed by the human conscience, under whose inspiration the demand for civic rights can transcend to protest, and from protest to resistance. (Cut: from the interview of Utpal Kumar Basu.)

A very young block development officer, possibly posted here just after clearing the civil service examination, said:

'During these floods, I find scams taking place everywhere regarding chira and jaggery. There is not even a fourth of what ought to be there in the sacks. But I keep reading in the newspapers about all the budgetary allotments being made, huge amounts of allotments. Why is it not reaching the people! Where does all the material disappear midway! Anyway ... forget it. It's a government job, it's inconvenient to open one's mouth. If relief supplies arrived, the flood victims would surely have got something. But everything vanishes midway...' It was the time ministers had set out to see the floods, a lot like going to the circus. Since it involved ministers, the most comfortable and exorbitant vehicle, a Scorpio, was assigned for each of the three ministers, so three in all; and if there's a minister there have to be security guards, and legislative assembly members have to be there too. Nonetheless only about fifty cars were allotted for the whole congregation, no more could be managed in those days of acute fuel price rise. The papers reported: 'Ministers visit flooded areas with a convoy of 53 cars.' Who knows how they found out. Scorpio, Bolero, Tata Sumo, Mahindra Marshall, Ambassador, Jeep – the flood relief convoy spanned about a mile. It was the first time in my life I had heard one or two of the vehicle names, I'm copying every now and then from the reports of Suman Batabyal of the *Dainik Statesman*, in the form of a cut up, like the names of these cars. A fierce debate was taking place in the Mednipur circuit house about the modalities of providing flood relief to the people. The aroma of fresh mutton cooking wafts in from the kitchen. The ministers and other personnel would all have lunch, and after that, taking their time, they would set out for flood relief accompanied by the convoy of vehicles. The people of Keshpur and Ghatal were then crouched on bamboo platforms erected on stilts, clinging to the branches of trees, perched on the roofs of two-storeyed pukka houses ... living together with snakes and suchlike. The chira and jaggery had arrived after three days ... let alone a sheet of tarpaulin to cover their heads, they did not even get a drop of water to drink. Loud lamentation everywhere – a mute mother stands under the open sky, clad in something like rags wrapped around her body, her child of a month or so held in a tiny bundle in her arms. From a distance, one could not surmise whether it was alive or dead. The ministers' Scorpios now reached Keshpur, accompanied by four dozen cars, a dozen and a half policemen, and half a dozen media persons. The convoy halted at Keshpur's Boshonchok. About six villagers had taken shelter on the highway after they lost their house in the floods. They were there with all their cows, goats, ducks and hens. The river of muddy water was then flowing over the villages. How would the ministers distribute flood relief? The ministers were somehow taken away quietly, avoiding the people. Quite a few well-decorated motorboats were ready and waiting in advance. There were almost a dozen and a half of them. The motorboats puttered along until they reached a relatively high, mound-like site. Only the minister for relief was able to get out of the motorboat into the knee-deep water. In order to help the remaining two ministers cross the water, the local school was ordered to be opened and high benches were brought. But how were they to get out by stepping on those high benches! After all the high benches could not be placed firmly on the water – they wobbled and floated. Two sturdy local leaders then came forward. They carried the ministers on their shoulders and took them across the muddy water. True, it was a bit difficult for them, but local leaders are well versed in all this.

All the transnational corporations rushing to set up industries
Get the Third World's
Water, earth, air and labour – all almost
Free of cost –
That's why they come running –
Running, running,
They want to come;
They act as if they are gushing over with care
For the Third World –
For the famished people of the Third World

Ministers tend to be on the heavier side. They agreed to be carried. The ministers sighed in relief, coming for flood relief was not exactly a cakewalk! Be that as it may, with great difficulty, avoiding the muddy slime and protecting the folds of their dhutis, they stepped on to dry land, and they asked the assembled populace: 'How are you all?' The people shouted out their reply in one voice: 'We are well, Sir. We are well.' They had to be well. Because just nearby, leaning against motorcycles, stood two mighty leaders from the panchayat. If someone said anything out of line, they would thrash him as soon as the ministers left and take the skin off his back. The people said exactly what had been taught and explained to them, they put smiles on their faces according to the instructions. They began clapping, again and again. The ministers distributed among them the contents of the few sacks of dry food they had brought along – muri, chira, biscuits and lozenges – and acting according to instructions, the people stood in queue and began receiving the ministers' handouts. All at once, half a dozen or so media persons began clicking photographs, these smiling faces were proof of the fact that flood relief was taking place, that people were receiving flood relief. Then, one minister wanted to visit the nearby village as well. Two panchayat leaders came running up to him and whispered into his ear: 'Beware, don't fall into that trap, that area is under the possession of the opposition party, there isn't a single person of our party there, they thrashed and demonized everyone and drove them out of the village, we did not spare them either, we too made this village completely devoid of the opposition, there's no opposition in this village, and none of our people in that village, a clear division, they are ready and waiting, they have hired and brought people to carry out a protest demonstration in front of the ministers.' Meanwhile, completing the handing out of relief materials, the minister for relief stood up straight and gave a tiny little speech for the benefit of the reporters: 'How contented the people are even after such a terrible flood, they are getting all the necessary relief materials under our administration. See it with your own eyes, take pictures carefully, show it to the people of the country.'

But the belly does not heed anything, Dada. We have to put our lives on the line all day in order to get a fistful of rice twice a day. I don't care about anything else now, but we also have to bear the disgrace from time to time of being accused of stealing. That hurts a lot. What do you want to hear about me, I lost my parents in my childhood, I have no family or relatives. I had an elder brother, all of a sudden he sold off the house and everything and went away to Bombay or somewhere. I heard he works as a goldsmith, he married someone there. When I was about thirteen years old, I was married off in a hurry, I mean he wanted to get me off his shoulders by any means. My husband drove a rickshaw-van, sometimes he went out with the vehicle, most of the time he lay drunk. I was barely fourteen by the time the girl was in my womb. How can I tell you the turn that things took after that, Dada. One morning, I woke up to find my husband had disappeared. He did not have parents or siblings, only a tiny homestead to live in. Later I found out that he did not find me suitable, apparently I was not a real woman. I heard from people that he got married elsewhere, he's probably living happily. My real life began. Carrying the baby in my arms, I walk from my remote village in the interior of Dhola, take the 7.10 local train from Lakshmikantapur and get down at Ballygunge, a maidservant in babu homes. Sometimes it's past evening by the time I return home. The gaze of the younger son in the house where I work is not decent. For that matter, the old bloke too looks at me weirdly sometimes, I don't feel comfortable even after covering my bosom with the sari. One has to go along very cautiously, taking care of all sides, I am not willing to lose my honour, but what will I eat if I lose the job! I didn't agree to the proposal of staying there at night, there's no telling what these babus can do at any time if they get the chance, they don't even heed mother or sister. I try to return home by evening. Returning to my father-in-law's homestead, the first thing I do is to light the lamp at the tulsi pedestal, I blow the conch, I bow down low in pranam, I pray, God grant me good sense, it's better that I starve to death, but I should not have to go the wrong way, driven by my belly. But can one ever be certain about that; on the street, there are boys and youngsters of course, but even men as old as my father or uncle look at me as if they would eat me alive if they got hold of me. Not having any other option, I hold the baby to my chest, I look down and walk away. When their eyes meet mine, some people make bad signs, and of course, they say bad things. I don't pay any attention, we can't survive if we heed all that. Sometimes there used to be the sound of knocking on the door at night, I would keep the chopper within hand's reach, I couldn't sleep the whole night, I was so scared that I couldn't even shut my eyes. One night it was unbearable. I lit the lamp. I wound the sari anchal around my waist. I held the chopper aloft in my right hand and screamed out: So your arse is full of juice after drinking cholai and you've come here to show off, have you, let the one who wants to break open the door and enter do that, you shameless fuckers – let's see your power. Come and see the chopper in my hand – the fucker who pops his head in first, I'll cut the head off his neck with one swipe. After that day, there's no more sound at night, but outside, on the streets, they torment me, sometimes I feel like cutting off all my hair, shaving my head and blackening my face with tar, so that male eyes don't fall on me ... I can't explain to you what a torment it is, Dada. And can one change one's fate! The husband remains the swami even if he keeps ten women, he remains the swami even if he marries ten times – swami is God, a relationship over lifetimes. We were married with the sacred fire as witness, according to Hindu custom, whether or not I'm able to feed myself, I apply sindoor and wear conch-shell bangles. I don't think about all this, whatever is in my fate will happen, I pray to God that I can depart with my sindoor and bangles intact.

All the transnational corporations rushing to set up industries
Get the Third World's
Water, earth, air and labour – all almost
Free of cost –
That's why they come running –
Running, running,
They want to come;
They act as if they are gushing over with care
For the Third World –
For the famished people of the Third World

This letter of mine is apropos of the report titled 'National flag in naked child's hands, theatre-worker arrested'. I had the opportunity to see this play in Bakuldanga. It was a powerful and pertinent five-minute presentation. The contention of the playwright is clear. What could be a more fearless symbol of the bad times afflicting the country even after sixty years of Independence than showing it through the medium of a naked child! Isn't '*Yeh azadi jhoothi hai*' true? Why did a hundred thousand farmers commit suicide in the last five years? Why are millions of children illiterate even today? Malnourished through starvation and ill health? Why is there violence everywhere, religious intolerance, caste war? Madhusudhan Babu and company have been successful in gifting the citizens with their programme on an opportune day (15 August 2007) and in an appropriate way. The destitute mother clothes her naked child, who smiles radiantly and holds aloft the national flag and sings '*Saare jahan se achchha Hindustan hamara*' – there can't be a more ideal advertisement on the occasion of the diamond jubilee of Independence. But I am amazed – how was the national flag disrespected in this play? Both mother and child held it aloft with great pride until the end. And a naked child is a symbol of innocence, a symbol of purity. It is never disrespectful of the nation. I request the administration, protect culture by unconditionally freeing the arrested theatre workers. (Subhashis Sarkar, Bakuldanga, Bankura.)

CUTOUT

From the news report titled, 'National flag in the hands of a naked child, 11 theatre workers arrested', it is learnt that the superintendent of police in Bankura has said, 'On a day as auspicious as 15 August, a street play with a naked boy holding the national flag is completely illegal. By this act, the national flag has been disrespected.' From the news report, it is further learnt that at some point during the play, the slogan, *'Yeh azadi jhoothi hai'*, was also heard. The theatre workers were supposedly arrested on those grounds. As an eyewitness to the incident, I would like to state that the song, *'Saare jahan se achchha Hindustan hamara'*, was also heard offstage. Besides, in some scenes of the play, incidents like the attacks by fundamentalists against Taslima, or against journalists by political rogues, and against farmers by hoodlums, had been depicted. Such acts weaken the very foundations of Indian democracy. If the honourable superintendent of police had studied the play properly, he would have realized that, first of all, nowhere was the national flag or the nation insulted. Second, a flag in the hands of a naked child can never be illegal. Besides it is only part of the play. A naked child is in no way obscene. In that case, my question: how did the superintendent of police reach the conclusion that the national flag had been insulted? Is this not an attack by the administration against culture and the right to free speech? (Priyatosh Sarkar, Hazra Lane, Bankura.)

They barged in with screams of 'Kill, kill!', saffron bands tied around their heads: Shall we remain silent when our great leaders are insulted? Are you trying to fuck with us? At first, they brutally thrashed a Class IV employee, spotting him alone. They broke an arm and a leg of a journalist. Next was the office of the weekly magazine *Outlook*. In the current issue, they had published a list of some villains, Bal Thackeray's and Narendra Modi's names were also on the list. For that matter, a cartoon caricaturing Bal Thackeray had also been published in the weekly. And that had led to terrible repercussions, the inflamed saffron-banded mob was not willing to listen to any reason, they wanted to vandalize and destroy the office of the weekly. Their assertion was that Bal Thackeray and Narendra Modi were great leaders of the great Indian nation, the upholders of the pride of Indian culture, to make fun of them by depicting them as clowns was anti-national. They would not tolerate this, no patriotic Indian should tolerate all this. Some time back, a similar anti-national act was committed by a Muslim bastard called Husain, oh, he's a real masterpiece, he makes a film with Madhuri Dixit but behind the scenes he draws the Goddess of Knowledge, Saraswati, naked in order to attack the Hindu religion. Just look at the temerity – to deliberately draw a Hindu goddess naked, in this country of Hindus! Can any real Hindu tolerate such insults to their religion, or should they even tolerate it! There needs to be a countrywide movement against it, we shall call for a Bharat bandh when necessary, in protest against the insults to these national leaders. But why don't the people of the country come together and come out to protest in large numbers!

And the intellectuals are the number one bokachodas of the country! You can't understand what they do, what they think and how they express themselves in words, but one can see that most of them are leftists, they were Russia's pimps at one time, and now they are China's. I've heard that some of them are changing colours like anything. Yes, that includes the grey-haired schoolmaster, I've seen him in the book fair, what the fuck was his name ... Subimal Misra or some Misra, he too – he's another bokachoda, a top-class bastard.

CUTOUT

A Muslim organization declared a fatwa offering a reward for the murder of Taslima Nasreen, in Dharmatala, Calcutta, in a public meeting, literally under the noses of senior police officers. The complaint was the same as that which had arisen against Rushdie – Taslima had offended the religious sentiment of Muslims. In this city of Calcutta, which is the capital of the left fortress, in this cultural capital of the India of some people's dreams, Majidullah Khan Farhad, one of the leaders of the group that just a few days ago had carried out the attack in the Hyderabad Press Club against Taslima and attempted to murder her, came and threatened to have Taslima murdered in order to punish her and announced a reward for that purpose. In the fatwa issued in the public meeting, Majidullah declared: The one who kills Taslima will receive a 'limitless monetary reward'. Incited by him, other Muslim leaders too kept announcing rewards for the act, accompanied by inflammatory speeches. Those who issue such fatwas know very well that the government would not have the courage to annoy them, no government was capable of touching even a hair of theirs, because that would be harmful for them, electoral prospects would be upset. The fatwa to murder was issued in the presence of the imam of the Tipu Sultan Mosque; it was this imam who, a couple of years ago, had announced a reward of fifty thousand rupees to anyone who blackened the face of Taslima Nasreen, and later, under pressure, had retreated, saying, 'I didn't say that', or maybe it was some cock-and-bull like that. Finally, a memorandum in writing was also submitted to the government. After that began the real democratic sports. At first, the chief secretary refused to speak about the matter; later, under pressure from journalists, he said in reply to a question: 'I will not be able to say anything in this regard.' Openly threatening to murder someone, or announcing a reward for someone's murder, in a left-ruled state like West Bengal, in India, the altar of democracy – even when asked what steps were being taken by the government in the context of such medieval barbarism, he was unwilling to make any comment. Everyone has a right to express their own views in a democracy. In public, individually or in an organized way, contrary views can also be opposed. Mass organizations can be built, public opinion can be created. But can a fatwa be issued, announcing a reward for someone's murder in a public meeting, under the noses of the police? The police commissioner clearly avoided replying to such questions: 'No, no one will be arrested for all this.' No political party or organization, whether of the left or the right or centre or the extremists has bothered about the matter. Not a single word has been said yet, no political party has noticed it yet. After all, in our democracy, which party has the courage to rock the vote bank...

No one knows how the death occurred, although everyone knows that it happened. Not finding any clue, a shaman was called from a faraway village. The whole day the shaman did things like chanting spells using the bamboo winnowing tray and reading the mirror of the thumbnail, and thus reached the conclusion: 'How the death occurred can be ascertained. Tonight, her ashes must be inserted into a large brass urn and its mouth sealed with Ganga clay. After darkening the room, I shall conduct a seance with the urn. During this time, under no circumstances must any light enter the room. A lot of things will be needed, like owl's blood, cow dung and urine and so on. I shall collect all that and bring it. Once the seance is over, lamps must be lit all around the urn and the room must be full of light. After that the water blessed by the seance spells will be given to every member of the family. The water must be consumed with a pure mind, wearing pure garments, and they must dream after falling asleep. And the mystery of the death will be revealed from the dreams, the mysterious death.' Everything was done accordingly. The room was made completely dark, the seance was conducted with the brass urn containing the ashes and a little bit of the blessed water was given to everyone. The urn had initially been covered by a blood-coloured sheet of jute, now the hundreds and hundreds of clay ghee lamps surrounding it came alight. All the lamps shone together magnificently. From that moment, the room was bathed in an aura of light and there wasn't the tiniest bit of darkness even in the farthest corners. After that, all the family members, clad in pure garments, drank the water blessed by spells given by the shaman and entered their respective bedrooms with pure mind. The girl's mother dreamt: a snake, two-headed, was wound around the navel region, and one of the snake's mouths was in the centre of the body. And someone went up and down the stairs, with lamps in their hands – descending once to the mouth of the pit, and then climbing up reverberatingly. No face was clearly visible, only hot ghee, molten, ran down the stairs, it melted and ran without let-up. After a time, everything suddenly came to a halt once again, and the dream family became hazy. Her father dreamt: his daughter was writhing in a half-burnt state, she screamed – Baba, can't you see, I'm burning! He could clearly see that his daughter's body was continuously burning into embers – a glowing pile of embers. The father woke up and rising hurriedly went to the room with the urn, the brass urn was truly burning, the blood-coloured cloth covering it was blazing, and as it burned, the urn containing the ashes began exploding loudly, emitting endless peril. The ghee lamps were toppling over, they exploded like country-bombs, they kept exploding. The whole aura of light was shattered, it was indistinguishable from darkness. Does the light contain darkness, or was it the darkness that contained light – who knows which was which one's edge, its complement!

All the transnational corporations rushing to set up industries
Get the Third World's
Water, earth, air and labour – all almost
Free of cost –
That's why they come running –
Running, running,
They want to come;
They act as if they are gushing over with care
For the Third World –
For the famished people of the Third World

Actually, I live in another part of the world, which is where I have a job, I came to the village house after almost ten years. Not exactly a village now, not a town either for that matter, not even what's called a suburb. A lot has changed, and again, a lot is unchanged too. The very first thing I did was to find out about Master-moshai, our Bairagi Master-moshai. I heard he was still alive, he still lived in the same house. It was this Master-moshai who taught us that we who belonged to the babu class and were privileged should think about whether we ought to call those who till the earth and reap the harvest 'crop artists' instead of farmers ... and that it was important to keep in mind that this shouldn't be just a fad, mere words, the thing should emerge from within. Be that as it may, after waking up in the morning and having my tea, I immediately went to visit him. But what do I see! Master-moshai, at this age, clad in quite a dirty lungi, bare bodied, squatting at the water tap and washing a pile of dirty utensils. His hands seemed to be unmoving, he looked very exhausted. Very unwell. But his bright eyes looked as large and as sharp as ever behind the spectacles. It took him a while, but he did recognize me after seeing me. He was surprised, he appeared to be embarrassed, and then straightening and standing up with effort, he began explaining: 'The daughters-in-law have so much to do ... that's why ... how are you ... after such a long time...' Suddenly, I had a sense, seeing Sir I understood the situation at once. 'Sir, your books – a few thousand books, Indian as well as foreign' – I screamed out, I hadn't even asked him, 'How are you, Sir?', I hadn't even greeted him with pranam, like a selfish person, only the lamentation about the books escaped my lips. I had grown up reading books from Sir's collection, I had obtained a job, teaching in a foreign university, I used to eagerly consume any book I found then, every kind of book, I had free access to this library of Sir's. If I have attained anything, it was from this collection of Sir's books on which I cut my teeth. It took him a while to gather himself. After that, he said slowly: 'You used to say then and write on the walls, "In this system, the more one studies the bigger the idiot one becomes." You people also set fire to the school library once, in the beginning of the seventies. I didn't understand the meaning of all that then. Now it continuously assumes meaning for me. Everything – I sold everything as scrap, by the kilo. What's the use of collecting all this rubbish, it only litters the rooms and occupies space.' How could I think to offer pranam, I was shocked! Master-moshai took some more time, he did not look me in the eye at all. 'Don't be sad, my eyes are so afflicted by cataract that the very formation of letters appears blurred now. And none of the grandchildren want to read books, for them Bengali books are like something from another planet, the previous generation's garbage. They don't even touch them. The meaning of books and so on has changed now, the meaning of knowledge has also changed. All this is really garbage now, the garbage of civilization…' Now the members of the laughing club have begun their final round. Is the mask of civilization called democracy continuously slipping away, democratic-ness? Stable identities were getting wiped away, all those wild marks of *Guernica*. What is the relationship between democracy and power, what is the nature of their hidden understanding – some people are raising questions about this. It was evening by the time I was done and sat down. Arriving in front of Writers' Building he swung around at an unstoppable speed, mind it, it won't do to move the focus. I say, was the thing called collective consciousness at work in all these murder plays, at least in some measure, to some extent! We shall win, we have to win. No, the magic box only looked to be opening, but nothing was revealed. In this dead of night, someone somewhere has begun singing about the love between one human and another. It's audible, and again inaudible too. And, because, yet, only, the punch flung by me reaches till the point, just till there – from where the hairy tunnel of your nostril begins, drunken oaf, in the middle of the road...

Acknowledgements

CUTOUTS have been taken in various ways based on current newspapers, sometimes to retain the character of news, sometimes directly too. *Aajkal*, *Dainik Statesman*, *Anandabazar Patrika* and *Sangbad Pratidin*, and in English, *The Hindu*, *Indian Express*, *Times of India*, and back issues of *Economic Times* – I am much indebted to them, directly and indirectly. The English reports were translated into Bengali. Because the prose is a story type text, the source and date could not be mentioned where necessary because the text matter would lose its sharpness, but I am indebted to them, I acknowledge my debt in all humility to all these newspapers. I could mention the names that I remember; the passages from Ranajit Guha and Mahasveta Devi were taken from the *Dainik Statesman* and *Anandabazar Patrika* of 15 August respectively ... And most definitely, the publisher is in no way responsible for the text, all responsibility is the writer's – all of it.

[Nappy Change, 2010]

A Green-Coloured Asur at the Idol under a Single-Roofed Pavilion and Below, Placed Visibly, the Symbolic Bride Made up of Nine Leaves

(In homage to the late Shibnarayan Ray, the life that men live)

While being a libertine
In battle or forest, through rape, ploughing or touch
Or any time you're in danger following an uproar when you're smashed
Remember me, just chill and call me
(I don't know what 'chill' means, my ears are ringing from hearing it so often
On the restless surface of the earth
For some reason, I shoved it in!)
And then you'll see something awesome
I'm the one who'll rescue you from all danger and adversity
Screw all your enemies
But yeah, every problem has a price
A-case-of-trashing-an-old-vehicle

CUTOUT

When Brinda Karat, the leader of the poor and destitute common folk of Hindustan,
Openly exhorts the people of Nandigram to deliver *'Dum-dum Dawai'*

As punishment, seeing her shiny face gleaming,
It seems she just stepped out of a beauty parlour –
Simply fabulous, she looked like a million dollars
I can't stop hiccuping when I look at that; meanwhile
There's Medha Patkar, looking like a rustic old woman ... Let the Karat-Bose-Bhattarcharyas be, I simply ought to be called
A traditional Marxist now, of whichever variety,
A traditional castrated goat – or else it's going to be dangerous;
Actually, we've gotten used to enjoying power for the last 30 years,
The tiger that's tasted human blood
Can't survive at all without human flesh.
Although I firmly believe that no matter which party
Comes to power – whether it's Mamata Banerjee or the Maoists – once they're
In 'power', they'll do exactly the same, as each day goes by, they'll turn into
Bloodsucking vampires, power's the last word, power's the *asli cheez* –
A red-hot casting couch
To the accompaniment of *tava-jaya-gatha*

(From my diary, 2007)

(A sample of establishment criticism)

In a commentary on Jean-Luc Godard's film *Keep Your Right Up!*
In *Desh* magazine, the Bengali weekly with the highest circulation
(Now a fortnightly, I don't know its current circulation), it was said:
'Only a lunatic can make such a film. And only lunatics

Can sit through the whole film.' Just these two sentences. The end of Godard. The end of film criticism in Bengali.

(*Desh* magazine, 23 April 1988, page 64;
taken from the epigraph of my book
Subimal Versus Subimal and A Lot of Provocative Stuff Apparently
[Published in 1988])

....

GAYATRI MANTRA

Those who wish to be popular – whether it's a film star or a peddler of spurious stuff, or a religious or political leader, or a rustic or rotund novelist – are hugely dependent on the fakery of advertising. It's steadily becoming impossible for talented people to gain public recognition through their talent. There aren't any takers unless one blows one's trumpet. Those who're honest and self-respecting spend their lives in the darkness of neglect. Those who're artful and shameless (perhaps they have a bit of talent too) seek refuge in the powerful institutions which own trumpets and are adept at blowing them. One could say that advertising is the 'contribution' of the capitalist economic system. But right now, this technology is being used even more successfully for brainwashing purposes by various kinds of governments. That's definitely the case within one's own country (there's no competition there), and at the same time, in other countries as well. Plenty of local intellectuals are enrolled in various ways, and they're given privileges and benefits so that they'll sing praises of specific governments.

....

A collection of essays of mine, titled *Against the Stream*, was published some years ago. According to a professor-critic who wrote about it in a widely circulated daily, my contention apparently 'doesn't go against any stream'. I'm used to reading adverse comments about my writing; it would be illogical on my part to expect that I'll go against the stream and not face revilement. But this scholar's complaint was indeed somewhat novel. I can think of three possible explanations for his conclusion. It could well be that what he says is true. That is to say, although I profess being against the stream but actually, like the above-mentioned critic, I too am mingling with the popular current. On the other hand, it's possible that I too couldn't present my stance, my argument and my confessions clearly enough to educated readers. Consequently, the esteemed professor-critic couldn't understand which currents I have been swimming against for so long, and what my orientation is. The third explanation, even if disrespectful, is possibly not entirely removed from reality. In the preface of my book, I had written, *en passant*, that 'those who write critically about a book without even reading it, or without understanding the argument of the book (whether it's a friend or an enemy or someone hoping to establish their intellectual credentials) have done great harm to Bengali literature'. Perhaps this gentleman too belongs to the tribe of critics who form an opinion about a writer even before reading a book, and then go through the cover, preface and contents page, riffle through the remaining pages and then write fervently, and if he's well acquainted with the higher-ups of widely circulated magazines, that piece of writing is usually published too. Most of what appears in Bengali commercial magazines in the name of criticism is of this nature. Reading the critique, there's no way of knowing what the argument of the book under discussion is, but one can gather what the attitude of the critic is towards the author of the book under discussion. **Finish those who refuse to be appropriated! There has been a lot of transformation in my thinking in the last forty or forty-five years, but even with all that, there has always been a specific orientation. That orientation has made me independent; it didn't permit me to join the bellwether flow.** Of the three streams that I think are most powerful among the educated sections in both the Bengals in the present day, the first one is religiosity, the second one is parochialism, and the third one is devotion to Marx. So one is supposed to flow in one or other direction according to the stream one is in, or even in an opposite direction. In East Bengal, or 'Bangladesh', nationalism has prevented the predominance of religiosity at least to some extent. Many among the Marxists in western Europe are critics of nationalism and religious thinking. But in West Bengal, in practical terms, these three streams are bound in mutual reinforcement, and from the point of view of thinking as well, their difference is ambiguous. However, the *ishta mantras* of many among those for whom the authority of Marx and Lenin is indisputable are the Bhagavad Gita and the *Kathamrita* of Sri Ramakrishna; and they believe that the reason for all the suffering and misery of West Bengal is the conspiracy of non-Bengalis against Bengalis. They think that the Bengali language is the sweetest and richest language in the world, and that Bengalis are the most cultured race on earth. Apparently at one time, British imperialism had almost destroyed the national genius of the Bengalis through economic exploitation and the spread of maleducation; and apparently now, state and economic pressures from New Delhi are deliberately preventing West Bengal's development at every step. I'm against all three of these streams. Because the readers of my writing in Bengali are principally educated Bengalis of West Bengal and it's among them that I currently reside, so therefore it's not possible for me to be indifferent towards or neutral about their thinking and behaviour. I can either release myself in their stream, or I can be involved in trying to draw their attention towards the orientation I consider to be the most excellent. **My writing is not suitable for whiling away time or to read in bed before falling asleep. Rather, my writing may seem a bit clearer if, in the course of reading while sitting upright, the reader gets up and walks a bit from time to time in order to think. If my reasoning seems unacceptable after that, that's important for me to know. Because I am eager to benefit from a well thought out critique. I have faith in those readers of mine, both male and female, who are questioning, who are keen on thinking, who are prepared for mental toil. It's them that I keep in mind when I write, although I don't know who the publishers have faith in when they bring out my books.** Although man possesses innate abilities despite originating from the assembling of inanimate matter and the process of biological evolution, pre-human tendencies and habits are not at all absent or isolated in his nature. A huge amount of effort and concentration is required to establish and develop special human abilities. One way of avoiding this toil is to return to pre-human dependence on repetition. The ability to stand erect is an inherent trait of man. But sitting instead of standing, and lying rather than sitting, requires less effort. It's clear to everyone that to float with the stream rather than swim against the current, to rely on collective behaviour rather than to take personal responsibility for a decision, to search for refuge in the ever familiar and the static rather than risking investigation of the unknown, to hold on to conventional relationships and codes of living rather than the uncertainties of an independent life – is easier and free of complications. Just as the establishment and development of his special abilities gives man the promise of his being successful, similarly, his tremendous desire for leisure makes him terrifying and suspicious. This inner conflict in man is recognized in the discipline of psychology. It's a difficult task to establish and develop man's special abilities all by oneself in a world lacking wisdom, imagination and conscience. The purpose of psychology is to make man self-confident and inspired in the course of the sadhana to attain his special abilities. **Unless a thorough and deep cultural renaissance takes place in India, mere political independence will not bring about any well-being in the lives of the ordinary men and women of this country. Political independence is expedient to a few people of the upper strata, who'll swell up; ordinary poor, illiterate, superstition-ridden folk will remain in the same darkness they were in. HOW FREE IS FREEDOM?!** At the core of all religions are some intrinsic beliefs, and the devotees of every religion claim that the intrinsic beliefs of their religion are indisputable, unbiased, universal and self-evident. No argument or evidence is provided in support of this contention; when some people try to advance an argument in refutation, then, as soon as the explanation begins, one notices that it's not an argument but mere declamation. Our knowledge about the universe and its origin, the inhabitants of the earth and their history, has grown through collection of information, experimentation, discovery and invention, and been refined over the last three- or four-thousand years. But it is revelation that is the principal prop of people who have faith in God or Allah or Jehovah, who is imagined in various religions to be the unseen creator, ruler or controller of the universe. **I'm used to reading adverse comments about my writing; it would be illogical on my part to expect that I'll go against the stream and not face revilement. But I don't know who the publishers have faith in when they bring out my books.** And merely accepting the existence of God or Allah or Jehovah without a second thought isn't all; together with that, the religious folk claim that the Vedas are infallible, or that the Bhagavad Gita is the voice of God himself in the incarnation of Krishna; that Jehovah chose Moses, or Allah chose Mohammad to proclaim his instructions to; or that Jesus is the only son of God; or that each one of the individuals like Chaitanya, Ramakrishna, etcetera were incarnated men, and so on. It is even claimed that the one who never had to refer to anyone like God or Allah or Jehovah in his support, the selfsame Buddha, attained absolute knowledge, and that knowledge is unquestionable and proven. **HOW FREE IS FREEDOM?!** If we accept such a claim, then we have to recognize many more claims as a corollary to that. For the promoters and preachers of religion, any supernatural act on the part of the authority who is beyond any proof – is possible. And so, for followers, the Buddha becomes a mysterious magician, Moses walks leisurely with his followers and crosses the sea, Mary gives birth to Jesus with her virginity intact,

Mohammad tours Heaven in bodily form, Krishna reaches many women simultaneously, Ramakrishna gives his disciple a darshan of vishwaroopa, a miraculous light is emitted from Aurobindo's navel after his death, and Sai Baba twirls his hand and produces rings, watches and other such wonders. If the supernatural and revelation are accepted, then issues of internal consistency or corresponding questions can't really be raised. That no evidence or proof is provided regarding supernatural events is not the principal philosophical objection of an atheist to religious belief; his principal objection is to the claim of religious belief to be above question. **Unless a thorough and deep cultural renaissance takes place in India, mere political independence will not bring about any well-being in the lives of the ordinary men and women of this country. Political independence is expedient to a few people of the upper strata, who'll swell up; ordinary poor, illiterate, superstition-ridden folk will remain in the same darkness they were in.** The origin of science and its development was on the basis of asking questions; it's because religious belief denies questioning that the atheist considers religion harmful. To ascribe unreal causes to real things or events is the only business of religion, and as a result, the difference between truth and falsehood becomes unclear, consideration and testing of a hypothesis is no longer necessary, and the advancement of knowledge is disrupted. **One of the principal objections of the atheist to religion is that religious institutions have helped to perpetuate the social system based on institutionalized inequality far more effectively than have any sentinels or the military.** Inequality, oppression, exploitation and persecution are present, to a greater or lesser degree, in every society. Consequently, it is expected that those who are powerful will engage the sentinels and the military to suppress the turmoil that naturally results. But it is far more attractive for the people in the establishment to inwardly mesmerize those who create trouble than to use force. This job is done most successfully by religion. If belief in 'original sin' or in 'birthright' can be made widespread and firmly rooted, a revolt against the shameful system becomes futile. Once people can be made to accept that there's nothing amiss about what exists, efforts and enthusiasm for change can never become powerful. **There has been a lot of transformation in my thinking in the last forty or forty-five years, but even with all that, there has always been a specific orientation. That orientation has made me independent; it didn't permit me to join the bellwether flow. My writing is not suitable for whiling away time or to read in bed before falling asleep. Rather, my writing may seem a bit clearer if, in the course of reading while sitting upright, the reader gets up and walks a bit from time to time in order to think. If my reasoning seems unacceptable after that, that's important for me to know. Because I am eager to benefit from a well thought out critique. Finish those who refuse to be appropriated!** In the final section of the *Tuhfatul Muwahhidin* (Gift to the Monotheists), Rammohun Roy had divided humankind into four classes. First, those who were deceivers, who invented various religious doctrines in order to charm the common people. Second, those who were the deceived, who blindly follow others without verifying actual facts. Third, those who were both deceiver and deceived, who accept what someone says without a second thought and try to make others also accept that without a second thought. And fourth, those who do not deceive others and are not deceived themselves either. The people in the fourth class are honest and seek truth. Rammohun had no doubt at all that social and cultural development depended on the growth, efforts and enthusiasm of the fourth class. Religion and the state are constantly at work to enhance in various ways the widespread and deep-seated fear and feeling of insecurity in people and use that to establish themselves. In the climate that I observe nowadays, I think it's becoming increasingly difficult for ordinary people to muster up and nurture courage. To kneel before the powerful and to pounce upon the weak, disregard reality or the poor folk in order to be viewed favourably by the wealthy, hover around the masters round-the-clock and be careful to avoid the company of respected people who are known to be critical of the establishment, all out of a lust for the security the establishment offers, its patronage and prizes – what memories will the offspring of those who have raised themselves to their advanced age in this manner, and are still doing that, be heir to? At present, the fourth class is a small minority in our country. Whether in this country or elsewhere, those who are wily and deceitful have since the beginning of time used the unthinking folk for their own ends. Wily people are not wise, and stupid people are not deceitful, but when it comes to deceit and self-deceit, the two complement one another. **HOW FREE IS FREEDOM?!** Therefore Marx-devotion. He himself was a first-class thinker. Not only was he adept at analysing society, he was also one of the visionaries and proclaimers of an ideal social system. There are flaws in his analysis and his ideals are opaque; nevertheless, in terms of the process of understanding modern civilization and making our thinking clearer, his contribution is undeniable. But the stream of

Marx-devotion in West Bengal that I oppose – many educated Bengalis are in that stream – is only feebly related to social analysis or ideals and zeal. After the Bolsheviks seized power in Russia under the leadership of Lenin, Marxism was established as the state religion there. Preachers of Marxism spread across countries in the same way in which, at one time, Buddhism, Christianity and Islam was spread in various directions. This propagation gained different degrees of support in various countries according to various social-cultural-political-economic circumstances. **My writing is not suitable for whiling away time or to read in bed before falling asleep. Rather, my writing may seem a bit clearer if, in the course of reading while sitting upright, the reader gets up and walks a bit from time to time in order to think. If my reasoning seems unacceptable after that, that's important for me to know. Because I am eager to benefit from a well thought out critique.** Almost from the beginning an extremist section of educated Bengali folk were drawn towards this doctrine. Its widespread influence, following sixty years of unceasing propagation, is visible. As a result of the Marx-devotees coming to power in West Bengal, Marx-devotion has grown. But if religion had only claimed that the supernatural and the revelation were beyond question, perhaps its impact on human history would not have been so malignant. Power is needed to establish such claims, and one of the principal means to such power is organization. When the one in whose imagination the core beliefs of any religion are first formed is active in preaching those beliefs among people, then he gets some devotees and followers, and with or without his consent, a religious organization comes up around them. This organization can be of different kinds; and even if a workable estimate is to be made of whether the impact of the religion will be widespread or otherwise, and if it is, then how much time that will take, one needs to be aware of various kinds of facts. But it can still be said with some degree of accuracy that it is doubtful whether the religion of those believers who are completely disinterested in the work of propagation and for that reason gladly dwell in mountains, caves, forests or deserts, has any widespread impact. Meanwhile, the basis of the propaganda and power of most influential religions is organization, and if the founder is not himself an organizer, then he would need at least a few devotees who can broadcast his message forcefully to multitudes of people, and whose organizational capabilities are exceptional. Jesus came by some preacher devotees like that, who had narrated and made people imbibe numerous supernatural tales and legends surrounding him. There's no dearth of examples like that in India. The branches of the organization that the virile and eloquent devotee Vivekananda built in various American cities towards the end of the nineteenth century, positing Ramakrishna as the religious authority, are still active. The model for that was possibly the Jesuit order, and again, modelled on his organization, in recent times many Hindu missionary organizations have come up who have considerable following in youthful circles in America. **Finish those who refuse to be appropriated! I'm used to reading adverse comments about my writing; it would be illogical on my part to expect that I'll go against the stream and not face revilement. But I don't know who the publishers have faith in when they bring out my books.** The principal and sole objective of advertising is the sale of goods. The business of advertising exists solely to tempt the buyer, no matter how trashy, flimsy and unnecessary the goods might be. What kind of bait can hook what kind of fool – is the subject of the research undertaken by advertising specialists. There was no need for advertising in the socio-economic milieu of the village; buyers and sellers knew one another; the quantum of surplus was meagre. But in large and small towns, trade and commerce is extensive, competition is fierce, and opportunities to deceive are much greater. If you want to win a young woman's heart, puff on a cigarette of a special brand; if you want to attract the attention of men, wear your brassiere in a special way; if you want to make your neighbours envious, buy a car of a special model; if you want your offspring to be secure, deposit your money in a special bank. Don't you have the household gadgets and equipment that everyone else has at home? Haven't you adopted the latest fashion? Won't you go for a holiday to the place everyone's going to? Earlier people used to decide on what's to be done by following traditions. But now, in a market society, it is what others are doing that determines people's behaviour. **HOW FREE IS FREEDOM?!** A self-regulating person is always a rarity, one sees them even less now. Everyone's seen the Hindi film *Ram Teri Ganga Maili*, everyone's read the Bengali novel *Shei Somoy*, everyone's heard Kishore Kumar's songs. If you and your family haven't seen, read and heard all these, then your life's been in vain. Newspapers, posters and television carry out assaults every day, with the objective of hypnotizing people. **Unless a thorough and deep cultural renaissance takes place in India, mere political independence will not bring about any well-being in the lives of the ordinary men and women of this country. Political independence is expedient to a few people of the upper strata, who'll swell up; ordinary poor, illiterate,** superstition-ridden folk will remain in the same darkness they were in. This is far greater in the West. But even in this country, the aggressive operations of advertising are growing, and there's almost no arrangement or initiative to resist that. Those who wish to be popular – whether it's a film star or a peddler of spurious stuff, or a religious or political leader, or a rustic or rotund novelist – are hugely dependent on the fakery of advertising. It's steadily becoming impossible for talented people to gain public recognition through their talent. There aren't any takers unless one blows one's trumpet. Those who're honest and self-respecting spend their lives in the darkness of neglect. Those who're artful and shameless (perhaps they have a bit of talent too) seek refuge in the powerful institutions which own trumpets and are adept at blowing them. One could say that advertising is the 'contribution' of the capitalist economic system. But right now, this technology is being used even more successfully for brainwashing purposes by various kinds of governments. That's definitely the case within one's own country (there's no competition there), and at the same time, in other countries as well. Plenty of local intellectuals are enrolled in various ways, and they're given privileges and benefits so that they'll sing praises of specific governments. One of the principal objections of the atheist to religion is that religious institutions have helped to perpetuate the social system based on institutionalized inequality far more effectively than have any sentinels or the military. Inequality, oppression, exploitation and persecution are present, to a greater or lesser degree, in every society. Consequently, it is expected that those who are powerful will engage the sentinels and the military to suppress the turmoil that naturally results. But it is far more attractive for the people in the establishment to inwardly mesmerize those who create trouble than to use force. This job is done most successfully by religion. If belief in 'original sin' or in 'birthright' can be made widespread and firmly rooted, a revolt against the shameful system becomes futile. Once people can be made to accept that there's nothing amiss about what exists, efforts and enthusiasm for change can never become powerful. There has been a lot of transformation in my thinking in the last forty or forty-five years, but even with all that, there has always been a specific orientation. That orientation has made me independent, it didn't permit me to join the bellwether flow. Once religious organizations come up, their work isn't limited to merely preaching. The precepts and supernatural tales and legends associated with them constitute their primeval capital, and if someone questions their veracity, the organization endeavours to stifle such voices. If one part of the programme of a religious organization consists of preaching the revelation, the other part then comprises a crusade to annihilate questioning. I have faith in those readers of mine, both male and female, who are questioning, who are keen on thinking, who are prepared for mental toil. It's them I keep in mind when I write, although I don't know who the publishers have faith in when they bring out my books. The form of the propaganda is more or less clear, but the process of instituting religions has not been the same everywhere. Both the aspects were extremely powerful in the history of Christianity and Islam; bringing the Bible and the Koran didn't depend merely on the magic of words, weapons had to be used time and again towards that end. Not only were those who belonged to other faiths, and those who were non-believers, forced to embrace their religion, in parallel, those within their religion who expressed doubts about the explanations provided by the authorities had to suffer great torture for their breach. This violent intolerance as a practical means of religion has in our times turned into two political systems, namely Fascism and Communism. At least in this aspect, the latter are the heirs of the religious tradition. Among the rationalists in our country, many are in a dilemma, they are hesitant when it comes to expressing their personal thinking against public opinion, they pipe down at the slightest pressure. They would like to make a compromise between reason and faith, and because it is faith that's predominant in their families and their environment, their intellectual vigour is usually short-lived. **Unless a thorough and deep cultural renaissance takes place in India, mere political independence will not bring about any well-being in the lives of the ordinary men and women of this country. Political independence is expedient to a few people of the upper strata, who'll swell up; ordinary poor, illiterate, superstition-ridden folk will remain in the same darkness they were in. My writing is not suitable for whiling away time or to read in bed before falling asleep. Rather, my writing may seem a bit clearer if, in the course of reading while sitting upright, the reader gets up and walks a bit from time to time in order to think. If my reasoning seems unacceptable after that, that's important for me to know. Because I am eager to benefit from a well thought out critique.** That's why in the history of modern Bengal, we see the initiatives of the Rammohun kind ending up in Dakhineshwar and Belur, and the termination of endeavours of the Vidyasagar kind in the Pondicherry ashram. The lifelong endeavours of the rationalist Akhoykumar Dutta, as well as his writings, have been almost entirely forgotten, but many artful entrepreneurs have made a fortune riding on the *Kathamrita* of Sri Ramakrishna. Most of the men and women in our country still live in villages and are still illiterate, poor and helpless. The influence of those who are in the business of temples and mosques, dargahs and sacred places, and of peddling amulets and faith healing is not at all insignificant. Meanwhile, I think the aura of supernatural miracles among educated urban folk just keeps growing by the day. Astrologers have a great following now (right from the prime minister to High Court judges, university professors, communist leaders, senior bureaucrats and bank managers, all are slaves to planetary placation); the procession of hundreds of thousands of disciples of 'Bhole Baba' to Tarakeshwar is now the greatest religious festival in West Bengal; Sai Baba, ISKCON and Ma Anandamayi. In Bengali newspapers, on one side are supernatural accounts of mendicants and saints; on the other side are utterly worthless and baseless accounts of how various planets will control people's daily lives. **HOW FREE IS FREEDOM?!** Squeezed in the crowd, drenched in sweat, suffocating in the darkness of a power cut, it seems we are submerged in a collective sadhana to return to the Middle Ages under a progressive leadership. **Religion and the state are constantly at work to enhance in various ways the widespread and deep-seated fear and feeling of insecurity in people and use that to establish themselves. In the climate that I observe nowadays, I think it is becoming increasingly difficult for ordinary people to muster and nurture courage. To kneel before the powerful and to pounce upon the weak, disregard reality or the poor folk in order to be viewed favourably by the wealthy, hover around the masters round-**

the-clock and be careful to avoid the company of respected people who are known to be critical of the establishment, all out of a lust for the security the establishment offers, its patronage and prizes – what memories will the offspring of those who have raised themselves to their advanced age in this manner, and are still doing that, be heir to? But although I'm completely atheist as far as my thinking is concerned, nonetheless it doesn't seem sensible to me to dismiss religion as merely a kind of psychological opiate. I hope that in the course of saying why it doesn't, some questions of mine regarding religion will become clearer. **There has been a lot of transformation in my thinking in the last forty or forty-five years, but even with all that, there has always been a specific orientation. That orientation has made me independent, it didn't permit me to join the bellwether flow.** Although the explanations presented in support of religious beliefs are extremely shaky, and in the history of religious propagation even if the effacement of questioning and the prevalence of masochism and sadism is especially observable, nonetheless, for at least three reasons I don't view religion as merely a kind of stupefaction. First, I've met and know a few people who are professed religious believers, but in whose character and behaviour there are qualities (like compassion, honesty, good humour, creativity, service, courage, equability, etc.) which I consider extremely valuable. That doesn't mean that all these qualities arise from their religious belief. But at least in the case of these special women and men, I think these qualities cannot be separated from their religious beliefs. And so, a question comes to mind: What's the relation of all these qualities to religion? **HOW FREE IS FREEDOM?!** No religious belief was necessary for the origin and nourishment of all the qualities whose assemblage occurs in the character of Jyathamoshai in the novel *Chaturanga*, by Rabindranath Tagore. The few special individuals of my time who I personally know have made a mark on my character and thinking – like Bertrand Russel, Manabendranath and Ellen Roy, Rajshekhar Basu, Sudhindranath Dutta, Albert Camus, etc. – none of them were religious believers. But I wonder whether the few people of religious faith I know, whom I respect, would have been able to protect their good qualities from the attacks of happy atheism but for their refuge in religion. If religious belief helps to protect and develop these fine qualities of theirs, then despite being an atheist, I can't disrespect those beliefs of theirs. **Finish those who refuse to be appropriated! My writing is not suitable for whiling away time or to read in bed before falling asleep. Rather, my writing may seem a bit clearer if, in the course of reading while sitting upright, the reader gets up and walks a bit from time to time in order to think. If my reasoning seems unacceptable after that, that's important for me to know. Because I am eager to benefit from a well thought out critique.** Responsible critique in the Bengali language is rare, a mutually respectful debate between one thinker and another is even rarer. Those who write critically about a book without even reading it, or without understanding the argument of the book (whether it's a friend or an enemy or someone hoping to establish their intellectual credentials) have done great harm to Bengali literature. **Unless a thorough and deep cultural renaissance takes place in India, mere political independence will not bring about any well-being in the lives of the ordinary men and women of this country. Political independence is expedient to a few people of the upper strata, who'll swell up; ordinary poor, illiterate,**

superstition-ridden folk will remain in the same darkness they were in. One could say that in its embodiment, man's creative imagination and varied artistic endeavours are to a large extent marked by religious belief. One cannot imagine a history of sculpture in this subcontinent by leaving out the Buddha in Sarnath, Vishnu in Mathura, Shiva in the Elephanta Caves, or Mahishasuramardhini in Mahabalipuram. One can see innumerable astonishing examples of religious sculpture in the much-loved Gothic cathedrals of medieval Europe, in the blue mosques and minarets of West Asia, in the Sanchi stupa, in the transformed temples of Bhubaneswar – Konark – Khajuraho. **I'm used to reading adverse comments about my writing; it would be illogical on my part to expect that I'll go against the stream and not face revilement. But I don't know who the publishers have faith in when they bring out my books.** It isn't only in Indian music that the most significant part is associated with religious beliefs, in European music too, the influence of religion has for long been powerful and also fecund. For those who cherish European music, whatever their philosophical outlook might be, Bach is no less beloved than Mozart, Beethoven, Wagner and Stravinsky. Also notable is the fact that in all countries, a very major part of pre-modern poetry is connected to religion. Dante's epic poem entrances me as much today as the Vaishnav padabali, or the Shyamasangeet of Ramprasad, does. **I have faith in those readers of mine, both male and female, who are questioning, who are keen on thinking, who are prepared for mental toil. It's them I keep in mind when I write, although I don't know who the publishers have faith in when they bring out my books.** Therefore, if an atheist is sensitive and an aesthete, if he has an inclination towards art, music and literature, then he cannot but notice that at one time much of this world was religious, and in the modern era too, this relation has not been entirely broken. Among the twentieth-century poets whom I especially love, just as there are Sudhindranath Dutta, Éluard and Neruda, there are also Rabindranath Tagore, Rilke and Eliot. Of course, there are examples of architecture, sculpture, painting, music and literature from the past that were not directly associated with religion; in the present era, this separation is much clearer and also more widespread. But despite that, the question arises: What is the nature of the relationship between religious belief and the artistic imagination? Is the relation coincidental? Was the proximity between the two that had been observed for long merely apparent and not real? Or were both born out of the same source of mind? So that ploughing or innovation in one makes the other strong or weak accordingly? T.S. Eliot and Jacques Maritain, among others, complained a lot about art being sought to be accorded the place of religion, and they were of the view that this effort is completely vile. Eliot wasn't just a religious believer, he was also one of the principal poets and literary critics of this age. How seriously would atheists who love literature take that complaint of his? **HOW FREE IS FREEDOM?! Religion and the state are constantly at work to enhance in various ways the widespread and deep-seated fear and feeling of insecurity in people and use that to establish themselves. In the climate that I observe nowadays, I think it is becoming increasingly difficult for ordinary people to muster and nurture courage. To kneel before the powerful and to pounce upon the weak, disregard reality or the poor folk in order to be viewed favourably by the wealthy, hover around the masters round-**

the-clock and be careful to avoid the company of respected people who are known to be critical of the establishment, all out of a lust for the security the establishment offers, its patronage and prizes – what memories will the offsprings of those who have raised themselves to their advanced age in this manner, and are still doing that, be heir to? If I believe that the notions of God, the soul and the supernatural are merely products of the human imagination, and that before man, or after, or if man is excluded from the pictures, they have no independent existence – nonetheless, to regard religion only as something harmful, is, in my view, not in keeping with human experience. In that case, the question arises of whether the qualities and actions that we attach value to have any necessary and universal connection to religious precepts and consciousness. Those who wish to be popular – whether it's a film star or a peddler of spurious stuff, or a religious or political leader, or a rustic or rotund novelist – they're hugely dependent on the fakery of advertising. It's steadily becoming impossible for talented people to gain public recognition through their talent. There aren't any takers unless one blows one's trumpet. Those who're honest and self-respecting spend their lives in the darkness of neglect. Those who're artful and shameless (perhaps they have a bit of talent too) seek refuge in the powerful institutions which own trumpets and are adept at blowing them. One could say that advertising is the 'contribution' of the capitalist economic system. But right now, this technology is being used even more successfully for brainwashing purposes by various kinds of governments. That's definitely the case within one's own country (there's no competition there), and at the same time, in other countries as well. Plenty of local intellectuals are enrolled in various ways, and they're given privileges and benefits so that they'll sing praises of specific governments. **Unless a thorough and deep cultural renaissance takes place in India, mere political independence will not bring about any well-being in the lives of the ordinary men and women of this country. Political independence is expedient to a few people of the upper strata, who'll swell up; ordinary poor, illiterate, superstition-ridden folk will remain in the same darkness they were in.** It is not easy to find a universally acceptable answer to such a question, but those who'll think about this question with an open mind need to remember a few things. First, in history and in one's personal experience, one comes across some individuals who possess the above-mentioned qualities, but who aren't known for their religiosity. Not much is known about the personal life of Epicurus; but one gets some indication about his character from the ideal that he held up, of making life into a playground, and that is not one of religiosity. Were the questioning Socrates or the rebellious Spartacus inspired by religious beliefs? Or the lonely social reformer of the nineteenth century, Iswarchandra Vidyasagar? Among those I know about, I can think of the atheist and man of conscience Manabendranath Roy, the Gandhian from Andhra Pradesh, 'Gora', or Goparaju Ramachandra Rao, Justice Tarkunde from Maharashtra, the Gujarati thinker A.B. Shah, and Nirmal Kumar Bose from Calcutta. **HOW FREE IS FREEDOM?!** No ordinary link is proven by all these examples. Perhaps all that can be said is that the presence of conscience and its operation is supported by direct experience. Based on that, is it illogical to conclude that qualities like non-violence, service, compassion, heroism, honesty, responsibility, etc. may be reinforced in the case of many by their religious beliefs, but that their source is not religious belief? Is their source some mysterious aspect of human existence from which both conscience and religion gather support for themselves? Isn't the proposition worth considering that the biological-social creature named man is known from its birth for possessing a different consciousness and sense of responsibility, and that religion, social organization, principles, education, law and order, and so on either nourish and expand that sense, or distort it? **My writing is not suitable for whiling away time or to read in bed before falling asleep. Rather, my writing may seem a bit clearer if, in the course of reading while sitting upright, the reader gets up and walks a bit from time to time in order to think. If my reasoning seems unacceptable after that, that's important for me to know. Because I am eager to benefit from a well thought out critique.** Many people confuse religiosity with conscientiousness or morality. It is through the effort of trying to give real form, out of a personal sense of responsibility, to what I consider necessary or a duty, in one's own life and activities, that the existence of conscientiousness or morality is proven. On the other hand, religiosity means viewing oneself as weak and powerless, and therefore establishing a reliance on some bygone, mysterious power, and trying to attain refuge in that power according to the prescriptions of scriptures, or a guru or of folklore. The more an individual in society views himself as insignificant, helpless and broken, the more pronounced does religiosity become. Religiosity has always been influential in this country's heritage – one finds that very few thinkers in this country have proclaimed the precept that man himself is the creator of his destiny, if one were to look at their views and sayings – but I can't recall witnessing, even in my youth, the extent to which religiosity has become manifest at present, in the educated section here. **Finish those who refuse to be appropriated!** Pujas of known, lesser known and unheard of gods and goddesses in one neigbourhood after another, crowds of young devotees outnumbering the elderly in Dakshineswar, Thantaniya, Kalighat and Tarakeswar, the appearance almost every day of new 'Babas' and 'Mas' claiming supernatural powers, the induction of salaried and advertised astrologers in every jewellery shop, consulting the almanac to ascertain auspicious times, whether for submitting nomination papers for political elections or applications for jobs, the emergence of temples overnight in the streets and lanes of the city, loudspeakers blaring non-stop, round-the-clock kirtans chanting the Name – it seems our educated folk are employing technology to return to the darkness of the pre-modern mind. Those who wish to be popular – whether it's a film star or a peddler of spurious stuff, or a religious or political leader, or a rustic or rotund novelist – they're hugely dependent on the fakery of advertising. It's steadily becoming impossible for talented people to gain public recognition through their talent. There aren't any takers unless one blows one's trumpet. Those who're honest and self-respecting spend their lives in the darkness of neglect. Those who're artful and shameless (perhaps they have a bit of talent too) seek refuge in the powerful institutions which own trumpets and are adept at blowing them. One could say that advertising is the 'contribution' of the capitalist economic system. But right now, this technology is being used even more successfully for brainwashing purposes by various kinds of governments. That's definitely the case within one's own country (there's no competition there), and at the same time, in other countries as well. Plenty of local intellectuals are enrolled in various ways, and they're given privileges and benefits so that they'll sing praises of specific governments. After returning to Calcutta, over the last few years I've been observing that almost seventy to eighty per cent of the programme announcements that are carried in *The Statesman* are for religious discourses, lectures, kirtans, havans, etc. In almost all the Bengali daily newspapers, there's a separate page declaring the fate of the zodiac signs, and in some of the dailies there's also an arrangement for a special page for religious propagation. Many of the popular writers are believers in the supernatural; perhaps that's a major factor behind their popularity. **One of the principal objections of the atheist to religion is that religious institutions have helped to perpetuate the social system based on institutionalized inequality far more effectively than have any sentinels or the military. Inequality, oppression, exploitation and persecution are present, to a greater or lesser degree, in every society. Consequently, it is expected that those who are powerful will engage the sentinels and the military to suppress the turmoil that naturally results. But it is far more attractive for the people in the establishment to inwardly mesmerize those who create trouble than to use force. This job is done most successfully by religion. If belief in 'original sin' or in 'birthright' can be made widespread and firmly rooted, a revolt against the shameful system becomes futile. Once people can be made to accept that there's nothing amiss about what exists,**

efforts and enthusiasm for change can never become powerful. There has been a lot of transformation in my thinking in the last forty or forty-five years, but even with all that, there has always been a specific orientation. That orientation has made me independent, it didn't permit me to join the bellwether flow. I have faith in those readers of mine, both male and female, who are questioning, who are keen on thinking, who are prepared for mental toil. It's them I keep in mind when I write, although I don't know who the publishers have faith in when they bring out my books. Businessmen seek profits, and political parties seek power. There's the possibility of greater profit if a lot of goods can be sold quickly with the help of loud advertising. The possibility of coming to power is greater if one can muster enough public support through loud rhetoric. Knowingly making false promises, provoking greed, violence and anger, hypnotizing people so that their thinking faculties and common sense are suspended, to belittle what is complex, difficult and subject to perseverance by labelling it as simple and easy to attain – the business of political rhetoric is about all that. Growth in a society's resources, the equitable distribution of its surplus, the reduction in the ordeals inflicted by bureaucrats and middlemen, expansion of opportunities for ordinary folk to advance in life – none of these are attained through the magic of any Aladdin's lamp. It is knowledge, endeavour, idealism, innovation, toil, cooperation, appropriate technology, institutions, etc. that are needed. **Unless a thorough and deep cultural renaissance takes place in India, mere political independence will not bring about any well-being in the lives of the ordinary men and women of this country. Political independence is expedient to a few people of the upper strata, who'll swell**

up; ordinary poor, illiterate, superstition-ridden folk will remain in the same darkness they were in. But explaining all that requires time; to build up endeavours on the basis of one's consciousness requires even more time. Where do those whose sadhana is power have so much time? By raising slogans such as 'Garibi Hatao', 'Larke Lenge Pakistan', 'Inquilab Zindabad', etc. they try to gain public support. And thus, the chanting of religious mantras or rhetoric in the case of politics. **HOW FREE IS FREEDOM?!** Obscuring reality and preoccupying the mind, rhetoric that frantically aims at creating bewilderment and dependency helps the artful manipulate and make use of simple folk. Poverty is not removed, rather the number of those who are poor, their proportion, as well as the gap between the poor and the wealthy, all grow, and leaders cheat the poor and occupy seats of power in New Delhi. There's no glimmer of revolution; the Congress government at the centre continues its efforts to keep the hackneyed system standing through importunate entreaties to the World Bank, multinational corporations, Japanese entrepreneurs, Birla, etc.; the leftists show the same adeptness as the right-wingers in underhand dealings; they are conscienceless in annihilating Naxalites and Gorkhas; yet, thanks to the mantra of revolution, the Marxists became the satraps of West Bengal. Massive efforts are undertaken to increase the influence of the party and its leaders by way of combining rhetoric and advertising. **I'm used to reading adverse comments about my writing; it would be illogical on my part to expect that I'll go against the stream and not face revilement. But I don't know who the publishers have faith in when they bring out my books.** Gathering accounts of various supernatural events that occurred in someone's life is thought of mainly to use on devotees. Meanwhile, the need for the deification of Socrates or the assembling of supernatural events in his life did not arise, because he was not the founder of any religion, and Plato was not interested in establishing any religious organization under the authority of his teacher. At least one of the reasons for the Brahmo religion not finding much public support in India, and for that matter, in Bangladesh too, is that although Rammohun Roy was a great personality, he never claimed any supernatural powers. And despite their feelings of deep reverence and affection towards him, Debendranath Tagore, or Keshabchandra Sen, or Sivnath Shastri made no attempts to establish him as a god or avatar. Actually, one observes an inner contradiction in the Brahmo religion. On the one hand, Rammohun was a great proponent of science education, applied philosophy and ever-expanding quest; on the other hand, the authority that he accorded to the doctrines of the Upanishad was avowedly indisputable. **Finish those who refuse to be appropriated!** A compromise between theology and science is unimaginable. Because in the case of the former, knowledge is thought of as eternal and changeless, and in the case of the latter, knowledge is admittedly limited, subject to consideration, changing, where an existing hypothesis may be proven to be wrong or incomplete through the acquisition of new data and careful analysis, and therefore knowledge there is not something fossilized, it is something that grows. **HOW FREE IS FREEDOM?!** By trying to make a compromise between the two, the Brahmo religion couldn't really spread much, and it didn't come to be established as a philosophy either. In contrast, by proclaiming the divinity of Ramakrishna, Vivekananda attracted followers not only within his own country but abroad as well, and the discipline, financial resources and influence of the organization he conceived of is greater than that of many political parties and business corporations. **There has been a lot of transformation in my thinking in the last forty or forty-five years, but even with all that, there has always been a specific orientation. That orientation has made me independent, it didn't permit me to join the bellwether flow.** In old times, the principal weapon in the practice of deceit was the sacred mantra, occult methods and incantations and the bribe-dependent demonstration of miracles. By declaring that the world was unknowable instead of seeking to understand it, by exacerbating people's sense of helplessness, and by explaining suffering, sickness, economic inequality, social oppression, state intimidation and abuse as one's destiny, the preachers, priests, clergy and missionaries of various religions used to try to lull to sleep the instinctive questioning tendency of common folk. After that, it would be explained to the helpless folk that the unknown supernatural powers that control their lives had a special relationship with the wily and sanctimonious flag bearers of religion, so if a bribe was given through them they could be made to act in their favour, and thus, if nothing else, the business of mythology and spells and charms, a miracle wrought by the middlemen of the supernatural! Through employing such means, various religious institutions swelled their power. **Unless a thorough and deep cultural renaissance takes place in India, mere political independence will not bring about any well-being in the lives of the ordinary men and women of this country. Political independence is expedient to a few people of the upper strata, who'll swell up; ordinary poor, illiterate, superstition-ridden folk will remain in the same darkness they were in.**

The religious texts, scriptures and puranas that were created in ancient times – the Vedas or the Tripitaka, the Mahabharata or the Bible, the Talmud or the Koran – the source of authority of each one is supernatural, and the entrepreneurs of religion have for ever been explaining their tales and the punishments for violating prescriptions. Hinduism, Buddhism, Christianity and Islam haven't fallen behind in this respect. There has been competition and conflict between them, but when it comes to preaching unthinking faith and suppressing logical questioning, they're all equally zealous, active, and have been at it for many centuries. **Finish those who refuse to be appropriated!** Even when religious believers speak of the transcendental and unworldly, the archives reveal that their attraction to the worldly was by no means modest. There are bound to be individual exceptions, but once an organization comes into existence, the need for land, property and financial power arises; and then, centring around the monastery or ashram, zamindari, usury, profit, etcetera begin to emerge. For the sake of worldly interests, the religious institutions turn into supporters of the established system – if they could accumulate adequate means, they were the ones who became the principal upholders and masters of the system. Alternatively, they endeavour to be close to kings, zamindars and merchants. In this regard, one doesn't see much difference between the experience in the East and that in the West. It wasn't just the Church that made an enormous amount of wealth; in this country, extensive zamindari and usury came up centring around the *mutts* and temples. I don't see any reason to think that the same process doesn't exist at present. Donning robes of white, black, yellow, saffron, red and several other colours, various religious organizations accumulate extensive amounts of wealth in the name of some authority, and they carry on employing their capital in various profitable exploitative enterprises. **HOW FREE IS FREEDOM?! My writing is not suitable for whiling away time or to read in bed before falling asleep. Rather, my writing may seem a bit clearer if, in the course of reading while sitting upright, the reader gets up and walks a bit from time to time in order to think. If my reasoning seems unacceptable after that, that's important for me to know. Because I am eager to benefit from a well thought out critique.** If I turned into an atheist on account of questioning, my atheism has become even more pronounced by observing the nature of religion's attitude towards the established order. I've seen beggars, leprosy patients, starving and semi-starved women and men on the streets from my childhood. In response to the question of why they're in such a plight, I was told that this was apparently the outcome of sin in past lives. There's no trace of what anyone did in past lives in recorded history. On the other hand, if one analysed the social system, it's possible to conclude about the cause of all this suffering; and once the cause is known, one can make the effort to eliminate poverty, or at least reduce it. As I grew older, I saw widespread famine and epidemic, wars and communal carnage, I heard terrifying stories about the annihilation of Jews in Germany, I read about the oppression of black people by white Americans, as well as accounts of the slave camps in the Soviet Union. It didn't seem possible for me to accept the explanations of those who, even after observing and knowing and reading about all this, sought to explain that there is a benign intention underlying everything on earth, and that in the final analysis, underlying all oppression, decay and agony there is a most merciful entity who is at work. Rather, it seemed to me that some indication of a reliable explanation of the human condition is found in the writings of Marx, Freud and Russel, among others, and although these explanations show the way, they are not above question either. **HOW FREE IS FREEDOM?!** Like with the human body, in the case of society too, if the cause of sickness is known, it's possible to move towards good health, and in the way a physician can be responsible and active even without claiming absolute knowledge (or as a result of not claiming so), similarly, by being aware of the limits of his knowledge, a conscientious atheist can involve himself in endeavours to redress oppression and inequality. He does not rely on God, or a guru, on mantras or supernatural powers; he relies on experience, reason, compassion, endeavour, cooperation and an unshakeable sense of responsibility for himself as well as for all mankind. **There has been a lot of transformation in my thinking in the last forty or forty-five years, but even with all that, there has always been a specific orientation. That orientation has made me independent, it didn't permit me to join the bellwether flow. Unless a thorough and deep cultural renaissance takes place in India, mere political independence will not bring about any well-being in the lives of the ordinary men and women of this country. Political independence is expedient to a few people of the upper strata, who'll swell up; ordinary poor, illiterate, superstition-ridden folk will remain in the same darkness they were in. I have faith in those readers of mine, both male and female, who are questioning, who are keen on thinking, who are prepared for mental toil. It's them I keep in mind when I write, although I don't know who the publishers have faith in when they bring out my books.** By Marx-devotion I mean the attitude that the authority of Marx–Lenin is beyond question, the belief that the medicine for all the ills in the world, the solution to all problems and the scientific explanation of all structures is sure to be found in some utterance or the other of Marx–Lenin. Just as for Hindu religious folk the source of all the knowledge in the world is the Vedas, or the Mahabharata, or the Bhagavad Gita, and for the religious Muslims it is the Koran, similarly, for the Marx-devotees, it is the collected works of Marx. Of course, there's no need to study those works carefully – just as those are enormous in volume, similarly, a lot of what he says is abstruse – the explanations of the mullahs and maulvis of Marxism, in the form of slogans and pamphlets, is adequate for most of the women and men who are Marx-devotees. **One of the principal objections of the atheist to religion is that religious institutions have helped to perpetuate the social system based on institutionalized inequality far more effectively than have any sentinels or the military. Inequality, oppression, exploitation and persecution are present, to a greater or lesser degree, in every society. Consequently, it is expected that those who are powerful will engage the sentinels and the military to suppress the turmoil that naturally results. But it is far more attractive for the people in the establishment to inwardly mesmerize those who create trouble than to use force. This job is done most successfully by religion. If belief in 'original sin' or in 'birthright' can be made widespread and firmly rooted, a revolt against the shameful system becomes futile. Once people can be made to accept that there's nothing amiss about what exists, efforts and enthusiasm for change can never become powerful.** Just like how, despite their pretentions about Mother Earth or all their hype about the illusoriness of life, religious Hindus don't feel any compunction in obtaining their ends through bribery or obsequiousness to the powerful, or like how it isn't difficult for religious Christians to combine hymns in praise of the crucified Christ with expansion of empire, war or exploitative processes, those who are Marx-devotees also raise slogans about class struggle, the proletariat, revolution and so on while being busy establishing their respective opportunities and benefits. Those among the Marx-devotees who do read and study a bit know that the revolutions in Russia or China do not conform at all to Marx's theory of history, that capitalism is still extremely powerful in the United States or the industrially advanced countries of Europe, that these countries do not conform to Marx's sociological analysis and prophecies, and that, like the interpretations found in Christianity, there's no end to differences of opinion within Marxists about the interpretation of Marxism. **HOW FREE IS FREEDOM?!** Most of the Marxist leaders of West Bengal (whether of the CPI or the CPI[M]) have proven through their actions that they are simply supporters of the established order, that all of them have reaped immense benefits and opportunities from this order, and that they don't have the slightest interest in social change. Many among them have acquired houses and cars, and after driving out the British, they sent their own sons, daughters, sons-in-law, nieces and nephews to 'God's country', America, they have dexterously blended together the rhetoric of revolution with the *'dehi dehi'* chants of community Durga Pujas. The Ghoshes, Boses, Dasguptas and Mukherjees are Marxist not just in the recesses of their minds, but by outward abandonment of the thread slung around their chests. **Unless a thorough and deep cultural**

renaissance takes place in India, mere political independence will not bring about any well-being in the lives of the ordinary men and women of this country. Political independence is expedient to a few people of the upper strata, who'll swell up; ordinary poor, illiterate, superstition-ridden folk will remain in the same darkness they were in. The Marxist chief minister of West Bengal travels in and out of the country carrying the shopping bag of revolution, in the expectation of patronage from the World Bank, multinational companies, Japanese capitalists as well as my swadeshi Birla family. The Marxist government thrashes Maoist Naxalites to death, and hands out plots of land, apartments, scholarships and grants to the mafia of followers of the party and the Left Front. **Finish those who refuse to be appropriated!** Despite all this, a large number of wily and conscienceless intellectuals have consistently declared that they are Marxist. They feel at peace if they can provide a quotation from the works of Marx–Lenin in support of their all-round compromise. They are disinterested in discussing the errors of Marx–Lenin. And however radical he might be in his writing and conduct, they don't hesitate to label or view the one who points out those errors as a reactionary, or a stooge of America or Pakistan. Like religiosity or parochialism, Marx-devotion is opposed to reason and questioning, they have no faith in the moral responsibility or the capabilities of the individual. Those who wish to be popular – whether it's a film star or a peddler of spurious stuff, or a religious or political leader, or a rustic or rotund novelist – they're hugely dependent on the fakery of advertising. It's steadily becoming impossible for talented people to gain public recognition through their talent. There aren't any takers unless one blows one's trumpet. Those who're honest and self-respecting spend their lives in the darkness of neglect. Those who're artful and shameless (perhaps they have a bit of talent too) seek refuge in the powerful institutions which own trumpets and are adept at blowing them. One could say that advertising is the 'contribution' of the capitalist economic system. But right now, this technology is being used even more successfully for brainwashing purposes by various kinds of governments. That's definitely the case within one's own country (there's no competition there), and at the same time, in other countries as well. Plenty of local intellectuals are enrolled in various ways, and they're given privileges and benefits so that they'll sing praises of specific governments. This trend has severely hurt intellectual growth in contemporary West Bengal. I am opposed to such trends because the establishment and expansion of objectivity, rationality, idealism and individual responsibility is desirable to me. **There has been a lot of transformation in my thinking in the last forty or forty-five years, but even with all that, there has always been a specific orientation. That orientation has made me independent, it didn't permit me to join the bellwether flow.** Many of my male and female readers complain about my word construction and use of language. They are unfamiliar with some of the words I use, and so they find my writing difficult to read. **Finish those who refuse to be appropriated!** My readers definitely have the right to complain. But I would like to say a few things from my side in this regard. Beyond the words that we usually use when we speak, write letters or newspaper articles, and create stories, plays and novels with, there is an extensive vocabulary in the Bengali language, and there is the possibility of creating words. There is some difference between the language used in reflecting on theoretical matters and the language used in jawing with friends. Besides, most of the Bengalis educated through the English language keep using English words arbitrarily in their conversations. I've been trying for many years to establish the practice of theoretical discussions in the Bengali language, and whether in speech or in writing, not to use English words in the Bengali language as far as I can. When it's necessary, I have used some Sanskrit, Arabic and Persian words that have been used earlier in the Bengali language, but with which the lethargic writers / readers of today are unfamiliar. Sometimes I have constructed a few words whose meaning would soon become clear from the way it is employed. If there is something of my own that I wish to say, it makes sense to say it in my own style. Perhaps the readers have to toil a bit, but such toil may help to sweep away the fatty deposits in the mind. **HOW FREE IS FREEDOM?!** My book *Radicalism* was published in 1946. A year and a half after that, *In Man's Own Image* was published. We were of the view that unless a thorough and deep cultural renaissance takes place in India, mere political independence will not bring about any well-being in the lives of the ordinary men and women of this country. Political independence is expedient to a few people of the upper strata, who'll swell up; ordinary poor, illiterate, superstition-ridden folk will remain in the same darkness they were in. For a cultural renaissance, public education is needed, which is founded upon a philosophy of life that believes in the creative potential of human beings. Humanism is the philosophy of life of such a renaissance. In the book *In Man's Own Image*, we presented this philosophy. I'm used

to reading adverse comments about my writing; it's illogical to expect that I'll go against the stream and not face revilement. I don't know who the publishers have faith in when they bring out my books. HOW FREE IS FREEDOM?! HOW FREE IS FREEDOM?!

Acknowledgements

I am grateful to the late Shibnarayan Ray for a variety of reasons. This great man of free mind and free conscience had encouraged me time and again to write, there is also mention of that a few times in the pages of the journal *Jigyasha*. Furthermore, in another book he undertook an indulgent discussion about my anti-novel, *This Could Have Become Ramayan Chamar's Tale*, giving it a lot of space. In this regard, I accord him the same respect as I do Kamalkumar Majumdar and Amiyabhushan Majumdar, and but for their encouragement perhaps I might have had to stop writing altogether, considering the way the public was after me. This marginal writer (I don't make a show of humility by calling myself 'unlucky') is grateful to these three people. Shibnarayan Ray mentioned in passing in one place that he was introduced to me by Sankha Ghosh; but that's both true and untrue, because I knew him long before that, I've spoken too in his sessions with his readers, when he used to visit Calcutta from Melbourne, I exuberantly praised his *Moumachhitontro*, and praised *In Man's Own Image* too, I used to search for his writing and read it, but it's true that I never told him about myself. There's unease only in one regard, despite his request, I didn't write for *Jigyasha*, I don't know why I didn't…

Reading Shibnarayan Ray's writing once again now, it occurred to me that a long presentation can well be made, but I don't feel hardy enough for that. This text has been created using extensive 'cuts' from just a few essays of his, with an apparently incoherent yet affordable outlook – not quotes, but *cut*. But again, it's not just cuts, but my present method (CUTOUT), this was constructed through the admixture of CUT CUTOUT OUTCUT and through employing a new approach, but without distorting a single letter, in order to see how much of Shibnarayan Ray could be captured through a few special essays of his, whether there's any unexpected spark dispersed anywhere, how he develops his argument, whether the upright arguments suffer from some other unpredictability, whether or not it seems un-ordinary to me – to tell the truth, writing from the personal plane, looking inwards – sometimes it would strike a personal chord as I read, and sometimes it wouldn't at all, I would begin to suspect myself, for good reason or no reason at all – I don't know how someone else would view it. There are those who read essays, etc. only to 'know'; in this method the sparks would be unusable, a postmodern response and indeterminate ... But it'll make you think and yet not let you arrive at any conclusion; barriers have been raised at the methods of arriving at that. The text can be read from any part, by making oneself rational (but never being stuck with rationality, because rationality is not something fundamental, and extreme, and quantum in circumference and HOW FREE IS FREEDOM?! too) and by chasing the current method of argumentation and by hurling abuses at Subimal Misra to confuse matters, and when the whole method of layout itself attacks itself, bites itself, and the subjects, by itself, and bad guys drink bangla while I stick to vodka and those who wish to be popular – whether it's a film star or a peddler of spurious stuff, or a religious or political leader, or a rustic or rotund novelist – they're hugely dependent on the fakery of advertising. It's steadily becoming impossible for talented people to gain public recognition through their talent. There aren't any takers unless one blows one's trumpet. Those who're honest and self-respecting spend their lives in the darkness of neglect. Those who're artful and shameless (perhaps they have a bit of talent too) seek refuge in the powerful institutions which own trumpets and are adept at blowing them. One could say that advertising is the 'contribution' of the capitalist economic system. But right now, this technology is being used even more successfully for brainwashing purposes by various kinds of governments. That's definitely the case within one's own country (there's no competition there), and at the same time, in other countries as well. Plenty of local intellectuals are enrolled in various ways, and they're given privileges and benefits so that they'll sing praises of specific governments.

[Ekchalar Protimay Sobujronger Asur Nichey, Besh Drishyoman Bhabei, Kolabou Rakha, 2010]

The Experience of Unremitting Abandonment

(I'll cut my anchal and give you a kerchief, let it fly in the wind, O friend)

Having set fire to himself
A man runs along the thoroughfare
With a burning tyre around his neck
And the tyre blazes furiously

The location of zero just keeps stretching towards infinity, in trauma, because
The limit of zero resides in zero, which has no beginning and no end either
He seemed to be talking to himself, and hiding in the distance was a man who lay entirely out of reach. The name he carried on his shoulder and went around with wasn't his own, he didn't know whose it was either, he wasn't really familiar with it, perhaps it belonged to some outsider. Perhaps it was he alone who was the one. And yet, one had to say perhaps, perhaps 'perhaps'. No discipline at all could grow in strength from his weak point of view now. The water would be visible even before entering, because of a reverse flute, because of a sacred vow of speechlessness, of secrecy. And there was the unalloyed emptiness. Limitless emptiness, a circle of emptiness. Because there's a nucleus of emptiness or zero in the material world, zero, the most successful emptiness, an impure fire, sandalwood. In the yellowish darkness, a desolate *thakur dalan*, beneath an

ancient aswath tree that soared towards the open sky. The brains of dead bodies, the lungs, pieces of the eyes, nose and face on the crowded road, people in the crowd kept liquifying and dropping on the road, they keep dropping. It had turned into evening then. A colourful signboard hung at the place where the hip-looking girl of twenty or so stopped the taxi and entered: Gents Beauty Parlour. A man sitting in a corner and playing a computer game on the TV screen. The gentleman took out a bottle of whisky and poured into a glass: 'Here, relax now, Rimi, the client'll be here very soon.' She was captive in a room, so she sat in anticipation of something ominous. She sat there, she yawned. And even before entering, the water was visible. Man begins by thinking he'll win all the games, but there were a couple of games involving life – which you bet on – a couple, which you commence knowing full well that you'll lose, where your life is at stake, betting your life on it. And that was how he walked. Somewhat haltingly. Halting and breathing in the air, of the greenery all around. That boipara, the river in the evening, that railing outside Presidency College on College Street, stacks and rows of old books. He was looking this way and that. And then walking along on his tiny feet. There was a great uncertainty in his gait, the method of not finding something he was looking for. From time to time, removing his spectacles and wiping the glass with a corner of his punjabi. The same old boipara of one's own, fifty years of going there – it was almost unrecognizable nowadays. From time to time, I had no clue where I was. However much one advanced, the horizon too kept receding just as much. In that case, who is Baneshwar of the novel *Shofolota Nishfolota* (Success and Failure) by Jibanananda Das? The place was really desolate. The pioneer Jibanananda who first ventured here hadn't ever imagined that one could be deluded enough to think that, compared to this imperilled region full of black rock and dense forest, the utterly dark, hair-raising, ghostly pasture didn't count for much. Emerging outside, he saw terrified folk running about at the entry to the lane. Halting the motorcycle, some three youths with shaven heads, all with rings in their ears, came forward: 'We'll make flowers bloom on every bud, on every bud, this is our locality.' At the foot of the inaccessible, forested hills on the two sides, stacks of books, high and low mountains, ice crystals and notched stone. From amidst that had arisen a black, triangular, winding, difficult terrain, the valley of our habitation. Every now and then, tiny, narrow-gauge trains, moving on tracks looking like veins and sub-veins, and going along sidings and valleys, suddenly descend, and also ascend just as suddenly.

However much one advanced, the horizon too
Kept receding just as much
The relentless searching around for the lost country lay all over the scattered bits of writing. He went on talking, uninhibitedly and incessantly. To himself. Was I trying to avoid the issue of the Partition, the greatest disaster in the lives of Bengalis, by singing paeans about the glories of fifty years of Independence! A people were permanently consigned to refugeehood to fulfil the aspirations of a few belligerent leaders. Permanent refugees. And then there was Marichjhhampi. It happened not so long ago. A government professing progressivism had flung even the small bits of bedclothes of suckling infants into the water. Was he, his deathly yellow thinking, sometimes momentarily transcending time-space and entering another time-space elsewhere! Pressure all around to freeze information. Roads

laid with stone chips extending till the next life, a rail track like an arrow of light crossing the paddy fields dotted with kingfishers, the non-stop sequence of scenes of the journey gave him a hint of the incessantness of fairy tales. It took fifty years to traverse a couple of hours' lowland. The country seemed nothing more than an abandoned rail yard to him. The land of one's own, imagined to be 'blessed with wealth, adorned with flowers', an imaginary homeland. College Street. Didn't leave anything behind for him. National fences scattered about, ground zero – it existed and didn't as well. The border protected by barbed wire. Far away, from within the forest at the end of the path on the opposite side, a thin plume of smoke rose. The smoke spiralled, unable to either ascend or descend. It was observed that a train with carriages was coming around the bend in front and advancing towards the station. Ritwik Ghatak had shown that in *Komal Gandhar*. I concealed myself somehow under a popular ideology, and just then, the train went by, making a clanging sound and spreading and splashing flashing hot sparks on our faces. The train seemed to be suspended at a point then. *Ashani Sanket* was also being shot just then, the famine in full colour. That day, it was past midnight, and while he was boozing he remembered, and said: 'Let's go and watch it.' Satyajit Ray had gone to bed, he was woken up, it seemed someone was shouting out, 'Ray! Ray!', from downstairs. Holding the window ajar, he saw that amidst all the darkness there stood Ritwik Kumar Ghatak, all by himself. Not exactly upright, he wasn't able to do that. Satyajit opened the door and emerged hurriedly, still in his nightwear, a look of concern in his eyes, and he heard the hoarse voice saying without further ado: 'Look Ray, you laid your hands on Rabindranath, I didn't say anything, you laid your hands on Bibhutibhushan, I forgave you, but beware … don't touch something like famine and Partition, these aren't your subjects…' I can't vouch for its authenticity, but apparently after *Ashani Sanket*, Satyajit didn't make any films on such subjects. This was such a game of dice where both sides had to use pawns and arrange them; because it wasn't that staying alive was entirely useless, rather than concern himself with problems for which the system was responsible, he now thought only about problems obtained from nature. Was this a kind of escape! Can you still enjoy, like you used to, the things that you couldn't obtain, you, even now!

Zero is a point which creates boundary lines from the centre
Of directional bodies, determines them
She said, 'But I didn't ask him for much, Didi. Only whatever any other girl wants in this world. To survive together, within ourselves. Why should we bother about what happens to others? He hasn't a clue about whether his own son learnt the alphabet properly – and he's teaching boys and girls in the basti, he's teaching the alphabet to the womenfolk, a night school. Sure, there are a few young women, a dim light from the kerosene lantern, apparently even their suppressed giggles and jokes can be heard from outside. Earlier, that's what I heard, there was a Chandana-di or someone. He didn't conceal anything, or suppress anything, not even her hundred blemishes. He was an amazing person. He wasn't aware of anything. Such people are incongruous in the real world, untenable. He was walking along the tramline in front of Deshapriya Park, thinking about a line of a poem, the babu had no clue that there was a tram behind him, that its bell was clanging. He escaped being run over by a whisker.' She broke down in tears: 'I worked so hard for

your dada, how much I tried to restore his sight with love.' He got gooseflesh. L-o-v-e! The corpse of love lay under the jarul tree beside the Dhakuria Lake. Intimate fondling in the darkness, couples making love. One couldn't bear to look at the battered face. Was there some intimate relation between that impassive look and the helpless death dance mixed with it! Afternoon had turned into evening. He was lying down. The experience of unremitting abandonment. Because if anything is adjacent to zero its value too increases. The place was truly frightening. The emotions and desires that were kept suppressed for eighteen to twenty years of his life were like a swollen stream, he was thrown into the pit of destiny and the water vapour belched out from there rose in a spiral. Belched it out. The pit into which the glistening stream was thrown was a hazy one, all around it was a covering of black hair. As it quivered continuously, it was turned into a boiling reservoir, which was foamy and abyssal. And that overflowing mass of water gushed out in hundreds of courses that emerged from the slippery mouth. The long, sepia-brown-coloured water stream rushed downwards – and the dispersed steam was merely a dense, trembling veil, hissing and foamy, overflowing. Standing at the edge of the mountain, we were looking at the coruscation of it breaking down as it struck a black-red rock way down below us and hearing the admixture of the spray emitted from the pit and the semi-human sounds that emerged, wintry. Because of wanting to buy pain by paying its price. Because when two bodies which are positive and negative become one, their sum is bound to be zero. If zero is added to a positive body, the sum is positive, and if zero is added to a negative body, the sum has to be negative, trauma, ground zero.

The wayward body then had its right hand raised and was a sepia-yellow colour, naked emperor
And showed the dead body of the poet lying spreadeagled in the middle of the road, single-syllabled
Was there really nothing! Isn't there anything? All the while Chandana-di lay clinging like bodily fluid ... When it's her turn. With her chin bone impossibly high, a masculine, dark-skinned, ugly girl. In those days, she had crossed twenty or twenty-two, but she hadn't got married. Only a mop of curly black hair reaching down to her back drew one's attention. Which she, from time to time, used to think to be poison-red like a snake! One person directly pulled his wrist: 'What book do you want, grandpa?' If it had been the College Street of fifty years ago, could he have pulled me by the hand on a book-lined pavement? He didn't look back, words would lead to further words, some callow youth, he sold school and college books and cram books – would he understand the heritage of the old books along the railing in front of Presidency College! None of those people were alive any longer, the one who was proud to have sold a book to Suniti Babu with his own hands, Hamid Asraf and the like – to Romesh Majumdar, to Nihar Ranjan Ray. And Hamid was illiterate, come to think of it, but he could recognize a book simply by touching it, he could tell whether or not it was a rare book by sniffing it. All those days gradually got lost somehow. Everything seems like a dream now. He was lying under the open sky now, sheltering from the blazing sun under an ancient ashwath tree. By being affectionate to the girl, he wanted to set at rest the surviving memory of Chandana-di. He stood in front of the mildewed toxic walls and the bare rooms of the abandoned *thakur dalan*. The doors and windows had been removed and taken away, it

would collapse in the coming rainy season. What a flutter there was in the eyes and face of a twelve- or thirteen-year-old girl from suppressed laughter. Her suppressed breathing went from rapid to even more rapid. In that *thakur dalan* that was spotted in the desolation of the yellow-black darkness, there was then the seasonal tidal bore of rivers and canals; life's first venom ejects the two persons, keeps on ejecting them. The conch blowing and ululation greeting the goddess rings out. Behind the scenes of the immersion, someone had once poured a full pot of holy water on his head, those underage years, he had got entirely drenched. He felt a bittersweet, salty taste all over his body, he got the flavour too. So what if you're young in years, after all you're my husband, dear – the sound of holy water being sprinkled rings out. One couldn't ever return anywhere except to memories, not even to College Street, the homeland of fifty years. Yes, that Chandana-di too got married one day, with someone who was a widower, with a lot of farming land. And by then, the environs of the waterfall had been excavated. A semi-circular pathway had been cut out. Its entire diameter and circumference had been rendered visible. But because it ended abruptly, the traveller had to return via the same path over and over again. In a kind of ashen and fatigued circumambulation. Before stepping down, he turned back to look one last time, but from there it was not possible to see the confluence of the waterway, definitely not on the part of humans and animals, only the circular path that went over the dais and descended there could be seen, as was customary. It could be touched too, one could be overwhelmed by the covering of hair over the flower of the hole. It was a terrible affair, public obscenity as well. One remembers the man had been advancing quickly along the thoroughfare. Over the shapeless background behind him were hazy, green-coloured silhouettes, one could well sight the forest. The stimulus was forested, but it suggested the inner soul. And in the throes of mutual sexual ardour, both of them embrace each other, and in those positions they tumble down. It wasn't possible to make any efforts to retrieve the dead bodies right then.

Suddenly one day all along the covered wayfaring wall, water with wild jasmine was visible

The girl's intentions seemed to not be above board. At least that was the complaint. Unlocking the door of the world beckoning to her with the key hanging on the wall and leaving a letter under her mother's pillow, she ran away with a vagabond lacking home and hearth who was thrice her age. The man apparently ran an uncivilized music group, an underground band, they sang with terrible screams. Sitting up hurriedly, he made the rounds of the bathroom and the roof. The matter didn't at all seem above board. After that, as soon as she sat on the bed for some reason and the pillow moved, the folded sheet of pad paper fluttered. As if it wasn't a letter in her hand but a fistful of fire. Yellow-blue fire. Legs, head, hair, the female organ, the male organ and the neutral organ, everything was burning in a blazing yellow-blue. Was the girl going around with hijras too, nowadays? How far away was the waterfall from here? You could only spot the water once you went deep inside. She wasn't bad at studies, but she was terribly stubborn. She would accomplish whatever she set her mind on, without bothering about anyone. Her small room was hers alone, no one had the right to enter there, not even her parents. She read tons of books, all worthless. She also wrote poetry or something. She took after her father. Sometimes she could not quite figure it out. She had seen letters stuffed between the pages of books. She flared up at once if anything was said. 'What's wrong with that, everyone my age has had the experience a few times, okay so I flirted a bit with Uncle, and accompanied him to the resort – so what? After all, times have changed completely, Ma, put aside your old, haggard values...' So had the girl grown up? Apparently, she had turned eighteen long ago. As he walked along the boundary wall of Presidency College, he discovered one day that obscene books with a newspaper cover were also being sold in a couple of places. Customers arrived and exchanged old books for new ones. He noticed female customers too. They didn't come alone, a group of them would arrive amidst mirth and laughter, without any inhibition they openly leafed through the books and guffawed in laughter. Each one prodded the other, showing them the pictures inside. All colourful pictures. Of various positions and various movements. Even after wandering around for fifty years, he had no inkling, he hadn't noticed anything for so long. The writer boy with a shoulder bag said: 'You're shocked seeing just this, if you heard what transpires on the Presidency College field once it turns dark you'll have a fit! The corners of College Square turn into a love carnival at night, – with different kinds of love. Various kinds of books. You don't need to know about them. Everything involves the young generation, school and college students. Old fogeys aren't infrequent too, standing shoulder-to-shoulder with them.' With a laugh, he said: 'According to your theory, if zero is multiplied by a positive number it's zero, and even when multiplied by a negative number it's zero. With the presence of the number line at ground zero, the sum of the entire body is zero. But the calculation is not that simple. If the shadow that's tied to a worldly man who's six feet tall is nine feet long, then how long would the shadow tied to a man who's destitute certainly be, how long could it be? Can you think of any calculation?' Some logic! And whether there were two shadows or one, they wouldn't be located on the thin line, wouldn't remain there. That distance was measured, and it was found that we had almost reached the wall of the settlement. The popularly acknowledged borderline, determined by the shastras too. An ancient *thakur dalan*, the kul-devata, the uttering of mantras. Abode of kings, ogress' abode. I now have to advance exactly three steps on the brick-mortared road, to the *thakur dalan* at Kalitola, but the household would be maintained in exactly the same way, the directed tantra, anxiety, the great monastery of bloody-soil. He has no use for the tantric pursuit of alcohol-meat-fish-money-sex here, any more, for a long time.

Zero is neither positive nor negative
The body of zero is ataractic
The bits and pieces of the final remains were scattered over the road, a thoroughfare. The wheels of cars and carriages went over those and the moving wheels spread the embolus. Crimson, trembling. Silently turning incorporeal. Once the rain descends, everything is washed away, monotonously. When the poet was run over on the bridge above, bits and pieces of his body fell upon the road below the settlement, disintegrated bits kept falling with the movement of cars and carriages, and the movement of people. The rotten brains of his head lay over the bridge like a nuisance, pale-yellow intestines, decayed, rusted lungs, leaking drops of blood, unshut-eyelids, an indifferent smile on curved lips. Drops of disintegrated flesh kept dripping through the gaps between the rail tracks on the road below. It kept

dripping, kept dripping for an entire lifetime, people stepped over that. At ground level, there were narrow streets, a crowd of common people walking. Ships-aeroplanes-cars-autorickshaws-motorbikes-bicycles-people were all moving through the gaps, progress, but in the midst of all that, marrow-flesh-blood-and-bone, all that, all of that – kept dripping from above. People returning from work went by with handkerchiefs pressed to their noses. Oh, how the rotted brain stank! A cluster of railway policemen gathering every moment at the bridge, some poet or someone from somewhere was apparently run over. Curious people gathered there, craned their necks to see, and once they had seen they went away. A thela-wala, who could be recognized by the zari-crown on his head, halted, he raised his arms and tried to stop the vehicles plying on the road. The wheels of time continued to move, no one stopped. Chandana-di was then looking at him with squinted eyes as she combed her hair with the comb from Jessore, holding the blue ribbon between her teeth, there was a mysterious smile on her face, observing the intensity of my sight, she brought her arms down so as not to expose her armpits. A railway station beside paddy fields, all around were paddy stalks, lush like the kaash grass of autumn, an incomparable electric-green spanning the horizon, the trusted fields. As one entered the village, there were waterbodies adjacent to one another, small and large ponds and tanks, all along the edge of the mango orchard a dalliance of dishevelment, the ghostly marsh. At the edge of the marsh, a massive aswath tree. Standing all alone amidst the water. Gnarled at the bottom, with baskets hung there. Blue-green fireflies hovered on the floating weeds on the ghostly marsh, crossing the high and dry land of the graveyards of life, slightly above were bits of bloated flesh, the lustre of the breast and the apex, its tip, sweating in trembling emotion, coming alight and extinguishing, extinguishing and coming alight. The boy crossed the ghostly path of water and putting fireflies inside a coconut shell he focussed it like a torch on the dark road as he walked towards his homestead. The room at the entrance of Chandana-di's in-laws' house, he was invited over as usual as he was her younger brother. Tender shoots of gourd with rice, mashed taro, and fish curry prepared with fresh carp from the pond. Thick, creamy milk from the household cow brimming in a bell-metal bowl from olden times, inlaid with floral motifs. All these were his favourite victuals, Chandana-di had remembered that too. The man had a goat slaughtered in his honour. A tender, black Bengali goat kid. You won't get all this in your urban areas. Just eat it and see, it'll melt in your mouth. Not tough at all. As juicy as it's tasty. He hadn't been able to eat more than one piece of the meat that had been cooked with lots of ghee. And how pained the gentleman had been about that, your stomach's shrivelled up, city boys just can't eat nowadays. A simple, easy going, prosperous household. Paddy fields, potatoes being cropped over ten bighas of land. Chandana-di bent down as she tucked in the mosquito net in the front room, her gold nose ring studded with a gemstone gleamed in the light from the hurricane lantern: 'I've kept water beside your head, you'll be thirsty at night. Anything else ... I think I'll finish my chores and at night...' The master's voice from the courtyard outside: 'Has anyone removed the pot from the well-side ... I say, has anyone removed it ... Where are you, Chhoto-bou ... I can't hear you ... Ghostly waterways and marshland, a ghostly settlement ... So late at night ... Aren't you asleep yet...' 'No, I'm unable to sleep ... It's been so sultry since evening ... The leaves on the trees are all still ... It's definitely going to rain ... Here, take the hand-fan ... Let me fan you ... Take your vest off, you'll feel more comfortable...' 'What about him...' 'Oh, it's late night for him now ... As soon as his head hits the pillow he's fast asleep...' The railway police authorities announced: 'The dead body has not been identified as yet. While a train was going along track No. 1, a man suddenly appeared on track No. 2, and that's how he got run over. So many people get run over like that. Who cares for anyone, who knows anyone?' A professor with thick glasses and an authoritative air ventured a glance: 'I know him, I often see him walking absentmindedly along the tram track opposite Deshapriya Park. A youth who looked to be a student was walking hurriedly, he came to a halt: 'I used to see him every day at the line of shops selling old books outside Presidency College. I don't know why he looks for books every day. After all, boipara is becoming obsolete day by day. What the fuck's to be gained by reading so much in these times of joblessness.' Bits and pieces of life keep disintegrating and falling to the road below, in blobs, leaving marks like the excrescence of time. It keeps falling continuously, the poet's life keeps dripping endlessly. The rail bridge keeps trembling dizzily with the sound of collapse, the walking route of people for so long. The railway police point with their fingers: 'Just look, the whole body is disintegrating into blobs, it's falling on the path people walk on, on the improper path that people aren't supposed to walk on. Baba, how the rotten brain stinks! Makes you want to throw up at once.' Gradually, the public's enthusiasm is exhausted, everyone walks on towards their respective destinations. And then after a time, rain descends under all the yellow-tinged darkness. Darkness and rain. Smeared with blood. Bloody. Bodies find each other again. The square of the zero-body turns out to be zero, the cube of the zero-body turns out to be zero, even if the zero-body is multiplied by the zero-body only a zero-body remains. The silhouette along the retina is in turn brought gradually, it's heated, all the incidents then begin to revolve behind one another of their own accord, they begin. Because he's endowed with a body, because it's a poet's death dance. Because the odour of the rotten, decomposing brain had then begun to spread all around, beyond the human settlement, yellow-pale, a static series of points, zero, ground zero. Because bodies found each other again, they had begun to find them.

[Anoboroto Porityag Korar Abhigyota, 2005]

The Earth Quakes

(Remembering Jibanananda Das's prime novel, *Shofolota Nishfolota,* in which the character Baneshwar was created.)

Come, let's go fluting
Arousing the Yamuna
Let's ravish Krishna Kanhaiya

People have an addiction to becoming great, they have this thing about leaving behind a mark. Just after that, one after the other, after crossing the nine-inch span of the stigma-line, that river, the river Monokamona; it was an elephant corridor, along the Bamni river, I left it behind at the horizon and entered the forests of jujube, polash, neem and custard apple to the ringing of anklet bells. It was a small river, but a thirsty one, flowing rapidly, which wanted to talk too, about all kinds of secret things, it didn't keep anything hidden or concealed, nothing. Can something desired ever be had for nothing, can it be touched! From atop the wooden bridge, I could see that the route of descent was jungly, you had to cross the secret chamber taking one slow step at a time, you had to descend, even lower – much, much lower, and only then ... and only then the Monokamona. And leeches on your legs, silently sucking away blood; at first you don't even have a clue, the moment you become absent-minded and inattentive they start sucking your blood – they suck blood and stick to you – that's a bloody tale, a sticky-viscous one. If you can descend properly, you can touch your way to the cave, it feels nice to sit with your feet in the water, the full moon is entrancing, beautiful birds chirp near your ears, the fragrant stamen hairs of a wildflower disperse, they seek to fly into space, at little Suntal, on the Monokamona. The spectators had started clapping then. The world-famous boxer crossed the ring and advanced. He shook his opponent's right hand with both his hands. His face with an exuberant smile next to his opponent's face. The spectators roared in support of his friendliness and courteousness before the duel, they welcomed him. An ace fighter pitched against an unknown Lilliput whose name no one had ever heard of.

An oxygen experiment at normal temperature

Everyone knew who would win. Ninety-nine per cent of the people were on one side. A handful of the other's supporters were sitting here and there. He had been through a few life cycles of realizing the fruits of his karma. Now, perhaps, maybe, he doesn't really know, he had only one truly secret desire: to find his own value. But even besides that, there are some dimensions, different ways and means of surviving death. He was standing all by himself in his own corner. The assistants had slid out through the rope with the boxer's stool. His opponent stood facing him in the opposite corner of the square ring. The battle commenced as soon as the bell rang. The whistles and cheers of the spectators resounded in the arena. The media reported: it's a prestigious battle. The great boxer had his target in clear view, he moved rapidly, closing the distance between them. His desire to knock out his opponent was no secret. He wasn't composed even after landing twenty or twenty-five punches. It was a veritable storm of punches, he wanted a knockout in the very first round. There was almost no sign of his opponent in the ring. Moving back in the face of the beating, back, through the prop-less void, he fell against the rope. The referee separated them and sent them back to the centre of the ring. But he was hit the very next moment, and as soon as he was hit, he fell against the rope once again. Gradually this ceased to be sport. One side wanted to completely efface the other side, without allowing him to even stand. If it had been anywhere other than the professional boxing arena, the public's enthusiasm would have come to an end in the first minute itself. They could hardly spot him. His survival, his very existence, was concealed under his opponent's secret techniques. A minute – before one knew it, two minutes went by. When they stood apart, the audience could see both of them, standing beside one another. His lip was cut, blood streamed out of his nose and there was a swelling like a cyst on his forehead. There was blood on the rope too, from his leaning against it, the boundary rope was a bloody red, slightly darkish blood. But the public present there weren't paying attention to something: even after being thrashed so much, he was still standing; beneath his feet was the earth, and the earth was quaking; he was panting, but he did not fall down, he was not running away. He would see it through till the end ... But where was it ending ... it wasn't ending at all! At the destination! But there wasn't a destination, or alternatively all of it was the destination! He couldn't clearly understand. And suddenly there was a flash of lightning, the dazzling contest came to a halt, he was standing all alone in the ring, he was alone; and confounding everyone, the world-famous man lay upside down. He lay there, he was recovering his senses, his body was trembling. His opponent was staggering of course, but defying reason, he didn't fall down. An unconventional hook of his own style made the other fall to the ground. The referee pushed him away and leaned over and began to count the seconds. According to the norms of professional boxing, if an outright knockout punch was delivered, the audience cheered, they would. But just the opposite happened here. Just a couple of hands were raised from here and there, the cheers were muted. No one was happy at all that he had won in this way, that such a big boxer was knocked out like this, everyone was perturbed.

A Bengali babu
Bought a few acres of property on the moon
He bought
Some part somewhere on the moon
Its boundaries too were measured
And explained to him
He was given the registration papers
For that matter, permanent citizenship too
Nothing was concealed, there was no fraud
In this lunar purchase

The boxer lay prostrate for about six seconds. At the count of seven, it was observed that he sat up on his knees, so that he could stand up straight at the count of nine, before it went to ten. If his knees touched the ground at the count of ten it would be taken to mean that he was unable to stand up, which would mean defeat. But according to boxing rules, as soon as his knees were no longer touching the ground, he would be considered to be in the act of standing up, of having risen, and from that very moment his opponent had the right to punch him and fell him again. As soon as he stood up, his opponent began circling around him, but the referee came in between and blocked him, he had begun to block him. He realized that the referee was giving him a long count, so that his opponent got a little more time. He smiled inwardly, this was inevitable in this system, everyone tilted in one way or another towards power, they would. That's why he had to change his strategy, make it different, which would be acceptable to everyone. Knives and scissors were boiling in boiling water, even before he could realize anything, a thin man came near him and began running his hand through his hair and then he suddenly held his head firmly. A robust youth with a shaved head got up on the bed from the other side, he sat with his legs folded at his tummy: 'You were killed in the duel. You'll attain nirvana now.' Just like how, if someone suddenly pushes you, you raise your hands towards the sky, as if to grab hold of the sky, in the same way, whether his hands rose up or not, that sort of thing. Now the referee seemed to burst out from the earth and at once he pressed his legs hard. The operation today is definitely without anaesthesia: the gaze of the bald-headed sergeant wearing a white gown informed him so. With a slight tug of his left hand, as he pulled the top of the indistinct stick below the lower abdomen, a thick stream of grey-red blood-pus began pouring out. The man pressed his two fat gloved paws down on his acutely painful spot. Had he been castrated, so that he could never again stand proud in any way? Bloody pus

Heat, temperature &
a heat-conduction experiment

kept gushing out like a fountain from the earlier incisions in four or five more spots, the white gown turned colourful with the reddish-yellow. He was writhing under the four or five hands that held him down. Why such a lot of foul blood? That meant all this had been inside him, and he had had no clue. The man ran his knife even deeper, even lower, right till the joint of the bone. Nothing could be discerned from above. As he used the knife, the man's face brimmed with immense satisfaction. His throat turned hoarse with moaning, but his reliance on speech was still unbroken, *shabdabrahma,* transcendental sound. The man continued working like a robot. His assistant stood beside him with the tray in his hand. He was now a soldier on the battlefield, his gaze unwavering as he held out knives, scissors and pincers one after another with swift hands. Now he began to bandage the spot, with a massive bandage around his waist, and so he looked different too. Fine, he wouldn't even go anywhere near protests again. His masculinity had been done away with,

History should never
Become history

and foul blood. As soon as the referee counted nine, he again gave him a gentle push, he wanted to keep him afar. But this was against the rules of the game. The opponent stood up in that bit of time. There was blood now on the corner of his lip from a cut; stooping down a bit and shielding his face and abdomen, he somehow grabbed hold of him. According to the rules of the game, it was separating two boxers locked together that was the real task of the referee. But the referee didn't do that. His opponent was holding off falling by holding on to him like a drowning man. But second after second went by and that provided him with the opportunity to regain strength in his legs. The last minute of the round was speeding along. If he could somehow stick out this round, he would get a full minute's respite. He stuck it out too. Badly knocked, but the smile on his face was intact, as if nothing had happened, as if he didn't even consider such a trivial person to be an opponent. There was hardly any fighting in the second and third rounds. The clever and nifty boxer was not short of experience. He had loads of experience. He was merely avoiding punches now, in self-defence mode. It was taking him time to regain his balance after the blow in the first round, so he was buying as much time as he could. He was back to his own self in the fourth round. His self-confidence seemed to have suffered a crack, but thanks to the supporters all around, he was regaining the ground beneath his feet bit by bit. Empowerment. He was not risking being punched right now, he was proceeding cautiously. He was employing his experience now. To tell the truth, this world-famous man was incomparable as far as power was concerned, he was a longtime practitioner, he still toiled for fifteen to sixteen hours a day, exactly like a highly seasoned man. He knew quite well how to win over the audience and have them clapping at every step. At this time, although he was not attempting any further deadly blows, he was making his opponent disoriented simply through small punches, he wanted to weaken him. For every punch that he landed by penetrating the gaps in the defence, his opponent returned three. But none of them were enough to win the fight. Although none of them were significant by themselves, it was infinitely significant as far as the final victory or defeat was concerned. Despite his reluctance, he seemed to be viewing him with a bit of caution now, he was wary. Both his left and right arms were moving continuously, his fast punches were most lethal, leaving no way to avert them, there was no way, he was making straight lefts now, he had to at least

The number of planets in space
Suddenly rises
It suddenly decreases too
What's called a planet is changing
As is its definition
There was a vote among space scientists
On whether Pluto is or isn't a planet
At the General Assembly
Of the International Astronomical Union
In Prague
2,500 space scientists from 75 countries
Participated in that
Yes, what's called a planet will be settled by vote

defend himself. Much as the famed boxer tried to hold him in a clinch, he kept him away with straight lefts, stormy punches, the impact of the stormy blows began to show on his face and eyes. But the boxer was versatile, just as he had experience he also had the practice of working with his arms. He could change the nature of his hooks, he could bring on a new variation the very next moment, without even giving the other boxer any chance of being prepared. He couldn't be blamed for that, this was the rule in boxing, to floor your competitor by any means whatsoever. He moved to another strategy now, he began in-fighting, exchanging punches at close range. He had attained mastery in in-fighting, he subdued his rising opponent again and again by this means. He was thus able to avert the straight lefts. So was his opponent losing, was he on a downward slope now! Was the colour of sunlight changing! The spectators in the arena exploded at such moments. The few supporters he had had turned silent, it seems the man can't be saved now. He was greatly preoccupied then – after all, he was losing by a bit every day – basically, it wasn't certain whether there was any difference between victory and defeat, no – and right then, his opponent skilfully freed himself in a trice and flung a vicious uppercut that set him afloat skywards and threw him to the ground. The exhilaration of the public rocked the arena. After all, an ordinary person like him was bound to receive dire punishment for humiliating the distinguished fighter, so that no other callow novice would have the gall to challenge him like this. His condition was really pathetic then, propping himself up somehow on one knee, he wanted to rise slowly, he filled his lungs as much as possible in the ten seconds of the count. But the damn referee was against him, he didn't want him to win at all, he clearly understood the counting was too fast, with two counts to the second.

HOME MINISTRY TELLS WOMEN
'DRESS PROPERLY'

In the seventh round, once again the same uppercut from inside landed on him. His legs had become unsteady, his opponent took advantage of his helplessness, and with another uppercut from close quarters coming immediately after, he now slid through the rope and fell outside the ring. He landed with a thud on the newspaper reporters' table. He even lost the shoes on his feet, it was scandalous. But he didn't fall, even there, he sat up resting on his knees. The referee wanted to complete the count at any event, he went through the count rapidly, very rapidly, and across the rope, inside the ring, the opponent stood waiting. He had to slide in through the rope and go and stand on the ring floor, face-to-face with the ace champion of the world who was waiting there, with his gloved fist raised. In just a few moments, once the referee ended the count, the man would be declared to be the winner, the public was screaming wildly in joy, they were witnessing a match victory after their hearts. But in a moment, everything turned topsy-turvy. Nobody imagined that the situation would change so drastically in such little time, all of a sudden, in a fraction of a second, by the time the count reached eight, his body leapt into space, he inserted his head in through the ropes and grabbed him in a clinch. Now the referee did just the opposite, he exerted force and pulled him away, meaning the stage was set for him to get thrashed. Everyone could understand the referee's partiality, but no one really bothered about that nowadays, such things happen, it happens in every sphere. It's an insignificant thing.

Basically I paint the kind of pictures
That sell well in the market
I paint hundreds of them at a time
I see that the art market too rises and falls in direct proportion
To the rise and fall of the stock market
When traders have loads of money at their disposal
The price of every kind of artwork immediately rises dramatically
And the price of nude paintings, of a particular style
For a particular class
So that together with bodily communication
Through a hint
Sexual ardour is overflowingly entwined

And with every line the language of physical
desire and pleasure
Is set to boil
Something even a gleaming photograph can't
provide.
Is all this art…
I understand everything but what can I do
After all, there's the market
Male nudes too sell well nowadays
Full-size male nudes in a particular kind of rendering
Women buy them   Some gay men too
Buy them straight away   There's no more
frustration
Apparently some of them are also in love with the
nude image
Masturbation
I paint pictures for a living
I'm in the business of art
That's why I don't want to reduce the number of
buyers
By bringing up such personal matters
Concerns such as 'Where shall I put up the nude
painting after I buy it'
Or 'How can it be hung at home'
Have become obsolete
In the last few years in the families
Of nouveau riche couples
Rather, such nudity is now
A sign of advanced society
It enhances one's status   It proves one's taste
Although I don't know how long it'll last

Given the way pornographic films have entered
the market
But there's still a niche market
For nude art
Even now
That's why I'm able to make a living

But despite all that, he stuck it out, he was regaining his composure, the fog all around was beginning to pale. A gleaming railway track running through the icy desert, Dostoevsky's death sentence was revoked at the final moment, he was now being deported to Siberia. Right in front of the Durga Puja, the crowd of flood victims, a queue at the community kitchen, he was standing with the battered enamel bowl from *Ajantrik* in his hand, a begging bowl! But the journey was not over. Casting his eyes from inside the ring, he could see that the audience was getting more and more infuriated with him. Why wasn't the idiot admitting defeat? But he was already defeated in one regard, only two or four people – yes, just two or four people – were eager about him. Their voices couldn't be heard. There were a handful of gambling folk who always took greater risk and bet on the weaker side. One or two people had staked their money on him too. They didn't love or support him, it was just a calculated gamble. There had also been bets on how many rounds he would last. Quite a few people had also bet that the fellow wouldn't last seven rounds. But there was no apparent sign of him admitting defeat. His opponent was unsuccessful in his effort to land another uppercut in the eighth round. But he had now become alert to this uppercut of his. He stunned everyone once again in the ninth round. Both of them were

Experiment on direction of heat flow

locked in an embrace, suddenly he stepped back and freed himself from all bonds. There was just that little bit of distance between the two, yet from within that his fists were shooting. His hands seemed to be rising higher and higher from near his waist and flinging punches upwards, right uppercuts in his very own style. There's this kind of usage in a few places in Godard's work, only in Godard's, but this was entirely his own. When the bell rang signalling the start of the ninth round, he once again decided on his method. The opponent was in a completely pathetic state, the way he was employing the right uppercut, that they had used for so long, in his own design had such a confounding effect now that the man had no option but to be simply struck dumb. But apparent difficulty was no difficulty at all, the way of narration becomes the subject, the method of throwing the punches becomes the real punch.

A tree stump gone to rot
And yet from within that emerged
Blazing flames
From the inner quarters of a rotten tree
A jet of naked flame emerged
Blazing Fresh

In the tenth round, he used his signature right uppercut a couple of times. His fists moved upwards from waist level and sprang out like an ascending jet plane. The opponent was in desperate straits. Through all the various devices he employed, the smile on his face remained intact. Under no circumstance would he outwardly express what was going on inside, the audience would definitely be disconcerted by that, the victory chants of this humanistic character would resound all over the country and the world. Huge pictures would be published in every newspaper, the sportsmanship of this great genius would be hailed, reporters would wax eloquent about his fraternal conduct with his opponent! Retaining his smile, he began punching fiercely. But however powerfully he might be punching, the man could not land him any terrible injury. Rather, discerning the moments of perplexity from the new uppercut, he had been able to dispatch the acclaimed man at least once to the floor. He wasn't able to be as speedy as before either. At the beginning of the fourteenth round, he was stooping down time and again. In the face of the novel attack, and in the process of fending off the attack, he was completely disoriented. He did not know how to combat such methods. It was as if he was retreating under his skin to conceal himself. It was only a question of going through the motions in the time remaining. He continued to employ whatever skill was required to control his opponent. Sometimes while hugging him, he pushed him as if it was involuntary, sometimes he held the other boxer's gloved fist tight between his body and his arm, and sometimes he actually thrust his full large, wide paw on his nose in a bid to suffocate him. But in such a situation, he realized that everyone from the ordinary spectator to the referee was on the side of this world-famous fighter, there was no one on the side of a mere nobody of a boxer like him, no one was coming over to his side either.

Convection experiment

That didn't bother him at all. After all, he himself had desired such a status, let people get up and leave, let the arena empty, let everyone tire of him, so long as he had the towel-carrying seconds. As long as someone could grasp the distinctiveness of his own uppercut, at least tried to grasp that, he didn't seek any other recognition, none at all. However few they may be, he didn't want any more; and if there were, then he would have to conclude that there was still a flaw, most certainly. Vivekananda had just returned from America. It was 1897, the site was Priyonath Mukhopadhyay's house in Baghbazar. A member of the nationally renowned cow protection society came up to meet him. He greeted Swamiji and presented him with a picture of Gau Mata, the Cow Mother. Vivekananda: What is the objective of your organization? The member: We save the Gau Matas of our land from the knives of butchers. Cow-shelters have been established in various places. Sick and barren Gau Matas purchased from butchers are cared for there. Vivekananda: Excellent. What is your means of income? Member: Whatever great souls like you are kind enough to provide. Vivekananda: How much money have you raised? Member: The Marwari trading community are our patrons. They have donated a huge amount of money for this noble effort. Vivekananda: There's a terrible famine in central India. The government of India has published a list of the nine hundred thousand people dead. Is your organization collecting donations for famine relief? Member: We don't undertake any famine relief. Our subject is the cow. This famine is a result of people's misdeeds and sins. As you sow, so you reap. But the cow is our mother. Vivekananda (smiling): I totally understand that the cow is your mother – otherwise who else would give birth to such fine offspring? As the man began to be overwhelmed by an unfamiliar astonishment, he now thought that he would deliver a resounding punch, a final blow, and show him what an ace's punch was like, he'd make him realize that all his artfulness was of no use, it never was at any time, actually you had to hit blows, you had to know to hit.

Where had the fellow been able to develop punches, he had just gone on bleating all his life solely with so-called form. But he was now a being from another world, he seemed to invite punches upon himself, and he moved back – all those incidental punches of the ace definitely hurt him, hurt him a lot, but he disregarded that. The man was confounded by the fact that even after being punched so many times, the fellow wasn't retaliating when the opportunity arose! No opponent lets such opportunities go, they don't. All this unbecoming conduct left him clueless, time and again – why would a man come to fight and then not fight! Why would

You've nothing to lose but
Your bad manners

he rein himself in! The world-famous boxer began to count the seconds as he waited for the sought-after opportunity. He had only one objective now – to get an opportunity – an opening – once he had that, he would shoot a punch with all the strength in his body. A checkmate with a single punch. Like a natural warrior, he used his left and right fists again and again and attacked the abdomen and jaws with a resounding flurry of punches – the very tide of the match would be reversed. He was a boxer with long years of experience, and he had ability too. People said that for as long as he stood in the ring with the support of his own two legs, the strength in his arms endured in full measure. But why wasn't this fellow fighting? In between rounds, even his own seconds didn't appear encouraging at all. He was a loser after all. Holding the towels up neatly, they were fanning him, but it was meagre, let alone reaching his lungs! How was it that one by one everyone turned against him, disgusted. After all, he himself knew that he was nothing but a loser, perhaps there was some flaw inside him which turned people away, friends included. But however few they may be, they did exist, and that was a lot, it was adequate. But was he actually against this entire matter of winning! Why had he at all got down to this game of winning and losing? A calamitous question. He never had any interest in all this, and yet he got down to it. He was boxing wasn't he. 'You've come smeared with glory-and-standing, pig shit, all over yourself' – oh that poem, 'Trirotno' (Three Gems), by Kalidas Roy that I had read when I was in school, meaning he was fighting now for – attaining – the smearing of pig shit like glory and standing on himself! A very – very marginal question. Yet he was losing. He was losing by himself. Losing to himself. Or was a new language of life and death being created that lay between surviving and not surviving, somewhere!

The media didn't really scream hoarse
About that girl from Madhya Pradesh
The teenager who in a burning condition
In blazing flames
Ran all the way to the police station
And stated
The rapists' names   the minister's grandson's name
Gradually everything was somehow
Hushed up
The whole incident
No one   No eyewitness came to court to give
evidence
No one in the village saw anything
No one knew anything about such an incident
Nothing was written in newspapers either any more
Nothing on TV

Dispersion experiment

Suddenly something happened. As the fourteenth round began, he turned around and landed a few punches on his opponent and stood panting. His arms hung innocently beside his legs. The referee was counting. Some suspicious talk could be heard from the south-west corner. As soon as he rose, he suddenly changed his battlefield. Clutching his opponent in a lock, he fell against the rope. Somehow or the other – he heard – the voice of a gambler-gangster – 'Come what may, Brother has to win – I've bet a whole lot of my money – If he sticks it out till the fifteenth round I'll be ruined. Offer the fellow some money – tell him to lose.' As the bell sounded, *dong*, a sense of foreboding seized him. But the spectators didn't have any clue about all this. Whatever happened would occur inside this ring, and he would be involved too. He suddenly became alert, as if he had regained his earlier self-assurance. The way he was advancing, setting each foot forward with fierce conviction, he was alarmed. But what exactly was this alarm! There was some deception behind that. He charged forward, but once again he started becoming moody: what was the point in winning! He wanted to move to one side and avoid the whole match. The opponent wanted to go into a clinch. He realized that was a ploy, there was certainly a motive. But he didn't feel like winning right now, everything seemed devoid of meaning – this little boys' game of fighting, this business of victory and defeat – he could not see any difference between them. Yet, despite all his reluctance he had to carry on playing the game – he must carry on; after all, he couldn't jump out of the ring and start running away; since he had entered the ring, he had to carry on until a decision was reached, what was called a result in the civilized world.

In trams and buses
They block you so gently you know
I can't say anything
If I stand quietly they turn more daring
And
We women
Have gotten used to all this
Once I alight from the tram or bus I brush it off my body
But there are also women
Our own friends
Who quite enjoy it
In other words, they encourage it
They pretend to move this way and that and give opportunity
And
And meeting male friends thereafter in college
Surrounded by friends
They tell juicy tales

He moved back as much as he could, he circled around his opponent, but how long could he do that! He would eventually have to be locked in that embrace. Only then would he find out their design. He moved forward desperately now, so that he could find out what was afoot. He couldn't restrain himself any longer, curiosity. Let whatever may happen happen, let's see it playing out! He conducted himself purely mechanically now, he kept tempting him in such a way that it seemed he himself wanted to be apprehended by him, in his clutches. It all happened in a strange way, out of the acquired habit of fighting to survive, every day. The opponent came charging, just the moment before their bodies touched, before he knew it, he somehow stepped back hastily. Most of the spectators began screaming, 'Foul! Foul!' The referee too was at first about to declare it a foul, but the very next moment he realized that the fellow had fooled all of them, he hadn't made body contact at all, so how could it be foul! The referee was dumbfounded, he didn't know what he ought to do; he remained standing. He clearly saw that it wasn't foul play, but the public wanted it to be declared a foul and that he, the referee, should do that. He was highly amused, observing the referee's plight. If he had been outside the ring, he would have burst out laughing at the referee's predicament. Between the two words, victory and defeat, there were lots and lots of other gradations too, other degrees. The spectators hadn't discovered all that, actually they had never been allowed to think, they simply avoided it, or a few had done it, done it with great depth, *Madness and Civilization*, there's nothing like the unidimensional victory–defeat binary, absolutely nothing. It's because a person can't do something that he does it, he does it all his life – or the alternative method of 'silence of politics' – the silent language of life.

Inspired by the call to jihad
A young mother with a baby in her arms
Volunteered
All these teenage mothers
Had been so animated
By the call of jihad
That their hearts didn't tremble the least bit
At the prospect of becoming human bombs with their babies in their arms
Following custom there was support from their families too

But their numbers aren't
Just two or five people
It grows by hundreds it keeps growing
Allah
Perhaps ~~God~~ will now go to sleep

The world-famous pugilist was extremely angry now, he wanted to get within reach of him by any means, as if he would then smash him with his fists. He was circling around, dancing. Would he let himself be apprehended and bring the battle to an end, in linear fashion! Suddenly he decided that he would not throw any punches at the body, or else they would attach screams of 'Foul!' to that. If he truly had to continue the fight, he would do that face to face, targeting only the jaw and nose, which was a very difficult proposition, impossible too. The opponent was experienced, skilled, winning had become a habit for him. Had he stepped into the arena to challenge that habit! But what of that! He was turning moodier every moment, but this wasn't really appropriate when he was standing in the middle of the ring. Through his demeanour he had to clearly show that he would definitely win, that he wanted to win. Such optimism was a hilarious creation – having faith in oneself. He wanted to laugh. For the last two rounds, he was being attacked again and again, he stood there unprotesting, he just stood there and got hit. Punch after punch landed on his body, all over his body, he wasn't defending himself, he wasn't defending himself at all, what was the point of pushing himself towards a fixed decision.

Experiment on water's poor conductivity

A star was about to die in space. An ordinary star. S.R. Ophiuchi. After all, the death of a star meant the most terrifying, brightest explosion. It's something beyond imagination. This explosion, or supernova, whose origins lay in an atomic reaction, would take place inside the star, it would go on happening, all within itself. The heat that would be generated was billions of times greater than the heat and light from the sun. The universe would be expanded. As light years went by, the death of the star would be visible from planet Earth too, the destruction of the star would be visible, and the expansion of the universe. At the final moments, the flurry of mind-blowing punches by the great ace was driving the spectators crazy, everyone was standing up and screaming at the top of their voice. They were excited that their beloved boxer was finally going to win. In enraged voices they challenged him: Fight, you bastard pussy-faced devil! – Advance, you son of a bastard! – Let's see your guts! At the same time, they were also encouraging his opponent: Don't spare him, finish him! – Just finish him off! – Make sure no other fellow has the audacity to show such daring in the future!

According to the government
Bison numbers are increasing rapidly in Gorumara
In order to reduce the number of bisons
Tigers will now be released
Inside the forests
And tiger cubs too
So as to stop the proliferation of bison

He wasn't paying any heed to such comments by the public, he had faced plenty of hostile environments like this, time and again. He had gotten used to that. In the seventeenth round, the opponent got a great opportunity. It was entirely the result of a moment's carelessness. After receiving a forceful punch, he was reeling now. He kept moving back.

He began doing that. The fellow was now in his control, finally. He didn't feel like doing anything; yet, seeing the opponent incautious for a moment he straightaway mechanically drove his fists to his face and nose. It was almost as if he was unaware of what his fists were doing, how they moved; he was merely observing what his fists were doing, he was enjoying that, a cruel pleasure. As soon as the man stood up again, a descending chop from him laid him sprawling on the floor again. It wasn't possible for any referee to declare the punch a foul. As soon as he fell, he rose up again, tottering. Perhaps they didn't die, they never died. He rose up, he unfolded new strategies and designs. Because civilization had taught that one must win, victory through any means, or else life itself would be in vain, would be ruined. A fubsy police officer was entering the ring through the ropes now. He had surely done something which they considered to be in violation of the law. He rose once again and tottered uncontrollably. But after all, he didn't want to win like this. So, did he want to lose then! Probably not that either. He didn't know for certain. He stood with his back against the rope, he took in some air, he inhaled fresh air. His knees were unable to withstand the weight of his body, at this untimely moment. Maybe he would tumble down just now, or maybe not. What was happening to him, was he losing to himself! Or was it that whatever was called winning had already happened a while back, and he hadn't realized it, the difference! Yes, the event had begun to transpire. There was nothing to be done. The last train had left. The blind beggar had now sat down to lay out the earnings of his day's fatigue at one end of the station platform, under the Persian lilac

Magnetism, static electricity

tree. That old Persian lilac of his. He had lit a red-stringed bidi. As he puffed pleasurably, he examined through the touch of his hand which coins were four annas, which ones were eight annas, and which ones were rupees. And which ones were coins that were no longer in currency, with which people had undertaken deceit, seeing a blind man. So he hadn't protected his life anywhere! Actually, he was only the gravedigger of the play *Hamlet*, the one who had to play the role of the priest of death sometimes. When a person died, did he realize that he was dying – perhaps he did, perhaps he didn't, it was entirely that politics of silence, political silence, via undercurrent, just that bit of destructiveness, it occurs again and again, keeps occurring, gets exposed, in death language, in the language of death...

[Mati Nore, 2007]

Acknowledgements

Needless to say, it's a cut-method piece, news from newspapers has been used, in my own 'cut' style, in my own way, the way I have been doing it. I have quoted verbatim from a serialized article by Sanjeeb Chattopadhyay about Vivekananda ('Swami Vivekananda: The Biography of an Unending Life') that appeared in a weekly publication, to bring discordance. The famous wrestler Gobor Guho's half-torn biography, a 'How to' series book about boxing, and several more things like that, all of which were kneaded and scrutinized in my own way, to break the reasoning process that's in currency, of vastu tantra – to say it correctly, vastu-tantric-ness, to knead that.

Translator's Note

V. Ramaswamy

All Those Moving Trails that Tumble Down Again and Again on the Way

Subimal Misra in Conversation with Swapan Ranjan Haldar

P.S.

Insights,
Interviews
&
More ...

Translator's Note

V. RAMASWAMY

This is the fourth and final book of my Subimal Misra translation project. It has been in the making for a long time. Some of the 'anti-stories' carried here were completed as long back as in 2011 and 2013.

I began translating Misra almost by accident in 2005, and soon after the publication in 2010 of *The Golden Gandhi Statue from America*, the first collection of his stories – his early stories – I took upon myself an ambitious, long-term project – a labour of love, a madness – of translating a selection of Subimal Misra's short fiction from his entire writing career of over four decades. I focussed on Subimal Misra's stories – or anti-stories – because they seemed to me to be more accessible to readers via translation. And thus a second collection, of his stories from the 1970s and 1980s, got done. The book *Wild Animals Prohibited* was published in 2015. But meanwhile, I had begun my study of Subimal Misra's oeuvre, and my attention was inevitably drawn to his 'anti-novel trilogy'.

Subimal Misra had decided to write only for little magazines. And so he thought he would never write a novel – how would that ever be published? But in the late 1970s, a story idea got into his head. That became *This Could*

Have Become Ramayan Chamar's Tale, which he self-published in 1982. This also became the first part of an anti-novel trilogy. The second part, *When Colour Is a Warning Sign*, appeared in 1984. I took these two works up for translation on Misra's recommendation. I thought the third part of the trilogy (published in 1990) was untranslatable as a creative literary work, as opposed to an annotated text. My translation of the two anti-novels was published in 2019 as *This Could Have Become Ramayan Chamar's Tale: Two Anti-Novels*. The book also carried Misra's essay on the 'anti-novel', a kind of manifesto.

Actually, the manuscript of *Ramayan Chamar* was ready in early 2015. And I had also begun working on the present book. But *Ramayan Chamar* took a long while to receive the publisher's approval, and so during this time my Subimal Misra project was in a kind of limbo. I put this book on hold, and during 2016–20 I translated other writers – Manoranjan Byapari, Adhir Biswas, Swati Guha, Ansar Uddin, Raghab Bandopadhyay, Shahidul Zahir, Audity Falguni and Mashiul Alam, the last three from Bangladesh. I returned to this book from time to time, and then more substantively in 2020–21, and completed the manuscript in early 2021.

In the course of my Subimal Misra translation project, I was not only a translator, but also, necessarily, a research scholar of sorts, and a fastidious anthologist and editor. At a personal level, the project became a means, a companion and a witness to my life journey over the last decade. Through it, I was able to deal with grievous life circumstances; translation became for me something akin to a devout seeker's repetition of the sacred name with prayer beads, a silencing of the mind through single-pointed concentration. In turn, this enabled an even deeper immersion – or higher ascension – into translation.

Through all this, and once again unwittingly, an audacious project of literary and cultural curation was undertaken – of the oeuvre of a powerful, anti-establishment writer in the Bangla language, a unique countercultural icon, largely unknown even to readers of Bangla in his own city, Kolkata. Because Subimal Misra assiduously cultivated his anonymity and marginality.

Taken together, the books give us powerful images of over four decades of the life of the city and people of Kolkata, of the state of West Bengal, the nation, India, as well as the world. From Haran Majhi's ghostly widow haunting the city to the grieving father of Tapasi Mullick seeking a shaman's help to communicate with his murdered daughter, and with Gandhi ever-present, Misra bears witness, like in a truth and reconciliation commission, to all that he has seen and known.

HarperCollins's commitment and contribution to this project is nothing short of historic.

While *The Golden Gandhi Statue from America* and *Wild Animals Prohibited* received positive but limited reviews in India, *This Could Have Become Ramayan Chamar's Tale: Two Anti-Novels* received wide and fulsome acclaim. Two of the Misra books, *This Could Have Become Ramayan Chamar's Tale: Two Anti-Novels* and *Wild Animals Prohibited,* were also published in the USA in 2020 and 2021, respectively. Both books received exceptional reviews from critics in the USA. At another level, Utsarga Ghosh, a literature scholar, was awarded a PhD from the Department of English, Banaras Hindu University, in 2022 for his thesis titled *Translating into English: The 'Afterlife' of Subimal Misra's Fictional Writings*.

***

In his preface to the first translated volume, *The Golden Gandhi Statue from America*, Misra likened his early stories to the beginning of a staircase, which readers needed to ascend to access the later phases of his writing. The book compiled fifteen stories from the late 1960s to the early 1970s. It was a book unlike any other. The subsequent books, *Wild Animals Prohibited* (which had twenty-five stories from the 1970s and 1980s) and *This Could Have Become Ramayan Chamar's Tale* (with Misra's first two 'anti-novels' from the 1980s) were also unique, and unlike the earlier Misra books in translation. This book lies at the top of the Misra staircase. It brings together twenty stories from the 1990s and 2000s. This is Misra's late work, as it were. Once again, and not surprisingly, it is as unique and unprecedented as each of the earlier volumes. It is the grand finale of Subimal Misra in English translation.

The anti-stories in this book are taken from six Subimal Misra books: *Lohar-Taar Bagh O Dorshoker Modhye Rokto Bhalobashe* (1993); *Sotyo Utpadito Hoy* (1997); *Kaatth Khaay Aangra Haage* (2001); *Chhottrish Bochorer Rograragri* (2004); *Kika Cutout* (2006); and *Haate Dhoriye Deowa Hoyechhe Shesh Hobishyir Malshabhog – Aar, Ebong, Haashte Haashte, Khorkutor Moto Bheshe Jaowar Ananda-Gourobe* (2010). I had begun listing Misra stories for translation as early as in 2006, and kept making additions and alterations over the years. Misra himself suggested only three of the pieces in this volume, namely, 'Memory Game', 'The Earth Quakes' and 'Nappy Change'. Procheta Ghosh (Lala) and Dr Mrinal Bose rendered invaluable assistance in terms of advising me on the selection, as did Swapan Ranjan Haldar.

The book has been a difficult endeavour. This 'late work' of Subimal Misra is opaque, and it is as if he tests readers because he seems to be doing all he can to alienate them, to drive them away! Translation is therefore difficult.

A good chunk of the initial work was done in 2014–15, but after that I began to feel weighed down by the sheer volume of what I had taken on. Just looking at the list of titles of the anti-stories awaiting translation filled me with dread and despair! I met Dolonchampa Chakraborty, also a Bangla-to-English literary translator, in 2019 and requested her to join me in completing this volume. She came on board, but then came the pandemic, and owing to personal difficulties Dolonchampa could not contribute.

Ultimately, I had to tell myself over and over again that this book was only supposed to be a *selection*, rather than an exhaustive collection. And thus, towards the very end, a practical and judicious excising had to be done, leading to this selection of twenty anti-stories from the 1990s and 2000s. The length of even this caught me by surprise. Yes, Subimal Misra's anti-stories in this phase were generally on the long side.

I feel a sense of deep satisfaction at having been able to complete this book, and also complete the ambitious translation project that I had embraced.

***

I see the stories, or anti-stories, as prose-text works of our times which the author has chosen to write and publish. It is not my remit as a translator to wonder whether that is vision or vanity. I only seek to convey as much as possible of the original text. The selection was entirely my own, through my own intuition, but always keeping in mind the responsibility of 'representing' or curating the work of Misra. The story order is mostly chronological and follows the order of their appearance in the respective Subimal Misra books. Thematically, the subjects range from the 'global' – the Gulf War of 1991 which heralded the post–Cold War unipolar world – to the very 'local' – the Singur movement of 2006 which began the process that led to the unseating of the all-powerful CPI(M), who ruled the state of West Bengal in India since 1977.

Misra had begun two books (*Kaath Khay Angra Haage* and *Chhottrish Bochorer Rograragri*) with the story 'The Great Renunciant' (although with different titles), and so I thought it fit to open this book too with that story, and its later title. This story is one of the rare Misra pieces from this period with a simple, straightforward and conventional narrative. But then in an end note, he seeks to exculpate himself by declaring that he simply filched and reproduced someone else's work! The protagonist of the story, Jharuprasad, a folk singer, may seem to some of Misra's close circle (like Lala) to be a kind of 'alter ego' of Misra, and hence our mirthful-affectionate reference to him as '*Amader Jharuprasad'*, our Jharuprasad.

The title of this volume, *The Earth Quakes*, and also of the last piece in this book, is from the first story in his last anti-story collection (*Haate Dhoriye Deowa Hoyechhe...*). It is autobiographical, and about a boxing match. As Misra explained to me, it is about him confronting another writer, someone who is famous and rules the cash registers.

'Memory Game' (which Misra called a 'novelette'), was not only the longest anti-story but also the most dense and difficult text in this book. The strategy I employed – to deal with the daunting task of translation – was to do it backwards. The last paragraph first, the penultimate paragraph second, and so on. The story translated here as 'The Great Reununciant' was originally given the Bangla title 'Madankatkati'. Misra subsequently titled it 'Mohanirgrothiyo'. And he transferred the title 'Madankatkati' to the story earlier titled 'Ram Naam Khamcha Khamcha'. I first translated this re-titled latter story as 'Madankatkati – Throbbing Passion'; subsequently this non-Bengali learnt that 'madankatkati' is the name of a crunchy-crispy savoury item in Bengal, and so I changed the title to 'Madankatkati – Crunchy-Crispy Passion'.

***

Translatability – is a key issue as far as Subimal Misra's work is concerned. His anti-story, 'Kokire Lonang Korar Moto', from the book *Sotyo Utpadito Hoy*, comes to mind. The first two words of the title are made-up words, like, say, the many made-up words in the poem 'Jabberwocky', by Lewis Caroll. To my mind, the title suggested 'Like Netting a Babe'. (When I later asked Misra, he said, 'Whatever you think.') But the title was the least of it. I started working on that text and completed my first round of translation. The story is written in at least two registers, *sadhu bhasha*, which was historically the literary register of the Bangla language, and *kothyo* or *cholito* or *cholti* bhasha, which is the spoken or colloquial language. How was that distinction to be made via English? I could find no satisfactory answer to that question. I recall reflecting inspiredly on the text at the end of one of the days I spent translating it, during a residency in Korea. In a certain flight of thought, as if having deciphered a secret code, I began to see 'meaning' and 'significance', and thus knew the grandeur of the unique genius and vision of Misra; and at the same time, I also realized that this was *not* translatable. But that did not cause me any grief. Rather, a smile of amusement formed on my face. The realization of the genius of the author necessarily meant the demise of the translator! The story in question was on my list for long, and I thought that I would have to do a Jabberwocky, but it was finally left out.

Subimal Misra's book *Sotyo Utpadito Hoy* (*Truth is Manufactured*, 1997), described on its back cover as 'Perhaps a story, perhaps a novel, perhaps the death of the novel too', must be one of the most unique works of literature in the world, and in the Bangla language. It consists of five 'episodes', which, in his words, are 'apparently different and separate, but again not so either. There is an inner connection between one and the other, although there is an apparent incoherence and lack of immediate connection.' Four of the episodes are carried here.

I have found no satisfactory solution to rendering dialect speech into English. Subimal Misra peppers his narrative with this whenever the context demands it. In short, through language, and also allusion, his texts are polychromatic in Bangla, while they are inevitably monochromatic in translation. Reading Misra's texts brings their own affects and effects for a reader. I hope my translation too does something in that direction.

Misra also invents words (and spellings) all the time. It is from the context of usage and the orthographical structure of the word that one has to derive the meaning. Sometimes the spelling is an innuendo. An example that comes to mind is from Swapan Ranjan Haldar's interview with Misra in the P.S. Section of this book. Misra used the word *khemota* – colloquially, disparagingly – for *khomota*, which means 'power', but it brings to one's mind the word *khemta*, with the retroflex 'ta' (instead of the dental 'ta' of the former word), which means 'nautch girl'. In my translation, I rendered it as 'wield a nautch girl's drawing power'.

***

Reading Subimal Misra is always educational. For instance, it was from 'The Hand – Rough, Severe, Blazing with Resolve, Pliable, Clenched in a Fist, Surrendered, and Deceived Too' that I learnt about the Paik Rebellion of 1817. The story 'Love Story' has a kind of epigraph, about a washerwoman. Only recently did I learn from the writer Niranjan Mondol that this story is taken from the fifteenth-century Bengali text *Manasa Mangalkavya*, and that there is an island in the Sundarbans that bears the name of the fabled washerwoman. Or consider 'The Treasured Art of Vocal Harmony'. The title in Bangla is 'Swaramelakalanidhi'. In November 2021, long after I completed translating this, and several months after I had already submitted the manuscript to the publisher, I attended a lecture on Hampi by the French-Indian Indologist couple, Pierre and Vasundhara Filliozat, at the National Institute of Advanced

Studies, Bangalore, thanks to the invitation of my dear friend Sharada Srinivasan. In his talk, Pierre Filliozat mentioned the Sanskrit text *Swaramelakalanidhi*. My ears picked that up at once. And thus I learnt that *Swaramelakalanidhi* was written by Ramamataya in the year 1550, and that it is a treatise on Vijayanagara musicology from the Post-Sangita Ratnakara period of South Indian music history. It is considered to be one of the most celebrated texts on Carnatic Music theory. Misra's writing gives clues to the discerning reader about the range of his interests and reading, and we always learn something new.

In the process of trying to be fastidious and judicious in selecting the anti-stories for this volume, I was too close to the texts to be able to discern the thematic unity or dissonance in the selection. So this is something I keenly look forward to hearing about from readers. But perhaps something that might strike the reader is the element of playfulness, or teasing, in the writing.

***

I read Michael Hofmann's essay 'My Life with Roth' in 2006, and that planted seeds in my mind of a long-term Subimal Misra translation project. As I was nearing the end of the work for this final volume, I was fortunate to be able to communicate with Hoffman. He wrote in an email: 'It's so interesting to hear from another "in the field" – a translator who is in happy possession of an author! It's a lovely thing for me to think of that piece – something like a grateful adieu to Roth – being picked up by your aunt, and then shipped on to you, and you still being able to gain some energy or determination or assurance from it.' The

Subimal Misra project made me a literary translator, and the mission I embraced in the process was *translating voices from the margins*.

Although I have lived in Kolkata all my life, I am an 'outsider' of sorts on account of my Tamil origins. An outsider who is a permanent spy on all things Bengali. An outsider who felt proficient enough in the Bangla language to have the audacity to start translating a writer like Subimal Misra without having the slightest notion about him. A writer whose work, by his own admission, is all about language. It was shocking audacity indeed as I now realize, something I am truly embarrassed about, but I grew inwardly through the project so that I could always be up to the challenge in my own growing 'Subimal Misra consciousness'. And it is only now, at the end of the project, that I realize that this was one more instance of 'outsider art'. I am neither Bengali, nor a reader of literature in Bangla, not a literary critic or scholar, and I wasn't even a translator. If anything, I was a lover of literature, somewhat proficient in the Bangla language from being a participant-observer of life in Kolkata. It is my 'language' ability that I brought to the Misra project. I spent a good part of over fifteen years on this outsider-translation project, undertaken with an ever-increasing fervour, to bring the name and work of Subimal Misra to the attention of the wider world of literature. I wrote an essay in Bangla 'Amar Subimal Misro Anubad Jatra' (My Subimal Misra Translation Journey) in 2018, and this was published in the journal *Alochonachokro*. The person who concluded the project was not the one who unwittingly began it. I had been transformed.

The Subimal Misra project has had its own rewards. Suranjan Ganguly was my contemporary in St Xavier's College, and when I reconnected with him after many years and he learnt of my Subimal Misra interest, he sent me the book, *Anti-Story: An Anthology of Experimental Fiction*, edited by Philip Stevick, which was published in New York in 1971. The book was a revelation. On the strength of Misra's short fiction by then, he could definitely have been included in that volume; the names of some of the writers included there are also to be found in Misra's own writing. He was the uncrowned prince of the little-magazine world of Calcutta by the end of the 1970s. But reading Stevick's anthology, I could see that Misra was also in the forefront of experimental fiction worldwide by the very beginning of the 1970s – the decade that Naxalites proclaimed would be the decade of liberation.

Rahul Banerjee, a natural resource scientist and lifelong activist in people's struggles, was my school classmate more than fifty years ago. I initiated a fundraising effort in 2017 towards meeting the expenses for Misra's care by selling his self-published books. Rahul made a hefty contribution, and thus he came to read the story 'Lenin…', which is carried in this volume. He wrote an essay about the anti-story on his blog soon after that. So I requested him to translate the story – which he did too. His translation formed the base upon which I then worked.

Eric Auzoux – who I met at Sangam House in 2015 – translated into French a collection of Misra stories from my English translation, which was published by Éditions Banyan. Like the book *The Golden Gandhi Statue from America*, this too was dedicated to Jean-Luc Godard. The publisher, David Aimé, sent the book to Godard, who was kind enough to acknowledge the gift, and express his apologies for his ignorance of Misra's name!

***

Translating Subimal Misra – made me into a translator of 'voices from the margins'. Once I began reading him, I was catapulted into another notion and imagination of what 'literature' is or means, or could mean, specifically in regard to the Bengali sphere I was dwelling in. And so I learnt about and approached and then began translating the autodidact writer Manoranjan Byapari. My translation work caught the attention of Swati Guha and Adhir Biswas, who gave me their books to translate. And in time, my own antennae pointed me towards Raghab Bandopadhyay and Ansaruddin. In 2019, I learnt about Shahidul Zahir, of Bangladesh, and soon after, I lived for a couple of weeks in the pages of Zahir's books. He was the first Bengali writer I read unstoppably, like someone greedy for his prose. I began translating him almost at once, and in turn, I began an engagement with Bangladesh, making regular visits, and building a circle of friends there.

I translated Shahidul Zahir's novella, *Life and Political Reality*, with Shahroza Nahrin. And thus I realized that translation is best done in collaboration. Two is unquestionably better than one, as long as each person is appropriate to the task and the duo can work together harmoniously and creatively. In that sense, a serious translation project demands, in the interest of quality, that it be a collaborative one. Although I was the sole translator of Subimal Misra, the project, however, was entirely a collaborative one, and in the Acknowledgements section of this volume, I have mentioned some of the people without whose assistance I could not have advanced.

Hopefully this journey of translating 'voices from the margins' – entirely a labour of love, a madness – will continue. An outsider literary project. And thanks to my experience of working with Shahroza Nahrin, I have now also started mentoring young translators.

***

Subimal Misra stopped writing in 2012 on account of poor eyesight and ill health. He was in hospital in the latter part of that year, and then bedridden since late 2014, needing day-long care. He was not able to read or write, and he found it difficult to speak. But his mind and spirit were as sharp as ever. I visited him regularly, sometimes accompanied by Lala or some other friend, and kept him abreast of my work, publication, reviews, and responses. I carried materials to read out to or play for him. Misra was suffering from cardiac problems and complications related to advanced diabetes and old age.

He had written somewhere that his 'official' birthday, 20 June 1943, was entirely fictitious, and that his mother had told him that he was born on a Wednesday, a bit before the middle of December. I declared once to Misra that 10 December – Human Rights Day – would be an appropriate date to adopt. And so, on 10 December 2018, Lala and I visited Subimal Misra to greet him on his '75th birthday'!

Misra had a medical emergency on 29 December 2022, and was admitted to the Calcutta Medical College Hospital the following day, thanks to the timely intervention of his publisher, Adhir Biswas. A host of people responded to our appeal for assistance via social media. Many people volunteered for hospital duty. We were amazed to discover that a whole new generation had discovered Misra and come to revere his name.

He was discharged on 6 January 2023, and thanks to the response to the fundraising appeal we were able to ensure that he received the best possible medical attention, treatment and care at his residence. Subimal Misra passed away in his sleep in the early hours of 8 February 2023. An era ended with him. It is difficult for some of us to come to terms with his absence. Although he was seriously ill, he saw through eight years with sheer grit. I was fortunate to have known him, and truly blessed to have been his chosen translator.

October 2023

All Those Moving Trails that Tumble Down Again and Again on the Way

SUBIMAL MISRA IN CONVERSATION WITH SWAPAN RANJAN HALDAR

Q. The society you write about is never outside the realm of politics. We too believe that any such writing is no writing at all, however much a label of 'universalism' is sought to be attached to that. So why didn't you get into active politics? Was that decision at least to some extent influenced by the fate of Ritwik Ghatak?

A. In this country, the respect accorded to the ruling party is about the same as that for democracy ... To put it very simply, in so-called politics there's a tendency to cast everything in the same mould, and analysis too follows the same path. Within the boundaries of the binary of good and bad. The tendency to deny a silhouette space pares down politics: everything about me and my party is correct, beyond argument, while everything to do with the opposing opinion is incorrect and bad. Writing, i.e. a different kind of writing, does not subscribe to this mould-centred division; here the narration of events is multidimensional, people are multidimensional, and the testimonies as well. This goes beyond the ambit of all the current political unidimensionality, it awakens, awakens the 'other', the testimony seeks to be 'constructed', the interiority of contemporaneity is rich with the shadow of the universal and the eternal, of creation, at least whatever little I understand, or ... but obviously stamina is needed, the capability is needed. Yes, I did have the lives of Manik Bandopadhyay and Ritwik Ghatak before me, but there was also Jean Paul Sartre. Politics would flutter its wings shabbily, and nothing more.

Q. Even after so long, as soon as your name is mentioned, at most one hears about 'Haran Majhi', or in a slightly more elaborate discussion, 'Ramayan Chamar'. That's all. Haven't you failed to draw the readers of Bengali literature? Rather, we've observed that you have many more readers in Bangladesh. You are also finding publishers there with ease. Why have we not been able to see you becoming acceptable here, to an adequate number of readers, or at least some publishers?

A. I have strong objections to the term 'drawing readers'. Given what I write and the way I write, I myself create the fate of my writing. There's a sentence I wrote a long time ago: 'If success comes, I am afraid, because if you try to do something new, success doesn't come. If I achieve success, that means I am doing something which is not that novel.'

Relatively more people have heard about 'Haran Majhi' or 'Ramayan Chamar', but very few people have actually read even those. And they haven't got to the other books. I'm glad they didn't. I don't want more than a specific number of readers to read my books. Although I live in the current era, I am generally not in favour of publicity. I put out notices about the publication of my books in a couple of little magazines that I like. I don't do the same with all little magazines, without consideration, I forbid that. After all, not all publications are worthy of carrying advertisements from Subimal Misra in the current state of this Bengali marketplace, the little-magazine marketplace. I don't do whatever will sell more copies of the book. Advertising and informing – there's a difference between the two, and I have also discussed this in detail elsewhere. On the other hand, I have a tendency to drive away readers: 'Subimal Misra will never be counted in the tribe of those of a half-brained mentality.' At the Kolkata Book Fair, prior to selling a book, I test the reader if necessary, to see whether he or she is capable of being a Subimal Misra reader. 'Subimal Misra's books do not have an exchange value, they never had. His books are not a means to make money, although one has to take some money in exchange, towards the cost of production, and that is by adhering to the clause, "whatever you think it ought to be as a Subimal Misra reader". And because Subimal Misra's books are not a commodity, they aren't easily available, and definitely not available everywhere' ... etcetera, etcetera.

I've heard that there are some readers in Bangladesh, I get letters quite often. I'm grateful to them – I'm amazed that they keep track of a marginal writer like me although they are so far away. I don't reply, I'm lazy, I keep deferring that and so I never reply, it's terribly wrong. As many as two books were published there recently after getting the rights from me. I believe they're selling well too. Nothing overwhelms me any more. And as far as West Bengal is concerned, I don't have any publishers at the moment.

Q. After becoming your readers, if some people then inevitably reflect your influence in their writing, or follow you in some way, how would you encourage them?

A. I'll ask them to try to demolish me. If I advance one step, then I retreat two steps in order to examine myself closely. I view my weaknesses critically. I would ask my readers to do the same, I would ask them to criticize me openly and privately and thus enrich me.

Q. Bengali literary critics too don't really want to touch you. And if they at all do that, they stop after saying a few words. But after all, academic criticism of writers' writing is important. Why isn't that importance given to you? Or is it that their knowledge shrinks when your shadow falls on them?

A. The teacher asked: 'Angona, whatever you've written for my essay on the dog, Shoumi too has written the same, verbatim. Did you copy what she wrote, or did she copy what you wrote?' Without being alarmed in the slightest bit, Angona replied: 'No, Madam, actually, you see, both of us wrote the essay after observing the same dog.'

Q. Contemporary politics in West Bengal, the winds of '*poriborton*', i.e., change – we'd like to hear something about that from you. In particular, what do you think about the schism in the intelligentsia? Is this division, in reality, anything more than scheming on the part of both sides?

A. *Dhanteras* has possessed the Bengali race, they must buy gold whether they can afford it or not – they simply must.

Q. Were the thirty-four years of Left Front rule truly a curse as far as Bengal was concerned? What do you have to say about Singur, Nandigram and Lalgarh?

A. It's not about having a simplistic opinion. Nandigram, Singur and Lalgarh have only thrown up some weeds of a hyacinth-covered pond, below that lie murky depths of black water – black as pitch.

Q. How would you explain the separatist movements all over India and especially in Kashmir?

A. Side by side with the awakening of national identity, we have the licking of the boots of power, and power-grabbing in the name of politics.

Q. We know from experience that even today, you are elated no end when you come upon a worthy little magazine. Couldn't a little magazine have come up under your guardianship? Why did that not happen? Is it that actually no one was willing to accord you that salience?

A. I have brought out at least five or six little magazines, but I couldn't sustain any of them. In the case of two, I had to suffer the customary blows and move away to protect my dignity. Because to run a magazine you need money, you need at least some marketing intelligence, and you need to wield something like a nautch girl's drawing power to procure advertisements. I had none of that. The first magazine, under joint editorship, *Onyorup Rupantor,* was entirely devoted to poetry in translation; I couldn't keep it alive. The second one, *Ekjon* – the whole issue was on one person's writing, his or her prose, and an interview – comprising one forme; only two or three issues were published. The third one, *Anquilosar,* was entirely a prose magazine – one or two issues came out. The fourth one was *Bigyapon* – I was able to bring out four or five issues. I was able to print and sell 1,100 copies of one of its issues, even in those days; it was the 'anti-establishment issue'. Later, for the purpose of registration, it was given the name *Bigyapon*

Porbo, and gradually the control of the magazine began to go out of my hands. The special issue on Jean Paul Sartre's turning down of the Nobel Prize – there were plenty of noteworthy articles in that issue; Godard's controversial essay on Bergman, 'Bergman's Mother', was especially noteworthy. I did the Amiyabhushan Majumdar issue based on an interview with him. I was completely driven out of this magazine shortly after that. The fifth magazine, *Adarsha Hindu Hotel*, was jointly edited; only one issue was published. The sixth, *Kobitirtho* – this magazine has done well since its appropriation. The lettering of its title was done by dipping a matchstick in Chinese ink, and that is still used. Each of the first five or six issues began with a piece by Kamalkumar Majumdar. I was driven out from there too, for the same reason: the control of the magazines lies in the hands of the one who can procure advertisements. Seventh, a magazine I brought out in more recent times in a fit of rage, *Patalgaddi* – every issue of which is its last issue – some three issues came out in the last five or six years – there are no advertisements in that, the magazine does not exceed one forme. So that's a very brief account of my association with magazine editorship – I could never compromise anywhere, I couldn't do that and stay on. I was 'driven out' of almost all the magazines – I was evicted...

Although you didn't ask about it, but some other things come to mind in this connection. Not just little magazines, I tried 'publishing' as well, going outside conventional processes, with new writers. That was Pathok Somobay, a readers' cooperative. We began that entirely as an experiment, publishing the books of reader-buyers on a cooperative basis. The first was a book of mine – *Nanga Haar Jege Uthchhe*. I don't exactly remember, but I think

I could manage to get about two hundred buyers, even Buddhadev Bose eagerly became a buyer. All the buyers' names were printed in the book, and the book was dedicated to all of them. It was running well, but squabbles arose because of the 'cold war' over whose book would be published first. It ran for a while through personal sales, and then it closed down. I am nostalgic – Pathok Somobay, an effort to publish books through advance readership, the readers' cooperative of my dreams.

From all this, I think that I lack any organizational capability, I don't have the capability to bring people together. I couldn't gather people, rather, quite the contrary, I pushed them away. No more; water boils in fire, and when reality sloughs off its skin, it creates a reflection.

Q. What advice would you offer to budding writers – which can guide new writers in new writing?

A. I don't have any guidelines. I don't possess the capability to offer any advice. Great folk can do all that, sages can do that. One has to learn as one treads the path, it's the path that teaches what ought to be done, how it ought to be done, what ought not to be done; the path will reveal what ought not to be done, it'll throw that up. But in order to recognize that, eagerness and love are essential.

Q. 'You write pornography' – we don't really hear this complaint being made today. Because the camps which used to make that allegation have started publishing pure pornography in their magazines and annual festival numbers. That signals your defeat – since you sought to establish beauty through sex, and by using sex. You sought peace through depicting violence. You summoned creation through destruction. But what was begun was akin to awakening the poisonous snake with a few drops of penis massage oil!

A. You have given a bit of the answer too within your question. Anyway, I try to attack 'sex supremacy' with sex supremacy, violence with violence, and there's no element of 'pleasing' in that. Instead of enjoying that, they're furious from head to toe. This is akin to a kind of fusion, I have been employing that for almost five decades to see what transpires. Of course, in the process there has been a lot of change in terms of viewpoint, in terms of the dimensions. I especially want to extricate where 'I' myself am standing, in comparison. However, I would be extremely grateful if this is not confused with the term 'fusion' that has come into currency in recent times, especially in the field of music.

Q. Whatever you might say, the fact is that Subimal Misra has ended up becoming an institution today. In the process of opposing the establishment, you yourself became an institution of sorts. Could one say that?

A. I don't know whether you know, a few years ago, in Bangladesh, annoyed by the torment of mice, people caught them, stitched up their anuses and then released them. It was observed that as they suffered the discomfort, they began fighting and biting each other and becoming fierce, and while they were busy with the turmoil and fighting, they kept dying.

Q. You are keen on learned readers. But is the extensive learning that's required in order to become your reader possible in the age of the electronic media? Why would a person look frantically for your books and try to read them? What is the means to enlighten them? Who would give them the cue? After all, you can't be contained within the narrow confines of contemporary pedantic discourse. So how would the youth seeking Bengali literature come to know about you?

A. Actually I am not exactly read by so-called learned readers. Educated folk, professors, academicians, even if only partially, become extremely foolish – extremely scholarly, extremely foolish. They don an air of having understood everything. But I also have very modestly educated, ordinary, middle-class readers. They don't have that arrogance, the arrogance of education; rather they eventually try to grasp the matter by doing their best to use their own minds. Badal Sarkar, the dramatist, Brecht and Ritwik Kumar Ghatak found such an audience, they found that. They, that audience, consisted of extremely ordinary folk, they did not belong to the so-called smartass set. In my case as well, I've observed that when I receive calls and letters from faraway places, there are quite a few readers of the same category, and I hold them in veneration. I bow before them. They point out mistakes, they argue with me, and even more significantly, through their arguments they help me to refine myself and my overall writing practice.

Readers of that kind, serious readers, are few, very few, in this age of electronic media, but one cannot say that there aren't any. They are my true readers, they number just a few, but they are true.

There's no easy way of finding my writing, my books. The books aren't available in the 'book market', many publishers and booksellers in College Street haven't even heard my name. Everything has to be searched for. Again, seen differently, extensive reading, both good and bad, everything, helps a bit, but it can misguide as well. People have to recognize that themselves, they have to advance through such recognition. They must journey on, discerning what's new and what's worn out. Why a writer describes himself as the most marginal of marginal writers, why he tries to say that, thinking about all that – it's especially essential to be thinking.

However, I've observed through experience that it's essentially the educated, the so-called educated writers who object. And let me say, it is writers, and writers in particular, who'll be terribly incensed by my writing, terribly. My writing tells them about the pre-history of their thinking. You'll hardly find any writers who pay lip service to my writing. After all, who is it that allows, or is powerful enough to allow, one's adversary to grow, who is it that possesses such daring?

Q. Have you come across anything in the writing by your next generation, or by the completely young generation, that makes you hopeful? No, I don't want to know any names.

A. While leafing through little magazines, I suddenly come across such writing, can you believe that! Writing that startles you. That alarms you. Essentially by young writers. But I'm unable to get most of the magazines. Nowadays, I wait eagerly to receive little magazines. Hoping someone sends something to me. I request some people to buy them from Patiram and send them to me. I'm unable to go to College Street nowadays owing to my ill health – it's been five or six long years. All my life, I have believed in buying little magazines, the genuine ones, but I'm unable to get such magazines. For some years now, Lala (Procheta

Ghosh) has been buying some magazines from the Kolkata Book Fair and delivering them at my residence. I don't know about others, but I buy books, and I'm happy to go bankrupt buying little magazines. And, even after doing all that, not even one per cent of genuine little magazines reach me ... Yes, as I was saying, whatever I obtain does startle me, even in little magazines. In the big magazines, in the so-called leading fortnightly publications in the field of literature-culture, it is only the second-hand stuff by established and semi-established writers that is published, hackneyed shit-and-dung, not even a single line is fit to be read. Observing all this, I think it might be better to read the classics again, read them anew, rather than waste time on that stuff.

Q. 'Kishenji is finished' – how do you react to that?

A. If you go through my writings, which are scattered here and there, you'll find some counter-questions, in disguise, in response to your question, although nothing is really clear to me, but again it's equally not really unclear either, and it's definitely not in-between. I am against the killings that are going on without let-up, every day, of ordinary toiling folk, peasants, shopkeepers, schoolmasters, nurses, doctors; and again, as far as Kishenji himself is concerned, there are no 'buts' in my opinion regarding his patriotism. Actually, I can't think about anything in such a simple, watery way, I'm unable to do that. But the pack of whys – perhapses – and ifs always create knots in my head, it's not possible for me to respond in a few words. One man issued a threat, and in a single day, the price of babui-grass rope rose, the price of kendu-leaves rose – how can I forget how much people living on the margins benefited from that. But I cannot support such indiscriminate killing of helpless, innocent people under any circumstances or pretexts (Maoism is only a means of exculpation – 'This is a battleground, and so such things will happen, always happen…'); just like I didn't support the erstwhile Naxalites' spree of killing poor home guards in the seventies … Yes, I firmly believe that state terror becomes much more terrifying than the Maoists, it's becoming like that, time and again. Then again, one should also think about whether, parallel to caste- and religion-based hatred and violence, Maoist terror in the name of so-called revolution will benefit or harm the poor, starving Indian masses.

[This is an excerpt from a conversation that was recorded by Swapan Ranjan Haldar in 2010 on behalf of the little magazine *Ultodurbin*, and subsequently appeared in the book *Adyoshraddho*, published by Dana, Kolkata, in 2012. Translated by V. Ramaswamy.]

Acknowledgements

This book has been in the making for a long time, and so acknowledgements are due to several people. I became a translator, so to speak, at Sangam House, and some of the stories in this volume were begun in the wake of my residency there in January 2011. I was also fortunate to be in residency at Ledig House (now Art Omi), USA, in 2013 and at the Toji Cultural Foundation, Korea, in 2015, where I worked on the anti-stories that appear in this volume.

My Subimal Misra translation project owes much to Dr Mrinal Bose, and he was involved in this book as well, in terms of helping me select the anti-stories for translation. I am grateful to Procheta Ghosh (Lala) for his constant and unstinting assistance. Tapas Ghosh and Swapan Ranjan Haldar were also constant sources of encouragement.

I was fortunate to receive the assistance of several people in my translation work. I am grateful to Nilanjan Bhattacharya, Sangita Roy, Anubha Daripa, Rahul Banerjee, Srishti Dutta Chowdhury and Nabina Das.

Anna Lena von Hellendorf, graphic artist, developed an interest in Subimal Misra's work, and contributed an exceptional cover for the book *This Could Have Become Ramayan Chamar's Tale: Two Anti-Novels*. I am delighted that this volume too carries her cover.

Some of the anti-stories carried here appeared in print or web journals. These include *Nether* (both the earlier print version and the current web version), *Bangla Journal*, *The Puritan*, *Cafe Dissensus* and *Monograph*. I am grateful to the editors.

I would like to express my gratitude to Rahul Soni, my editor at HarperCollins, for his interest and support, which enabled me to complete the Subimal Misra translation project. Finally, a happy thank you to Anandhi Sethuraman, who did the unenviable job of copy-editing this volume; we knew each other from childhood through family connections, and were propitiously reconnected last year after more than four decades when I learnt that she had been a professional copy-editor.

About the Author

Subimal Misra was born in 1943 and his writing career spanned over four decades. The cliched label, 'anti-establishment', is often applied the moment his name is mentioned. But since 'anti-establishment' now seeks to become the establishment, he opposed that too. He was entirely a little-magazine writer, not having written a single letter outside little magazines in his career. Some say Misra brought a different genre into Bengali literature, which made his writing distinctive. From a stance of all-round opposition he said, 'I try to think differently and yet people make an uproar about me – the two can't coexist, that can't be. If I attain instant recognition and popularity, then I would think that what I'm doing is not new.' *When the way of saying becomes the subject* was one of his favourite expressions, with a debt to Jean-Luc Godard, of course. He also maintained that he didn't believe in any prevalent one-dimensional label: *Whatever is accepted as correct is what has to be examined much more.* Misra passed away in February 2023.

About the Translator

V. Ramaswamy lives in Kolkata. This is his fourth book of Subimal Misra in translation, the others being *The Golden Gandhi Statue from America: Early Stories*, *Wild Animals Prohibited: Stories, Anti-Stories*, and *This Could Have Become Ramayan Chamar's Tale: Two Anti-Novels*. He was a recipient of the Literature Across Frontiers–Charles Wallace India Trust fellowship in creative writing and translation at Aberystwyth University in 2016, the New India Foundation translation fellowship in 2022, the PEN Presents award in 2022, and the Bangla Translation Foundation (Dhaka) prize for the best translated book of 2022.

HarperCollins *Publishers* India

At HarperCollins India, we believe in telling the best stories and finding the widest readership for our books in every format possible. We started publishing in 1992; a great deal has changed since then, but what has remained constant is the passion with which our authors write their books, the love with which readers receive them, and the sheer joy and excitement that we as publishers feel in being a part of the publishing process.

Over the years, we've had the pleasure of publishing some of the finest writing from the subcontinent and around the world, including several award-winning titles and some of the biggest bestsellers in India's publishing history. But nothing has meant more to us than the fact that millions of people have read the books we published, and that somewhere, a book of ours might have made a difference.

As we look to the future, we go back to that one word—a word which has been a driving force for us all these years.

Read.